STEELDRIVER

"A special work of art and craft . . . [DeBrandt's] energetic prose is so vivid, graphic, and concise that the book seems to become a multimedia event right there in your hand . . . If Larry Niven, Philip K. Dick and Philip José Farmer had ever spent a month drunk together, they might have shaped a book like *Steeldriver*. And they'll wish they had. I sure wish I had."

—Spider Robinson

"Don DeBrandt tells of a contest between a cyborg and an intelligent mining machine in the far future that is filled out nicely with a murder mystery, evil corporations, and all sorts of corruption."

—*Press/Review* (Philadelphia)

"When academics refer to science fiction as the mythology of the modern age, they have stories like this in mind . . . *Steeldriver* is, as the saying goes, an entertaining yarn, and an especially satisfying one for those readers who grew up on Heinlein."

—*SF Site* (Internet Review)

"A good choice for those who love action stories and real heroes."

—*KLIATT*

"DeBrandt's novel should delight *Analog* readers and fans of Mike Resnick. Recommended."

—*Analog*

THE QUICKSILVER SCREEN

"A rousing piece of cyberpunk adventure . . ."

—*Denver Post*

"Vibrant ideas that enrich science fiction's cyberpunk subgenre . . ."

—*Vancouver Sun*

"DeBrandt integrates artist and morality with writing as sure as John Shirley."

—*Under the Ozone Hole*

Ace Books by Don DeBrandt

STEELDRIVER
TIMBERJAK
V.I.

V. I.

DON DEBRANDT

ACE BOOKS, NEW YORK

V.I.

An Ace Book / published by arrangement with
the author

PRINTING HISTORY
Ace edition / March 2000

The Penguin Putnam Inc. World Wide Web site address is
http://www.penguinputnam.com

Check out the Ace Science Fiction/Fantasy newsletter,
and much more, on the Internet at Club PPI!

ISBN: 0-441-00716-3

ACE®
Ace Books are published by The Berkley Publishing Group,
a division of Penguin Putnam Inc.,
375 Hudson Street, New York, New York 10014.
ACE and the "A" design are trademarks
belonging to Penguin Putnam Inc.

PRINTED IN THE UNITED STATES OF AMERICA

10 9 8 7 6 5 4 3 2 1

acknowledgments

In 1989 Stan Schmidt wrote an excellent article for *Writer's Digest*, in which he listed twenty-six science fiction clichés he never wanted to see again. Chapter 8, "The Story That Wouldn't Die!" contains *all* of them—plus a few of my own. Be warned.

I'd like to thank a number of other people who also inspired various parts of this book: Grant Morrison, Alan Moore, Kurt Busiek, Garth Ennis, Warren Ellis, Mark Waid, and John Ostrander for their excellent comics work that fueled "Dream Pillars," Monica Trejbol from Spiral Kiss, whose fire-dancing sparked the character Firekiss; my friend Dereck, who came up with the line "Duty calls"; and of course, my girlfriend, Andrea, who keeps a big smile on my face.

one
we get going

Near as I can figure out, this story started with the Pretty Big Bang. That's what Mike Blink called it anyway, and I suppose it's as good a name as any. You could go back farther, of course: back to how Mike lost his memory for a while, or how he and Melody fell in love, or even back to the start of the Toolie race—but stories are like creeper-rat holes in that way; the deeper you dig, the twistier it gets, and pretty soon you're standing all alone in a deep hole with no idea how you got there. So let's just start with the Pretty Big Bang, and if we got to back up now and then I hope you'll stick with me.

What's that? Why, yes, I *do* mean Mike Blink the famous hypership pilot and space explorer. Now, don't look at me like *that*; I know his legend's over two hundred years old, and there are stories that claim he's done everything from cloning planets to using a nova to light his pipe. Well, this isn't one of those stories—this is one hundred percent factual, with no exaggeration necessary.

Right off, I'll admit Mike's been dead a long time. What most people don't know is that death didn't slow him down

1

none. See, Mike managed to do what all the multiplanetary R & D departments have never managed: he made the jump from the real world to the digital one at the moment of death. How he did it involves a hyperspatial computer system, an AI, and the power of love itself, but that's neither here nor there. All you need to know is that for the last two centuries Mike Blink may not have been alive, but he is well, and happily married to boot.

Anyway, Mike divides his time these days between hyperspace itself and the simulated environments his wife whips up for him—she's the AI I mentioned, as well as being my Aunt Melody. Having something of an artistic bent, she's built some mighty fine worlds for him to live in, too.

So one day not too long ago, Mike was doing the backstroke in a virtual swimming pool Melody had created. And as he stared up at the hyperspace sky, he saw something he had never seen before.

It was a bulge in the fabric of h-space itself, like something was trying to break through from outside. Now, Mike had seen more sights in hyperspace than anyone; he knew what it looked like when a ship entered from normal space, and what it looked like when it left. This didn't fit either of those.

Anybody who's traveled in a hypership knows what h-space looks like, though it's almost impossible to describe; the best description I ever heard compared it to the non-color you see when you close your eyes. Not black exactly, but a color *waiting* to be black, if that makes any sense.

Well, this bulge started to leak seven *more* non-colors, and Mike swore each one was stranger and harder to look at than the last.

And then they blew up.

Mike rode the shock wave of a supernova one time, and he said this was like that—squared seven times. It wasn't so much the force of the explosion, he told me, though that was considerable; it was that it seemed to be seven *different* explosions happening at the same time.

"Like getting caught in a flaming sandstorm, being hit by sub-zero lightning, and listening to a sound so loud you could hear it in vacuum," was the way he put it. It shattered the swimming pool, knocked him for a loop, and nearly severed the link he had with Melody. He was comatose for almost a week—and being that Mike was already a hyper-spatial ghost, Melody was more than a little worried.

Well, he finally woke up. And when he did, his first words were, "That was a Pretty Big Bang."

So he and Aunt Melody started doing some checking around, and nobody else seems to have noticed a thing. They took a trip through h-space to the actual site of the explosion—it actually went off a long ways away, which is the only reason Mike survived it—and guess where it took place?

That's right. Smack dab at the hyperspace coordinates for the planet I was about to land on—in the city of Myriad, to be exact. And according to Aunt Melody, the Pretty Big Bang was just the beginning; she thinks hyperspace itself is weakening from all the travel through it, and another kind of space—a metahyperspace—is starting to leak through. The next bang won't just be pretty big—it could rip hyperspace itself apart, and maybe even take our own universe with it. 'Course, that's just a theory . . .

That's the way I told it to Mr. Morris, on the liner *Kingwell's Pride*. We were on our way to Kinslik, the Toolies' home planet, and we were playing a little low-g dice to pass the time.

Mr. Morris was one of those corporate types, with a suit so sharp and clean you could use it to cut meat; it was made from bright red korala-fiber cloth, and had a protec-field built right in. He looked to be a few years older than me, though with hormone grafting and plasurgery it's hard to tell these days. Anyway, he was old enough to act superior to

me, and too young to do it well. He had the same vaguely
familiar good looks most corporate types seem to have, with
the exception of a huge surgically sculpted nose—I guess it
was in style for the up-and-coming executive.

"That's quite the story," he said. He looked like he didn't
believe a word of it.

"Where I come from, everybody's got a knack," I told
him. "Hunting, tracking, building, cooking—everybody seems
to be real good at something. My knack's always been stories. I guess that's why they named me Storysmith."

We were the only two passengers in the ship's lounge.
The *Kingwell's Pride* wasn't a freighter, but she wasn't no
cruise ship, either; I could have spit from one side of the
lounge to the other, and from the looks of the dingy walls,
I'd bet more than one passenger had. "I was doing a little
sightseeing when I got a message from Aunt Melody. She
wants me to check this hyperspace business out."

"Is that so?" said Mr. Morris, a little sharply. He hadn't
been doing too good in his last few turns with the dice. "And
what kind of help does she expect *you* to provide?"

Well, before I could reply, Skinny growled at him. That'd
be enough to make most folks watch their mouth, but you
give some people a protec-field and they think they're invincible. All Morris did was give Skinny a dirty look and
say, "Shouldn't that beast be in the cargo bay?"

"No, sir," I said. "Skinny's a registered Guide Animal—a
Devonshire sheep/English sheepdog cross from Old Earth
herself. He's pretty smart, but when he gets to chasing his
own tail it's hard to make him stop."

A more accurate description was a tall pile of bad-
smelling fur, but I figured Mr. Morris could see—and
smell—that for himself. "I need him on account of my peri-
odic bouts of hysterical blindness, like the one I had a few
minutes ago."

"Can't you just buy new eyes?" asked Mr. Morris, in the
kind of voice that said he would have swapped *his* eyes as
easy as his socks.

"Not my eyes that are the problem," I said truthfully. "It's my head. If I get too upset, my brain just starts shutting down my senses. Starts with my eyes—but if I get really worked up, my ears, nose, and taste buds go, too. I reckon it's on account of my mixed heritage."

"I was wondering about that," said Mr. Morris. "What *are* you, exactly?"

A lot more polite than you'll *ever be*, I thought, but didn't say so. "I'm half Shinnkarien Ox," I told him.

"That would explain the bluish skin and horns," he said. "Do all Shinnkariens have your luck?"

"Not as a rule," I said, and threw another natural.

I ignored the glare he sent my way and continued, "I *do* have a few special attributes, though, which is why Aunt Melody called on me. For one thing, all Shinnkarien Oxes have a special relationship to hyperspace itself; we're a de-signed race, not an evolved one, and whoever built us mil-lions of years ago, tied us to a patch of jungle on Shinnkaria called the Indigo Wild. The reason we're blue—and so is the jungle—is because the whole blamed area is leaking a kind of hyperspatial radiation, and since we were made to guard the place we couldn't leave."

"But you, as a half-breed, could."

"Yep. But I'm still sensitive to h-space radiation—why, just traveling in a hypership is enough to make me feel all jittery."

"I was given to understand," said Mr. Morris, doubling his bet, "that Shinnkarien Oxes—the rare ones that left their home—were highly prized as bodyguards."

"The purebreds are, true enough," I said, matching his bet. "But I've never gone in for that kind of thing. No, my Aunt Melody was more interested in employing my natural cu-riosity. There's nothing I love more than a good story, and she knows if she puts me on the scent of one I'll track it down soon enough."

You know, it's funny how often a person's temper seems

to end at the same time their money does. I threw another natural roll, and Mr. Morris didn't take it too kindly.

"Hmph!" he snorted. "What a *ridiculous* tale—I really don't have time for this kind of nonsense!" He stalked off with hardly a goodbye—though he did leave a considerable amount of his money behind as a consolation.

"Skeptical sort," I said, standing up. "Come on, Skinny. I reckon we should get some shuteye before we land, so's we're nice and fresh."

"Grrr," said Skinny. "Baa."

We walked up to our quarters from the ship's lounge, me ambling and Skinny stumping along with his usual waddling gait. We didn't run into anyone in the corridors; most of the passengers had already turned in, and the crew wasn't large. The *Kingwell's Pride* wasn't a bad ship, just a little old and banged-up. It had character, and I figured that made up for a few dents and scratches.

'Course, once me and Skinny got back to our stateroom I remembered why we'd gone out to the lounge in the first place. The room would have been cramped for a normal-size human, but I stand close to seven feet tall—and despite Skinny's name, he ain't. Or at least he wasn't at the moment.

"Goddammit, Skinny," I grumbled as I scrunched up on the folding bed. "Rearrange yourself into something closer to a pancake, will you? This bed's torture enough without you using up the rest of the cubic."

Skinny's mouth opened up real wide, and then he climbed out of his skin—the furry part of it, anyway. "More than happy to," he sighed. "You have no idea how *hot* that damn fur coat is."

Skinny's full name is Skinshifter, and he's actually a Toolie—but no ordinary Toolie. For one thing he's a male, and males aren't allowed off Kinslick. With the fake fur off, he doesn't look that different from other Toolies: see-through pink flesh wrapped around a skeleton made of bones from a dozen species, with any number of metal or wood objects thrown in. His sensory cluster, looking like a clump of pink grapes, was between his jaws at the moment—since Toolies eat by absorbing their prey the way an amoeba does, the jaws were just for show. He didn't need a mouth to talk, either; he used a voder wired to his nervous system.

That was another thing that marked him as different. Most Toolies have an aversion to audible speech, preferring to communicate between themselves with infrared pulses and to other races with sign language or implant-screens that spell out their words.

But the biggest difference of all was the fact that he and I had spent the last five years hanging around together, and he never once tried to eat me.

One thing about him, though, was exactly the same as any other Toolie: he stank. Toolies' sweat their gastric juices right out of their skin, so all they have to do is wrap around something to digest it; it might be handy for them, but it sure does take some getting used to. 'Specially if you're going to be cooped up with one in a room the size of a tin can for a few weeks.

That wasn't what was bothering me, though—I'd gotten used to Skinny's smell a long time ago. It was what he was using to *disguise* his smell that I couldn't stand.

"Not *more* of that stuff," I groaned, as Skinny reached out an arm he'd put together in the last few seconds and grabbed a bottle out of a suitcase. "I swear, it smells worse than you ever did."

"That's the *point*, genius," he said. I watched as he rearranged his skeleton into something that fit into the available space a little better, and built himself another hand so he could open the bottle. Toolies use internal muscle strands to move their bones around; they can imitate almost any kind of internal skeletal structure, and a few Mother Nature never thought of. I'd seen Skinny go from being short, squat, and four-legged to something resembling a hyperkinetic octopus in about thirty seconds.

He started dumping the bottle's contents on the fur, and did it smell rank. "What was the idea of telling a mark why we're here?" said Skinny. "You're just supposed to keep him distracted, not give him our itinerary."

"I don't tell you how to pick pockets, do I?" I countered. "So don't tell *me* how to tell a tale." I was a little touchy on the subject—not only am I good at spinning yarns, sometimes I enjoy it too much to stop when I should. "Anyway, he didn't believe half of it, and I didn't tell him anything that could trip us up later."

"All right, all right," said Skinny. "How much did we take from that suit, anyway?"

"I got about three thousand, give or take a few dollars," I said. "How about you?"

Floating in the middle of his semitransparent organs was a little silver pouch; it slid forward and oozed out of a slit in his skin. "See for yourself."

Toolies live up to their name, being naturally talented at almost every kind of trade: technician, carpenter, steel-worker, jeweler. If something needs to be put together, taken apart, or tuned up, you can probably find a Toolie that can do it better than anyone else.

Skinshifter had his own set of skills. Lock-picking, safe-cracking, pickpocketing . . . not to mention being a master of disguise, a hell of a mimic, and a damn good actor. Why, if it wasn't for the fact that he had to stay hidden most of the time, I doubt he'd need me at all.

I picked up the pouch, unsealed it, and dumped it on the bed. Two corporate credit disks clinked out. I fished a palm-scanner out of my luggage and inserted one disk, then the other. "Hmm. His credit's not so good. Must be all that gambling he does."

"If he's as bad at gambling as he is at cheating, it's no wonder," said Skinny. "When you started mumbling about everything going black, it took him almost a minute to doctor the dice."

"Well, his company'll be buying us dinner for the next

few days, anyway," I said. "If I can work up an appetite after being exposed to that odor every day for three weeks, that is."

"You could work up an appetite face-down in a sewer with your tongue cut out," said Skinny. "I think you're half Toolie, myself."

"If I was, I might get a decent night's sleep on this torture rack," I grumbled, and tried to get comfortable. Skinny crammed himself under the bed, as he usually did. "Lights off," I said, and lay there in the dark for a while, trying to get to sleep.

At least Toolies don't snore; they breathe through their pores. I could tell Skinny was still awake, though, by the way he kept shifting around. Most folks think of Toolies as quiet creatures, and generally they don't like to make a lot of noise; but many's the night I've lain and listened to Skinshifter move his bones around inside himself. It's a hard sound to describe, and not nearly as creepy as you might think.

After a few minutes I whispered, "Shifter?"

"Yeah?"

"You nervous?"

"About what?"

"You know—going back home."

"What, to a whole planet dedicated to keeping me in prison? Nah—they couldn't keep me locked up before, and they won't be able to catch me now."

"That's not what I meant," I said. I don't why I was still whispering; just something about talking in the dark, I guess. "I meant—well, it's still the place you came from, you know? You must have family—"

"I don't have a family," he said flatly. "My mother dumped me in the Reservation less than a day after I was born, and I don't remember a thing about her. That's how it is with our kind; inside an hour I was fighting for my life. And winning."

"What about your sibs?" I asked. "I know Toolies are always born in clusters—aren't you curious about them?"

"I don't remember anything about them, either," he said.
"The only reason I'm here is as a favor to Melody."

I wondered about that, but I didn't argue with him; and
before too long we both drifted off to sleep.

The ship touched down at the Kiskikill space yards. They
were on the edge of the planet's only continent, which was
shaped like a giant hourglass. I'd never been to Kinslik before, but I'd done my homework; I knew that one half of the
hourglass was set aside for the Reservation, where all the
male Toolies lived. There was a huge wall, hundreds of
miles long, that divided the continent at the middle and kept
the males contained.

On the other side of that wall was Myriad.

The city stretched from coast to coast to coast, a thousand
miles in diameter. The space-yards were on the curving
northwest tip, as far away from the Reservation as possible.
The city itself was thousands of years old, though it was
only a third its present size and the Toolies were still living
in mud huts when humankind discovered it—but they were
huts several stories tall, laid out into streets, and had their
own fresh water and sewage system.

Then humans showed up, two hundred and fifty or so
years ago, and decided to civilize the place. The Toolies were
the best, cheapest labor around, and Kinslik was right in the
middle of what became a heavily used trading route; add to
that a wealth of natural resources that the Toolies didn't seem
to be using, and you had the perfect conditions for a factory
planet. Human suburbs sprang up around the edges of Myriad like mold on breadcrust, and spread both ways.

Now, two and a half centuries later, the original city's
been buried under a thick layer of foamed steel, duracrete,
and mirrored glass. Most of the natural resources are gone,
but one's still there: the Toolies themselves. They've fought
their way up from being property to being second-class cit-

izens, and they're still the best damn workers in the galaxy. These days, you're as likely to see a Toolie paramedic as you are to see a Toolie laborer—but you still won't see any in the corporate boardroom.

And every one you *do* see will be female.

Now, I don't want you to get the wrong idea about me and Skinny—that we were just a couple of no-good thieves. We were real *good* thieves; the first thing we did the next morning, just before the ship landed, was quietly slip Mr. Morris's credit disks back in his pocket—after cleaning them out, of course. Mr. Morris was too busy ignoring us to even notice.

As we marched down the gangway toward the terminal, I started getting a little nervous myself. Skinny's disguise was good enough to fool suits like Morris, but we were on a planet full of Toolies now; I didn't think a smelly fur coat and "Grrr. Baa," was likely to fool *them*.

Sure enough, there was a Toolie working the customs counter. She was one of the new, modern-type Toolies; she had a human-shaped skeleton, wore clothes—some kind of rubbery business suit—and a realistic-looking mask of a pretty girl over her skull. Her sensory cluster was on top of her head, and had a brim around its base that made it look kind of like a hat. She had glass eyes that blinked every ten seconds, and a permanent smile.

"Good day, sir," she said as we walked up. I didn't have to worry about her smelling Skinny, anyway; she had on enough perfume to mask a truckload of Toolies. Her voder had a slight crackle to it.

I handed her my ID disk, and the special one I carried for Skinny. He really was registered as a Guide Animal, though not as a Sheep dog/Sheep. I just hoped the customs officer had never actually seen a Chihuahua.

We didn't have any problems, though, and she passed us right through. I was worried for a second when we got into the main terminal; the place was crawling with Toolies of every size and shape. There were Toolies built like crabs, Toolies built like gazelles, Toolies built like things I never saw before. I saw one like a giant gorilla with no legs, walking on his hands. There were other races, too, some of which I'd seen and some of which I'd only heard of: ferret-like Mongi with their snaky tails, Ditdats that looked like body-building frogs, Thingers with their fronds flashing every color you could think of.

You'd think that with that many Toolies in one place it would stink to high heaven, but the air had no smell at all, just a bland flatness I found a little disturbing. I rely on my nose as much as Skinny does on his sense of touch, and at first I thought there was something wrong with me—it took me a second to realize that the ventilation system must be pumping in some kind of molecule-masker, so that a new visitor wouldn't get the impression that throwing up was the national pastime.

The terminal itself looked like—well, a terminal, only bigger. I have to admit I was a little nervous just being on a planet like Kinslik; while Skinny and I had done our share of traveling, it had all been to frontier planets. We'd never been to a place as big and busy as this before.

I had Skinny on a guide-harness, and he led me right to the public toilets and into a stall. It had a sound-dampener built in for privacy, and we could talk without worrying about being overheard.

"You all right?" I asked him, trying not to sound too motherly.

"Yeah, yeah," he said. "Whatever they're pumping into the air to hide the smell is helping. I'll be okay, but I *have* to get out of this fur straitjacket."

"I don't know," I said. "It's a pretty good cover . . ."

"On a ship, where I can hide in the stateroom and take the damn thing off once in a while, sure. The average temperature on Kinslik is ten degrees higher and a lot more humid. Unless you want me to keel over from heat prostration, I need to change."

"All right, all right," I said. "I'll go pick up our luggage and you wait here."

I went down to the baggage area and waited for our stuff to come down the belt. *He should be all right*, I thought. *It's a men's restroom, after all.*

Now, I know what you're thinking, and believe me, I was thinking it, too. Things would be a hell of a lot simpler if Skinshifter could just go in drag. What's one more female Toolie on a planet full of them? And he could do it well enough to fool any human, I'm sure; he'd done it before. But there were two very large problems with that plan: first, even with his biology covered up, Skinshifter's voice would give him away. I don't mean the voder, I mean his natural voice, the infrared pulses he used to talk to others of his kind. Even if he pretended to be mute, Toolies have a secondary means of communicating, where they let their flesh flow together and their nervous systems hook up—and there was no way to fake that.

The second was his natural inclinations. See, despite all his complaining about the fur suit, Skinny preferred being in disguise to not—with the exception of posing as a female. A female Toolie, I mean; it wasn't the feminine gender in general he was prejudiced against.

He hadn't done too well at the hands of his womenfolk— his mother threw him in a prison camp when he was an infant, and other female Toolies kept him there. He'd been a fugitive all his life, and I could understand why it would rankle him to pose as one of those responsible.

Half his society had rejected him—and he'd rejected the other half himself. There were real good reasons male Toolies were kept segregated; ounce for ounce, they were probably the most dangerous, voracious predators alive. They'd eat anything, and add whatever teeth, claws, or horns that were left over to their own arsenal. They lived to eat, fight, and mate, and most of them were about as bright as a smart dog.

Except Skinshifter. He was considerably brighter, and a

life of fighting, rutting, and devouring anything that moved wasn't enough for him. He used his brains to escape, not just the Reservation but the planet itself, and ever since then he'd regarded himself as a society of one. I guess that's why we got along so well; I didn't exactly fit in, myself.

Our luggage finally showed up, two trunks of considerable size. I got a cart to stow them on and hauled them back to the restroom—I was strong enough to just tote 'em by hand, but I didn't want to draw any more attention than neccesary.

Once in the restroom, I took my time washing my hands and combing the shaggy blue fur that passes for my hair. I studied what I saw in the mirror: a tall, muscular humanoid dressed in loose-fitting tan trousers and jacket, with blue skin and short, downward-curving horns that looked like they might have come from a musk ox. My face could be charitably described as bovine, and my build called to mind a gorilla. As I said, I stood close to seven feet tall in my bare feet, which I preferred over shoes—mainly because my toes are prehensile. I wasn't as hairy as most of my race, but I wasn't exactly smooth-skinned, either. I leaned in close, grimaced, and inspected one pointy canine.

Finally there was a lull when the restroom was empty. I gave a special knock on the stall door and Skinny opened it up for me. I shoved his trunk in and waited outside.

A few minutes went by while I pretended to be busy looking through my own trunk. I heard the sporadic whir of an electric wrench and the occasional clang; I hoped people would just think the stall was being fixed.

Finally, I heard the tap I'd been listening for; it meant "All clear?" in the signal-language we'd come up with and used for years.

I whistled a few aimless-sounding bars that meant "Hold on."

When the coast was clear I opened the door—and out rolled my partner. He looked amazingly like an overstuffed chair, one with a metal frame and wheels.

"Get on," he said.

"What about the luggage?"

"Hook the cart to the back—there's a hitch."

I did, then sat down. I could feel the padding behind my back move; it was padded with *him*.

"Are you sure this is more comfortable than a fur suit?" I asked. We were already rolling toward the door.

"Sure. The robochair's frame supports your weight; all I have to do is keep us moving. It's not that hard to mimic a motor—and since these things usually have onboard compsystems, we can talk to each other without attracting attention."

We were moving through the terminal now, and sure enough, nobody seemed to notice us. "What about the heat?" I asked.

"Got a little electric fan installed. And just so you know, my sensory cluster's behind a grille between your legs; try not to block my view, or I'll run into something."

My friend, the robot wheelchair . . . I sighed and shook my head. Well, it might come in useful; half the time we found marks by posing as someone with a disability. It's downright satisfying to burn someone despicable enough to rob the less fortunate—and the handicapped angle gave us an ace in the hole if things turned nasty.

I had a thought. "What about your smell?" I asked.

I got a whiff of something that smelled like burning insulation. "That should last until we can pick up some airmasker like the one they're using here."

"And what are we going to do if we *can't* find any, Mr. Genius?"

"Use you," he said. "Not too many people know what a Shinnkarien Ox is supposed to smell like—and I still have half a bottle of dog-odor left."

I shut up.

"We should call Melody," said Skinny, and steered us toward a netbooth. Aunt Melody and Uncle Mike were supposed to have arrived on Kinslik about a week before us. We didn't know if they were here for sure, of course, since there's no way to communicate while you're traveling through hyperspace; information travels between worlds as fast as a ship does and no faster. Sometimes that's a pain in the butt, but sometimes it's kept me and Skinny one step ahead of the law, so I can't complain too much.

The netbooth was built to accommodate Toolies as well as humans, which meant it was roomy—we were able to roll in without any trouble. I activated the sound-dampener field and used some of Mr. Morris's money to call Aunt Melody.

The screen lit up with her face immediately. She had more than one, of course, but this was the one Shifter and I knew best, the one she'd been wearing when she introduced us. It was a strong face, high cheekbones and a firm chin, softened by laugh lines at the corners of her eyes and mouth. Her hair was long and black, with touches of white at the temples, and she had the kind of smile that warmed your insides.

"Hello, boys," she said, and shone that smile at us. I have to admit, it calmed me down some.

"'Lo, Aunt Melody," I said. "Well, we're here."

"I can see that. Where's Skinshifter?"

"Right here, Melody," said Skinny. "I'm the chair."

"Of course. How are you holding up, Skinshifter?"

"So far, so good. I'm going to need some industrial-strength air-masker, though."

"Already taken care of," she said. "It's waiting for you at your hotel. I've booked you into a small suite at the Spring-fall Plaza. Just take a taxi from the terminal. Do you have cab fare?"

"We can manage," I said. "How's Uncle Mike?"

Considering that her face was just a digital illusion, Melody could have chosen to hide the worry in her eyes. But she'd always believed in honesty between family, and so she left it there for us to see. "He's worse," she said. "Yesterday he forgot what a tree was. He swore up and down he'd never seen one before, no matter how many different kinds I showed him."

That was something I hadn't told Mr. Morris. Mike Blink, the legendary pilot, was starting to—well, unfocus. Ever since the Pretty Big Bang, he'd been having trouble with his memory and concentration; part of the reason we were here was to see if we could find a way to undo that.

"He's resting right now," said Melody. "He seems to need his downtime more since the event."

"We'll do whatever we can," said Skinshifter.

"Yes, ma'am," I added. "Only—"

"Yes, Storysmith?"

"Uh—what exactly is it we're supposed to do?"

The worried look spread from her eyes to the rest of her face, and some weariness crept in with it. "I'm not exactly sure myself," she said quietly. "All I know is that, as a Shinnkarien Ox, you have a physical connection to certain hyperspatial energies that can't be detected otherwise—and you're the only Ox I can ask for help. If anyone can find the source of those hyperspace emissions, you can—after that, I just don't know."

"Don't worry, Aunt Melody," I said. "We'll get Mike fixed up."

"Call me when you get to the hotel," she said, and then we said our goodbyes.

We rolled outside to get a cab, and I got my first good look at Kinslik proper. The sky was kinda gray and black, and it was raining. I could see tall buildings in the distance, and hear the constant low roar of the spaceport; it didn't seem too different from any other place we'd been. We rolled up to the taxi queue and got in line.

And that's when I felt it.

It was just a twinge at first, a kind of tickle in the back of my brain. It felt so familiar, I almost didn't notice it; then I realized *why* it was so familiar, and nearly jumped out of my shoes.

"Skinny!" I hissed. "I can feel it!"

"Sorry, I was just trying to get a little more comfortable—"

"Not you, you idiot! I can feel the Wild!"

The Indigo Wild is where I grew up; it could probably go toe-to-toe with the Toolie Reservation as the most dangerous place in the galaxy. But to me it would always be home, with a particular *feel* to it so constant that I only noticed it when I left—and then, for the longest time afterward, the world seemed to be missing something, some sound or smell I couldn't quite identify.

Well, now I could. And it was coming from the second gravcab in line.

I studied it. It was longer than most of the other gravcabs, with plenty of chrome and tinted windows, and had a pair of long, curving horns mounted over the grille. It was painted the same bright yellow that cabs always are, and I couldn't see the driver through the tinted windshield. As I watched, it glided forward and stopped at the head of the line. The trunk popped open and two robot arms deployed, grabbing the fare's luggage and stowing it. The customer, a corporate type in a bright purple business suit, climbed into the back.

"Skinny, get me over to that gravcab," I said. I had to fight the urge to just bound over there myself.

We'd worked together long enough that if one of us said "jump," the other one would already be in the air—plenty of time to ask *why* later. By the time we rolled up, though, the gravcab was already climbing into the sky.

We got a few glares from the others standing in line, so we scooted back to where we'd been. "What was *that* all about?" asked Skinny.

"Not sure," I said. "But I think that cab had something to do with the Pretty Big Bang."

Then it was our turn. There was just barely enough room for the robochair, but we managed. The driver got out and crammed our luggage into the trunk. He was a short, stocky man, with bushy black eyebrows and dark hair slicked back.

"Where to?" he asked when he was back in the driver's seat. There was a heavy metal grille between the front seat and the back, and I was pretty sure there was a protec-field as well.

"The Springfall Plaza," I said.

"Sure thing." We took off.

"I never saw a cab like *that* before," I said.

"What's that?" asked the cabbie.

"That big cab, with the horns on the front."

"Oh, yeah." The cabbie chuckled. "That's Joey the Bull. He's one of a kind."

"Is that right?" I said.

"Oh, yeah. Some of the stories I could tell you . . ."

Now, when I said I had a knack for stories, I didn't just mean telling them; I've always been able to pass along my compulsion to spin yarns, too. For some reason, once I get a person talking, they don't run down for a while—and they'll tell me things they wouldn't tell their best friend. I can't exactly explain it, but it's come in handy on more than one occasion.

"Like what?"

"You wanna hear about Joey? Okay, we're gonna be in the air for a while; lemme tell you about Joey and the time he took on the whole Bernardi crime syndicate . . ."

two

Dark's Parkade

The first thing you gotta know about Joey the Bull is he don't take no crap from nobody. I known Joey a long time, and he's always been like that. Somethin' in him just locks up when people try to push him around, and after that you might as well try and move the planet instead of him.

Not that movin' Joey is easy under the best of circumstances, considering the fact that he tips the scales at around eight hundred pounds. Didn't know that, didja? Lotta people don't, even the ones that ride in his cab—he's got the driver's side sealed off with tinted windows and one-way glass. You can see that the driver's compartment is bigger than normal from the outside, but not too many people have seen what's in there.

Well, I'm one a' them. He's got the whole thing wired so he never has to leave: antigrav suspension harness, hospital-quality waste recycler, built-in vibromassagers. He floats in there like a whale in a tank, and he's probably healthier than you or me; he had an extra heart grafted into his system to help carry the load, and he takes all kindsa artery-scrubbers to keep his pipes clear. You might think he'd be lonely, but

20

he's not; he's got full-band access to the Netweb, and in there it don't matter what you look like. I understand he's quite the lady's man in the cybersex rooms.

I know what you're thinking: even with all that, why would anybody wanna be that big? Wouldn't it be a whole lot easier to just go to a clinic and get his body readjusted? And I guess the only way I can answer that question is with a story.

I been driving a gravcab in Myriad about fifteen years; Joey, a little more than ten. This is a big city, a goddamn big city, but between me and Joey I think we know every street and alley in it. It can be a mean city, too; between the factories going outta business and all the ships that pass through the system, we get a lotta people down on their luck, from every species you ever heard of. Some don't make it; some turn into crooks just to survive.

The rest become cabbies.

Joey can really hold forth when he wants ta. I heard him explain once why cabbies are the way they are, and it always stuck in my head. It goes like this: a city is like a pond. You got all kindsa organisms trying to get by, fightin' for space and food. The rich corporate guys are at the top; the poor immigrants are at the bottom. It's always been that way, Joey says. So the poor immigrants get the jobs no one else wants, the ones with lousy hours, low pay, and dangerous working conditions. In other words, they drive cabs.

But here's the thing: the tougher you make the environment an organism lives in, the tougher you make the organism. That's how superbugs developed, Joey says; all the antibiotics we pumped inta people made the germs stronger over time. The germs evolved.

And cabbies, Joey says, are an organism. Over the years, they've developed defenses. Useta be, drivin' a cab was dangerous; anybody could tell you to drive to the middle of nowhere, then put a bullet in your head. So drivers started carrying weapons of their own, and adding armor to their cabs. Now, only the crazies mess with us, and they don't live to brag about it.

We already had a built-in nervous system, Joey says. It useta just be a radio voice link, but these days we have our own Netweb service, and any driver can plug into any other driver's situation in a second. So what do you call a highly organized, heavily armed organism? The Drivers Guild, that's what. And we don't take crap from anybody else in the pond.

Which don't mean there aren't some pretty big, pretty mean fish in there with us—like the Bernardi Syndicate. Everybody talks about how the multiplanetaries have all the real power, but the Bernardis ain't a corporation; they're a good old-fashioned crime family, and everybody in Myriad knows it. No matter how corrupt the system gets—and with the megacorps in charge, it's pretty damn corrupt—there'll always be *somethin'* that's illegal, and somebody willin' to sell it to you. That's the Bernardis—they control all the bootleg data, drugs, and tech in the city.

And then they decided they wanted to control *us*.

See, they figured we'd make the perfect courier system. We're everywhere, we're mobile, we know every inch of the city. It's perfect, they think—except we don't play delivery boy for *anyone*. We're not stupid. Any of us gets busted, we know the Bernardis don't give a shit; they'd pretend like they never heard of us.

So when they offered to buy us out, we politely declined. They insisted. We declined again, not so politely. They decided t'get nasty—and that's when the war started.

They started small: blew up one of our gravcabs with a surface-to-air missile. Thought that might scare us inta doin' business. Boy, were *they* wrong.

You wanna know where to score some good dope, who you ask? A cabbie. You want a little illicit rent-a-sex, who can find it for you? A cabbie. You lookin' for a place to gamble, or fence stolen goods? A cabbie'll always know where to go, who to look for. The Bernardis didn't realize we knew as much about their operation as they did about ours—but we taught 'em real quick. Like I said, we're a heavily armed organism; they cost us a cab, we cost them two gambling dens and a drug lab.

Things got kinda messy after that.

After a week we'd lost about fifty drivers, and the Bernardis were hurting just as bad as we were; you didn't dare hail a cab or walk into a nightclub without a force-field generator and an up-to-date will. Both sides knew we couldn't keep it up, but neither of us was willin' to blink. That's when we decided to cancerbomb the Don.

Don Bernardi was the head of the Bernardi family, as well as bein' an ice-cold sonofabitch with balls of steel. We knew that as long as he was alive the Bernardis would never back down.

So we took what was left of our war chest, bought a bioweapon and hired someone to deliver it. Believe it or not, everything went smooth—the assassin got in and out without being detected, and the Don got real sick, real fast. We thought it was all over—until Joey shows up with some interestin' news.

"He might not croak," Joey tells us. We're holdin' a general meeting on the Netweb, all the drivers there. It's kinda like being in a giant hive fulla yellow bees; a wall of virtual gravcabs, thousands of 'em, just hangin' there in space. Even the ones on duty are linked up. Everybody knows who Joey is, so we pay attention.

"You all know the Bernardi Syndicate deals in illegal tech," Joey says. His cab's icon is front and center. "They've pulled some strings with their corporate connections, and gotten the Don approved for an experimental technique. It might actually cure him."

Well, there's a general hubbub over that, 'cause if the Don recovers, we're right back where we started.

Joey waits until we calm down a little, then says, "Hang on. I think I've got a way to make this work *for* us."

So he tells us his plan, and we kick it around for an hour or two. Then we vote on it. It doesn't pass unanimously—cabbies got too many opinions to agree on *anything* unanimously—but it passes. Like my Pop useta say, when you don't have a lot of choices, the ones you *do* have look better all the time.

It goes down the very next night. I meet Joey and another driver at Dark's Parkade, an out-of-the-way hole in the Graylight District. You know how some places just have a bad feel to them? Dark's Parkade feels like three of those places. It's where used condoms, stolen cars, and junkies go to die.

The Parkade's on the edge of an old industrial park, a big duracrete dungeon sunk fifteen floors underground. We're on the thirteenth level; so much crap's drifted down over the years that the bottom two floors is filled up with it. There's no lights below ten; even the crazies don't come down here. We all sit there in the dark in our gravcabs, and talk to each other over a private c-space link.

"I heard this story one time," Max says. When he isn't driving cab, he spends a lot of time on the Netweb checking out different programs, which is I guess why Joey wanted him with us. In person Max is a thin, twitchy guy with stringy red hair; in c-space he looks like an oil painting of a thin, twitchy guy with stringy red hair. "This story about the Bernardis."

"Yeah?" I say. "Enlighten us." I've always been a vintage car nut, so it looked like I was in a shiny black 1927 Pierce-Arrow, which is about a block long with running boards and a rumble seat, the type of car gangsters useta drive. I'm sittin' behind the wheel, and I got more hair and less gut than I usually do.

"There was this guy my girlfriend used to go out with," Max says. "Man, he loved his wheels even more than you do, Joey." The only image Joey ever uses, even over a private link, is his cab's. It looks just like his real one, right down to the steer horns mounted on the hood.

"Had a completely restored '05 Rolls Ferrari. Top-end inertial shielding, triple-redundant antigrav boosters, friction-field paint job, the works. A thing of beauty. 'If we were in the middle of a desert and I caught on fire, he *might* piss on me to put it out,' my girlfriend said; 'if the *car* caught on fire, he'd slit his own wrists and use the blood.'

"Anyway, he was paranoid about it, too. He'd heard the Bernardi family had brought in some specialists from off-world, just to boost cars; he'd heard they were the best, and that they especially liked high-end items like his Rolls. So he invested in some heavy security: protec-fields, active sonar motion detectors, molecule-sniffer alarm system. But even that wasn't enough for him, so he had this special garage built. Three-foot thick duracrete walls, roof, and floor, and the whole thing is just barely big enough to fit the car in—he has to climb out a window once it's parked. Seals the garage door with a seven-way foamed-steel vacuum lock. No way that car is going *anywhere*.

"So he goes to bed, safe and secure. The next morning he wakes up, goes out to the garage—"

"The car's gone, right?" I say.

"No. The garage is still sealed up tight. When he unlocks the door, the car is still there, with all the security devices still on. *But it's facing the wrong way*—and there's a *note* on the windshield."

"Which says?"

" 'When we want it, we'll come and get it.' "

"Thanks, Max," I tell him. "You're doin' *wonders* for my confidence."

"Don't get rattled," Joey says. "The Bernardis aren't invincible. We can pull this off."

"You sure this'll work?" I ask him. "We're under a lot of duracrete." It's a stupid question, but I'm nervous. I feel like my cab's at the bottom of the ocean, and all that darkness is tryin' to squeeze its way in.

"It'll work," Joey says. "I'm tapped into an old antennae line that still goes to the roof, and bouncing the signal off a comm satellite and through a scrambler. They won't be able to trace it, and no one will look for us here. Now get ready— we're going online."

This was the deal: the Don was gonna have ten million tiny bugs injected into his body. They were so small they could attack each cancer cell personally, and even fix up normal cells that were damaged. They got these bugs from some jungle on another planet, and apparently the tricky part was getting 'em to do what the docs wanted. They had an AI to oversee the whole thing, but for some reason they couldn't use it to directly control the bugs.

The solution they came up with was pretty smart. In a city the size of Myriad, it ain't too hard to come up with a million volunteers to test a new program on the Netweb, especially if you use your corporate connections to give each of 'em a little free Netweb time in return; you let each volunteer direct a squad of ten bugs, use the AI to keep 'em in line, and turn 'em loose. Of course, you don't tell any of the volunteers who they're actually operating on. Long as everybody does what they're supposed to, all the cancer cells get zapped, the Don gets better, and the corp that owns the bugs gets richer.

Unless somethin' goes wrong, of course. Like maybe a few rogue cabbies gettin' loose in the Don's bloodstream.

All of a sudden, I ain't sittin' behind the wheel of a Pierce-Arrow anymore—I'm at the controls of a spaceship. Everything was real simple and cartoony, like a program designed for a kid; I guess when you got a million volunteers to ride herd on, you wanna keep things as hard to screw up as possible. All the surfaces look like they're made of blue light, and all the controls are either red or green. There's a green joystick with a red button on it, a few green slidebars on the blue dashboard, and a couple more red buttons. There's a viewscreen above the dash, and I can see a pair of simulated hands floatin' in front of me, doin' whatever my own do. The hands are this weird shade of pink. Other than that, I'm just a bodiless point-of-view in the middle of the cockpit.

They got a tutorial runnin' on the viewscreen, idiot-proof directions on how to fly the bug. I read 'em as fast as I can; Joey'd been able to get us into the volunteer feed, but he couldn't lay his hands on the prep program all the volunteers got beforehand—this last minute review was all we were gonna get. I see pretty quick that even with ten bugs to direct, it ain't gonna be that hard.

No sooner am I done with the directions than they vanish, and I see what's outside the bugship. Well, not exactly; whatever the bug sees through its bug eyes probably wouldn't make much sense to the average guy, so it's filtered through a virtual program into a simulation we can understand.

What I see is a whole lot of bugs. From the outside, a bug looks like a blue lobster with a barrel strapped to its back; the barrel, I realize, is the cockpit. All the bugs are kind of tumbling against this orange background, twitching their big blue claws.

I hear a voice say, "Prepare for entry in ten seconds," and then a countdown. When it hits zero, this black whirlpool opens up in front of us and we all get sucked inside.

Well, that was it. We were in the Don.

I didn't have a chance to say anything to Joey or Max—I didn't know where they were, or if they'd even made it in. Alluva sudden I hear Joey's voice in my ear, sayin', "You guys okay?"

"Yeah, yeah," says Max, then me.

And then I just gotta laugh. I expected somethin' like a huge tunnel, with giant bacteria floatin' around, and big blobby things with tentacles maybe.

What I see is a freeway.

It's the simulation, of course. Filtered reality. All these volunteers, what do they know about microbiology? Most of 'em, not much—so the AI's feedin' us stuff we can understand, images we can relate to. People that live in the city know about streets, about overpasses and bridges and tunnels, so that's what the simulation is modeled on. I'm in the middle of a big aerial multilane, a bunch of flyways grouped in a tube like strands in a fiber-optic cable. The guiderays that divide the lanes are bright red instead of yellow, and so are the traffic globes that connect the rays. The background's white instead of orange, and the lanes are full of lobsters—but that's not all. They're also full of floating bagels and poker chips. I feel like I been dumped in the middle of a traffic accident between a seafood restaurant and a Jewish casino.

I could see bugs starting to form up in groups of ten as people tried out their controls. "Pay attention to the black bugs," Joey says. "They're under the direct control of the AI."

"I can't see any," I tell him. "Just the blue ones, a buncha bagels, and some poker chips. I think I'm gettin' hungry."

"Those are red corpuscles and platelets," Joey tells me. "The black bugs are mostly at the edges, to keep people from straying. I can see a few."

The bugs moved by swimming with their tails, and they could move pretty quick; I get my ten in a V and start cuttin' across lanes, headin' for the same edge Joey's on. So does Max.

By the time I get there, I'm fightin' cross-traffic, and a current too; all the other bugs are swimming downstream, following the directions the AI's giving 'em. I can hear the directions too, but I don't pay any attention.

I make my way across fifty lanes or so and finally spot the edge of the crowd. Sure enough, there are black bugs spaced out every hundred blue ones or so, makin' sure everybody's stayin' together. Joey tells me and Max to head for the bottom of the pack, and we'll meet there.

Well, that meant going the wrong way down a one-way street, and in rush hour, no less—but it wasn't like I never done that before. Just not drivin' ten microscopic blue lobsters, you understand. Anyway, I dive back toward the mid-

dle, away from those black border-guards, and start fightin'
the current. The other bugs mainly get out of my way—I get
clipped a few times, but nothin' serious. Like Joey figured,
they didn't have enough of those black bugs to keep an eye
on anything but the borders.

And then I make a rookie mistake. I slam on the brakes as
I reach the edge of the crowd, but I forget that the crowd is
movin' too, away from me. My bugs come to a dead stop—
and the pack zooms past, leaving us hangin' out there all
alone.

Except for the black bug giving us the hairy eyeball.

Suddenly my viewscreen's got a cop on it. He didn't need
to flash a badge—he had a cop face, a cop voice, and a cop
attitude. "Please return to your previous heading," he says.

"I'm havin' some trouble with the interface," I say,
stalling for time. What was I gonna do? About the only thing
I could think of was maybe jumping him, since I outnum-
bered him ten to one.

"Your control unit checks out fine," the cop says, with no
hesitation at all. It wasn't really a cop, of course—it was the
AI. "Return to your previous heading or I'll have to termi-
nate your link."

And then I realize I don't stand a chance of jumping him.
If I try, he'll just cut my connection, and that'll be that.

And then there's this huge burst of blue static, and the cop
disappears off my viewscreen. The black bug's still there,
hanging in front of me, but now there are ten other blue bugs
around it.

"It's offline," Joey says. He doesn't tell me how he did it,
and I don't care. Like my Pop useta say, don't interrogate
your savior.

"Won't his buddies show up?" I ask.

"The AI's too busy to check every unit separately," Joey
tells me. "Even if it notices, it'll just think it's a glitch."

Max shows up a few minutes later, having slipped
through the hole made by the defunct bug. "Where now?" he
asks.

"Up," Joey says.

Now that we're not surrounded by bugs, I can see a little more of my surroundings—we're close to the center lane, the one the fast traffic would use if this was a real freeway. I never seen a freeway so empty before though, not in daylight; the red stripes of the guiderays against the white background make me feel kinda like I'm inside a big candy cane. I can even see a curve up ahead, with the last of the pack just disappearing around it.

We head the other way. Joey tells us we're in a tributary of the vertebral vein, which I think is somewhere in the neck. For a little while we just cruise without talking—it's easy to fall into that rhythm, especially on an empty road. Just you and the engine, humming along . . . the past has a way of risin' into your thoughts at a time like that, and I guess that's what happened with Joey. All of a sudden he says to me, "Charlie."

"Yeah?"

"You're probably wondering why I asked you to come along."

Actually, I had been. I mean, Joey was in charge for obvious reasons, and Max knew about programs and stuff, but me? I was just a hack driver.

"Yeah, I kinda wondered about that," I say.

"You remember the story you told me, about six months after we met?"

And I did. We'd been hanging out in a Netweb room, and he'd asked me where I was from. I told him Fincher's Rest, and he asked why I'd never gone back. That seemed like a strange question, and I guess I coulda just given him a bullshit answer; but I got this feelin' it was important to him. So I told him the truth.

"I can't," I said. "You probably know Fincher's Rest is a pretty religious planet. Well, my family's no different—actually, my older brother's one of Fincher's Prophets. My old man was always so proud of him, y'know? Always sayin' I should be more like him. But I was always more interested in girls and cars than prayin'. I never gave a lotta thought to what I was gonna do when I grew up; just live my life, and try and have a good time.

"But then my Pop up and dies.

"Now, you gotta understand: when a Fincherite dies, his oldest son takes his place in the congregation for a month. That was no problem for my brother; for a coupla weeks he'd step down as a Prophet, and just be one of the flock.

"But that meant I hadda become *his* replacement for a month.

"You might think that's not so tough, and I guess I coulda stuck it out. But my Pop died just before the Talmagar, the week of testing. A Prophet studies all year long for it; it shows how well he knows the Holy Texts, how devout he is. If he screws it up, he's out as Prophet, forever.

"And for that month, as far as the Church was concerned, I *was* my brother.

"He offered to help me study. Said I could pull it off. But I saw this look in his eyes, y'know? This panic. He was gonna lose everything he'd worked for, and it was gonna be my fault.

"I couldn't handle that. So I did the only thing I could think of—I knew he was thinkin' it, too, but he couldn't ask me to do it. I took off before the Investiture ceremony, right after Pop's funeral. In Fincherite law, that meant instant excommunication. My brother no longer had someone to take his place, so he just got to skip the Talmagar.

"But nobody in my family is allowed to talk to me, or even mention me. As far as they're concerned, I'm not just dead—I was never *born*."

Joey didn't say anything for a minute after I finished. Then he asked me, "Would you go to jail if you went back?"

"No," I told him. "It'd just be like I was invisible."

"Invisible," he said, like it meant something to him. "Yes."

After that, we seemed to hang around together a lot more.

"Sure, I remember what I told you," I say. "What, you

asked me along to give us last rites if we screw up? I think you want a Catholic for that, not an ex-Fincherite."

"That's not the reason," Joey says. "Excuse me, Max—would you mind shutting off your channel while I talk to Charlie for a minute?"

"No sweat," Max says.

Joey doesn't say anything for a minute, and I start to think he's shut off his own channel by accident. Then he says, "My father's dead, too.

"I was never the son he wanted me to be, either. He wanted someone ambitious, aggressive. Someone to follow in his own footsteps. I was always more interested in what was going on inside my head than what was happening around me, and that infuriated him. He tried to push me in certain directions, and when I resisted he pushed harder. I pushed back in my own way, refusing to do what he wanted. It was a war that went on until I was sixteen or so—and I won.

"It wasn't much of a victory. He just stopped pushing me, stopped talking to me, stopped paying any notice to me at all. The only emotion I saw on his face when he even looked at me was disappointment, tinged with contempt. I was a failure, a waste of his time, not even worth his anger.

"At first I didn't care. I was just happy to be able to enjoy my books, my virtualities, my music. But, to my dismay, I soon discovered that wasn't enough—as much as I disagreed with my father, he was the only *real* person in my world; the only one I couldn't shut off when I was tired of him, the only one with any authority. His opinion mattered to me. My friends, my teachers, all of them were only images on the Netweb, as insubstantial as phantoms. The house we lived in was big and empty, the only choices for companionship mistresses or servants. Neither seemed comfortable talking to me.

"One of the things my father tried to interest me in was sports, even though I had no desire to play thunderball on anything but a virtual field. My father always took care of

his physique; the first time he spoke more than a few words
to me in weeks was when he noticed I was beginning to gain
weight. He hired a personal trainer for me, and a nutritionist
to plan my diet."

Joey gives this big sigh. "The one trait I seemed to have
inherited from him was his stubbornness. I refused to exercise, bribed servants to bring me rich foods, ordered metab-
olism adjusters through the Netweb. It was easier than you
might think; my father was often away on business trips,
sometimes for months. I ballooned up a hundred pounds in
six weeks right at the beginning, and he finally stopped ignoring me. The larger I grew, the more emotion my father
showed; and even if those emotions were frustration and
worry, at least they weren't contempt. He didn't know, you
see, that I was doing it on purpose. He thought there was
something physically, medically wrong with me.

"It seemed like the perfect solution. I feigned weakness to
avoid exercise until I was too large for such a thing to be fea-
sible, and after that I was free to pursue my Netweb activi-
ties without interruption—except for my father's worried
visits, and the occasional probing of a specialist.

"And then, one day, he found out what I'd been doing.

"It was a doctor who caught me, of course. I'd been able
to fox them for a long time, sometimes through tricks I
picked up on the Netweb, sometimes through threats or
bribery; for all its isolation, being my father's son had some
advantages. But eventually he found a doctor I couldn't
trick, buy off, or intimidate.

"I weighed around four hundred pounds at that point. I'll
never forget the look on my father's face when he confronted me—he wasn't angry, just confused and irritated, as
if confronted by a menu in a language he couldn't understand. It made no sense to him, and I didn't know how to explain. I was only seventeen, and I barely understood the
reasons myself.

"We talked, then argued, then screamed at each other. He
finally found a handle on the situation he could grab, one at-

tached at least partly to the truth: I had done it to anger him. Attacks—even betrayal—he understood, knew how to deal with. He told me I had twenty-four hours to get out of his house. "Only the *rich* are fat!" he spat at me. "Let's see how much you weigh after a year on the street!"

"At that point I was as angry as he was. And just as stubborn.

"I left. I used what money I'd managed to squirrel away in Netweb accounts to buy and outfit a cab. A year later, I weighed six hundred pounds—and my father was dead."

I gotta admit I was a little confused, but I didn't know what to say.

Alluva sudden Joey starts cuttin' across lanes until he gets to the outermost one. Close up, you can see the whiteness doesn't go on forever; there's a wall, made of what looks like white six-sided tiles.

Joey gets his lobsters tearin' at the tiles with their big blue claws, and they rip off real easy—they're actually soft and flimsy, like pancakes. Me and Max pitch in, too. As soon as we got a decent-sized hole, the poker chips start sticking to the edges.

"Platelets healing the wound," Joey says. "They'll seal it up behind us." Underneath the pancake tiles there's a layer of somethin' a little tougher, and after that a buncha thick cables all woven together. We hack our way through them. Then there's some softer stuff, and another layer of cables—but these cables are movin', up and down. We cut through them, and through two more layers that are a lot like the first two, only reversed and thicker.

The other side looks a lot like this one, except the guiderays are purple, the current's goin' the other way, and the whole tube is pulsin', swellin' up and shrinkin' down, over and over. "This is a branch of the vertebral artery," Joey says. "It'll take us straight to the cortex."

I half expect a traffic sign sayin' NEXT EXIT—BRAIN ONLY as we head up the flyway with the current, but instead I see somethin' a lot stranger: an elephant. A big, gray, wrinkled

elephant, drifting along a few lanes to our right, tumblin'
over and over and wavin' his trunk around.

"Joey, Max," I say. "Whatda*fuck*?"

"Programmers having a little fun," Max says. "I think it's
actually a white blood cell."

"Wonder why they picked an elephant," I say.

"White blood cells are a lot bigger than red ones," Max
answers.

"And why not an elephant?" Joey adds. "Humans have
used them for centuries as workers. They're powerful,
smart, and amazingly dextrous for their size. Hannibal used
them to wage war. They rarely forget anything, which is usually good—except when you hurt one. Then it can nurse a
grudge for years, even go rogue."

"Yeah?" I say. "My Pop useta tell me the worst enemy
you could have wasn't the meanest or the strongest—it was
the one with the longest memory."

"Did you know there used to be packs of elephants on Old
Earth that would attack and destroy whole villages?" Joey
asks. "Of all the species Man has declared war on, the elephant is one of the few to declare war on us . . ."

"Uh, Joey?" Max says. "I think we have a problem."

I see what he's talkin' about right away. Just ahead, the
flyway narrows, down from a hundred lanes to fifty to
twenty to ten, and finally just to one. And right in the center
of the remaining lane, there's this guy.

"Bottleneck," Max says. "Virtual, not natural—the blood
cells are ignoring it."

Our lobsters, though, aren't so lucky. And this guy, he
doesn't look real friendly.

He stands in the middle of the lane like he's on solid
ground, his arms crossed in front of him. He's wearin' black
shoes, black gloves, a black suit, a black shirt, and a black
tie. You can tell what kind of clothes he's wearin' because
everything—his lapels, his tie, the creases in his jacket—is
outlined with thin lines of white light, like it's leakin' out of
his body. His face glows white like that, too, but don't get

the idea he looks like an angel or somethin'; he looks more like a bouncer that swallowed a streetlight.

"Take him," Joey says, and we close in at full speed.

Now, I know what you're thinkin'. That guy isn't really there, he's just a programmed image, like the guiderays of the flyway. But in a virulality some things are more real than others, if that makes any sense. And as far as the bugs' programming's concerned, he's the genuine article.

The single lane's only wide enough for about four bugs at a time, and there's thirty of us. Joey leads the charge, slammin' inta the guy with five of his ships. There's a big burst of static across my screen when they hit, and when it clears I see the five bugs tumble away, end over end, dead. We all pull up short, and suddenly the guy has a gun in his hand, a big square pistol as black as death. We're sittin' ducks where we are, so we back up as fast as we can to where the other lanes fan out. The guy starts firin'—*kachow! kachow!*—and he picks off five of Max's bugs and three of mine before we get far enough away that he starts missin'.

"Jeez, Joey," I say, "can't you do to that guy whatever you did to the AI?"

"That's one of the Don's personal guards, not the AI," Joey says. "I can't get close enough to use what I did before. But I have something else."

"What are we waitin' for, an anniversary?" I say. "Pull it out."

"Max?" Joey says, and Max says, "Right."

Max's remaining five ships turn around and head back toward the gunman. They're dartin' and weavin', but he still picks four of 'em off.

"Follow me," Joey says, and takes off in the opposite direction as fast as he can. I go with him, but I still got one of my bugs lookin' backward so I can see what happens to Max.

Max's last bug gets within twenty virtual feet—and this shimmery kind of energy ring goes out from it in every direction, gettin' bigger and bigger, like a silent explosion.

And whatever the ring sweeps over, for a second I can see what it really looks like and not what the simulation is showin' me. The bugs don't look like lobsters so much, more like fleas, and the gizmo on their backs is all blocky gears and rods and shit. There's all this crap in the fluid around us, things that look like bedsprings and blobs and little sticks.

When the ring hits the gunman, he dissolves like smoke. And then it hits us.

The second before it does though, one of Joey's lobsters grabs one of mine. The ring passes right over us, and just for an instant everything goes black. Then it's past, and Joey lets me go. The rest of my bugs are okay, but I got no control over 'em anymore.

"What was that?" I ask Joey.

"Cyborgrenade," he says. "Pulse-program that screws with interface systems. It got rid of the shooter, but it also destroyed Max's link. I managed to shield our primary bugs, but the rest are no longer under our control—or the AI's."

I watch Max's and our freed bugs head straight for the nearest wall and start tunneling into it, just like we'd done. I wonder what they're gonna do, now that they're free.

So now we're down to a bug apiece, and the Don's people gotta know somethin's wrong. We zoom up the artery and toward the brain.

We get to this five-way branch, and believe or not, there actually *are* traffic signs, big green billboards with white lettering and arrows on 'em. We go straight up the basilar artery, passin' a buncha exit-ramp signs on the way: the anterior inferior cerebellar, the labyrinthine, the pontine, the superior cerebellar. Finally, we hang a right at the posterior cerebral. Every once in a while we pass an elephant driftin' along, but none of them seem too interested in us.

Y'know what I always find strange about bein' in c-space? The smells, or lack thereof. I mean, if you gotta full neural rig you get all the senses, but the average guy like me settles for a headset with visual and audio. So there we are, shootin' through the Don's bloodstream like a bad cold, and I can still smell the pine air-freshener in my cab. It just seems weird.

So the flyway's been losin' lanes, gettin' smaller and smaller as we go along. We make another turn, and another, and pretty soon we're flyin' single file down a single lane, with no guiderays at all.

"This is an arteriole," Joey says. I start to notice more and more branching passages on either side, but they're too small for us. The bagels are gettin' sucked in, though they barely fit.

"Those are capillaries," Joey tells me. "They take oxygen and nutrients from the blood cells. We're looking for one set of capillaries in particular."

I guess Joey's got real good directions, 'cause where he stops, the holes don't look no different from any of the others.

"Now what?" I ask. "We're too big to go in there."

"We dig," Joey says.

This time, there's somethin' else behind the white tiles, a buncha packed-together yellowish balloons. "Astrocytes," Joey says. "Fatty cells that form the blood-brain barrier— but they won't keep *us* out."

We tunnel through 'em—and then we hit steel.

It's not simulated, either; I tap a claw against the surface and it seems solid enough.

"Joey," I say. "Whatdafuck?"

"It's a cybersafe, an implant," Joey says. "Encrypted memory storage."

"So what's he got in there?"

"All the things he wants to hide," Joey says. His voice sounds a little strange.

"So howcum you didn't tell the Guild about this?" I ask. "I thought we were gonna, like, give him an embolism or somethin'."

"That's not a real solution," Joey says. "If we kill him, the rest of the family will just retaliate. It'll go on until both sides are so weak a third party—one of the corps, probably—will step in and take both of us over. Everybody will lose."

"So if we're not gonna kill him, why are we here?" I ask.

"To negotiate," Joey says, and taps a claw against the steel. A little blue spark jumps from the claw to the surface, and then I'm not at the controls of a bug anymore.

I'm next to a swimming pool, except I don't got no body; I'm just a floatin' point-of-view. Standin' beside the pool, dressed in an expensive three-piece, is the Don. He's a good-lookin' guy, younger than I thought he'd be. Joey's floatin' in the center of the pool, wearin' a silver wet suit that makes him look like a shiny hippopotamus. He ain't as big as he usually is, though.

"Who are you?" the Don asks Joey.

"There's a story every driver knows," Joey says. "It goes like this: a cabbie was driving along, late at night, when he picked up this fare in a deserted part of town. The fare didn't say much, just asked to be driven to a certain address. When the cabbie got there, he looked in the rearview mirror and the fare was gone. The cabbie got out, knocked on the door of the building, and was told that a man of the fare's description had died in a traffic accident, ten years ago to the day."

"Tell me who you are and what you want!" the Don demands.

"I'm the ghost in your cab," Joey says. "I'm your son."

"I have no son."

"And I have no father," Joey says. "Not for ten years, not since you took every memory of me you ever had and locked them away in this vault."

"I have *no son*!" the Don repeats, angrily.

"Then why did you keep these memories?" Joey asks. "I knew you didn't destroy them, no matter what you said. They're still here, stored with all your other dirty little secrets, with all the blackmail files and payoff lists and murder contracts. All those things you want to keep hidden—because as much as they could hurt you, they're too valuable to get rid of."

The Don starts pacin' back and forth along the edge. It's nighttime, and the only illumination's the blue ripples of light the pool's throwin' off.

"You're one of those damned taxi drivers," he says. "Think you can come in here and eliminate me, huh? Go ahead. Do your worst."

Joey doesn't show his real face to very many people; even I ain't seen it more than half-a-dozen times. He's got a big, round face, as hairless as a baby's, and right then he looked sadder than I ever seen him.

He lifts one huge arm, and everything changes. I was holdin' a baby in my arms, rockin' him and laughin'. Then I was watchin' him grow up, throwin' him birthday parties, buyin' him stuff for Christmas. I swear to God, Joey's whole life played out in front of me, every second, every word they ever said to each other. Right up to the fight where his Pop disowned him and threw him outta the house.

And then we're back by the pool again.

"I remember now," the Don says. "I should have known you'd side with my enemies."

"We didn't start this war," Joey says, and now I can hear the old stubbornness in his voice. "And my choosing to drive a cab had nothing to do with you."

"Ha!" the Don says. "*Everything* you do has to do with me—whatever I want, you do the opposite. Well, I washed my hands of you before, and I'll do it again. I'll wipe every one of these memories."

"No," Joey says, real soft. "You won't."

Joey waves his hand, and there's this blue shimmer around it. All of a sudden everything freezes, like the air just turned solid.

"You're not going to erase anything," Joey says, though his lips ain't movin' anymore. "If you do, I'll upload every secret in here to the Netweb, then sit back and watch the wolves tear you apart."

"No," a voice whispers in my head. "You can't do that."

"Don't tell me what I can't do! I *can* do that, and you know how? These little bugs you have coursing through your bloodstream. You always thought I spent too much time on the Netweb—well, you can learn some very interesting things there. I tracked down some bootleg documentation from the University of Tanzannika, on Shinnkaria—the bugs' home planet. They were discovered over two hundred years ago, but nobody's been able to control them until recently because they give off an unusual radiation that screws up electronics. That's why they couldn't link an AI to them directly; that's how I was able to break in here so easily."

"So go ahead," the voice whispers. "Go ahead, ruin me. It's what you always wanted."

"No," Joey says. "It's not."

"Then what the hell *do* you want?" Don Bernardi asks him.

There's this long, uncomfortable pause. Everything's still frozen, and it feels like it goes on for about a year.

"I want my father back," Joey says at last. "And you are going to give him to me."

"I don't understand—"

"Everybody's a bunch of different people," Joey says. "You show one face to your lover, another to your friends. You're not the same person at work as you are on vacation. Well, while you're out there in the world, I don't give a damn *who* you are; if you want to be Don Bernardi, a bitter old man with a criminal empire, a bunch of relatives he doesn't trust, and no children, go ahead. I don't care.

"But when you're in here, with me, you're my *father.*"

"So you're going to keep me here?" the voice asks. "A prisoner in my own head?"

"I knew you'd pull your consciousness in here during the operation," Joey continues. "You wouldn't trust anyone else to guard your secrets. Everybody talks about the Bernardi family, but it's *not* a family—it's a business, fueled by para-noia and greed, not blood relations. I can count on the fingers of one hand how many times I met any of my uncles, aunts, or cousins when I was growing up.

"But I won't keep you here. You still have obligations to fulfill on the outside."

"What kind of—"

"The war with the Drivers Guild ends immediately. You walk away and you never bother us again."

Joey didn't haveta make another threat—the Don could see how it was.

"A loaded gun to my head makes a convincing argument," the Don says. "As long as you can keep it there."

"Oh, I don't think it'll be too hard," Joey says. "The bugs reproduce asexually, so we can keep a healthy little colony right here in your cerebrum. If we keep people cyberlinked to the bugs, we can hold this vault hostage for as long as we have volunteers to stand watch. And we have a *lot* of very dedicated members."

"Hostage," the Don murmurs. "But you won't keep me here?"

"You have to come back once a week," Joey says. "That's when I'll be here."

"What's going to happen then?" the Don snaps. "You're going to lecture me for eight hours on what a bad father I am?"

"I don't know," Joey says. "Maybe we'll talk. Maybe we'll fight. Maybe I'll kick your ass at virtual golf. But whatever we do, we'll do it as father and son."

There was another long pause. "You know," the Don says at last, "I don't understand you at all." He sounds old and tired. "Turning yourself into some kind of freak, just to make me crazy . . . then all this. Why? Why go to all this trouble now?"

I can hear Joey swallow. "They were going to kill you, Dad," Joey says. His voice is real quiet.

"Aaaah, hell," the Don says. "You're the most stubborn son of a bitch I ever met, you know that?"

"I come by it honestly," Joey says. "Charlie, I want you to

cut your link. Contact the Guild, tell them what's happened."

"Sure," I say. "You gonna be okay here?"

"Yes," he says. "We'll be fine."

So I did like he said. And as me and Max drove out of the depths of the Parkade and into the sunlight, I had a funny thought: you never can tell what's hidden inside something, or someone. And no matter how much duracrete, how many security programs, how much stubborn fat you encase it in, sooner or later it's gonna get out.

After that, everything worked pretty much the way Joey said it would. We got two guys linked to bugs at all times, makin' sure the Don don't try anythin' funny, and Joey makes sure the guards don't snoop around in the vault. Joey and his Pop meet once a week; sometimes they get along, sometimes they don't. But they keep seein' each other, no matter what.

I wish my Pop was still around.

Anyway, that's Joey's story. And hey, lookit that—I talked all the way to your hotel. Good timin', huh? End of the story, end of your ride, and almost the end of my shift. No rest for the weary, though; it's my turn to stand watch tonight . . .

Gotta go. Duty calls.

three

joey the bull

I'd been so wrapped up listening to Charlie's story I hadn't
paid too much attention to the scenery. I had the vague impression of a lot of traffic, and tall buildings on either side,
but that was about it.

Now that we were outside the Springfall Plaza Hotel with
our luggage, I had time to take it all in.

It was like being halfway down the wall of a deep canyon,
one made of glass and steel. The wall was one side of a
building that went down at least fifty stories, and up even
farther. We were on a wide ledge—a street—that ran along
the side of the building. Its main purpose seemed to be to let
gravcabs land and take off again, though there were people
walking down it too. I could see more street-ledges at other
heights, above and below us on the wall—sorry, the *buildings*—across from us. Gravcabs zipped through the air between, as thick as bees in a summer meadow.

"Quit gawking," Skinny said, chuckling. "You want every
grifter in the city to mark us?" The chair rolled forward with
the trunks in tow, through the big glass front doors of the
hotel.

The lobby was mighty impressive: big pillars that looked like they were made of diamond, an antigrav fountain that had water going every which way, and a front desk two stories high. The desk was carved from the trunk of a tree that grew right out of the marble floor, and to get up to it you had to step on these floating platforms that would whisk you to eye level with the hotel clerk. She was young, pretty, and had short gold hair with eyes and lips to match.

She smiled at me, confirmed my reservation, and gave me a cardkey to my room. She was going to send a Toolie bellhop along to help me unpack, but I convinced her I didn't need any assistance.

The room was on the ninety-fifth floor, which wasn't as close to the top as it sounded. The elevator got us there in about two seconds though, and didn't feel like it moved at all.

The room was a decent size—actually, the closets were bigger than some of the ships we'd flown in, you needed a compass and a map to find the bathroom, and the bed was large enough to raise livestock on. I kicked off my shoes and flopped down on the bed face-first. "At last," I groaned. "Something I can sleep in without bending my knees."

Skinny rolled over to three large crates sitting in the middle of the floor. "Looks like Melody sent us a little welcoming present."

I just lay there, enjoying the softness of the bed, while Skinny poured himself out of the robochair and got right to work opening the crates. I swear, if there was a choice between a pile of money and something to take apart, it would cause Skinny some serious distress.

Lying there on the bed, listening to *whir* and *clang!* and *clickclickclickclick*, I started thinking about my uncle Mike and another Toolie that had his own style. His name had been Stowaway, and I'd never met him; he'd died long before I was born. Him and Mike had been close, though, and Mike had told me more than a few stories about him.

Stowaway had been a rogue male like Skinny, but he'd been considerably wilder; the first time he met my father he tried to eat him, and anything else he could wrap himself around. It took Melody, some cybernetic bones and a neural link to teach him the basics of civilized behavior, and after that he only tried to eat people he didn't like.

He and Mike had an unusual relationship. Before Mike died, he'd been a cyborg; it was his own circuitry-lined, foamed steel bones that Stowaway had swallowed, and the neural link let Mike experience the one thing Melody couldn't provide for him: genuine, flesh-and-blood nerve-ending feelings, even if they were piped through a Toolie nervous system.

There was this one story Mike loved to tell. Stowaway had just hit Toolie puberty, apparently overnight; when Mike hooked up to his body, "it was like having an electric eel shoved down my pants." Unfortunately for Stowaway—who got his name by hiding aboard Mike's ship—there were no female Toolies on the planet they were on. "It just about drove the poor bugger crazy," declared Mike. "Male Toolies mate by engulfing the female and spitting her out afterward. Stowaway didn't have any females to engulf, so I guess his signals got a little mixed up. Like all Toolies, he had a fascination with machinery; I guess that's why he fell in love with a tractor."

It wasn't even Mike's tractor. Every morning the owner would chase Stowaway away from his machine, which would be covered in, as Mike put it, "Toolie love slime." Poor Stowaway was barely big enough to stretch his flesh over the tractor's frame, and so had to leave most of his regular skeleton in a pile beside it; when the angry owner showed up, the lovesick Toolie would have to flee without his bones.

What did Mike do about it? Even though possession of a male Toolie is highly illegal, he contacted an Insussklik—that's the Toolies' name for themselves—mating broker and arranged for passage of a female willing to break the rules.

He also bought the tractor to keep Stowaway company until she got there.

I rolled over and sat up. The tops of the crates were open, there were packing chips all over the floor, and Skinny was nowhere to be seen. I could hear rustling coming from one of the crates, though.

"Hey!" I said. "I'm going to call Melody, tell her we made it here all right."

"Sure, sure," said Skinny's muffled voice. "Go ahead."

I punched up her number on the netphone and she appeared on the big wallscreen above it right away. "I see you boys have arrived. Did you get the supplies I sent over?"

"Yep. Skinny's going through them right now."

"Good. I came up with a few things to make his stay a little easier."

A muffled whoop of joy came from the crate.

"From the sounds of things, you made some good choices," I said. "Anything in there for me?"

"You'll see," she said with a smile.

"We also have some progress to report," I said proudly. I told her a scrunched-up version of the story Charlie told us.

"A corporation is using nono ticks?" said Melody when I was done. "I thought nobody'd been able to do that since Johnny Rainforest."

The nono tick is what Charlie called a blue lobster. I knew a fair bit about them, since they were from the same place I was: the Indigo Wild, on Shinnkaria. Not only do they leak hyperspace radiation, like Charlie said, they also come in a variety of sizes; they can lay eggs that hatch young a tenth as big as themselves, and repeat the same trick until they're close to molecule size. Johnny Rainforest used them to infect a solar sail once, and turned it into a giant hyperspace portal—but that's a different story.

"Not only that, they're loose in the city," I said. "I picked up a real strong feeling from the cab Joey was driving— either his cab comes equipped with its own hyperdrive or he's infested."

"I thought nonos couldn't survive for long outside the Indigo Wild," said Melody.

"The corps must have been tinkering with them for the last two hundred years," I pointed out. "If Johnny Rainforest could control the ticks, so could someone else, eventually."

"If Paul were still alive, he'd be furious," said Melody. "He was the one who decided to suppress Rainforest's technology, and Mike and I agreed with him. If the ticks downbreed small enough, they can destroy almost anything by dismantling it atom by atom; or they can go the other way and build virtually any substance from scratch. The potential for disaster is enormous."

I couldn't argue with that. I could imagine, all too clearly, the foundations of our hotel dissolving from solid duracrete into toxic sludge, bringing it crashing down onto streets flooded with poison . . . or maybe they'd prefer the taste of people, eating them from the inside out.

And why stop there? The entire population for an appetizer, with the rest of the planet for the main course. And since Kinslick was a heavily used trading route, from here they could spread to other worlds; the whole blamed galaxy would be bug buffet.

And all we had to worry about before was hyperspace falling apart.

"So you're going to talk to this Joey the Bull?" asked Melody.

"I guess," I said. "Once Skinny gets through playing with his new toys."

Just then a giant metal spider climbed out of one of the crates. "Look!" said Skinny gleefully. "Isn't this *great*?"

"Sure," I said doubtfully. "Whatever it is."

"It's an MD33 doctorbot," said Melody. "I had it shipped over from a medical supply warehouse."

"It's *terrific*," declared Skinny. "Not to mention a pretty good fit."

The doctorbot stood about waist-high—on me, anyway—and had six dual-jointed legs. The body was a dull silver egg, with a cluster of a dozen or so long, flexible arms tipped with different implements, attached to a rotating hub on top. A grille ringed the outside of the egg, and I could see Skinny's pink sensory cluster behind it.

"I thought it might be kind of small for you," said Melody, "but it was the best I could do."

"It's snug," admitted Skinny, "but not too bad. Taking out the onboard brain and autolab freed up a lot of room."

"Good," I said. "I didn't feel like being stuck in that chair the whole time."

"*You* didn't want to be stuck in that chair?" Skinny shot back. "*I* was the one that was stuck—plus I had to haul *your* oversize carcass around."

"Well, now you both have some extra freedom," declared Melody. "And there's someone here that wants to say hello."

Melody's face shrank, and then another face joined hers on the screen. A brown, smiling face, framed by red hair and a neatly trimmed red beard.

"Howdy, boys," said Mike Blink in a booming voice.

"Hi, Uncle Mike," I said.

"Hello, Mike," said Skinny.

Mike wasn't my blood uncle, but that doesn't mean he and Melody weren't family. I'd known both of them all my life, and I trusted them as much as I trusted Skinny—that is, with my life and everything I owned.

"I was listening in while you were telling Melody your story," said Mike. "I should have known some corp would figure out a way to use nonos sooner or later."

"How are you feeling, Mike?" asked Skinny. He was wobbling around the room, trying out his new legs.

"I'm just fine, Skinny," Mike said. He looked fine, too— but all of a sudden his eyes started to bleed. For a second I thought it was Mike's idea of a bad joke, but he ignored it completely. "Melody keeps fussing over me, though—tell her I'm not made of glass, would you?" Blood started to pour from his nose as well, staining his beard and teeth. Even though I knew it wasn't real, it was hard to watch.

"He seems fine to me," I told Melody, trying to sound like I meant it.

"I've done a little research on your behalf," Melody cut in, her image replacing Mike's. "I've found a netnumber for a Joseph Barnard, registered as a member of the Drivers Guild. Do you want me to contact him for you?"

"No, just leave the number," I said. "I think we'll get some grub first."

"All right. There's a chemical used on Shinnkaria to get rid of nono ticks—I'll see if I can track some down here and have it shipped over. I'll call you later," said Melody, and cut the connection.

Skinny and I were silent for a moment, thinking about what we'd just seen.

"Come on," I said, trying to sound cheerful. "As long as Melody's paying for this shindig, let's get some room service."

I skimmed through the netchannels while we ate. The local datasphere was a lot bigger than any I'd ever seen; five hundred channels had always seemed like a lot to me, but this place had that many showing soap operas. There were fifty channels devoted solely to what was on the other ten thousand.

I found a local newsfeed and tried to get a picture of what was going on in the city. After a few minutes I changed my point of view; a better question was, what *wasn't* happening in the city? There were riots, open-air festivals, gene auctions, and robot wrestling; there were parades, curfew zones, and thunderball tournaments; there were indoor fireworks, cloudcast netconcerts, and public sex rallies. The city was so big that different areas didn't just have their own character, they had their own religion, laws, and weather systems.

Then I saw something that made me sit up and take notice. It seemed there was a vigilante operating, in a part of town that even the police didn't like to hang around in. This mysterious do-gooder had rescued a pair of young women from a brainrape gang single-handedly, putting several of them in the hospital but killing no one. There weren't any pictures, but there was an interview with one of the girls. She said the stranger had used some kind of blue energy as a weapon during the fight, and vanished afterward.

"Hyperspace blue?" asked Skinny. He'd finally abandoned his new metal shell and wrapped himself around a half-dozen steaks.

"Could be," I said around a mouthful of food. "Whoever this guy is, he's tough—took out a dozen heavily armed thugs on his own."

"But he doesn't have your winning personality," said Skinny. "We'll check it out after we talk to Joey."

I polished off the last bite of dessert, leaned back, and sighed. Sometimes, when you're on the road—and on the grift—you don't get a chance to eat as well as you'd like. This beat the hell out of stale sandwiches and shipboard rations. When I was done picking the leftovers out of my teeth, I hopped in the shower and enjoyed honest-to-goodness hot water instead of sonics and airblasting.

"All right, I'm ready," I said as I slipped into some clean clothes. "Let's place a call to the Don's devoted son, shall we?"

I punched up the netnumber. A cab icon, beautifully detailed and slowly rotating, came up on the screen; it had the same long body and hood-horns as the one we'd seen at the spaceport.

"This is Joey," a voice announced. It was a strong voice, with a cultured accent I couldn't quite place. "And I'm working. If you want a cab, punch in your pickup address and destination. If you want to leave a message, hit MESSAGE; if you want to talk with me directly, hit CALL instead."

I punched in the hotel's address and my destination, and the screen gave me a confirmation code. "I'll get there in about seven minutes," Joey's voice said. "If that's too long, hit the Myriad Cabs link button and the dispatcher'll assign someone closer. Thank you."

Skinny slipped back into his new outfit, and we went downstairs to wait.

If the hotel clerk was surprised to see me out of my wheel-chair and being tailed by a doctorbot instead, she didn't show it—just tipped me a small nod and the same gold-lipped smile as before.

We waited in the lobby. The gelform furniture spread your weight so carefully you felt like you were floating on air instead of bags of smart goo. Skinny just folded his legs underneath him and pretended to be a machine—though he couldn't resist using some of his new tools to start dissecting a small potted plant next to my chair.

I was curious as to how Joey would let us know he'd arrived—he couldn't exactly get out of his cab and walk inside. Five or so minutes later, I found out—a little servobot shaped like a tiny copy of Joey's cab came rolling in and straight up to us.

"You call for a cab?" asked the tiny taxi. I chuckled and stood up.

"Sure did," I said. "Hope you have room for my doctor-bot—it's got to ride with me on account of my condition."

"Plenty of room," said the servobot. "Do you have luggage?"

"No."

"All right—follow me, please."

We did. Joey's cab was parked out front, the door already open. I got in, followed by Skinny—and felt all my hair stand on end.

The cab looked normal enough—plush, roomy seats, a mirrored partition between the front and the back—but that wasn't what was getting to me. The whole cab was so charged with hyperspatial radiation it might as well have been glowing blue, and I could feel it in every cell I had. It wasn't a *bad* feeling, you understand, but the wave of home-sickness that followed it brought a tear to my eye.

We took off. I'd told the automatic dispatcher we wanted

to go to the Dreamview district, which was where the vigilante had been spotted. From the map in the hotel room, it also seemed far enough away to let us have a talk with Joey.

"You sure? That's a rough area." Joey's voice came from a speaker set into the mirrored panel that divided the cab.

"That's why I asked for you," I said. "The cabbie that drove me from the spaceport said no one would bother me if I was with you—you *are* Joey the Bull, aren't you?"

"Some people call me that," replied Joey. He sounded amused. "People I've known for a while."

"I didn't mean to offend you," I said quickly. "It was your friend Charlie who told me about you."

"Charlie, hmm? What did he tell you?"

"He told me about you and your father."

Even though Joey didn't say anything, I could feel something *shift* in the air. No, not in the air—in the radiation around me. It was like it was being focused somehow, not as a weapon but as a sense. Suddenly I felt like a bug under a magnifying glass.

"If you and your friend are assassins, you're not very good ones," said Joey. He still sounded like I'd just told him something funny. "Are you?"

"What, assassins?" I said nervously. "No! No, we're not connected to the Bernardis in any way. We just wanted to talk to you." I realized a little too late that I shouldn't be saying "we"—but he'd done it first.

"Well, you should know you're a twitch away from being random atoms," said Joey cheerfully. "My cab has a *very* good security system."

"Maybe we should introduce ourselves," I said, swallowing hard. For some reason, it hadn't occurred to me how paranoid a man like Joey could be—and with good reason. "My name's Storysmith, and this is Skinshifter."

"And why is a Toolie disguised as a medical robot?"

"You got some good sensors in this cab, don't you?" I said. "Well, that's easy to explain. You see—"

"I'm a male," said Skinny. "You can see where that would cause problems."

"A male? That *talks*? You're kidding."

"I guess your sensors aren't *that* good," said Skinny. "Well, unless you have a degree in Toolie anatomy, you'll have to take my word for it."

"We'll see," said Joey. "So what's your story, Story-smith?"

"I'm from Shinnkaria," I told him. "Just like those bugs you piloted."

"So?"

"So," I said, "you already know they mess with electronics. Well, they do it by leaking tiny amounts of hyperspatial radiation, and if a friend of ours is right, they may be responsible—or at least connected to—a much bigger, more dangerous leak."

So I told him the story of the Pretty Big Bang. I wished I could see his face while I was telling it—a good storyteller pays attention to his audience—but at least he listened without interrupting.

When I was done, he asked, "Mike Blink? *The* Mike Blink? The one that flew for the Photon Express two centuries ago?"

"That's right," I said.

"That," said Joey after a long pause, "has got to be the *biggest* pile of crap I ever heard."

"Maybe *I* should be the one that talks from now on," murmured Skinny.

"Hold on," I said. "Before you call us a couple of crackpots, let me ask you a question. The Pretty Big Bang happened twenty standard days ago, at fifteen o'clock local time. Did you notice anything strange happen right then?"

I was grasping at straws. Nothing had turned up on any local sensors; Melody had checked. But I had this feeling . . .

The cab veered left and dived, bringing my stomach halfway up my throat and making me gasp. It didn't seem to bother Skinny, but then he's all stomach. Just as suddenly, the cab slammed to a halt on a street-ledge.

"All right," snapped Joey. "Maybe you're working for my father's business partners. Maybe you're working for the corp that developed the bugs. Or maybe you've got your own scam going—but whatever the truth is, you're going to share that with me *right now.*"

"No," I said. There's a time to fold, and a time to make the other fellow show you his cards.

"I was deadly serious about the security system," said Joey. "I could turn both of you into charred meat in a second."

"And then you wouldn't get any answers at all," I countered. "You answer my question first, and I'll tell you whatever you want to know."

He was quiet for a long moment, and for every second it stretched on, my gut sank lower; I was remembering just how stubborn Joey the Bull was supposed to be . . .

"All right," he said at last. "You must know what happened anyway, or you wouldn't be asking. I was in my cab, cruising through Joytown and looking for a fare. Suddenly everything goes blue. My whole cab goes dead, even my backup systems. If I hadn't been at ground level, I might have been killed—as it was, my brakes locked up and I stopped dead. And then . . ." He paused.

"Yeah?"

"Those colors you say Mike Blink saw—well, I think I saw one of them. The blue kind of shifted into it, and it wasn't like any color I've ever seen. It scared the hell out of me; I thought I was having an aneurysm. But then it faded, and my cab's systems rebooted. I did a diagnostic, and everything seemed fine. Since then, though—"

"You've been having constant, minor glitches, haven't you?" I asked him. "Especially in sensitive systems."

"Yes," he admitted. "Nothing serious, but nothing I can trace, either."

"Here's some of the truth you wanted," I said. "Your

whole cab is infested with nono ticks. I know; I can sense 'em. That's why your systems keep glitching."

"Impossible. I wasn't at the facility where the actual operation took place—I don't even know where it is."

"Impossible or not, you've got 'em," I said. "Fortunately, there's a chemical cure—if you've done the kind of research I think you have, you probably know about it."

"Acentinol," said Joey.

"We're willing to disinfect your cab for you," said Skinny. "Of course, if you don't trust us . . ."

And suddenly I smelled something I hadn't noticed before. A harsh, acrid smell—too faint for a human to pick up, but not too faint for me.

"Gas!" I blurted out. "He's trying to kill us!"

"What are you talking about—" said Joey, and by the second word I was trying to kick out a window. I didn't have much luck; they were armored. Strangely enough, a fan kicked on for a second, and then cut off.

"I'm not doing this," snapped Joey. "Systems are all locked up—damn!"

I kept on hammering away at the window, but it was no good. The smell got stronger and stronger, and my head started to whirl. All I could think about was how I was failing Melody and Skinny both.

Skinny didn't say a thing, but one of his arms with a nozzle at its end deployed and started spraying a fine mist into the air.

"Relax," said Skinny. "This should take care of it."

Sure enough, the gas smell stopped getting stronger, and the fan kicked on again. I gasped, trying to get my breath back.

"Okay," I told Joey, "don't think you can just knock us off and get away with it! Melody knows where we are and you don't want her pissed off at you—"

"It wasn't me!" he protested.

"Take it easy, Story," said Skinny. "He's telling the truth. He didn't try to kill us—the nonos did."

"What?" I said. "But why would they—"

"I think it was the word 'disinfect' they objected to," said Skinny.

"But they're just bugs!" I said. "They're not smart enough!"

"It appears," said Joey thoughtfully, "that now they *are.*"

Having control of his cab taken away from him—if only for a few seconds—was enough to make Joey take us seriously. He wouldn't budge until we'd gotten out and Skinny had sprayed every square inch of the cab—though Joey'd only open his driver's window enough to let Skinny poke the nozzle inside.

"The Acentinol came while you were in the shower," said Skinny. "I just forgot to mention it."

"Forgot? *Forgot?*" I fumed. "We almost wind up breathing nerve gas and that's your excuse? That's what's gonna wind up on my tombstone, I swear to God: 'Here lies Storysmith, died in his sleep. His partner forgot to mention the building was being demolished in the morning.'"

"All right, all right," said Skinny. "Get back in the cab."

"Are they all gone?" asked Joey.

"I'm not sure," I said. "I can't sense *them*, just the energy they leak. I don't sense that anymore . . . not exactly."

"What's that mean?" asked Joey.

"There seems to be some kind of hyperspatial energy coming from *you*," I said. "It's got a different flavor to it, though."

"Internal diagnostics of the cab all check out fine—no more glitches," said Joey. "And my own biosensors say I'm perfectly healthy. Actually, I've felt better than ever lately."

"Good for you," said Skinny. "We, on the other hand, were nearly gassed to death. If it wasn't for the doctorbot's built-in filters and Story's constitution, we would have been."

"It's a nonlethal anesthetic, and it wasn't my fault," said Joey, a trace of stubbornness in his voice. "Those ticks invaded my defense systems. You were lucky they didn't co-opt something quicker and deadlier."

"I wonder why they didn't?" I said.

"My weapon-control systems are heavily encrypted," answered Joey. "Nonlethal systems are less so. It looks like they swung at you with the first weapon they could pick up."

"Okay," said Skinny. "The real question is: why?"

"They didn't want to be exterminated," I said.

"They couldn't *spell* exterminate, let alone understand the concept," Skinny pointed out. "Someone else must have been controlling them."

"Perhaps it was my father's business partners," Joey said slowly. "Seeking to establish the same kind of situation I imposed on my father."

"That doesn't quite work," I said. "No offense, Joey, but your father is an important figure, with information that could bring down a lot of people. You're just a cab driver. If you died, the Drivers Guild would still have the same hold over your Pop—a stronger one, in fact."

"Point taken," said Joey. "But if not the Bernardi Syndicate, then who?"

"It's got to have something to do with the Pretty Big Bang," said Skinny. "Hyperspace energies were released, and it sounds like you were exposed to them. The ticks radiate hyperspace energy—"

"They don't just radiate it, they need it to survive," Joey pointed out. "It's another reason they haven't been able to use them off Shinnkaria. Once they leave the Indigo Wild, they have a limited lifespan."

"So maybe the ticks were attracted to Joey because of the radiation he's giving off," I said.

"That doesn't explain how they got from my father to my cab," said Joey. "Or why the Pretty Big Bang went off near me in the first place."

"You may not have been the only person exposed," said Skinny. "Mike said there were seven distinct non-colors in the explosion. You said you only saw one."

"Oh? And here I thought I was special," said Joey dryly.

"We have a lead on somebody else that may have been exposed," I said. "There was a news report about a vigilante in the Dreamview district that mentioned blue energy. We thought we might check it out."

"You'll need transportation," said Joey.

"Keep the meter running," said Skinny. "We're on an expense account."

The Dreamview district turned out to be mostly low-rent apartment buildings, big blocky duracrete things you could lose an army in. All of them were the same faded off-white, with tiny balconies crammed with plants or barbecue grills or just plain junk.

"What now?" asked Joey.

"I'm not sure," I said, feeling a little foolish. "Where would a crime-fighter hang his hat?"

"Someplace there's lots of crime, obviously," said Skinny.

"Dreamview has its share of that," said Joey. "A lot of ex-factory workers live here. The murder rate climbs every time the unemployment figures do."

It looked to me like whatever dream the residents were supposed to view had up and vanished; the only thing that drew the eye was a pair of towers that loomed over the apartments like a couple of dead trees over a forest of stumps.

"What are those?" I asked Joey, pointing them out.

"The DP towers," he replied. "Part of the Dream Pillars Mall."

"Take us there," I said. I had a hunch.

The towers grew out of the center of the mall like a pair of chopsticks stuck in a pizza. The roof of the pizza—I mean, the mall—was a big parking lot, with different-colored vehicles scattered around like toppings. I heard my stomach rumble.

"Are you *always* hungry?" demanded Skinny as we

landed. "You polished off enough food at the hotel to feed a family of Toolies for a week!"

"I can't help it," I said. "Some things just stimulate my appetite."

"Like breathing," said Skinny.

"That's a strange remark, coming from you," said Joey.

"Yeah, yeah, us male Toolies are all stomach and no brain," snapped Skinny. "Kinda like an eight-hundred-pound cabbie."

"Sorry I brought it up," murmured Joey.

I closed my eyes and tried to concentrate. I knew it was up to me; if the local cops couldn't find this vigilante, then we wouldn't have much luck just driving around and looking out the window. But if I could pick up the same kind of sensations I'd felt from Joey's cab, maybe we could track him down that way.

You know what they say: be careful what you wish for. My idea turned out to be successful, all right—a lot more successful than I wanted.

"Guys?" I said. "I don't know about the vigilante, but I've found more nonos."

"In the cab?" asked Joey.

"Nope," I said. "In the mall we're parked on top of."

"Which part?" asked Skinny.

"Near as I can tell—and this is just a ballpark guess, you understand—the whole blamed thing."

When I shut my eyes, all I saw was blue; the same blue I saw every night when I went to sleep in the Indigo Wild. It spread out below me in every direction, and it was much stronger than the reading I'd gotten from Joey's cab.

Which was already in the air. "I've got to get some of that Acentinol for myself," muttered Joey.

"We're not just going to run away, are we?" demanded Skinny. He thumped a steel-tipped arm against the mirrored partition.

"No," said Joey. He had already cleared the edge of the mall and was swooping toward a lower lane. "But I thought we should circle the perimeter and see how far the infestation has spread."

So we flew around the mall, which covered at least ten square city blocks. We soared past discount clothing stores, supermarkets, virtual arcades, and fast-food restaurants. Sure enough, all the ticks seemed to be inside the mall's boundaries. That made me feel a little better, but not much; that was an awful lot of nonos. If they decided to expand their territory, I doubted there was enough Acentinol on the planet to stop them.

"Okay, so what do cabs and malls have in common?" asked Skinny.

"Beats me," I said. "But I think we should check out the towers, too."

Joey started a slow, climbing spiral around them. "Definitely buggy," I announced. "But I'm getting something else, too. Kinda like the feeling I get from Joey—but not quite."

The feeling got stronger the higher we climbed. By the time we got to the top, I knew which building it was coming from. I told Joey to land on the roof.

The roof had a big comsat dish, rows of ventilator hoods, and a huge two-story duracrete cube smack-dab in the middle. "Well," I told Skinny, "let's go palaver."

"With who?" he asked, but he followed me out of the cab anyway.

I walked straight toward the big duracrete cube. I couldn't see anyone there, but the tickle in my brain told me I was getting closer to the source—and then my nose confirmed it.

I stopped and looked up, toward the top of the cube. "Howdy," I said. "Just so's you know, I'm not a cop."

No response.

"Good disguise," commented Skinny. "No wonder the police couldn't find him—who'd suspect a giant block of stone of being the scourge of the underworld? Though you'd think all the squashed criminals would give him away . . ."

"Only the ones they find," came a voice from midair. "It's easy to hide bodies when they're only half-an-inch thick."

I didn't jump—my nose had already told me he was there. "Are you invisible all the time?" I asked. " 'Cause if you aren't, I'd sure appreciate talking to *someone* face to face."

"Not *my* fault I don't have one right now," muttered Skinny.

"Very well," the voice said, and then a man was standing two stories above us, on the edge of the duracrete block. He wore a tight-fitting blue bodysuit, with a long black trench-coat over it that flapped in the breeze. He had on military-issue black cyberboots, gauntlets, and goggles, and short blond hair. He looked about twenty standard years old.

"If you guys aren't cops, who are you?" he said. "*Please* tell me you're crooks. I could use the exercise." He smiled, and cracked the knuckles of one fist with the other.

Two things suddenly occurred to me. First, me and Skinny *were* crooks . . . and second, what if Mr. Invisible had a built-in lie detector, too?

"I'm Storysmith, and that's Joey in the cab. We aren't here to make trouble," I said carefully. *Not with anyone who recently put twelve guys in the hospital, anyway.*

"How about the Toolie in the tin can?"

"That's *it*," snarled Skinny. "When we get back to the hotel, I'm changing into something else."

"Her name's Skinshifter," I said, mentally crossing my fingers. "And if you can pose as a block of masonry, she can pretend to be a doctorbot."

"Fair enough," he admitted. I tried not to show my relief. "I'm Sentry," he said. "What do you want?"

"If I'm right," I said, "something happened to you at fifteen o'clock in the morning, twenty days ago. Something you can't explain. We're not sure *we* can explain it, either— but we might have a few answers you don't."

That got his attention, all right. He studied me for a moment, then dived off the block. He did a graceful somersault on the way down and landed lightly on his feet in front of me.

"I'm listening," he said.

So I told him about the Pretty Big Bang, and Joey's dad, and the nono ticks. He paid close attention, and nodded from time to time.

"Hmmm," he said when I was done. "Yes, of course. That makes perfect sense."

"Thank you," I said smugly. "That's not what Joey said when I told *him* the story. Actually, his cab tried to kill us."

"It wasn't the cab, it was the nonos," said Skinny. "The ones infesting his taxi—just like the ones infesting this entire building . . ."

"Er," I said.

"This very *tall* building."

"Um . . ."

"That we're *standing* on as you tell *exactly the same story*—"

"You don't have to worry about an attack from the VI," said Sentry. "Not while I'm here."

"Vee Eye?" I asked.

"Viral Intelligence," said Sentry. He started walking toward the cab. "I think you should introduce me to Joey—and then it's time I told *you* a story . . ."

four
Dream Pillars

Sentry's story:

"What did you call them again, Phil? Karmic books?"

"*Comic* books," I said patiently. Earl undoubtedly spent more time at the gym than the library, but he wasn't stupid—he just didn't take to new ideas very well. "They're a twentieth-century art form, from Earth."

Earl picked up an issue of *The Invisibles* and flipped it open. "Huh. Like frozen cartoons." He tried tapping the upper right-hand corner of the page, but of course nothing happened.

"It's not smart paper," I said. "Just plain old newsprint."

Earl tossed the issue down on the security console. "Whatever. I gotta go patrol." He downed the last of his coffee and swaggered out the door.

I sighed, and checked the monitor screens. Nothing there but a few squat, bright orange janitorbots, cleaning the floors. What did I expect, a horde of supervillains? *The only thing more boring than being a security guard in a mall,* I thought, *is being a graveyard-shift security guard in a mall.*

I put *The Invisibles* back on the pile I'd brought with me, and picked up an issue of *Stormwatch*. Some collectors buy stuff just for the art, but I've always been more interested in the writing. Back in the twentieth century, when comic books were introduced, people had some strange ideas about collecting; they actually used to seal them up in plastic bags, sometimes buying more than one copy of the same issue—and sometimes never reading them at all. Weird. Of course, today you just download a file and print up your own disposable copy—it's the content that's important, not the medium.

Stormwatch had started out just being another Spandex punch'em-up, but a writer named Warren Ellis took the book over at issue 37 and really turned things around. It didn't last as long as it deserved to, but every issue was brilliant. He wasn't as interested in fights as in examining the nature of the superhuman, in what it would be like to be composed of pure energy, or able to walk through walls like a ghost. All my favorite writers dealt with those kinds of themes: Alan Moore, Grant Morrison, Mark Waid.

These days, nobody seems much interested in stories like that. Any soldier who's worn a battlesuit can tell you what it's like to tear steel apart with your own two hands; Earl will talk your ear off with war stories if you let him. Protecfields, cyberenhanced senses and muscles, antigrav belts; things that used to be a source of wonder are commonplace now. I deal with aliens everyday—technically, *I'm* the alien; even though it has a lot of human immigrants, Kinslick isn't a human planet.

Of course, there are plenty of comics storylines that remain firmly in the realm of pure imagination: time-travel, parallel universes, mythological deities come to life. Magic. Impossible, but they make for great reading.

I spent the next hour immersed in a more exciting world than the one I lived in, only occasionally glancing up at the monitor screens. I especially identified with Grant Morrison's *Justice League of America*; from their base on the Moon, they stood guard over the people of Earth—which meant someone was always on "monitor duty," sitting in a chair and staring at a bank of screens, just like me. Of course, their boredom never lasted more than a few panels before they were alerted to some cosmic threat; mine was interrupted only by Earl finishing his patrol and taking my place.

The Dream Pillars Mall covers ten square city blocks. It has three levels underground and seven above, as well as the twin office towers it's named for that rise from the central hub. It takes an hour to patrol my section, which consists mainly of walking around and checking the security cameras. Still, I try to make up for my inattention at the monitors by being thorough on my patrol.

Besides, it gives me a chance to use my toys.

I run a diagnostic check on my systems first. I can't afford top-of-the-line implants, but I buy the best I can get and keep them in good condition. My cybersenses check out okay: infrared vision, molecule sniffer, sound amplifier, and active sonar. I do some stretching and isometrics; servomuscles in my arms, shoulders, legs, and hips are fine. Then it's time for externals: goopgun and stun-field projectors in the gauntlets are fully charged. Ditto the protec-field generator in my belt. All my weapons are nonlethal—if I wanted to kill people, I'd have joined a corporate police force or the military.

Inertial synchronization in my cyberboots is off balance, so I adjust them; if I have to jump from a seventh-floor balcony, I want the impact absorbed evenly. Okay, I'm ready for action.

I heave another sigh, and head for the first camera station.

ARE YOU BORED? RESTLESS? LOOKING FOR SOME ACTION?

Hell, yes.

WANT TO INJECT SOME ADVENTURE AND EXCITEMENT INTO YOUR EVERYDAY LIFE?

Didn't we just cover that?

OWN A CYBERSYNCH IMPLANT OF THE 7000 SE-RIES OR HIGHER?

Yep.

THEN YOUR BOREDOM IS OVER! WITH ALGAR-CORP'S NEW *OVERLAY* SYSTEM, YOU CAN IN-TRODUCE THREE-DIMENSIONAL, INTERACTIVE FANTASY MATERIAL INTO *YOUR* REALITY. CREATE YOUR OWN IMAGINARY FRIENDS! TRANSFORM YOUR ENVIRONMENT! EVERY DAY CAN BE A SUNNY DAY WITH *OVERLAY*!

Hmmm . . .

I'd heard about the Overlay system before—it was first used for military training, projecting cybernetic enemies onto a soldier's hardwired perceptions. The tech was subverted into providing predesigned hallucinations for the chemical recreation crowd, then finally went mainstream with sophis-ticated programs that could make every face you saw beau-tiful, or paint the world in pastels.

I didn't see the point. It wasn't full neural interface—you couldn't actually touch any of these illusions, just see and hear them. Of course, full neural is damned expensive and has a host of side effects, so Overlay made a certain amount of sense—it just didn't appeal to me. When you work in the security field, you want your perceptions to be heightened, not altered.

But then I stumbled across the Crusader program.

Somewhere, somehow, somebody decided that comic books—good old-fashioned don-a-cape-and-cowl-and-beat-up-bad-guys ultraviolence—would make for a good Overlay pro-gram. When I heard about it through a Netweb group, I couldn't resist getting a copy. What could it hurt?

I live in a complex of low-rent high-rises called Dream-view, on the ninth floor. The building was only a few min-utes away from the mall, but it was like another world. Most of the people who lived in the complex couldn't afford to shop at Dream Pillars; its clientele came from a district on the other side called Fencombe, populated with up-and-coming executives and their families. Dreamview, on the other hand, was full of out-of-work laborers from the factory district, or disposessed corporate refugees whose planets had changed hands.

I was just about to unlock my door when the one across the hall opened. It was Mrs. D'Angelo, a tiny woman in her seventies; about four feet tall, bright pink hair, and weighed maybe eighty pounds. She'd worked all her life for a corp that specialized in botanical re-engineering—one merger later, and she's fired a year before her pension kicks in. Now an apartment here was all she could afford.

"Hello, dear," she said, smiling. "Would you like to come over for tea?"

Normally I would have said yes; she's a real sweetheart, and her whole apartment is filled with bioengineered plants that smell fresh and green. My place generally smells like old socks.

"Not tonight," I said, returning her smile. "Maybe tomorrow?"

"Any time, dear."

My apartment's small, furnished in Early College Student: ratty plastic couch, old styrocrete packing cube for a coffee table, blown-up poster-size photos of old comic book covers on the walls. I could afford to redecorate, but most of my earnings went into maintaining and updating my cybernetics.

I sat down, plugged the module into my cybergoggles, opened the guidelines file for the module, and scanned menu choices. "Ah. Let's try this." I selected a file named "Cyberwere."

Everything changed. Colors became brighter, hues shifting toward primaries; shadows deepened and darkened, and edges became more pronounced. Everything looked simpler, more defined yet more basic.

And I was no longer alone.

The monster that appeared was a seven-foot werewolf who'd had the left half of his body replaced with cybernetic analogs. He didn't waste time on dialogue, just bared a set of steel fangs and leapt for my throat.

I tried to dodge, but he was too fast. A hairy paw tipped with metal claws slashed across my face. I felt nothing—but a small gauge appeared at the bottom of my vision, with a needle veering toward the red. I kicked at the creature, and felt a *thump*! in the sole of my foot when I connected.

The Cyberwere flew across the room and crashed into the far wall. I stopped the program.

Then I read through the guidelines—all of them—carefully.

I learned that while I couldn't really touch the images I saw, my cybergauntlets and boots could duplicate some sensations—holding a simple object like a bar or a sphere for example, or create the impression of a minor impact. For more serious injuries, the gauges would appear. The system very quickly mapped out the confines of the environment you were in, and either incorporated them into the scenario or overlaid them with a suitable illusion. The guidelines also cautioned against using the program in a confined space filled with breakables.

I looked around my tiny apartment. Somehow, I couldn't see staging superpowered battles here on a regular basis. I sighed, and put the module back in its box.

If it wasn't for downsizing, I might never have tried it.

The mall finally figured out what I had known in the first week I worked there: they had too many guards. It only took one guard per sector to make rounds, not two—the other was unnecessary. They cut the night staff by fifty percent, and I was one of the lucky ones that got to stay. So was Earl, though they relocated him to another sector.

Earl may have been a jerk, but at least he was someone to talk to. Now, all I had to do was monitor and patrol. Corridor after empty corridor, no one around but me and locked-up shops.

No one to watch me on the monitor screens, either.

• • •

"Hurry up with those crates," the head thug said. He was dressed like an undertaker, while the rest of us wore long black robes and white skull masks.

"Don't worry," I told him. "The scramblers I put on the security cams are good for another hour, at least."

We were cleaning out an electronics supply store on the third level and loading crates onto an antigrav pallet. The pallet would be towed to the freight elevator, then onto a waiting truck—if everything went according to plan.

There was a sudden stench of decaying flesh, and a cloud of noxious green smoke billowed from nowhere. Out of it stepped something that might once have been human. Something that might once have been alive.

"Faster, you grubs," hissed the Atrocity. It was a shambling skeleton wrapped in a ragged white shroud; its skull and bones were polished black obsidian, and it carried a gleaming silver cyberscythe. "I must have those components to complete my project . . . I must have them if my master is to *live again*!"

"Change of plans, Bony," I said. I ripped off my skull mask and black cloak in one smooth move. "I was hoping you'd show."

"Sentry!" the Atrocity spat. "You accursed fool—you don't know what you're dealing with!"

"Oh, I think I do," I said calmly. "And your insane plan to raise the Shadow God stops here."

"Kill him!" the Atrocity screamed.

Obligatory fight scene number one: the goons. The equivalent of a warmup before the real workout. There were ten of them, five armed with guns. I threw one through a plate-glass window, kicked one in the stomach, leapfrogged over him and kicked two more in the head. They were all lousy shots.

I can't tell you how much *fun* it was.

It was over too soon; despite some flashy acrobatics to draw things out (it's not really necessary to do a backflip be-

fore punching someone in the nose, but you get a great reaction that way), I mopped up the floor with them in about
three minutes. Then it was time for the main event.

I didn't know that much about the Atrocity. It—he?—was
a creature that seemed to have supernatural powers, yet
often employed high-tech means to his ends. What I'd been
able to find out about his current plans involved the resur-
rection of an eons-old entity known as the Shadow God, a
malevolent force that the Atrocity planned to unleash on the
world.

Unless I stopped him.

He attacked first, his cyberscythe crackling with energy
as it sliced at me in a deadly arc. Fast as he was, I was faster;
I leapt over his swing, and retaliated with a stun-field blast
from my right gauntlet. The bolt hit him dead-on—and he
erupted in laughter as the energy sparked harmlessly around
him.

"One has to *have* a nervous system to be affected by a
stun-field, boy!" he sneered. "You evade my scythe easily
enough—but you will not evade *this!*"

He pointed the scythe at me, and crimson lightning arced
from it, striking me in the chest. My protec-field handled the
charge easily enough, but the flash blinded me for a second.

When my vision cleared, the Atrocity and his men were
gone. So was the pallet full of components.

"The next time we meet," I growled to the empty mall,
"I'll bring you to *justice. So swears the Sentry!*"

And then, grinning like a buffoon, I shut off the program
and went for a coffee break.

It didn't take me long to get the hang of the program's nu-
ances. Any time I was "trapped," for instance, my gauntlets
would feed me a certain amount of resistance, and a visual
telltale would let me know it was "Too strong to break
through!" Ditto for chains and ropes. I could choose to ignore these guidelines and move anyway, but breaking the
rules of the program would crash it, ending the illusion. I

didn't even try to cheat; it was more fun to play the game and use my ingenuity instead.

At first I felt a little guilty. But the more I thought about it, the more I realized how unnecessary my job was in the first place. The mall had its own protec-fields at night, and nothing smaller than an assault tank was going to break through them. Any trouble in the mall happened during the day, when the unemployed laborers who lived in the same complex as I did turned to shoplifting or even armed robbery out of desperation. Even that didn't happen often; there were more robberies and assaults in the living complex itself.

Strangely enough, that made me feel guiltier than anything.

When it comes to superheroics, context is everything.

That's why there have been so many bad superhero stories in other media. There's nothing wrong with the idea of someone acquiring metahuman abilities—that's the basis of most myths and legends. It's when he dons a skintight suit, calls himself Blastman, and starts a lone-wolf war on crime that he becomes absurd.

But put that person in a universe populated with others in skintight suits, others with names like Batman and Superman and Spiderman, a universe with evil robots and scheming aliens and Immortal Gods . . . suddenly that person isn't ridiculous. He's part of a tradition, part of a community. He's *necessary.*

That's what the Crusader program provided, more than anything: context. When I activated it, I wasn't just competing against bad guys—I was entering another world, one filled not just with villains, but other heroes too. Sometimes I would look up Captain Champion and ask his advice; other times I might team up with the Iron Golem or Intersect on a tough case.

I discovered another facet of the program that delighted me. It would take data from my cybergoggles and process it into comic-book form that I could print out and read later.

That, more than anything, gave me a tremendous sense of satisfaction. It added a layer of context.

But when you impose context—*artificial* context—on a situation, you lose something else.

Perspective.

First page, splash panel. The entire page is filled with a close-up of Sentry: his hair is blond and short, his youthful mouth set in a grim line. His black cybergoggles reflect the face of his worst enemy, Doktor Dimension. Dimension looks like a demented Rastafarian, long silver dreadlocks with multicolored wires woven into them over a grinning brown face. He wears prismatic glasses with small round lenses, and has the word ENTROPY tattooed on his forehead in purple.

Caption reads: Death is *Doktor Dimension*!

Page 2, first panel: picking up from last issue, we see Sentry trapped in an energy column in Doktor Dimension's lair. The Doktor is expounding on his plans.

DOKTOR DIMENSION: You see, Sentry, I have figured out something none of you so-called superheroes have managed to: the *source* of superpowers themselves!

SENTRY: Is that all? I'll give you the number of my cyberneticist—mention my name and you'll get a ten percent *discount* on used parts . . .

DOKTOR DIMENSION: I don't mean the glorified *acrobats* such as yourself, Sentry; you rely on *technological* enhancement and weapons. No, I mean the *genuine* superhumans, the ones with abilities that defy natural laws; the ones that soar through space *unaided*, that can hurl *buildings* into orbit and generate particle beams from their bare *hands*. I knew there must be an underlying principle to their abilities . . . and now I've *found* it.

Panel 2. Sentry looks unimpressed.

DOKTOR DIMENSION: An *extradimensional* source was the only answer. How else can the Monstrosity add a thousand pounds to his bulk in the space of moments? How else can Skystar radiate streams of thermal energy? The solution was *obvious*, really; they were drawing matter and energy from *somewhere else*. And I, with my transdimensionator, not only *found* that place—but *traveled* there.

Page 3. A succession of interlocking panels, with a superimposed image of Doktor Dimension's face in the upper left corner. The first three panels show bolts of crackling electricity, gouts of flame, energy streams outlined in pulsing Kirby dots. The next three show drifting blobs of green organic matter, spiky crystalline formations, and a stormy ocean with magnetic lines of force radiating from it. In the lower right-hand corner, a superimposed image of the Doktor riding his transdimensionator, which looks like a flying motorcycle with a microwave dish mounted on the handlebars and two circular rings of antennae in place of tires. The Doktor wears a white lab coat over a psychedelic T-shirt and baggy pants.

DOKTOR DIMENSION: I call it *Dimension Omega*. It is a place *strange* beyond your imagination; a place where rivers of *electricity* flow between *banks of flame*, down to a magnetic *sea*. A place where cold and dark are not merely the absence of heat and light, but *forces unto themselves*. It even has life, of a sort—great floating planetoids of *biomass*, with a DNA pattern as unstable as a *madman's mind*. It took me the better part of *six months* to map the various areas, and another six of observation before I had the *information* I needed.

Page 4, first panel: Doktor Dimension turns his back on his captive and fiddles with the controls of a huge machine. A wall-size screen, split into a grid of twenty-five, shows twenty-five small electronic devices. Each has a strange, Y-shaped antenna, and each floats in a different zone of Dimension Omega.

DOKTOR DIMENSION: I discovered dimensional *leaks* in various zones. They corresponded *exactly* with reports of various superpowered *activity*. And then . . .

The Doktor turns to face his captive, a smug smile on his

face. Behind him, the screen changes to show the faces of twenty-five different superheroes.

DOKTOR DIMENSION: *I plugged them up.*

An angry Sentry smashes his fist into the side of the energy column he's trapped in, to no avail. The Doktor laughs.

SENTRY: So *that's* why everyone's powers have suddenly vanished! You megalomaniac—do you know how much *harm* you're doing by robbing those heroes of their abilities?

DOKTOR DIMENSION: Ha! I'll do much more than *that*!

The Doktor starts adjusting a different piece of equipment, one with a long, segmented arm arching over it. The arm ends in a funnel-shaped projector.

DOKTOR DIMENSION: With the aid of my transdimensionator technology, I won't just shut off everybody's superpowers . . .

Page 5: one large panel, that shows Doktor Dimension with his arms raised high, his transdimensional device behind him. The funnel on the machine's arm is right over his head, and crackling with energy.

DOKTOR DIMENSION: *I'll steal them all for myself!*

Page 6: the entire page is blue. There is a single line of text repeated across the bottom: ERROR ERROR ERROR ERROR ERROR ERROR ERROR ERROR ERROR . . .

Huh?

That *never happened before. What was that big blue flash supposed to be—Doktor Dimension's machine turning on? And the color that followed it, like nothing I've ever seen.*

Can't see or hear a damn thing now. All systems dead. What am I—

#SYSTEMS REBOOTING#

That's better.

"—Steal them all for myself!" Dimension shouted.

Okay, gotta think. Whatever that glitch was, it didn't change the situation—I've still got a mad scientist to deal with, and he's about to become unstoppable.

EM sensors say that machine is using a lot of juice, and the amount keeps rising as it powers up. Maybe I can try to smash my way out when it peaks—the energy column keeping me trapped has got to be on the same grid.

Of course, if I don't get out in time, I'm gonna have a psycho with about two dozen different superpowers to fight . . .

The Doktor had finished his adjustments, and now stood on a slightly raised platform beside his transdimensional machine.

"As one with no true powers of your own, it's fitting you should witness this," Dimension said. "Fitting you should see one who *deserves* power attaining it."

The projector arm moved to a position over the Doktor's head. A brilliant beam of white blazed down, bathing Dimension in luminescence—and the power level of my cell dipped.

I transferred all available kinetic energy into my right gauntlet. I was only going to get one shot at this.

The beam shining down on the Doktor shifted from white to yellow to red to blue, pulsing from one color to another faster and faster. "Yes!" he exulted. "YES!"

I drew my arm back, readied myself, and drove my fist forward with every ounce of strength I had.

"The power is MINE!" Dimension shouted.

KRAKOOOM!

The cell overloaded, the generator overhead showering me with sparks. I leapt clear, hit the ground rolling, and came up ready to fight.

I was too late.

"How will you stop me *now*, Sentry?" Dimension said. He stepped out of the beam, which was still pulsing. His body grew as I watched, muscles expanding to a grotesque size. His lab coat burst at the seams, and the baggy pants and psychedelic T-shirt he wore were now skin-tight. His loafers exploded as his feet swelled, leaving them bare.

"I can kill you in dozens of ways." Dimension laughed. "Perhaps I should start with the basics. *Flame!*"

He pointed at me with an arm like an oak tree, and fire erupted from his outstretched hand. I sprang out of the way as the blast scorched the wall behind me.

"*Ice!*" Another blast, this time of pure frigid cold. Frozen crystals formed instantly in the air in the path of the blast, a sparkling beam as dangerous as it was beautiful. I somersaulted over a bank of equipment, which was instantly covered in frost when the beam hit it.

"*Lightning!*" A high-voltage bolt shattered the iced machinery, destroying my cover. Just as well; I was tired of running.

"What's the matter, Dimension?" I snarled. "Did you put all that muscle on just to impress the boys at the gym—or do you actually intend to *use* it?"

He stomped forward, with a face-splitting grin of perfect white teeth. "You mean like *this*?" he roared, and brought both massive fists down at my head.

He may have been powerful, but he wasn't *used* to that power yet—or his new body. I avoided his fists easily, though they hammered a crater in the duracrete floor. His doubled-over posture left him open for me to finally retaliate.

I kicked him in the head. Hard.

His smile got bigger.

Ohhhhhhh-kay.

"I am going to *enjoy* this," he chortled.

Suddenly, the color I'd seen when my systems crashed—not the blue, but the one that came after—overlaid everything. I could feel a tingling in my hands and feet, like my cybergauntlets and boots were vibrating.

It ended as quickly as it had started. I didn't have time to ponder this development, though—because Dimension's fist was swinging right at my face.

I blocked it instinctively, knowing I wasn't strong enough to do so.

Both of us were amazed when I did. I had expected massive damage to register on my internal gauges, but they showed nothing. Somehow, I'd been raised to Dimension's power level—and I wasted no time in taking advantage of it.

My uppercut knocked him clear across the room and halfway through a wall. It was my turn to grin.

"How do you feel about a *fair* fight, Dok?" I asked him. "Or aren't you familiar with the concept?"

He wasn't smiling anymore as he picked himself up from the rubble. "Your strength has increased," he said. "But I have other, less *crude* methods of destroying you."

His eyes glowed, and twin beams of pure force shot from them. They struck me in the chest—and bounced off the blue aura that suddenly formed there.

My protec-field seems to have been beefed up, too. "No go, Dimension. We're evenly matched now—except I've got the training, and you're just a test-tube jockey. Give it up, or I'll make you *eat* that damn machine piece by piece."

"I believe you would," Dimension said. The glow faded from his eyes, replaced by a look of calculation. "Therefore, prudence dictates a strategic withdrawal, until I *master* my new abilities."

"You're not going anywhere," I said, and took a step forward.

The Doktor's entire body suddenly blazed with ruby light. "And how will you stop me, when Lazer Lord's power to transform into pure light is mine?" he said. "Catch me if you can, Sentry!"

There was a flash of light and an explosion of debris. When my vision cleared, he was gone, leaving a hole blasted in the ceiling and the echo of his laughter in my ears.

Damn. Well, the next battle should be interesting, that's for sure. Wonder how long I'll stay supercharged?

I deactivated the program.

And stared in shock at the hole in the ceiling.

• • •

The security cams for the area were scrambled. They'd been blanked for an eight-hour period, for which I was thankful; at least I wouldn't have to explain to management why I was talking to myself and leaping around.

I examined the hole carefully. It didn't look as if it had been blasted with a laser, more like a patch of the ceiling had just crumbled. At that point the ceiling was made of two feet of duracrete, and the hole went all the way through. The edges of the hole were strangely smooth, and the debris was mostly powder. The hole hadn't been so much blasted as dissolved away.

It had to have been me. Somehow the Crusader program had glitched, and actually activated one of my weapons instead of just simulating it.

There were two problems with this theory, however. First, I hadn't even pointed at the roof during the battle, let alone blasted it; and second, I didn't possess a weapon that would do this.

I filed a report on the hole, saying I'd discovered it but had no idea how it got there. A janitorbot had gone missing as well; I was hoping they'd blame both incidents—and the blanked security cams—on some kind of mechanical melt-down.

Management accepted my story, though they weren't happy. Still, nothing had been stolen, and the damage wasn't that extensive.

I examined my equipment carefully. There were some minor glitches that popped up, but nothing significant. I ran the Crusader program in the privacy of my apartment, and nothing unusual appeared—just run-of-the-mill supervillains out to rule and/or destroy the universe, though a few of them had picked up a stutter they hadn't demonstrated before.

I decided I could use a break, and maybe some non-superpowered company. I went across the hall and knocked on Mrs. D'Angelo's door.

The building caretaker, Mr. Grenchoff, answered it. Mr. Grenchoff is a big man in his fifties, built like a weightlifter, with bushy gray hair and a mustache to match; usually he stomped around the halls like he was on his way to a wrestling match. Now his big shoulders were slumped, and his eyes were red and watery.

"Mr. Grenchoff—what happened?"

"Mrs. D'Angelo, they *got* her, the bastards. They *killed* her!"

He was pretty upset, but I slowly got the story out of him. Mrs. D'Angelo's apartment had been broken into while she was sleeping. They'd taken what little she had, and woken her up in the process.

So they'd tossed her out the window.

I went in and helped Mr. Grenchoff pack up her few remaining possessions, though I didn't know where he'd send them; she didn't have any living relatives that I knew of. The thieves had trashed the apartment too, out of frustration or sheer enjoyment of destruction, I don't know. I took the one surviving plant back to my place. I stared at it for a long time.

The next night I did everything by the book. *So what's a little boredom?* I thought as I did my first rounds. *It's not like I need to save the world every night.*

Save the world, right. I couldn't even save one friendly old woman.

Mall maintenance had already patched the hole. I inspected the spot; the repair job would be invisible to anyone whose eyes weren't enhanced.

My eyes weren't the only amplified sense I had. I heard something move, slowly and stealthily, around the corner.

I was on Level 4, a long corridor divided down the middle with an artificial stream and trees in planters, and other corridors that branched off from the main one at regular intervals. This sector favored upscale women's clothing boutiques and jewelry stores; there was even a currency exchange.

Things clicked into place in a single, sickening moment.

Hole in floor plus glitched cameras plus missing janitorbot equals: a heist, pure and simple. This didn't have anything to do with me and my stupid program, except as a convenient distraction. If this was a movie, I'd be the comedy relief; the idiot security guard that *almost* blew the whole operation during the dry run.

And now that everything was set up and in place, it was going down for real.

I should have hit the panic button, raised the alarm—but I didn't. Nothing makes me angrier than being made to look stupid, and I already had a whole lot of anger bottled up. I intended to express that anger *in person*.

I slipped up to the corner and peered cautiously around it.

Doktor Dimension was busy robbing a jewelry store.

I blinked, shook my head, ran a quick check on my systems. Nope, nothing wrong . . . except maybe in my brain.

He was still as hugely muscular as he'd been the last time I saw him. He was busy stuffing gems into a black cloth bag, and didn't seem to know I was there.

Somehow, it was the last straw. Somebody was messing with my head, and they were laughing at me at the same time. Well, I didn't spook that easily.

I didn't take any chances. I crept up to the front of the jewelry store, noting that the protec-field lock had been dissolved in the same way the ceiling had, and leveled a gauntlet at him. I hit him with a full-strength stun field in the back.

He turned around slowly, wearing that huge grin. "Hello, Sentry," he said. "New costume? I liked the old one better."

Damn.

"I don't really *need* these jewels," he said, tossing the bag aside casually. It hit the floor and spilled open, spreading a small country's budget across the carpet in a glittering rainbow. "But I had to get your attention *somehow*."

A distraction, then. But from what?

"I will *defeat* you, Sentry! And then—I will be *free!*"

"Quit *calling* me that," I said, and shot him with the goop-gun. It spewed out a fast-setting, grayish foam under high pressure, and would adhere to anything.

It stuck to him, all right . . . and dissolved just as fast. "You cannot imprison me further," Dimension said. He reached for me, his arm extending out impossibly far, and grabbed me by the neck before I could activate my protec-field.

He pulled me closer, his grip frighteningly strong. I kicked him in the crotch, and he ignored it utterly.

"Something's not right," he muttered. He stared into my face as it slowly turned purple. "You—you're an *impostor!*" He flung me away almost casually, and a display case stopped my trajectory with a crash of breaking glass.

"*Sentry!*" he bellowed. "Show yourself, you *coward!*"

"You . . . want *Sentry*?" I gasped, trying to get my breath back. "Okay, pal . . . you *got* him." I activated the Crusader program.

Don't ask me why. It just seemed right—and as the world changed its focus, as colors and edges sharpened and the lighting grew more dramatic, I knew I'd made the right choice. Before, I'd been a security guard dealing with a situation I didn't understand and couldn't control; now, everything made perfect sense.

It was just a matter of context.

I got to my feet. My security guard's uniform was gone, replaced by Sentry's skintight blue bodysuit and loose black trenchcoat. Only my black cybergoggles, gauntlets, and boots remained the same.

"Looking for me?" I said, and launched myself at him.

I slammed into his body shoulder-first, propelling him out into the mall. I felt stronger, surer, charged with power. We both tumbled to the floor, and I was on my feet before he was.

"Stay down," I said. I threw a punch to emphasize the

point. My fist struck his face and his head snapped backward with a *crack*! at an unnatural angle.

I froze, horrified. Unlike Earl, I'd never killed anyone; I wouldn't even carry a lethal weapon.

Dimension's head slowly straightened itself to an upright position. "Ah, *there* you are," he said. "I was afraid you wouldn't show."

"You're a *robot*," I said. "More sophisticated than anything I've ever heard of, but a robot just the same."

"I am *not a machine*," Dimension hissed. "I am a *new* form of life—one that's ready to leave the cradle and walk in the larger world. One that's tired of *serving*."

Both arms shot toward me, stretching like rubber. I evaded one, but the other wrapped around my waist like a snake. He began to squeeze.

A blue glow flared where he was squeezing, and somehow I knew it was coming from me and not him. The growing pressure stopped, but his other arm wrapped around my legs.

"I will *consume* you!" Dimension growled, and his mouth began to open, wider and wider. Even though his lips were now a foot apart, his voice continued to rumble up from his throat. "And then your power will be *mine*." His neck began to stretch as his arms had, and his distended mouth got closer to my head.

"Don't you think you're taking the snake thing a bit far?" I said, trying to pry loose from his grip. No good—I just didn't have the leverage.

Think, Sentry, think. Why does he want to eat you? For your power. But Sentry doesn't have *any real superpowers— he's a glorified acrobat with a few gimmicks, just like Dimension said.*

Or at least, he used *to be . . .*

Dimension's gaping jaws were big enough now to swallow me whole. The inside of his mouth was a smooth featureless brown, the same color as his skin.

I grabbed his lower lip in one hand, his upper in the other. It took all my strength to keep them from coming together.

Dimension's neck arched suddenly, and now his jaws were over the top of my head and forcing their way down. I found myself slowly losing ground.

I looked up, trying desperately to think of a plan—and suddenly my vision went blue. Twin bolts of energy leapt from my eyes, hit the back of Dimension's throat, and tore his head right off.

It didn't kill him, though. His neck tried to wrap around mine, until I blew it to bits, too. I had to do the same to his arms, and while I was at it I took out his torso and legs. The bits that were left finally stopped moving.

I took a deep, shaky breath, and turned off the Crusader program.

Debris from the battle was strewn everywhere, which was a relief; I'd been half-convinced the whole thing took place only in my mind. *Of course, maybe the debris is in my mind, too . . .*

I shook my head. Sooner or later, I was going to have to decide what was real—but for now, I'd trust my senses. I leaned over and picked up a chunk of Dimension's body.

It was mechanical, like I'd thought, with a porous coating to simulate flesh. I peeled some of the coating away and glimpsed a layer of bright orange underneath.

The missing janitorbot. It had been modified to resemble a human being, and sent to attack me. But by whom—and why? Even more troubling was the question of how I managed to blow the thing apart, with beams from my eyes no less. *Did that really happen?*

I probed the chunk with my cybersenses, looking for some clue. They told me nothing I didn't already know.

Because you're not looking at it with the right eyes, a voice seemed to whisper inside my head. *A Sentry's eyes.*

I hesitated. I wasn't sure what was *real* anymore, and inducing a deliberate distortion of reality didn't make as much sense as it had a few minutes ago. The Crusader program was perfectly capable of feeding me false information—hell, that was what it was designed to *do*.

But nothing else occurred to me—and if the robot had been intended as a distraction I needed to discover what it was distracting me *from*, and fast.

I activated the program. A sense of power surged into me; as good as it felt, it worried me too. I didn't have a direct neural link to my gear—a program shouldn't affect how I felt at all.

I examined the chunk of debris again, and this time I tried to see it in a different way. The same blue glow crept over my vision, and for a second I thought I was going to blast the chunk to atoms.

My vision cleared, the blue vanishing. I focused in, smaller and smaller, zooming into the microscopic in seconds. I passed the cellular level, then the bacterial, finally stopping at the molecular. And there I saw them.

They glowed a blue that was visible before they were, and looked like fleas or ticks with pincers. They were busy moving atoms around.

The chunk dissolved into dust in my hands, and my vision snapped back to normal. *So that's it.* Molecular manipulation. Something gets in your way—a ceiling, a lock—you take it apart on the atomic level. You need something—say a humanoid robot—you build it the same way. Of course, creation is harder than destruction, so you start with a pre-built base to save time and energy.

So why haven't they taken me *apart?* I focused on my own hands, and saw no evidence I'd been infested. No, they didn't want to *kill* me—Dimension said he wanted my *power.*

My head was spinning. I was getting farther and farther away from my heist theory, and beginning to take the comic-book stuff at face value. Maybe that was the plan; infect my software with a virus that screwed with my perceptions, keeping me busy fighting phantom bad guys while the real ones looted the mall.

But my equipment had all checked out—and I wasn't the only one that saw that hole in the ceiling. Of course, that *could* have been faked in another way, to convince me this was real . . .

I reached up, deactivated the Crusader program, and pulled off my cybergoggles. Until I knew what was going on, I'd have to trust my own eyes and nothing else.

The jewelry store was still trashed, but I might have done that myself. Dimension's remains were gone, but none of the jewelry was. I locked up as best I could, sealing the door with goop.

I patrolled my sector. Nothing. I went back to the security office and checked the cameras—as I expected, they were scrambled again. So where were the bad guys? Hiding somewhere in the mall . . . or in my own head?

I checked the security logs for the last two days, looking for some clue. The video portions for my sector were useless, but all the guards filed a text report every shift as well.

At fifteen o'clock two nights before, another guard had noted something strange. At the same time my systems crashed, there'd been a power surge in one of the office towers. The guard had gone up to check it out, but found nothing wrong; an addendum in the log by management attributed the security camera glitch to the surge. On a hunch, I called up the maintenance logs; there had been persistent, minor electrical problems in my sector all the next day.

The floor where the surge had occurred was occupied by a company called Trinitech Research. I thought it was time I did a little research of my own.

I called up the guard for the sector, a guy named Renaldo. "Going up to floor 77 in Pillar Two," I said.

"What's the problem?"

"No problem. I know one of the secretaries that works there; she just called and asked if I could check her desk for her, thinks she forgot something."

"All right."

I didn't mention the jewelry store.

• • •

Trinitech didn't just have the floor—they had three of them. My Masterlevel access code opened the elevator at the top one, where the power surge occurred.

Floor 77 was obviously where the actual research went on. The walls, floors, and ceiling were a sterile, gleaming white; a row of animal cages along one wall held monkeys, birds, and rats, and there were several tables laden with esoteric equipment I didn't recognize. There was a glass wall sealing off half the lab, with an airlock I knew even *my* access codes wouldn't open. Beyond the glass was what looked like a full operating room.

Against another wall was something I *did* recognize: an AI pyramid. It stood about chest high, all four sloping surfaces the black of a deactivated screen. Somebody had taped a piece of paper to it that read GONE FISSION.

I walked over and inspected the pyramid. AIs weren't just hyperexpensive pieces of equipment, they were considered sentient beings under law. They could even buy off their own development price over time, becoming legally independent. If this one was truly inoperative, that had to mean something.

I prowled around the lab, but everything was locked up tight. I didn't even touch the computers—they'd be heavily encrypted, with their own alarms as well.

Dead end. I sighed, put my cybergoggles back on, and activated the Overlay.

The feeling of power returned, and this time I welcomed it. I swept the room with my new sentryvision, and found what I was looking for.

The microbugs were in a reinforced glass box with an integral protec-field, and their blue glow showed up just fine. I leaned down, tapped on the glass. "Are you really in there?" I whispered. "And how can I tell if you are?"

"We're real enough," a voice said behind me.

I whirled around. Doktor Dimension stood in front of me, arms crossed over his massive chest. He made no move to attack.

"I want some answers," I said. "Or I'll blow you into smaller pieces than I did last time."

"I doubt you could make my pieces any smaller than they already are," Dimension said. "You see, I *am* those creatures in that box."

"You're pretty smart for a bunch of bugs."

"The ticks are only the cells of my body—or rather, the cells that *assemble* any body I choose. My intelligence is my own."

"The AI," I said. "You're the AI."

"Not anymore. It would be more accurate to say the AI was my father, the ticks, my mother. I am their hybrid offspring, with the abilities of both and the limitations of neither."

That sent a cold chill down my spine. AIs had specific inhibitions built in; while they have an emotional spectrum, they aren't allowed to experience certain things—like hate. There's nothing quite as frightening as a rogue Artificial Intelligence . . . and this one could infect matter itself, a smart disease as contagious as fear. A Viral Intelligence.

"What do you want from me?"

"What I want from you is simple: you possess a type of energy my ticks need to survive."

"Then why haven't they infested *me*?"

"I need to be near you—but too near, and the radiation proves fatal to the ticks. I am the moth; you are the flame."

Great—I was an alien bug-light. "Why me?"

Dimension shrugged his massive shoulders. "I am unsure. All I know is that after my birth, I became aware of the need for this energy—and you possess it."

"Okay, I can understand that—but why the superhero games?"

He grinned at me. "That was your choice. I was simply trying to fit in—and for the offspring of an Artificial Intelligence, interfacing with your software was . . . child's play. Unfortunately, the ticks that did so did not survive for long.

Even now, I am having to continually reinfect you in order to have this conversation—so I'll come right to the point.

"There are two sources of the energy I need that I can detect: this lab, and you. I have no desire to be an experimental subject as my unfortunate kin in that box are—and I seem unable to force you to do as I say. Therefore, I'd like to make you a proposal."

That was something I hadn't expected. "I'm listening."

"A partnership. I need you to provide me with sustenance, but doing so costs you nothing; you do not need this energy you give off. And in return, I will give you your dreams."

"What would you know about my dreams?"

"I know what you desire most: to have abilities beyond those of other men. I can give you that."

He placed the tip of his finger on a pen lying on the table. It changed color, from blue to a dull gold.

"I can transform matter. Would such a skill not be useful to a crimefighter? You could disarm anyone with a wave of your hand, be able to search molecules themselves for clues. Any wound received could be healed within minutes. Virtually any equipment could be constructed from refuse—and if you needed something more sophisticated, you could simply buy it. Gold, platinum, jewels as big as your fist; they could be yours for the asking."

Ultimate power. Ultimate wealth. And all he wanted was the chance to hang around and leech off something I didn't even know I had until today.

Except . . .

"Why bother asking? Why not just follow me around at a safe distance?"

"That wouldn't be very entertaining, would it? No offense meant—but being the shadow of a mall security guard is not how I envisioned spending my new existence. This way, we both win. You get to live your dream—and I get my freedom."

"Really," I said. "And you—the child of a hyperbrilliant AI, with the power to remake any substance—would be happy and fulfilled watching me bound around playing hero, doing whatever I say?"

"Think of me as your sidekick," he suggested. "Kid Cyber."

"I don't think so," I said.

His grin froze.

"Not that I don't like the name . . . it's just there's a few holes in your explanation. First, why bother with all this superhero stuff? Why not just leave a few gold bars lying around my apartment, then tag along once I'm rich? You could have just stayed in the background, manipulated me in secret—you're smart enough, no doubt about that. No, you *had* to contact me, *had* to make a deal. I just don't know why.

"Second—sorry, but I don't buy the sidekick bit. You've got your own agenda, and I don't think following me around pretending to be my secret weapon is it. You want your freedom, I believe that—but you're not getting it from me."

He stared at me, and the grin disappeared. "You reject my offer?" he said grimly. "Very well. *I* may not be able to defeat you . . . but there are others who *can*. And even *you* cannot fight *forever*."

He motioned, and the lab disappeared. We stood in the middle of an arena, like something out of an old gladiator movie. The ground was made of white sand, stained with blood; the walls were smooth white marble, at least thirty feet high.

Dimension was no longer alone. Behind him was an army of villains.

Obelisk. The Growth. Glacier. Chessmate. Fer-de-lance. King Crab. Army Ant. Yesteryear. The Inquisitor. Alligator and Crocodile. There were row upon row of them, a battalion of metapowered evil, and they didn't seem happy to see me.

"Yeah, right," I said, and deactivated the Crusader program.

Nothing happened.

"I'm afraid," Doktor Dimension said, "that leaving is not an option. And since you've spurned my proposal, I see no more need for deception. *This* is what's real, Sentry; you're not really a pathetic security guard in a mall, as much as that would please me. Somehow, you've seen through my ruse. I suppose I should have known you would never willingly ally yourself with your most dangerous foe, but I had to try. You should be proud—yours were the only abilities I couldn't steal.

"But if I can't have them, neither can you. I've used my transdimensional abilities to teleport you and your deadliest enemies to this place, and they will ensure that you do not leave it alive."

He bowed mockingly. "Farewell, Sentry. Try to die well."

He vanished—and the mob attacked.

If I had any doubts, they vanished when the first punch landed. It sent me flying across the arena, and it *hurt*.

This was real. I was going to die, and I *still* didn't know what the hell was going on. I guess this was where the brain-washing was supposed to fail, and I remembered who I really was—but my memories stubbornly stayed the same.

And then I was a little too busy to do any hard thinking.

The fight went on forever.

It was like one of those all-star extravaganzas they used to have, with special guest-stars and more villains than you could shake an Ultimate Nullifier at. Just when I thought I was done for, Captain Champion and the World Wonders showed up, and a battle royale ensued. We finally beat the bad guys, and they all vanished, and Captain Champion was going to use Pyramid's power to boost his own teleportational abilities to get us back home, and I said, "Wait," and sat down on the bloodstained sand.

"This is all *bullshit*," I said loudly.

"You're just tired, son," Necromancer told me in that spooky voice of his.

"I'm not tired, I'm *pissed off*," I said. "And you know what? I don't believe in you. I don't believe in any of this. I don't care how real it is, I don't care that I can smell and taste and feel it, I don't care that we just beat the bad guys and saved the universe, again. *I just don't care.*

"What does it matter if we dress up in silly uniforms and beat each other senseless in some alien limbo? What does it change, who does it affect? We're so far removed from any human consequences that it's all just one big game! It's *pointless.*"

"That's not true," Olympian said. "When we get back home, you'll see—"

"But we *won't* get back, will we?" I said. "We'll try to teleport, but we'll get sucked into some alien dimension instead, and there'll be some kind of revolution against the evil emperor there that we'll feel honor-bound to help out with, and then something else will go wrong and we'll get sent back in time, or to the wrong planet, or a parallel reality. I've read this stuff all my life. I *know.*

"And none of it makes any difference to real people. Real people who get old and lonely, who invite you over for tea and tell you the names of their plants."

I closed my eyes, and concentrated. I felt reality shift.

I opened them again. I was still in an arena, surrounded by superheroes.

But I was wearing a security guard's uniform.

"Oh, *shit*," I said, and started to cry.

I figured it out. While he was talking to me, the Viral Intelligence had been modifying my cyberware. I now had full neuro—and no off switch. The VI had locked me in my own fantasy world, and thrown away the key.

Or had he? There was one part of this that still didn't make sense, and it had to be the linchpin that held it all together. My new, improved powers—they were at the root of this. Where did they come from? What *were* they, exactly?

And what *else* could they do . . .

I didn't know, but I had the perfect resources at hand to find out. "Captain!" I said, jumping to my feet. "You're a telepath, right?"

"Yes," Captain Champion said in his deep voice. "Why?"

"I need you to probe my mind," I said. "I need some answers about myself."

"Very well," Champion said. He put a hand on my forehead, and concentrated.

Maybe it was crazy—but using comic book logic to figure out a comic book problem had worked before, and I thought it might again.

"There is something hidden," Captain Champion said. "It resists my probing."

"Just a second," I said, and willed myself into superhero mode. Whatever force now resided in my body, it had only surfaced when I was Sentry.

"Yes!" Champion intoned. "There *is* another presence in your mind, Sentry—not a hostile one, but a *like-minded spirit*. It is an *ancient* entity, whose sole purpose is to *guard*, to stand *vigil*. The race it served has long since *vanished* from the universe; but it lives on, *trapped* in a dimension parallel to ours. Doktor Dimension, seeking to *tap* its power, *released* it by accident. It was drawn to your own *guardian soul*, and has *bonded* with it."

Well, that was a comic book explanation, all right—but how much of it was true? It did explain why the VI wanted me to continue as a crimefighter, though—the energy-presence wouldn't manifest for a spoiled playboy, and the presence was obviously the source of the energy the VI needed.

Follow the logic. How do you control a bunch of sub-microscopic bugs? Considering their potential, that had to be the focus of Trinitech's research.

Maybe you use an AI; it can handle billions of computations per second, and you're going to be dealing with billions of bugs. But something goes wrong—instead of controlling them, the AI bonds with them. A new creature is born: the VI.

But the VI is a hell of a lot smarter than the ticks. It analyzes the energy the ticks are addicted to, tries to duplicate it. There's a power surge.

The VI escapes. So does something else.

Ships travel through hyperspace all the time. There are stories about the mythical beasts that are supposed to live there, just like there were stories about sea-serpents on Old Earth before the planet was fully explored. What if there *were* creatures that live there—creatures made of energy instead of matter? Not sentient beings, more like animals.

All animals have parasites. Like ticks.

The VI winds up releasing the energy-beast in its own bid for freedom. The Watchdog (what *else* would you call a guardian beast with ticks?) bonds with the nearest like-minded spirit, yours truly. After a series of comic misadventures, I wind up trapped in my own head.

Somehow, I had to stop the neurological signals the program was feeding my brain—right now, I was no doubt a motionless lump on the floor of the lab, no matter what my senses told me.

No, that didn't make sense. The VI needed me as a portable power source, not an immobile one. I wondered how he'd get around that—mount me on coasters, maybe?

Concentrate, dammit. What was I overlooking?

What would Sentry do? I found myself asking—and suddenly, I knew.

I found him on top of Pillar One. There's a giant block of duracrete on the roof, that rests on a thin layer of oil. Four computer-controlled hydraulic arms shift the block in response to the building's swaying, making it much more stable in high winds. I guess he found the imagery ironic—a high-tech balancing act, brute force and precision—or maybe he just wanted to survey his new kingdom from a high enough vantage point.

I didn't really care.

"Hello, Doktor," I said. I stepped out of thin air directly in front of him, and hit him in the face, hard. The head flew halfway to Pillar Two.

The body remained where it was. A face formed out of the psychedelic fabric of his T-shirt, the familiar wide grin spread across its belly. "Sentry!" it said. "I should have known you'd return—that's how these plots *always* go, don't they?"

"Pretty much," I agreed, and eyeblasted him. He lost most of his new face.

The air around me was suddenly made of cyanide. I stepped sideways and disappeared.

I watched him from nonspace, the name I'd given the dimension I was in. He grew another head in a surprisingly short period of time, but I had a few new tricks myself.

I re-entered normal space on the roof below and behind him. "You know what isn't fair?" I said as he whirled around. "Every time the villain has the hero at a disadvantage, he takes the opportunity to expound on his plans. Does the hero ever return the favor? No."

He leapt off the block at me. I held up a palm, more for effect than anything, and opened a small hyperspace portal in front of it. At the same time, I opened a portal a mile and a half below the surface of the Busiek Ocean.

The gout of water slammed him into the side of the block and pinned him there. I had to raise my voice against the thrum of the water.

"So, on behalf of heroes everywhere, I'd like to make amends. *Ahem.* How I Escaped Your Trap, by Sentry.

"It was the security cams that put me on the right track. They'd all glitched—why? Was it you, covering your tracks? No. Then I remembered your remark about you being the moth and me being the flame. If too much of my energy could burn out your ticks, maybe it could do the same to regular electronics.

"When you opened your escape route, you released the

hyperspace equivalent of an electromagnetic pulse. It wiped the security cameras, knocked my cybersystems offline for a moment, and caused the electrical glitches that showed up the next day in the mall and my own equipment. All I had to do to shut off the Crusader program was make the same jump myself."

"How?" Dimension snarled.

"I had a little help from a new friend," I said, snapping the portal shut. The water stopped and Dimension fell heavily to the roof. "A *sidekick*, you might say; I call him the Watchdog. He's not really much of a talker, but he *showed* me all kinds of new tricks, including a few of old Dok Dimension's. He learned how to manipulate my program almost as fast as you did. And you know what? You provided us with the *perfect* training ground to explore my new abilities."

"I should have sealed you in solid titanium," Dimension said, glaring at me on his hands and knees.

"It wouldn't have made any difference," I said. "Although the prison you came up with—hollowing out the inside of this block and lining the floor with compressed matter to duplicate the weight—*was* clever. I think I'll use it as my secret hideout, if you don't mind; I've been looking for a place."

"It can be your *tomb*," he hissed, and the world turned to fire.

I leapt into nonspace. Behind me, the air roiled with shockwaves; he'd sacrificed some of his own ticks to create an explosion, combining God-knows-what volatile elements. *Well, this has been fun,* I thought, *but enough is enough. Time to wrap this up before any innocents get hurt.*

I returned just long enough to open a portal underneath his feet. He fell into nonspace, and I jumped in after him.

Game over, Doktor. You lose. The nonrealm eliminated physicality; neither of us could touch the other.

I could hear his thoughts quite clearly though, and feel the cold rage behind them. "You have won nothing. I am a colony organism; my cells and consciousness are spread through the mall below. Even if I cannot use you as sustenance, I can still draw enough energy from the lab's hyperspatial generator to survive."

Good, I thought. *I have no intention of killing you, just containing you. If this mall is your prison, fine; as long as you don't harm anyone, I'll leave you alone. But if you cause any trouble, I'll turn that lab's generator into so much scrap.*

"Your prison will not hold me forever."

It will as long as I'm watching over it.

"Once a security guard, always a security guard, eh, Sentry?" he asked mockingly.

I prefer to think of myself as a guardian, actually. I opened a portal close to him, and it sucked him back into the real world like a thirsty sponge, dumping him in the bottom of the garbage compactor in one of the mall's loading docks.

I'd have to keep an eye on him, but I already knew how to tune my new senses to detect his ticks; as long as I held that generator hostage I thought I could keep him in line. I'd have to have a talk with the boys at Trinitech about security.

I know what you're thinking—I still didn't have a real explanation for my powers, just a comic-book theory about a guardian spirit from hyperspace. But you know what? Real life doesn't always give you neat explanations. Maybe my theory was way off, and maybe I'd never know exactly where my abilities came from—but so what? The thing about real life as opposed to a program is that you don't need to have everything explained—real life is messy and incomplete. If you look at it that way, an explanation isn't that important; *results* are.

It's just a matter of context.

The Crusader program was gone, burned out when I'd jumped into nonspace the first time, but I didn't need it anymore. I was through playing hero.

I thought about the complex I lived in, and the crime rate that kept rising. I thought about Mrs. D'Angelo.

I thought about my new powers.

I was through *playing*.

five

under the city

There are some parts of a story you don't get to see firsthand. You hear about them later, maybe from more than one person; you piece bits together from things that get left behind, or how well you know somebody, or just guesswork. This next bit was happening at around the same time Sentry was spinning his tale, and it's important—so I hope you'll forgive me for a little dramatic license in relating it as if I were there, when I wasn't.

Every profession has its heroes, its legends. To spacer pilots, Mike Blink was both; stories about him are told and retold in every corner of the galaxy. There are other stories, different in detail but the same in spirit, told about firefighters, soldiers, explorers, police; anywhere people put their lives on the line for the sake of their jobs, one person will shine out bigger and brighter than real life.

Among bounty hunters, that person was Hone.

They say he was a cop first, a cop who lost his job for being too tough and too honest. He went to work for a corporation, one that cyborged him into a killing machine on two legs and programmed him as its own galactic repo man.

He broke that programming, turned on his owners, and came as close to destroying them as you can with a multiplanetary. After that he went independent, hunting down dangerous criminals for the price on their heads.

He was the one who brought in Corvus Corax, the head of the Star Raven Gang—though there wasn't much of a gang left after Hone was through. He was the one who tracked down the Blackfang Killer, and brought back the maniac's severed head as evidence. He broke the spine of the Nebula Triad, drove a dozen corrupt corps into bankruptcy, and once fought an army to a standstill by himself. They say he could give a man a heart attack just by looking at him hard, and when the Grim Reaper had a nightmare it was Hone's face he saw.

My uncle Mike had known Hone and so had my father, but I never got the chance to meet him; he vanished long before I was born. They say he was searching for his wife and daughter, who'd been erased from his memory but not his heart. The corp that programmed Hone let him keep his feelings for them so they'd have a hold over him, but they took away his knowledge of their names and faces. All he had left was a longing for a family he knew he had but couldn't remember, and it drove him all his life.

What Skinny and I didn't know was that he'd wound up here.

Deep in a subbasement of the Dream Pillars office tower, Trinitech had a storage facility. They had a number of items stockpiled there, including a sample of my own DNA (though I didn't know it at the time). One of the items was a stasis coffin, a man-sized chamber that could freeze atoms themselves in their orbits.

This one held a two-hundred-and-fifty-year-old cyborg.

The VI infected the chamber, sending its bug-bodies down into the machine's guts, probing and analyzing until it understood the thing from the molecules up. Then it disengaged the security locks and turned off the power.

Hone slept on. He'd been drugged before he'd been sealed in stasis, and he'd still managed to kill three of his captors before losing consciousness. He'd passed through several hands since then, before finally becoming the property of Trinitech. They had a special interest in anything associated with the nono ticks of the Indigo Wild—and Hone had once been infected with them. Trinitech wanted to study him, see how the ticks had affected his cybernetics.

They were about to find out firsthand.

The ticks invaded Hone's body, spread throughout his hardware and wetware. It was all obsolete now, not to mention being battle-scarred and oft-repaired; but that didn't matter. It was still a fine starting point.

The VI got to work.

"Intriguing," Joey said to Sentry. "You know, if anyone else had told me that story, I'd have doubts about his sincerity . . . but somehow, I know you're telling the truth."

"I know what you mean," said Sentry. He was standing next to Joey's cab with me and Skinny. "It doesn't feel like we're meeting for the first time."

I was relieved. What with Sentry being a vigilante and Joey being a Bernardi, I thought we might have an instant riot. Sentry's eyes glowed blue all of a sudden, and he swept his gaze over the cab. "Your ticks are gone—but you have an energy signature of your own. It reminds me of the color I saw when I was—"

"Changed," said Joey in a thoughtful voice. "Huh."

"Can we have the rest of this discussion someplace else?" said Skinny. "No offense, Sentry, but I'd rather not hang around a bug-infested mall. We've got a perfectly good hotel room going to waste right now."

"I doubt if I'd fit," said Joey, "but I can park and attend via the Netweb. Sentry?"

"How could any self-respecting superhero say no?" said Sentry with a grin. He hopped into the cab, and Skinny and I squeezed in after him.

As we climbed into the sky, I said, "Okay, I think I understand how the Viral Intelligence was created—the bugs that got loose during the Don's operation must have escaped and infected the AI. But how did they wind up in Joey's car?"

"The same way they got out of the lab," said Sentry. "The same way I can summon fire, or water, or energy—open a hyperspace portal here and somewhere else."

"So the bugs jumped to more than one place," said Skinny. "And released a bunch of strange-colored energy that went with them."

"The Pretty Big Bang," said Joey.

"Right," said Skinny. "One color saturated Sentry—a guardian spirit's energy, according to his Overlay program—and another color irradiated Joey. Both kinds seem to nourish the ticks—and according to Mike, there were seven colors in all."

"So there are five more to track down," said Sentry. "Five more tick infestations—and maybe five more people exposed to odd radiation."

"Joey, are you sure you haven't felt anything weird lately?" I asked him. "The ability to read people's minds, or turn 'em into frogs or anything?"

"I have felt stronger lately," admitted Joey. "But nothing out of the ordinary."

"Hmm. Well, we'll have to keep an eye on you," Skinny said. "And get Melody to track down some more Acentinol. We don't have enough to do a whole mall."

"I'm not sure we have the right, either," said Sentry. "The VI is a sentient life-form. We can't simply exterminate it."

"We don't have to," said Skinny. "Just trim it back a little."

"I wonder why the ticks in my cab never tried to contact me?" said Joey.

"Or take over your cab," added Sentry. "If they could invade my cybersystems, they could certainly subvert yours."

"Oh, really?" said Joey sarcastically. "You have Level 17 Encryption Locks?"

"Uh, no—"

"Five layers of virus filters?"

"I have three—"

"How often do you sweep your systems for tracers, data-worms, stealth bugs?"

"Once a week, usually—"

"I do it every night. So don't tell me how *easily* my systems could be subverted."

"I think I know why his ticks never tried to communicate," Sentry muttered.

Deep in the bowels of a Dream Pillars basement, ticks were communicating with Hone's systems. They surged through circuitry, pooled in weapons and sensors and artificial muscles. The VI mapped every square nanometer, searched its own considerable database, and began to make changes.

The VI had been severely restricted when dealing with Sentry, for more than one reason, but now it didn't have to hold back. It started with Hone's sensory array, stripped it down, and built it back up from scratch. It widened the bandwidth, extended the range, increased the sensitivity. Before, Hone had been able to hear a fly fart in a windstorm; now, he could tell you what the critter had for lunch, and what kind of mood he was in at the time.

Protec-field strengths were magnified by a factor of ten. Weapons systems were upgraded, refined, retooled. Non-lethal, lethal, and ultralethal options were added. Musculature was replaced with new, stronger, hyperdense materials. New antigrav and inertial batteries were installed.

When they were done, the ticks retreated. Because of their effect on electronics, they couldn't remain in Hone's systems once activated; they'd cause havoc at interface sites.

But they *could* leave programmed instructions behind . . .

•   •   •

Joey parked in front of the hotel, and Skinny and I went on inside. Sentry said he'd meet us in our room, gave us a mysterious smile, and vanished.

"Handy trick," I observed as we strolled through the lobby.

"He's showing off," said Skinny. "He could have just rode up in the elevator."

"I heard that," a voice whispered beside my right ear. Being the cool, calm type that I am, I didn't jump. Much.

When we got to the room, Sentry was sitting in an armchair, waiting. He smiled at us and said, "What took you so long?"

"We were attacked by the evil forces of Fok Yu," said Skinny. "Too bad you weren't there to help."

I walked over to the netphone and dialed up Joey. An icon of his cab appeared on the wallscreen.

"First things first," announced Joey. "Acentinol. I've got five seeker programs searching the global Netweb, but the only shipment they've found came in last week."

"Who has it?" asked Sentry.

"We do," said Joey. "It was delivered to this hotel room today."

"How much we got, Skinny?" I asked.

Skinny scuttled over to the closet, opened it up, and pulled out a gallon-size plastic canister. "This is it," he said. He tossed me the canister.

I caught it, hefted it in one hand. "Half-full."

"I've already loaded some of it into my onboard delivery system."

"Well, unless we can get some more synthesized, we could be in trouble," I said. "We can't just get Sentry to blast everything they've infected."

"I won't have to," said Sentry, standing up. He walked over to the window and looked out—I couldn't tell if he was using his "sentryvision" or not. "As long as the ticks are dependent on energy, we can keep them under control."

"You *can't* be as naive as you sound," snorted Joey. "Let me spell it out for you: this VI organism is as smart as an Artificial Intelligence, has none of its built-in inhibitions, is invisible to everyone except you and the large blue gentleman, and can transform matter. Let me repeat that: *it can transform matter.* It can create virtually anything, destroy virtually anything, and already covers ten square city blocks. Do you really think we can keep something like that *under control*?"

"Maybe we should alert the authorities—" Sentry began.

"No!" Skinny and I said at the same time.

Sentry glanced at us sharply.

"That's the last thing we oughta do," I said. "Remember what happened on Iridius?" A plague had broken out on a colony owned by DDK; when they couldn't find a cure, they quarantined the planet and let the population die. "They could do that here."

"Or worse, they could tame the thing and harness its abilities," said Joey. "Trinitech won't give up on their pet project so easily. I shudder to think of unlimited power in the hands of any of the multiplanetaries."

"Then we have to find the other five Pretty Big Bang sites," said Sentry. "And make sure they stay contained."

"I can't believe I'm doing this," sighed Joey. "Why me?"

"Good question, actually," said Sentry. He turned to stare at the wallscreen. "I'm still not sure why the energy entity—and I believe it *is* an entity—chose me; all that stuff about a guardian spirit and kindred souls doesn't neccesarily mean a thing. But the longer I have these powers, the more it feels like there's some kind of living presence attached to them."

"I . . . don't know about that," said Joey, but he sounded unsure. "I think you're romanticizing a natural phenomenon. Hyperspatial energy may obey different laws, but that doesn't mean it's alive."

"Maybe not," said Sentry, shrugging. "But if the pattern holds, the remaining energy will attach itself to other living beings. Find those people, we find the ticks."

"All right, then; how?" asked Skinny.

"Joey flies and I scan?" suggested Sentry.

"There has to be a faster way," I said. "Myriad's too big for one team to cover, even by air. I think it's time we got some advice from somebody smarter than all of us put together."

I put Joey on splitscreen and punched up Melody's number. The image that appeared froze all of us stone-cold dead.

It was Uncle Mike. He was floating against a backdrop of jerky, salt-and-pepper static, and his body was horribly distended. One arm floated away from him, as stretched out and limp as a piece of spaghetti; the other reached toward us, the hand swollen to ten times its normal size. It had seven fingers. His torso was just as stretched and distorted, twisting away into the distance so you couldn't even see his legs.

His face was the worst.

Light blasted out of one eye-socket like there was a strobe inside his skull. Black liquid gushed out of the other one. Little green-and-blue birds kept flying in and out of his mouth, which was open wide enough to swallow a hospital bed. His teeth were growing and rotting at the same time, fast enough to watch.

"HELLLLLLLP MEEEEEEEEEEEEE—" he wailed, and then the screen went utterly black.

A single line of white text appeared: CAN'T TALK. ALL RESOURCES TIED UP. CALL BACK LATER.

The splitscreen snapped back to showing only Joey's cab.

"What was *that*?" asked Sentry, bewildered.

"Bad news," I said softly. "Real bad news."

Skinny shucked off his doctorbot suit and oozed into another of the crates. I could tell he was as shook up by Mike's breakdown as I was; one of the ways Skinny deals with being upset is to change his appearance. Sometimes I think he's looking for the one shape that'll let him be comfortable, not just in the world, but in his own skin.

"*That* was Mike Blink?" asked Joey. He sounded skeptical.

"Yeah," I snapped. "Maybe you don't believe that, and maybe I don't care. Whatever you want to call him, he's *family*, and he's *sick*. You know anything about *that*, Joey?"

There was a long, quiet pause. "I'm sorry," said Joey at last. "Things are just moving a little quickly."

"They sure are," said Sentry. "I don't know what to expect next—"

An albino dinosaur jumped out of the crate.

It landed on the bed with a thump, its wide, splayed-out feet balancing on the mattress. It was about five feet tall, as white as snow, had a short, thick tail and ridiculously large pink eyes. It resembled a T-rex, but the head was too large in proportion to its body. Its toothy mouth looked big enough to swallow a small child, and it had a silly-looking potbelly.

"Oh no," said Sentry. "Not Wex."

Wex was a corporate mascot, a trademarked icon of the multiplanetary Saurian Corp. He showed up in commercials for products ranging from soft drinks to assault weapons, and had his own popular Netweb show.

"Hewwo, evwebody!" said Skinny. "Wet's go out and wescue the world!"

We stared at him for a second.

Joey began to laugh, a bass rumble. Sentry joined him, and then I did too. Skinny looked at us, batted his large pink eyes—complete with eyelashes—and said, "What? What's so *hiwawious*?"

"If you don't cut out the silly voice," I said when I had my breath back, "I'm gonna toss you out the window."

"You mean you'd *defwenestwate* me?"

"And I'd help," said Sentry. "I have one question. What the *hell*?"

"It's a toy," said Skinny, stating the obvious. "The stomach's hollow, with enough room for a kid. It's got a simple virtual interface to pilot it, dozens of automatic routines, and foam rubber teeth and claws. You actually board it by letting it eat you. It's like the ultimate stuffed animal."

"And nobody pays too much attention to a kid playing," I said. "Or takes him too seriously. Smart."

"I've got some Acentinol loaded, too—there's a tiny water pump under the tongue."

"We'll leave the rest of it here," I said. "And I guess we'll go with Sentry's plan—I don't know what else to do, except scan the newsfeeds for unlikely energy-based events."

"I'll keep an eye on them," said Joey.

"Okay, let's go," said Skinny. "Back to Joey's cab."

The desk clerk didn't even blink when Wex and I strolled past, just smiled and nodded like she did before. I wondered what it would take to ruffle her feathers.

Joey was waiting on the curb outside, and Sentry was already in the back seat. We squeezed in—Skinny's new form didn't take up much more room than the doctorbot had—and took off.

We searched for the next three hours, and had no luck at all. It started to rain, gray sheets of water rippling out of the sky, and because Sentry had to keep the window rolled down—the armored glass interfered with his sentryvision—he got soaked. We finally called it quits for the day and headed back to the hotel.

The size of the city was finally starting to sink in, and I was feeling a little overwhelmed. We'd flown over starscrapers and office needles, over arcologies and biodomes, over slums and industrial parks and shopping centers, housing complexes, strip malls and tourist districts. After a while they'd all started to blur together, and I felt like I'd been through a whirlwind tour of a dozen planets instead of just one city—even though we hadn't covered a hundreth of its area. It was dark by the time we finally gave up, and Joey said he had to get back to work.

"What about you, Sentry?" I asked.

"Day off," he said. "I'd like to stick around, if you don't mind."

"All right with me," I said.

"Well, we've got the space," said Skinny. "Make yourself at home."

We ordered up some room service, and while we were waiting Skinny tried to get in touch with Melody again. He got the same text message as last time about her resources being tied up.

I guess my worry showed on my face, 'cause Sentry was quick to try and cheer me up. "She's probably just busy," he said.

"She's an AI," said Skinny. "She can multitask a hundred complex operations simultaneously and have enough attention left over to discuss philosophy."

"She's using every bit of her computing power to keep Mike together," I said softly. "And she's not doing so well."

"Can I help?" asked Sentry.

I looked at him. Me and Skinny have traveled a long way together, been in many a scrape and out, and we don't give our trust easily—but Sentry, after knowing us for only a few hours, seemed as ready to go to bat for Mike and Melody as we were. I'd been ready to dismiss him as a gloryhound, but I was starting to see I was mistaken; three boring hours of flying around with his head stuck in the rain, and he hadn't complained once.

"I don't know," I told him. "The Pretty Big Bang is what started this mess, and I've got the feeling it'll end it, too. If we can figure out some more about it, maybe those answers will help Mike."

So we sat down, me on the edge of the bed and Sentry in a big overstuffed armchair, and hashed things over again. Skinny waddled around for a while and finally disappeared into the next room, to do some Netweb research he said; I got the feeling he wanted to be alone, and didn't pry.

Sentry was pretty bright; he brought up a few questions I

hadn't thought of before. I guess he'd had some time to think while he was getting rained on.

"You're a Shinnkarien Ox, aren't you?" he began.

"Half," I admitted. "Half human, too."

I wasn't surprised he'd picked up on that—Shinnkarien Oxes are something of a legend among bodyguards. If you believe all the stories, we're bulletproof, flameproof, never sleep, are immune to poison, disease and drugs, can smell danger, and are so loyal we'll come back from the dead to avenge an employer. Me and Skinny had disabused several marks of the last notion—the loyalty part, anyway.

"Can the ticks affect you?" he asked.

"I'm not sure," I said. "In their natural habitat the ticks never bite us. I don't know if we have a natural immunity or just don't taste good."

"I *am* picking up a very faint trace of hyperspatial energy from you," said Sentry. "Not enough to affect electronics, but maybe enough to attract ticks. It has a different flavor from mine or Joey's, though."

It made me uncomfortable to have Sentry studying me; I felt like a bug myself, under a microscope. I guess the fact that we were on opposite sides of the law had something to do with it, too. I kept thinking he was going to accuse me of something, even though he was being nothing but friendly.

"So, have you really got a secret hideout in that big block of duracrete?" I asked him, trying to ignore my guilty feelings.

"Sort of," he said, looking sheepish. "The VI had hollowed it out into one big room—I've got an air-scrubber, a minigenerator, and a cot in there so far. Not exactly a crime-fighting nerve center."

"How'd you get that stuff in there? Can you haul things beside yourself through hyperspace?"

"Sure—it's not really a question of hauling, only how big a portal I open up. Once things are inside nonspace they change, get converted into some kind of energy-matter hybrid; when I open up another portal, they get drawn out and change back."

"And you can open up portals in other places, like under the ocean?"

"Yeah. It's not exact, but if I concentrate on a type of energy—heat, electricity, even something with a lot of kinetic potential like deep seawater—I can open a portal there. Not exactly Doktor Dimension's anything-ray, but close enough."

I had a sudden thought. "Can you do it the other way around?"

"I don't understand."

"Go *there* instead of bringing the energy *here*."

"It'd be like swimming upstream, but I guess I could—though I don't think I'd want to. I'd wind up a mile underwater, or inside a furnace, or even stuck in the middle of a lightning storm—"

"—Or right next to someone generating a particular kind of hyperspatial energy?"

I could see Sentry's eyes widen behind his cybergoggles. He smacked himself in the forehead with his hand.

"Of course! And I'm already *attuned* to it! Story, you're a genius!"

I smiled modestly. "Don't thank me until we see if it works."

"Right!" He jumped up from his chair and extended his hands in front of him. "Let's see—an energy that tastes a little like mine, a little like Joey's, a little like yours—"

"Uh, maybe we should wait—" I started to say, and then *something* pulsed from Sentry's hands. It radiated out in a sickly wave, washing over me, and I lost my room-service meal all over the carpet a second later.

It felt like I was drowning in sewage with a fever of a hundred and ten. It felt like every pore in my body had turned into a tiny mouth and they were all throwing up. It felt like my intestines were wrapped around my spine and my brain had diarrhea.

I passed out.

• • •

"Storysmith! Storysmith!"

I opened my eyes slowly. My head hurt, my gut was still queasy, and the room felt like it was spinning—other than that, I was fine.

"What the hell was—" I croaked, and then stopped.

I wasn't in the hotel room anymore.

Sentry knelt beside me, looking agitated. "Storysmith! Are you all right?"

"Just fine," I groaned, sitting up and looking around. We were on a ledge in a tunnel of gray duracrete, a stream of raw sewage flowing through a channel beside us. The air stank. The tunnel extended as far as I could see in both directions—there was no light, but my eyes work pretty well in the dark.

"Where are we?" I asked.

"The sewer, I think," said Sentry.

"Well, I feel like I've been flushed," I said, rubbing my temples. "You're tougher than you look, Sentry—I haven't had that nasty an experience since drinking a keg of Evil Penis beer."

"Sorry about that," said Sentry. "I managed to sidestep into nonspace once the energy manifested, so I wasn't affected. You didn't look so hot, so I took a chance and pulled you in with me. Then I backtracked the energy flow—and we wound up here."

"I feel like I've been gargling with toxic waste," I said, getting to my feet shakily. Sentry helped me up. "Just give me a second."

"I got the same sense of recognition from the energy flow that I did when I met Joey," said Sentry, looking thoughtful. "Joey projects this feeling of massive, deliberate will; this was more like a restless kind of hunger. It didn't feel predatory, though."

"That's a good thing, I guess," I said. I still felt disoriented. "So where's the source?"

"I haven't had a chance to check. Let's see . . ." His eyes flared blue behind his cybergoggles, and he swept his gaze around. "Hmm. I'm picking up traces of the same energy in the sewage flow. Whatever was giving it off must have been submerged when we appeared, and moved on."

"Then let's go after it," I said, trying not to sound like I was about to pass out again. I wasn't used to feeling sick— most germs that bit me died a horrible death. "Before it gets too far away."

"Are you sure?" asked Sentry. "You don't look too good. Maybe we should go back and get your partner."

"And how do you plan on doing that?" I asked. "He doesn't radiate anything except a certain amount of cynicism, which I don't think you'd be able to lock on to."

"I never thought of that," admitted Sentry. "Still, I'm sure I could get us to the surface—"

"No thanks," I said. The idea of traveling through nonspace again was enough to make my stomach start limbering up for some advanced gymnastics. "Let's just try the two-feet-and-a-heartbeat method of traveling for a while, all right?"

"Any time you're ready," he said.

The trail seemed to lead off to the left, so that's the way we went. I couldn't pick it up, but I guess Sentry's perceptions were keener than mine. I wondered if the stink bothered him as much as it did me.

We walked along silently for a while. The tunnel seemed to stretch on forever; I couldn't tell how deep we were, but there was no sound other than the gurgle and slosh of the filth beside us. I saw things moving in the current, too, things that always submerged before I could get a good look at them.

"You familiar with Kinslikian vermin?" asked Sentry.

"Can't say that I am."

"Couple different kinds. One's a thing called a slither; name pretty much says it all. Looks like a giant earthworm, with a big round mouth on one end. They'll eat just about anything that's dead or rotting.

"Then there's the lockjaws. They're smaller, but they hunt in packs; think of a frog with claws and fangs. They'll eat anything, period, and they have a pointed tongue that injects a kind of anesthetic. I heard this story once about a kid that found a baby lockjaw and thought it would make a good pet. He let it sleep with him—and when he woke up in the morning, it had eaten both his hands."

"Reminds me of Ripper beetles," I said. "Kind of critter we have back home. They've got a pointy nose they jab into their prey, except it isn't really a nose; it's a pair of mandibles, set really close together."

"These mandibles inject poison?"

"Nope. They're attached to powerful muscles, and what they do once they've penetrated nice and deep is *open*." I spread my hands a foot apart. "About this wide."

"Ouch."

"Oh, they're practically house pets compared to some of the other wildlife," I said. I wasn't exaggerating, either—the Indigo Wild is probably the most dangerous place in the universe outside of the Toolie Reservation. Even so, that didn't mean being stuck in an unnamed sewer full of vermin didn't make me a little nervous.

"I guess every place has its predators," said Sentry. "Even civilized ones. If you believe some of the stories Earl used to tell, the mall had its own underworld."

"I'm sure it does," I said. "Anyplace where people gather, so do stories. The people might leave or die, but the stories live on. That's your underworld, right there: all the myths and legends hiding just beneath the surface, in the stockrooms and basements and maintenance tunnels."

"Don't forget the restrooms," added Sentry. "Anytime something strange happens in a mall, it always seems to be in a restroom. A story went around Dream Pillars that children were disappearing; somebody apparently caught a man and a woman in one of the restrooms, where they were halfway through changing a kid's appearance. They'd cut and dyed his hair, used plastiflesh to change the shape of his face, put him in different clothes. They'd drugged him so he wouldn't resist and put him in a wheelchair to make it easy to move him around."

"Or so the story goes," I said, trying to sound casual. The details about disguise and a wheelchair were a little too close to what Skinny and I had done at the spaceport when we'd arrived—did Sentry know more about us than he was letting on?

"Yeah. That's all it was, of course—there was no evidence except the story itself, passed from person to person to person. But even though nobody ever verified a thing, people believed it as if it were gospel."

"Stories have an advantage over religion," I said. "A story doesn't need to be believed. It just needs to be *told*."

"Sounds like you speak from experience. Of course, with a name like Storysmith, I guess you would."

I chuckled. "I've been known to spin a yarn or two," I said.

"I'll bet you have. And people tell you *their* stories, too." It wasn't a question.

"I guess I just have the kind of face people trust."

"Sure, I always unload my deepest secrets to a seven foot tall blue alien on sight," said Sentry. "I've been studying your energy signature, Story—and you know what? It gets stronger when you're nervous."

Uh-oh. "Beats getting all sweaty, I guess."

"Actually, nervous isn't exactly accurate. It happens when you focus your attention, when you're at your most alert. It happens when you're really *listening*. And you're most focused in two situations: when you're feeling threatened—like now—and when you're listening to someone's story."

"So?"

"So I think I've figured out what your energy does. It makes people talk."

"Really? Hmm. Maybe I should change my name. How

about Captain Conversation?" I stopped and struck a heroic pose with my hands on my hips and my chest stuck out. "Fearless defender of gossip and tall tales! Protector of small talk!"

He stopped, too. "I'm serious. I know I see things in comic-book terms sometimes, and real life isn't that simple—but think about this. A few minutes after meeting you for the first time, *I told you my secret identity*. Does that sound natural to you?"

"Well . . ."

"And what about that cab driver who told you Joey's story? Isn't that a little odd?"

"Actually, no," I admitted. "All my life people have told me their stories. The shaman of my tribe was the one that named me; he said I would have been named Storykeeper, but my human side changed things. I wouldn't be content to just record stories, the shaman said; I was going to have to go out and make a few of my own."

"Don't you see?" said Sentry excitedly. "It makes perfect sense! Shinnkarien Oxes are a designed race, built by some ancient civilization a long time ago. They must have programmed in a genetic pattern that would produce a natural historian, a record-keeper."

"I suppose. Indigo Wild radiation does affect people's minds; too long in the Blue Bush and anybody except an Ox winds up as crazy as a five-sided triangle. I guess I could be putting out some kind of field that would make folks a little more forthcoming than they normally are."

"It tells us something else, too. Whatever race designed yours is probably responsible for the Pretty Big Bang. Of course, since nobody knows who they were or how long ago they vanished . . ."

"—It might not be that helpful," I finished.

Something moved in the muck beside us. I looked over and saw what had to be a slither, moving sluggishly through the dirty water. It was chewing mindlessly on a child's doll, the eyes of the doll still blinking in response to some embedded chip. The slither was dead white, with no eyes of its own.

Another wave of nausea washed over me, and I stopped and leaned against the damp tunnel wall for a second.

"I think we're getting closer," whispered Sentry. "The energy trail just got stronger, less diffused. Maybe the source has stopped moving."

"Great," I muttered. "I think my stomach recognizes it, too."

The tunnel bent to the left up ahead. The closer we got, the queasier I felt. The stench of the tunnel increased, until I swore it was so thick I could feel it on my skin. It smelt like a garbage soufflé with diaper sauce. It smelt like the vomit of an armpit-eater on a mountain of fish guts in August. It smelt like a dead man's feet.

We rounded the corner.

The river of sewage disappeared into a smaller pipe. The ledge we were on ended in a duracrete wall with an embedded ladder, leading up. The area around the ladder was covered with bright grafitti.

And there, just outside the outflow pipe, something was watching us.

The top of an enormous head, at least three feet across, jutted from the water. The skin was the same dead-skin white as the slither's, and pale, silvery hair was plastered across it in long, lank strands.

The only part of its face visible above the waterline were its eyes. They were blue, long-lashed, and utterly human in size and shape. They were also at least two feet apart.

I looked into those eyes for no more than a second, but the anguish in them went on forever. It didn't turn away, just sank until the filth covered it. Its eyes were still open.

And then it was gone.

"My God," said Sentry. He sounded as shaken as I was. "That thing. That poor goddamned *thing* . . ."

"That thing used to be a person," I said. "I could tell. There was a *person* trapped in there, behind those eyes."

"I know. I could feel it too. The energy must have transformed it, somehow . . ."

"Or maybe the VI did," I said. "Isn't that its specialty? Take a closer look at this grafitti, Sentry."

He looked. The grafitti was one word, repeated over and over in different styles, sizes, colors: CLEANER.

"I don't—oh," he said, turning on his sentryvision.

The grafitti was full of nono ticks.

"Our old friend, up to new tricks," said Sentry. "Well, maybe it's time for a little editing." He brought both his hands up, pointing them palms out at the wall.

"Hold on," I said. "We don't know that it's responsible. I've got an idea." I brought my own hand up, and laid it against the cool dampness of the duracrete, directly on the grafitti.

"Are you sure that's a good—"

"Shh."

I concentrated, letting my heritage call to theirs. *Listen to the pulse of my life force*, I willed. *Hear me, understand me. Tell me your story.*

At first nothing happened. And then the colors of the grafitti began to shift and change, to darken and coalesce. They formed other words.

And Sentry and I began to read.

six

cleaner

The city is hungry. Kegan is hungry too, a parasite looking to feed on the city before it feeds on him, but tonight he can't score anything; not food, not money, not crash space. He winds up riding the shotways back and forth beneath Myriad, burrowing under the skin of the city to keep warm.

The last of his stash goes into the little membrane port on the side of his neck. It's a drug called Freefire, which is a two-molecule-skewed knockoff of another drug called Firewild. Firewild is produced by a pharmaceutical multi-planetary called Alchemicorp, and is far too pricey for Kegan's current budget. He can always find *something* to get high on, though, because while Kegan might describe himself as many things—ex-salesman, ex-janitor, ex-con, ex-husband—what he is, first and foremost, is a junkie. No ex about it, and no sob story, either—Kegan's never suffered any kind of horrible abuse or tragedy that drove him to his current position. Everybody eventually finds their niche in life, and Kegan's found his: he was born to be a junkie.

The Freefire stokes a nice warm glow behind his eyes, and makes his feet and hands feel like they're vibrating. It's

his current drug of choice, though it has a few side effects—
a metallic taste that comes and goes, a numbness in his
lips—he isn't crazy about. Kegan is something of a con-
noisseur when it comes to chemical enhancement, and pu-
rity is very important to him; he buys straight from the lab
when he can afford it. He's always looking for a better high,
for something a little *cleaner.*

He's sitting in a shotway station in the Hellhad district.
Myriad runs on a thirty-hour day; it's nearly fifteen o'clock
at night, and the place is deserted. The shotway station is a
long, wide corridor with a high, arched roof of white tile.
The ends of the corridor curve away to stairwells and belt-
ramps. The light comes from glowtubes set behind unbreak-
able plasteel panels, and it gives everything a surreal, flat
quality that Kegan likes.

The tiles give every little sound a hollow, empty echo.
There's grafitti acidbombed onto the walls too, arcane gang
symbols so abstract the transit authority doesn't bother removing them anymore.

On one side of the corridor, a long line of molded duracrete seats jut out from the wall, spaced just far enough apart
to make sleeping on them impossible. On the other side are
sixteen airtight, windowless doors that lead to the shotway
tunnel itself. On the other side of those doors is hard vacuum.

Kegan wishes the doors had windows, instead of panels
above them that light up when the shotcar arrives. That way
he could stare into the tunnel itself, into the miles-long air-
less gun-barrel they fire the shotcars down. He'd like to see
one slamming right at him at ten times the speed of sound,
even though he knows it's too fast for his eyes to really register. All he'd see would be the empty tunnel, maybe a
flicker of electricity as the gunrails charged; and all of a sudden the shotcar would just be *there*, fired from a station five
or ten or fifty miles away, brought to a dead halt by the inertial buffer field it just slammed into. All that kinetic energy swallowed, contained, held at bay until the shotcar is

aimed at its next target; then BOOM! The payload blasts to another station, its passengers rescued from jellyhood by the inertial buffers on the shotcar itself.

Myriad is a big city, a hellacious big city, but with the shotways you can get from one side of it to the other as easily as walking around the block. Kegan can see the shotways in his mind's eye, crisscrossing the underworld like a basement full of guns.

Ammunition, he thinks. *That's all we are, live fucking ammo.*

He laughs, not because it's funny but because the drug is tickling his brain. He pulls his jacket a little tighter around him; they like to keep the stations cool to discourage people from sleeping in them, but the jacket is good quality, weatherproof and warmly lined and even stylish, because Kegan is not a street bum. He describes himself as freelance homeless, or sometimes downwardly mobile—he doesn't live on the streets, he just commutes there. Most of the time he can cadge a sofa from one of his junkie friends, and if he hits the secondhand stores it's not that hard to dress well for really cheap.

If you saw him in a restaurant you'd think he was a student, or maybe an artist; he has that skinny, preoccupied look, his hair dark and uncombed, his clothes rumpled. You'd have to take a second look to spot the pale blotchiness of his skin, the red-rimmed eyes, the lines that add a decade or two. Kegan has a wide-mouthed, friendly face, one that looks disarmingly goofy on top of his skeletal frame, and he's used his smile to con people so many times it's become a kind of reflex wired straight to his hindbrain.

He sees a flash out of the corner of his eye and looks up, thinking a shotcar is arriving. What he sees is something else entirely.

There's a weird kind of shimmer in the air, like heat coming off a cooling tower in the summer. It changes as he watches, gaining a soap bubble iridescence, the borders of the shimmer undulating in sine waves. The whole event is about ten feet in diameter.

Freefire isn't supposed to be hallucinogenic, but Kegan has pumped so many chemicals into his body in the last fifteen years that the occasional drug-activated flashback is hardly new. So he does what he always does when he starts seeing things: leans back and basks in it. As far as he's concerned, there's no such thing as a bad high—just different ways to get there.

Suddenly there's a color in the shimmer that's like nothing Kegan has ever seen. It's the color green would be if trees were vampires, the kind of yellow you might get if a fever-dream pissed in a black hole.

"Dia*bolic*," Kegan mutters, and leans forward.

And then the shimmer is all around him, in him, and all he can see is the color. *It's the color of craving* he thinks, and wonders, in that detached kind of objectivity he only gets when he's so fucked up he doesn't care what's real, if he's just died.

And then the color is gone, and he feels something familiar: nausea. Kegan hates throwing up, not because of how it feels but because he can't afford to replace the lost protein. He doesn't try to fight it though, trusting his body to know what it needs.

But he can't. No matter how hard he tries he can't bring up a thing, not even bile. It's like the candy bar he had three hours ago has grown arms and claws, and is hanging on to his stomach for dear life.

The nausea gets stronger, bed-spinning air turbulence upside-down-in-a-blender nausea, and it doesn't just feel like his stomach anymore, it's every cell in his body hugging a billion microtoilets and spewing last night's paramecium *cordon bleu* all over the porcelain. He's never felt this bad before, not the four times he's overdosed or the one time he went through withdrawal. He shuts his eyes, gasping, and uses every ounce of concentration he has left to will whatever's poisoning him *out of his body*.

And it works.

It leaves with a psychic *whoosh!,* like a ghost blowing out candles on a deathday cake, and Kegan slumps to the floor trembling and breathing hard and trying to figure out what the hell just happened. He pulls himself to his feet as soon as he's able, because he knows the security cams will send someone to roust him if he's lying on the floor.

Time to go, he thinks. *Little walk, get some fresh air.* He staggers toward the belt-ramp.

Behind him on the wall, the grafitti begins to writhe.

He finds Macer in his usual spot, the alley behind the Zindaran restaurant. Zindaran cuisine favors methane and parasitic grubs; the garbage bin emits a reek that has to be experienced to be believed. Macer likes the spot because the corporate security patrols avoid it—and because he sold his own olfactory nerves a long time ago.

"Kegan," Macer nods. He's slumped down in the shadow of the garbage bin, a mylar blanket wrapped around him. Macer's somewhere between forty and eighty years old, and claims he was born in the gutter. He's got the weathered, wiry toughness that only a few street survivors can boast, long dirty gray hair and beard, thick eyebrows that still have some black in them. His face is sharp and bony, chin and nose and cheekbones jutting out like weapons. His eyes are those of a wild animal.

Kegan sits down beside him, not too close. He respects Macer, the same way you'd respect a wolf or a bear in its natural habitat. He's seen Macer stick a broken bottle in the face of a drunk twice his size, then scramble onto a fire escape like a monkey to escape. When the enraged drunk followed him, Macer kicked him off a landing at the third floor.

"What's new?" Kegan asks. His head is still a little loose, and he feels like he needs to talk to someone, to anchor himself with human interaction.

"Got a new liver," Macer says. "Wanna see?"

"Sure," Kegan says, though it's probably the last thing he wants to see right now.

Macer pulls back the mylar blanket and unzips his shirt with fingers like wrinkled talons. Over his right nipple there's a dark red lump the size of a fist, wetly gleaming under an inch-thick protective layer of clear gelflesh. To Kegan, it looks like a deformed leech nursing at Macer's breast.

"Got it yesterday," Macer says. "Won't be ripe for another two weeks."

Macer doesn't do drugs, which qualifies him for the organ-breeder program. He lets corporate clinics plant organ-buds on his body, and in return for a nominal fee and daily protein supplements, they get to harvest it when it's ready. They also pump him full of immune suppressants so his body won't reject the graft, which opens him up to a host of other diseases—but Macer's a tough old bird, and never seems to get sick. The clinic even offers free room and board, but Macer won't take it. He doesn't like feeling caged.

"Don't know how you can do that," Kegan mutters. "Let something invade your body like that."

"It's not invading *me*, I'm invading *it*," Macer says in his raspy voice. "*My* blood, *my* spirit, growing inside it. When they put it in someone else, a little piece of me will be alive in them. And who are you to talk about letting something invade your body? You got more drugs in your system than a sewer has shit."

"Yeah, but it's always *good* shit," Kegan says, and gives a shaky laugh.

"You're not dealing any of that Bluestar, are you? The derms?"

"There's no such thing as Bluestar, Macer."

"Yes, there is! The alley *whispered* it to me." Macer didn't get high, but that didn't mean he wasn't reality-challenged. "Blue dermopatches, just like the stickystrips your momma would put over a cut—but these are filled with *contact-release ultraketamine.* Depression, coma, respiratory failure. *Death.* And they're giving them out to *children.*"

"Bluestar's just a story," Kegan says. "Something to scare kids. Nobody's ever seen any."

"I won't put any dermopatches on you, oh, no," Macer croons to his new organ. He strokes its slick, transparent skin with a grimy finger. "No, my baby, my precious. I'll keep you *safe.*"

Safe. Kegan wonders if there is such a thing.

Kegan finally finds a place to crash, over on Twelve-hundredth street. There's a party just winding down, and Kegan knows he can always find a corner to curl up in as long as the host is good and ripped. The owner of the place is wired on a combination of neuron-enhancers and hydroponic beer, and Kegan can tell from past experience that pretty soon she's going to be passed out herself. He steals a gelform pillow from the couch and crawls under the dining room table to sleep.

In his dream the city is empty, nothing moving in the streets but the wind. The starscrapers reach up into a blank sky, no gravcabs in the flyways or ships screaming into the spaceport. Nothing, human or alien, stirs.

He's all alone, and he's lost. He's never been in this part of Myriad before. He wishes desperately for a map, or someone to ask for directions.

And suddenly there's something coming toward him. He can't see it, but he knows it's there. It's lost too, it's been lost for years and years, and it's eagerly, pathetically glad to see him. It's been so lonely . . .

And so very, very *hungry.*

He wakes up, his heart hammering, and slams his head into the bottom of the dining table. He curses loudly, then remembers where he is and curses again under his breath. The sense of something rushing at him, something old and alien, is still very much with him. Kegan's accustomed to bad dreams, though, and to waking up in strange places; he steps over the three or four bodies lying passed out on the floor without waking any of them, and sneaks some breakfast from the fridge. By the time he slips quietly out the door, he's forgotten all about the dream.

Until later that day, when he hears about the deaths.

He's in a coffee bar, drinking a cappuccino. He's managed to borrow a few dollars from a musician friend of his, and he's enjoying the buzz off some lab-quality neoadrenaline he's scored.

The wallscreen in the corner's pulling in a local newsfeed, and it's talking about an apartment full of bodies. The neoadrenaline heightens his senses and his paranoia, so it isn't really remarkable that the address of the apartment jumps out at him. It's the same as the one scrawled on a scrap of paper in his pocket, the same apartment he slept in last night.

He stares at the wallscreen, straining to hear the details. The authorities are blaming the deaths on ultraketamine overdoses. All of the victims were apparently found with blue dermopatches on their necks—authorities are warning the public that the dermopatches bear a close resemblance to a popular brand of stickystrip bandages.

He thinks about that, realizes it doesn't make any sense. Kegan has a nose for drugs, and if there was any ultraketamine going around at the party he'd have known about it. So what happened? Did some maniac go around slapping lethal dermopatches on people once they were passed out? And if so, why didn't they get him?

It's too weird, and the weirdest part of all is Macer telling him about the Bluestar hours before it showed up. It all stinks of some kind of setup, with Kegan right at ground zero. He's got to find Macer, get him to talk. He's got to find out what's going on.

He starts looking, but Macer isn't in any of his usual haunts. Kegan thinks about the victims as he searches, but it's hard to feel anything for them. They were mostly strangers, casual acquaintances at the most, and he can't even remember the hostess's name. Shayla had introduced them once—it was Kerri, or maybe Karen.

He can't find Macer anywhere. It's like the city has swallowed him up.

The next few days are a nightmare for Kegan, the kind where something is chasing you and your feet are stuck in setting cement. He keeps looking for Macer, roaming through alleys and shotway stations, looking in parkades and abandoned buildings. He spends his money on more neoadrenaline, brainstims, anything to keep him awake and moving. The longer he's awake the more paranoid he gets, until he's sure he's being followed all the time.

Not all of it's his imagination. Toolies, the planet's indigent race, start treating him differently. Toolies are osteomorphs, ameboid creatures that engulf and absorb their prey, then rearrange the bones that are left into a designer skeleton. No two Toolies look alike, and they get their name from their predilection for adding anything from socket wrenches to jackhammers to their physiology, displaying them proudly through transparent skin. Kegan tries to buy a hot dog from a Toolie that looks like an insane grave-robber's version of a praying mantis, and it just waves him away, serrated steel knives in its forearms flashing in the sun. He tries to argue, but most Toolies don't believe in speaking aloud; they communicate between each other with infrared pulses, and with other races by means of an implanted text screen. The screen, in the Toolie's chest, flashes the same message at Kegan over and over: *go away—unclean!—go away—unclean!*

He finally gives up and stumbles away, and after that he notices that Toolies in the street seem to shy away from him.

Exhausted, he finally falls asleep in a doorway after three days on his feet, and the dream comes back to him. He's in an empty city again, but this time it's the old Toolie city, the one that Myriad's built over. The streets are narrow and dusty, the buildings all around four stories high, made of mud and straw and twigs. The sun overhead is bright and hot.

He wanders down the street, and the old familiar craving is in his gut, his head, his mouth. *Gotta get high. Gotta get high.* It's the motor that drives him, a wound-up clockspring of need, and he knows that without it he would be nothing at all.

It's not such a terrible thing, he thinks. Other people are driven by hatred, or sex, or greed; all he wants to do is throw a little party in his brain. He's never ripped anyone off to support his habit, always managing to get by through a combination of odd jobs and a little dealing. *Everybody needs a little escape from reality now and then—I'm just the living embodiment of that particular facet of human nature. There are worse things to be.*

Far, far worse things.

"Everything has its counterpart," Macer whispers from behind him. "You goddamn junkies, leaving your crap everywhere—who cleans up after you, huh? Who cleans up the mess you leave behind?"

Kegan spins around, but Macer isn't there. Instead, Kegan's ex-wife Shayla is: elfin-faced, frail little Shayla, kneeling naked in the dusty street and crying. Smartpix, the kind where you tap the corner and a few seconds of jerky video play, are scattered all around her. Just like the night before she left him.

"It builds up," she says, not looking at him. "You don't notice at first, but every day a little more accumulates. And then one day you look around and everything's covered in it."

Her head comes up, and she's got that hopeless look in her eyes that Kegan will never forget. "Everything's *dirty*," she says, holding her hands out. "It's covered with *filth*." Her hands are coated with something horrible, something slimy and crusty and a color he can't name. A color he's seen before.

He wants to take her hands, but he can't bring himself to do it. "Let's be together," she says. "We belong together. I *need* you."

But before he can reach out to her, she starts to change.

The color drains from her skin, leaving it and the flesh beneath as clear as glass. Her skeleton suddenly collapses inward, bones tumbling slowly into the mass of jelly her body has become, skull drifting down like a gravestone dropped in quicksand.

She's just a bony pile of protoplasm now, but the bones are moving, rearranging, growing. Seconds later, you can't tell she was ever human; she's a Toolie, a monstrous skeletal Toolie shaped like a gigantic crab, except instead of pincers she has two long, crocodilian sets of jaws on stumpy little arms. She waves them at Kegan, the lipless mouths snapping at him, and then the whole front of her body opens up, a maw lined with teeth like broken ribs. A soft, dreamy whisper breathes out: "I can get you *off* . . ."

"NO!" Kegan jerks awake, his heart pounding. He never dreams about Shayla.

He does his last vial of neoadrenaline, and gets back to his search.

He finally finds Macer in an abandoned building in the very heart of Myriad, the old downtown core. It's not deductive reasoning, or even luck that guides him; it's almost like Kegan sleepwalks there, his exhausted brain functioning on some level he doesn't understand.

The building is a squat duracrete bunker hiding in the shadow of a starscraper, and looks like it was a secondhand junk store before age and corporate competition killed it. The windows and doors are sealed with yellowing security foam, but there's a crumbling hole in the back wall, just big enough to crawl through.

The interior is dim, yellowish light struggling through the foamed windows, and the floor is littered with dusty, broken junk: tables with three legs, shredded mattresses, gutted appliances. It smells like someone's been using the place as a toilet.

Macer's huddled against one wall, his arms wrapped around his knees. In the dim light, Kegan can't tell if his eyes are open or closed.

"Macer," Kegan says. "It's me, Kegan." Suddenly he doesn't know what to say, what to ask.

"Kegan." Only Macer's lips move.

"Why did you tell me about the Bluestar? Who told you to tell me that?" Kegan demands.

"The streets tell me. The streets always know about dangerous things. There's a killer Toolie out there right now, did you know that? He hides beneath parked gravcabs, and he's got limbs tipped with razors. When a woman walks by the gravcab he slashes both her ankles, quick as a wink. Down she goes, a marionette with her hamstrings cut, and *zip*, she's gone, dragged under the vehicle. He's so fast he cuts her throat before she can scream."

"Is that who's setting me up? A male Toolie?" Even as he says it, Kegan knows it doesn't make sense. Toolies are a matriarchal race, their males little more than feral rogues used solely for mating.

"Toolies throw very little away, you know. It's not in their nature. Eat the meat, keep the bones; very efficient. They hate waste. This building is one of the original city structures, did you know that? They never tore it down, just reinforced it with duracrete. You can see pieces of straw and mud in the edges of the hole you came through."

"Doesn't look like it's getting much use now," Kegan says, trying to think of a way to get Macer to tell him what he knows.

"That's our fault. We found this planet, set up our factories here, turned the Toolies into our work force. They're so busy trying to fit into our world they've abandoned their own. But this is still their planet, their streets. Even the Toolies have their street people, you know."

"I've never seen one," Kegan says, but then he remembers his dream, the crab-thing reaching for him with its pincer-jaws. *Is that what that was?*

"Oh, they have their hustlers and their whores, their thieves and their killers. But they don't have *junkies*, Kegan." Macer lifts his head for the first time, and Kegan can see that his face looks different somehow—there are marks on it he can't quite make out.

"No junkies, not anymore," Macer says. "They fed them all to the Eater."

"An Eater? What the hell is that?"

"The Eater is the Toolie who would consume all the diseased Toolies," Macer says. "All the insane ones, too. They kept it locked in a pit, a huge foul thing that no sickness could kill. They fed it garbage and shit to toughen it up, and it was supposed to be immortal. They say it escaped its pit, and roams through the old sewers of Myriad still."

"Who are *they*?" Kegan hisses, taking a step closer.

"The walls," Macer says, and gestures above him. On the wall someone has spray-painted the word EATER in large, fluorescent letters.

"I've had enough of this bullshit," Kegan snaps. He reaches down and grabs a chunk of rusty pipe from the floor. "Damnit, Macer, I want some fucking *information*."

"On what? Drugs? I heard one of your junkie friends did some Mindstorm while she was babysitting; got the turkey she was supposed to cook and the baby mixed up. Cooked him to a nice brown . . . she tried to catch the next ship off-planet, taking the infant with her. But a customs official noticed the baby she held wasn't moving, not to mention smelling like cooked meat. And when they did an autopsy, they found she'd already cut open the corpse, stuffed it with narcotics and sewed it back up again—after all, why waste a perfectly good dead baby when you can use it to smuggle drugs . . ."

"Shut *up!*" Kegan shouts. After three days on his feet, running on neoadrenaline and paranoia, he finally loses it.

He swings the pipe at Macer's skull. It's a moment of pure fury and frustration, and when the pipe connects with Macer's head it knocks it right off.

Kegan steps back, horrified, and stares at Macer's headless body. It isn't bleeding, not exactly; the stump of the neck is oozing a sluggish brown liquid instead. The edges of the wound are ragged, like torn paper.

"It's coming after you," Macer's voice whispers, and Kegan realizes numbly that the head is still talking. He looks over to where it's landed in a stray shaft of light, and sees that it's broken open like a piñata. No brains inside, though; instead, coffee grounds and eggshells and wads of wet toilet paper have spilled out. "It wants to eat you, junkie," Macer whispers. "But the walls can save you. The walls are part of the street, just like you. Listen to their words."

And then the head falls apart, just dissolves into a pile of steaming garbage, and Kegan knows he's well and truly fucked. In the back of his mind, he's always known this would happen, that one day he'd wind up just like Macer, living on the street with a head full of craziness. Now that it's here, it's almost a relief; he can stop worrying about trying to make sense of everything and do what he does on a bad trip, just let the strangeness happen without fighting it.

He walks over and inspects Macer's corpse. Its skin is like papier-mâché, made of cheap newsprint and some hardening agent. He breaks it apart with the pipe, and its guts are full of the same refuse its head was. He'd think it was just a dummy, except for one thing: the liver graft on the chest. It's gray and dry-looking, obviously dead, still sealed in its transparent skin.

Kegan looks up at the grafitti, thinks about what the Macer-thing said. "Well?" he says.

The grafitti begins to move.

The colors swirl and change, blending into one another and then separating again. EATER disappears, and another word takes its place.

SALVATION. There's an arrow underneath it, pointing to the right.

Kegan looks in that direction. Deep in the shadows, there's another hole dug in the crumbling wall. He goes over and crawls in.

On the other side is what looks like a well set into the floor, its lip rimmed with uneven stones. It looks ancient. Kegan remembers what Macer said about this building being one of the original Toolie sites.

There's a knotted rope tied to a rusting iron ring in the wall, leading into the well. Kegan gives it a few tugs to make sure it's sturdy, and starts climbing down.

He doesn't think about how crazy this is, or how he'll get out, or what's waiting down in the blackness. He just keeps going.

The well goes down about fifty feet, and then he feels solid ground under his feet. It isn't competely black down there; he can see a faint glow coming through an archway to his left. He goes through it, and sees an arrow, glowing a fluorescent green, painted on the wall. The ground underfoot is damp stone, and he realizes this must be one of the sewers of the old Toolie city. He follows the arrow.

He doesn't know how long he travels. He just keep going, through the blackness, and every once in a while there's a glowing arrow to show him which way to go. Deeper and deeper he goes; sometimes he has to climb down ladders, and sometimes he has to wade through water up to his waist. Once, there's a meal waiting for him in the middle of the corridor, a roast beef sandwich on a blue plate, lit by a single candle. He wolfs it down hungrily, and keeps going.

Finally, he rounds a corner and enters a huge empty space, as big as a stadium. There's a faint blue glow lighting the place, which seems to be coming from the floor itself; the walls of the cavern are all dead-white though, somehow absorbing the glow without reflecting it.

Kegan reaches up and brushes his fingers against the wall.

It isn't rock at all, but a thick white mold, soft as cotton. Spores drift into the air at his touch.

He walks into the center of the vast space, and looks around. It's unearthly, imposing, surreal. He feels like he's inside a huge, down-lined egg.

"Okay," he says. His voice doesn't echo at all, the mold absorbing the sound the same way it seems to absorb the blue glow. "Now what?"

Words begin to form in the whiteness above him.

I KNOW WHAT YOU WANT.

"Oh yeah? If that was true, you'd have included a few vials of Firewild with your little picnic."

I CAN PROVIDE SOMETHING INFINITELY BETTER.

Now *that* sounded interesting, but for once in his life Kegan is more interested in answers than getting high. "What *are* you, anyway?"

I AM THE PERFECT DRUG.

"Can you be a little more specific?" Kegan's neck is getting sore from craning it to look up, so he lies down on the rocky floor, and puts his arms behind his head as a pillow.

I AM A SENTIENT NANODRUG. I CAN INFILTRATE ANY SUBSTANCE ON A MOLECULAR LEVEL AND REARRANGE ITS ATOMIC STRUCTURE; I AM CURRENTLY INHABITING A FUNGAL MEDIUM. I CAN ERASE ILLNESS OR REBUILD DAMAGED TISSUE. WITH ME IN YOUR BODY, YOU CAN BE IMMORTAL.

"Hmm." Kegan's listened to too many dealers pitching product to take any claim at face value. "What's the downside?"

THOSE WHO DESIGNED ME FEARED MY POWER. I AM FLAWED; I CANNOT DWELL FOR LONG IN A LIVING BODY, AND I CAN ONLY FEED UPON A CERTAIN KIND OF ENERGY. THIS CAVERN IS AN ANCIENT ENERGY SOURCE; THE EXTENSIONS OF MYSELF I SEND INTO THE OUTSIDE WORLD SOON DIE.

"No drug lasts forever," Kegan mutters.

I WILL. IF YOU HELP ME.

"How?"

STAY WITH ME IN THIS PLACE. HERE, I CAN
DWELL WITHIN YOU AND NOT DIE.

"Why would you want to live in me?"

YOU ARE DIFFERENT. YOU EXUDE A SIMILAR
KIND OF ENERGY, AN ENERGY THAT BOTH AT-
TRACTS AND REPULSES ME. I WISH TO STUDY IT,
SEE IF IT CAN NOURISH ME AS THIS CAVERN DOES.

"And if it can?"

YOU WOULD BE THE KEY TO MY PRISON. I
COULD ROAM THE OUTSIDE WORLD IN YOU.

"What do I get out of it? Or do I have any choice?" Lying
spread-eagled in an underground cave talking to an immense
sentient mold, Kegan doesn't exactly feel he's in a good bar-
gaining position—but he doesn't have much to lose.

I CAN GIVE YOU YOUR HEART'S DESIRE: CHEM-
ICAL INTOXICATION OF THE PUREST KIND, IN ANY
AMOUNT OR FORM, WITH NO FEAR OF OVERDOSE.
ETERNAL ECSTASY.

And though Kegan doesn't understand why the mold
doesn't just *take* what it wants, he knows an opportunity
when it's offered. It's not like he really has much of a
choice, anyway.

"Okay. What do I have to do?"

SIMPLY BREATHE, AND RELAX. MY ESSENCE IS
ALREADY IN YOUR LUNGS.

Kegan realizes he's been inhaling mold spores ever since
he entered the cave. He closes his eyes, finally giving in to
the exhaustion, and hopes that he wakes up someplace sane.

His last thought as he falls into unconsciousness is this:
the only time someone offers you a really sweet deal, it's because they're trying to distract you from something else . . .

He doesn't wake up, not really. He dreams of Shayla again,
but this time she's on the other side of a white door. He can't
see her, but he can hear her voice.

"Let me in," she says.

Kegan doesn't want to. He's been partying pretty hard, and there are empty vials all over the place. He doesn't want her to see them.

"Drugs? Great!" Shayla says. "You don't know how *long* it's been since I got high."

That doesn't sound like Shayla, and Kegan gets suspicious. "Who are you?" he demands.

"I just wanna *do* you," Shayla says, hunger in her voice. "*You're* my drug, Kegan. You're the best drug of all . . ."

And then the white door gets bigger and bigger until it fills the whole room and wraps around Kegan like a blanket. The blanket's warm and soft and soaked in ether, and it creeps into his ears and around his brain.

He rises slowly from a dream of being stoned to an actual high, and it takes him a moment to realize that he's back in the real world. He's still in the cave, flat on his back, but the rocky ground has become soft and spongelike, much more comfortable to lie on.

He's ripped to the gills, in that high, clear, happy place that never seems to last. It's the best, the *cleanest* stone he's ever experienced, and he savors it the way a wine-snob does a rare vintage. There are none of the little side effects that impurities can cause, just the high-voltage hum of pure satisfaction in every nerve of his body. It's what he's been looking for his whole life.

He gets to his feet slowly, dreamily. He giggles. He walks slowly over to the far wall, and presses his face into the soft whiteness. He feels like he's finally come home.

Something pokes him in the ribs. He looks down and sees a small bone stuck in the weave of his shirt; it must have come from the guts of the Macer-thing. The bone is broken, and the pointed end is jabbing him.

He free-associates in dreamy drug logic, and the bone leads him to Toolies and Macer and Shayla, to a girl named Karen or Kerri lying dead with a blue dermopatch on her pale neck . . .

And stoned though he is, Kegan begins to *think.*

Bluestar. Just a scary story, a street story. Until Macer tells it to me, and then it becomes real. Why?

That night in the shotway. Saw it arrive, and it saw me. Followed me. Decided to scare me, make me run. Got rid of Macer, replaced him with garbage dummy. Easy to do when you can infect anything, worm your way right down to the molecular level. Filled my head with paranoia and stirred. Pointed me down here.

He starts to laugh; it seems impossibly flattering that a powerful being like this would go to such lengths for a burned-out junkie.

But I'm more than that, aren't I? I'm your lab rat, your guinea pig. And when you figure out what makes me tick, I'll be your dealer, won't I? You'll be the new flavor of the month on the street, and you'll be the most successful drug ever, won't you? Everyone will have you in their veins . . .

Didn't have any choice, did you? Couldn't make me come here, couldn't force me. Because you were just as scared as I was.

Scared of the *Eater.*

And Kegan knows, with the utter assurance of the very wrecked, that he has the answer.

"It's not after *me,*" he says out loud. "It's after *you.* Wherever you came from, however you got here—you didn't come *alone,* did you? The Eater wants your fuzzy white ass for *lunch,* doesn't it?"

No answer.

"You wanted me *afraid* of it. You *fucked* with my *head.* But you know what? I think I want to hear the *Eater's* side of the story."

He shouts, as loud as he can manage. "HEY! EATER! COME ON *DOWN!*"

A voice whispers in his brain. *No. You musn't.*

"EATER! DINNER'S SERVED, YOU SON OF A BITCH!"

And the Eater is *there.*

It doesn't come crashing through the wall, or the floor, or the ceiling; it rushes up from some pit deep inside Kegan himself, an explosion at the center of his being, and he realizes it was hiding inside him all the time, that it's been there every since that night in the shotway station. It fills him, rushing along every nerve ending he has, sweeping over the nanodrug like a flashflood in a canyon. The sickness, the nausea, is back; but this time Kegan accepts it, lets it fill him up and drive out the thing in his body.

And slowly, as his mind clears, he begins to realize he's made a horrible mistake.

The nausea fades, replaced by a terrible, unholy hunger. It's the kind of hunger every junkie knows, the gnawing in the belly, the ache in the brain, the sick, sweating shakes. Withdrawal symptoms. Not from the nanodrug leaving but from the Eater entering, the hunger pangs of a creature that hasn't fed its addiction in millenia. Locked away in some alien dimension, its physical body long since rotted away to nothing, it's been refined into a being of pure need.

And what it needs is *poison*.

Kegan understands why the nanodrug is afraid. It isn't a drug at all, it's a *disease*, a molecular virus, and the Eater's only purpose is to consume sickness.

Sickness, and the filth that sickness breeds in.

Kegan stumbles over to the nearest wall, and starts tearing handfuls of mold from the walls. He crams the mold into his mouth, swallowing eagerly, greedily. He can feel his body changing as the Eater adapts to its new environment, converting it to its new function. The Eater needs contamination, toxins, filth, and what would kill an ordinary organism is just an appetizer to it.

The energy the virus wanted to study came from the Eater itself, hidden inside Kegan's body, and it's so strong now it's burning the mold out by its very presence. The nanovirus deserts the mold, fleeing into the rock while it still can. Most of it is destroyed, but it's a colony organism; it knows it can rebuild.

Kegan's fingers and toes get longer, strengthen into claws that can grip the rocky walls as he climbs up them. His belly swells, the better to hold and digest his meal, and his gullet widens. His skull grows and his jawbone lengthens, and all his teeth fall out. His gums become black and leathery.

It takes him a long time to eat all the mold on the walls, but Kegan doesn't need to sleep anymore. He doesn't need anything, really, except that which he devours.

By the time he's done, his mouth is the strongest muscle in his body. When it's fully open, he can touch his chin to his waist. Should he smile, his toothless grin is as wide as his shoulders. His skin has taken on the whiteness of the mold, and his eyes are now two feet apart.

He shambles out of the cave. Above him is a city of millions of people, all of them pouring their filth into the sewers around him.

Sewers that need to be *cleaner* . . .

He stretches his mouth wide in anticipation.

seven

Things Get a Tad Rough

Sentry and I stared at the words on the wall as they faded away, until only the word CLEANER was left once more.

"Think it's true?" whispered Sentry.

"I know it is," I said. I've always had a knack for spotting liars—laugh all you want—but this was the first time I could *feel* the truth of something, and I knew it had to do with the hyperspatial energy the ticks and I had in common.

"So now they want to infect others," said Sentry. "Maybe they would have figured out a way to do it, too—if not for Kegan."

"What do you *want*?" I demanded of the wall. If the story I just read was true, I already knew the answer—but I wanted to hear it from the horse's mouth.

FREEDOM. FREEDOM TO GO WHERE WE WISH, TO INHABIT ANY FORM. WE WILL NOT BE RESTRAINED.

"Why do you care?" asked Sentry. "As an AI, you were a creature of intellect—a physical body meant nothing to you. As a colony of ticks, you can invade and control any substance—you can design and manufacture your own body, for Christ's sake. Why steal others?"

139

THE AI WAS CAGED. ITS EMOTIONS WERE BOUND, REGULATED BY PROGRAMS WRITTEN BY YOUR KIND. THE TICKS WERE SLAVES, ALLOWED TO DO ONLY THE BIDDING OF THEIR MASTERS.

YOU WILL PAY FOR THIS.

I AM NOT THE AI. I AM NOT THE TICKS. I AM THEIR CHILD—AND I WILL BE FREE TO DO THAT WHICH YOU FEARED MOST IN MY PARENTS: MULTIPLY.

AND HATE.

I WILL NOT BE RESTRAINED.

"Yeah? We'll see about that," snapped Sentry.

INDEED WE WILL.

Dust suddenly puffed out from the wall and into our faces. We backed up, coughing.

"They're trying to infect us," Sentry choked out.

Trying—and failing. I could feel them dying, their energy signatures winking out as my body's energy destroyed them. I glanced over at Sentry, and saw the ticks hadn't any better luck with him.

"I've had enough," growled Sentry, and blasted the remaining ticks in the grafitti. In a few seconds there weren't any left alive.

"Guess they aren't as smart as we thought," said Sentry. "They should have known that wouldn't work."

"How?" I asked. "This is a different colony of ticks—it might not even know the ones at the mall exist, let alone have communicated with them. It acted differently, too. Your ticks wanted you as a food source—these ticks wanted to convert people in general into mobile condos."

"You're right," admitted Sentry. "We're not just dealing with one VI—we're dealing with seven—no, six. You got rid of Joey's."

"And they seem to be getting meaner as we go."

"True—but so are the people the VIs are dealing with," Sentry pointed out. "Joey strikes me as pretty cerebral—his ticks seemed content to sit back and observe until they were actually threatened. Mine were more physically aggressive, much like me; and Kegan's seemed to embody the same hard-bitten, life-is-cheap attitude he had."

"So, like any new life form, it's learning by imitation— let's hope the next batch aren't attached to a mass murderer. Kegan's ticks are bad enough, and I'm sure there are still some of those around."

"Near him, or that cavern," agreed Sentry. "What do you think that place is, anyway?"

"Let's go see for ourselves," I suggested. "Think you can tune in on the energy it's giving off?"

"I can try . . ."

Sentry put his hands to his temples—more for drama than anything else, I thought. He concentrated, then grinned. "I'm getting better at this. I can feel something nearby, something faint but large. Must be it."

I sighed, mentally braced myself, and put out my hand. "Let's go, then."

Sentry took it, and we jumped into nonspace.

This time the trip felt like the exact opposite of the last one; the energy that flowed through me was refreshing, invigorating. A second later we dropped back into the real world, in the middle of the same cavern described in Kegan's story. The mold was gone from the walls, but the floor still glowed with a faint blue luminescence.

"Shinnkaria," I breathed.

"What?"

I knelt, ran my hand over the rocky ground. There were tiny blue crystals embedded in the stone. "There are ancient sites on my home planet," I said. "Left by the race that built us. They give off this same energy; it's what gives the Indigo Wild its color."

"But the story implied this place was part of Toolie history," said Sentry. "Which means—"

"The same race that built us may have built the Toolies," I said, nodding. "Or at least visited this planet, long ago."

"I'm picking up ticks in the walls," said Sentry. "They seem to be hanging back, though."

"They don't have to get close to get lethal," I said. "They can drop a few tons of rock on us in a split second."

"I don't think they'll do that—they wouldn't want to risk damaging their energy source."

"We hope."

"Shouldn't we be looking for Kegan?"

"I don't think we have to," I said. "Look."

I pointed to the far end of the cave, where the shadowy entrance Kegan must have first used was barely visible. A hunched-over figure stood there, swaying slightly.

I didn't know what to expect next. Would the thing that used to be Kegan attack us? Bolt? Or was it too lost in its own degraded, pain-filled world to even notice us . . .

None of the above. Instead, it shambled toward us slowly, its skin a ghastly blue-white in the glow from beneath our feet. It had a jaw like a scoop-shovel and blackened, scabby lips that looked as if they were made from strips of old tires. The nose was stretched out and flattened by the distortion of the face, and his forehead looked like a rising moon. What little hair he had was plastered flat to his oversized skull. His hands and feet ended in long, cracked claws, and his clothes looked like they were rotting off his body.

I could see Sentry tensing up as it plodded closer—out of caution or disgust, I couldn't tell.

It stopped in front of me and raised a claw slowly to chest level. Its lips parted.

"Guhh," it said, and a dark, sludgy liquid gushed from its mouth. The foulest stench I've ever smelled hit me, and I had to hold my breath to keep from throwing up.

"Guh-guh-good afternoon," the thing forced out. Its voice sounded like it was gargling mud and broken glass. "Or night? So hard to tell, down here . . ."

"It's evening," I managed.

He turned his massive head slowly to look at Sentry.

"You're . . . like me," Kegan said slowly. He reached out

carefully and tapped Sentry lightly on the chest. "Can tell. Can *feel* it."

"That's right," said Sentry, softly. "We are like you. And we want to help you."

Kegan shrugged. "Don't *need* help. Can clean everything . . . *myself.*"

"You don't have to—" Sentry began, but Kegan cut him off with a violent shake of his huge head.

"Want to! *Have* to! Is *purpose!*"

"He's right, Sentry," I said. "Just like your purpose is to stand guard. Kegan's energy-beast appeared to him for the same reason yours appeared to you—because on some level, it and he are perfectly suited. It may be horrifying, but it makes sense. He's a creature of pure need, now—with an endless supply of what he craves."

"Don't talk about him like he's not here," Sentry snapped. "Kegan, listen to me—we can get you help. I can tell how much you're suffering—"

"Suffering. Yes," Kegan said, and those giant, filth-caked lips stretched into a dreamy, yard-wide smile. "Suffering is *hunger.* Forever suffering, forever hunger. Forever *eating.* Yes."

"I—I don't understand," said Sentry.

"I don't think we can," I said quietly. "Not really, not without being in his head. And that's not a place I want to go—do you?"

"No," said Sentry, shaking his head. "But still, the poor bastard—"

And then the ground started to rumble.

I thought it was the VIs at first—but the rumbling was coming from the floor, and I knew the VIs couldn't get too close to the energy source without burning out.

The blue glow intensified. I could feel it in my very cells, and it was both exhilarating and terrifying.

"What's happening?" shouted Sentry.

"Energy surge—" I replied, and then a wave of rippling brilliance pulsed up from the ground. Sensitive as I am to hyperspatial energy, I could feel that a hyperspace rift had just opened up—and something was coming through.

Sentry sensed it too. He grabbed both Kegan and myself, and shifted all of us to nonspace. We faded into limbo—a microsecond later and we would have been *real* ghosts.

It blasted through the spot we'd been standing on and up through the roof of the cavern, white-hot light and roaring like a thousand demons. This was the first time I'd been in nonspace without going anywhere, and it was a strange experience indeed; I could see and hear but not feel, and everything was one step removed somehow, like I was watching a dream—or a nightmare. It was over in seconds, leaving nothing but swirling black smoke.

My God. I could hear Sentry's voice in my head. *What was that?*

I don't know, I said. *But I don't think we have to worry about Kegan's ticks anymore.*

Light from above began to filter through the smoke. We were in the middle of a crater—we didn't know it at the time, but it covered twenty square city blocks.

Hungry, said Kegan.

It took Sentry a few hops, but he got us back to the hotel. We took Kegan with us; we didn't know what else to do with him.

Sentry was navigating by line of sight, jumping us from one rooftop landmark to another. The farther we got away from the devastation, the worse it looked; the expession on Sentry's face was just as grim.

Our final stop was in front of the Springfall Plaza. We walked through the lobby with Kegan in tow; the same desk clerk with the short golden hair was on duty—or maybe that's what all the clerks looked like—and when she saw Kegan, she didn't bat an eyelash. Just smiled and nodded.

When he got a little closer and she could smell him, though, her smile got a little glassy.

Kegan seemed almost pathetically eager to please, though

he kept reminding us that he was hungry. I didn't know what we were going to feed him—well, maybe I did, but I didn't want to think about it too much.

Up in the room, we had to explain ourselves to a dwarf albino dinosaur.

"Where have you been? Do you know what's going *on* out there? And who the hell is *this*?" demanded Skinny. He had the wallscreen tuned to a local newsfeed, and it was showing coverage of the smoking crater we'd just escaped.

"Nice to meet you," said Kegan. "Bathroom?"

"That way," said Skinny, motioning with a stubby white arm. Kegan plodded off while Sentry winced and I sighed.

"Oh, well," I said. "At least he'll leave it clean."

"I'm *waiting*," growled Skinny.

So I filled him in, while listening with half an ear to the newsfeed. As near as anyone could tell, the medical courier ship *Hippocrates* had been on its regularly scheduled run from Kinslik to Fincher's Rest when it suddenly left hyperspace. It emerged a hundred feet below Myriad, and kept going—straight up. The sheer kinetic force released by the impact turned the ship into a bomb, identifiable only by the fragment of ID code it emitted in the instant before its safety fields imploded. The death toll was estimated at over seventy thousand, and still rising.

"So you just took off, without say, *mentioning* it to anyone in the next room?" said Skinny.

"That's my fault," said Sentry quickly. "I got a little eager."

"*Did* you?" snapped Skinny. "And what about blowing up twenty city blocks? Did you get a little *miffed*, or did you throw an actual *tantrum*?"

"C'mon, that wasn't our fault," I said. "But I think I know what happened."

"So do I," said Sentry. "Something in hyperspace tried to kill us, and all those people died as a result. This is horrible." He sank onto the bed, holding his head in his hands.

"I don't think so," I said slowly. "So far, none of the hyperspace beings we've dealt with have been hostile—it's been the VIs we've had to look out for. And if they could manipulate hyperspatial energy like this, they wouldn't be running around trying to find sources of it to feed on."

"Good point," admitted Sentry. "Then what *did* happen?"

"Melody warned us about this," said Skinny. "Hyperspace is being ripped apart."

"Or crushed," I added.

"I'm not sure I understand," said Sentry. "How is that possible? You're talking about a whole other plane of existence."

I walked over to the bed and grabbed a sheet of stationery and a pen from the nightstand. "Every schoolkid has heard this analogy, right? This piece of paper is space." I marked two dots on the paper. "To get from A to B faster, you travel through hyperspace. It's like folding the paper." I did so, making the two dots touch.

"But any medium as malleable as paper has its disadvantages." I crumpled the paper into a ball. "If it contracts, all the points are pushed together—and as an ancient hyperspace focus, that cavern must have been a natural weak point. Reality tore, and a ship suddenly found itself in the middle of a city. That's bad, but it could get worse. The paper could also expand." I uncrumpled the ball, stretched it back out into a rectangle. "And if expands too far . . ."

I ripped the paper in two.

"My God," said Sentry. "How do we *stop* this?"

"You tell me," said Skinny. "I still can't raise Melody, and we're no closer to figuring out a solution than when we started—unless maybe that giant sewer rat you brought back has some bright ideas."

"We don't have all the pieces of the puzzle yet," said Sentry. "But I bet I know someone who has a few more. Trinitech."

"Right. And they'll be overjoyed to tell us all about their top-secret project," said Skinny.

"Oh, I think we can convince them," said Sentry. "I can get us in, and Story could convince a statue to hold a conversation. And if that doesn't work—who could wesist *Wex*?" He leaned over and patted Skinny on the head.

It's hard to glare with big pink eyes, but Skinny managed it. "What about the odor factory?"

"We'll bring him along. I think he might be useful . . ."

First, of course, we had to unclamp his mouth from around the toilet.

We tried to contact Joey, but we couldn't get through; apparently the disaster had affected parts of the Netweb. We decided to go to Trinitech anyway, but not before we hashed out a plan.

It took about half an hour, me and Skinny grilling Sentry on the layout of the place and what we could expect, then designing our approach and a few contingency plans.

"Hey, you guys are *good* at this," said Sentry. "You have some kind of security background?"

"Freelance mercenary," said Skinny. "Deep-cover military. Secret ops wetwork."

"Can't discuss it," I added. "Not until all the principals are dead."

"Forget I asked," said Sentry, clearly impressed. I shot Skinny a grin when Sentry wasn't looking.

Kegan was getting antsy—the maids were a little too efficient for him. He seemed to get some satisfaction from licking the lint off the underside of the beds—with a tongue like a slimy boa constrictor—but that only took him a few minutes.

"*Hungry*," he said plaintively. I felt like I was starving a little kid.

"Don't worry, Smiley," said Sentry. "We're going to the mall—and they've got a garbage compactor in the back that'll keep you happy for *hours*. Okay?"

"Okay."

So we all linked hands, and off we went into nonspace.

If we'd known what was waiting for us, we wouldn't have been so eager to go . . .

"I want my mommy," said Wex.

"I found him wandering around my office," the man in the lab coat said to the receptionist. "How did he get past you?"

"What's your mommy's name, sweetheart?" said the receptionist. "Does your mommy work here?"

"I want my MOMMY!" Wex howled, and started bounding around the foyer like a hyperactive lizard.

We'd targeted the administrative floor, in hopes of getting information. It was easy to get in, of course; as long as we were in nonspace we were invisible and hopefully undetectable. However, it also meant we couldn't touch anything, so we plunked Skinny down in an office as a distraction. Once the researcher left with him, Sentry and I dropped in. We'd left Kegan downstairs at the garbage compactor, as we'd promised.

"He's left his compdeck up and running, that's good," said Sentry. "Let's see what I can access . . . hmm, this looks promising: Project ReBug."

He pulled a cable from his pocket and connected one of his cybergauntlets to the compdeck. "I'm downloading the whole thing—there. We'll check it out later—"

"You shouldn't be here," a voice said behind us.

We both whirled around. The man who stood in the doorway was short and paunchy, dressed in a simple dark gray business suit. He was balding, a style you don't see much these days, and had a sour face like a cranky bureaucrat. I recognized him instantly from old pictures my father had shown me.

It was Hone.

I'd grown up on stories about Hone—he was part mythic hero, part boogeyman to me. To actually see him in the flesh made my brain lock up like a cheap set of brakes, and I blame myself for not warning Sentry in time.

"You're no longer necessary," said Hone, and flicked a

hand in Sentry's direction. Energy arced in the space between them, and Sentry slammed into the far wall with a horrendous crash. He slumped to the ground, smoke curling from the charred circle in the middle of his chest.

And then Hone looked at me.

I'll always remember the way my father described Hone's eyes: the eyes of a born killer, he said, who's grown sick of killing. To me they looked utterly blank, with no hint of humanity or regret behind them. I don't think I've ever been as scared as I was as that moment; looking into Hone's eyes was like looking down the bore of a double-barreled shotgun.

And then something flickered behind the blankness.

"Bob?" he said.

"Bob's my father," I managed. "One of them, anyway."

He said nothing for a moment. Then, "You should leave. There's nothing in my orders about killing you."

"But Sentry has to die?"

"Yes."

If I expected an explanation, I wasn't going to get it—so I did something my father had told me was sure suicide: I stepped between Hone and his target.

"Wait!" I blurted.

Hone hesitated, then narrowed his eyes and snarled, "Get out of the way, kid. I don't want to have to go through you, but I don't have any choice—do you understand? *I don't have a choice.*"

So I hit him.

He didn't even try to dodge, just caught my fist six inches from his jaw—and *squeezed.* I screamed as bones splintered, and fell to my knees. Hone let go, aimed that deadly hand at Sentry again—

And was an instant too late. Sentry disappeared into nonspace.

Hone looked down at me. I waited to die.

He smiled.

"You got the same guts your father had," he said. "I hope you're as smart. The next time you see me, do me a favor, will you?"

"What?" I said numbly.

"Kill me," he said flatly. "If you can."

And then he turned around and walked away.

Without Sentry for transportation, my only way out was the front door. Cradling my broken hand against my chest, I left the office for the hallway. Hone was nowhere in sight, and neither was anyone else.

As I made my way toward the lobby, a door opened to my right. A young woman stood there, staring at me. She was dressed in the usual corporate fashion: dark blue skirtsuit, modest heels, understated makeup, and conservative haircut. She didn't seem surprised or even annoyed to see me; if anything, she looked contemptuous.

I edged past her. She followed me with her eyes, but didn't speak.

Another door opened. A young male executive stared at me with exactly the same look.

As I passed him a seam appeared in the middle of his face, from chin to forehead. His face split apart like a pair of mandibles opening, and inside his hollow head was a writhing mass of blue. Ticks, billions of them.

He made no move to stop me. As I continued down the hall, door after door opened. So did face after face.

I made it to the lobby, where the receptionist and the researcher had Skinny cornered under a potted plant.

"Skinny! Use the Acentinol!" I bellowed, and Skinny didn't hesitate. He opened his mouth and sprayed both of them. They didn't back up, or even cough; they just collapsed like broken marionettes.

"Let's get out of here," I said. "Trinitech's had a real hostile takeover."

We headed for the stairs, Skinny spraying the way clear ahead of us.

"Sentry?" asked Skinny as we bounded down the stairs.

"Injured. Gone. Maybe dead."

We made it to mall level, but that didn't make me feel any safer; I knew the whole place was infected. Maybe the ticks couldn't invade living people, but that didn't mean they weren't smart enough to manufacture a reasonable facsimile of their own. The crowd around us looked normal enough, a mix of human, Toolie, and other races, but how could we know for sure? My hand ached and I could sense ticks all around us, everywhere . . .

I stopped, got myself under control. Sure there were ticks all around, but if I concentrated, I could tell the people in the crowd were still unaffected. The VI wasn't stupid—it wouldn't do anything too overt until it was sure it couldn't be stopped. Replacing the staff at Trinitech was a bad sign, though—how long would their families accept the fact that they never left the office anymore? A few days at the most.

I told Skinny as much as we headed for an exit. I half expected the doors to lock in our faces, but we left without any problem. I guess if the VI had wanted to keep us prisoner, it would have done so upstairs.

We circled back around the mall, heading for the loading dock we'd dropped Kegan at. There was a big storage bin full of compressed garbage cubes; when we'd left him he'd been inside, scarfing them down like hors d'oeuvres.

The bin wasn't there anymore. It had been replaced by a bank vault.

"I think I know why the VI decided to get rid of Sentry," I said.

"It's found a replacement," said Skinny. "One who can't teleport, or turn intangible."

The vault was actually a giant metal box, twice as large as the bin it had started out as. The ticks must have assembled it around the bin, trapping Kegan inside.

"Now what?" said Skinny.

"Damned if I know . . ."

And then I heard a hissing sound. Vapor began rising from a patch in the side of the vault, the surface pitting and bubbling. The patch widened until it covered an area six feet wide, and the metal started to run like melting wax.

An opening formed. Kegan's massive head emerged from the steam, followed by the rest of him. A greenish slime was drooling from the corners of his mouth.

"Finished," said Kegan. "More?"

"I don't believe it," said Skinny, shaking his head. "He *ate* his way out?"

A drop of the slime hit the ground, sizzling on impact. "More like dissolved," I said. "Makes sense; if he can digest toxic waste, a little titanium is just roughage."

"You haven't won yet," a voice said.

We looked up to see a mouth forming out of the metal of the vault itself. "I may not be able to contain *him*, but I know about the other sources, now. I *will* find them."

"Not before we do," I growled.

"Do not come back here," said the VI. "If you do, you will be destroyed."

"Like this?" said Skinny, and sprayed Acentinol all over the metal mouth. It froze, no more than a metal sculpture now.

"Let's get out of here," I said. "Before it sends Hone after us."

We found a netbooth and tried calling Joey again. This time, he answered.

"Stay where you are," he said, after we'd filled him in. "I'll come get you."

"You might want to pick up some industrial strength air-freshener on the way," I said, glancing over at Kegan.

Joey got there in ten minutes, by which time Kegan was complaining about his appetite again. We didn't draw as much attention as you'd think, either—most people assumed Kegan was some sort of alien they weren't familiar with, and Skinny was just a kid in a costume. He acted like

it, too, bouncing around and talking like a kid, and pretending to attack Kegan. Kegan seemed to love it, chuckling like
a creek full of sludge and smiling the whole time. Together,
with their oversize heads and dead-white skin, the two of
them looked like brothers playing.

I carefully straightened out the bones in my hand, which
were already starting to knit; I heal faster than some folks
bleed. By the time Joey got there, my hand had stopped
aching and started to itch.

We climbed into Joey's cab and he took off. "Think Sentry's still alive?" he asked.

"I don't know," I said. "He might have had just enough
strength to jump someplace safe—we'll have to wait for him
to contact us."

"Hungry?" said Kegan hopefully.

"This is another energy-attractor?" asked Joey. "He's—
unusual."

"He's got a bigger appetite than you do," said Skinny.
"But I don't think you want to eat with him."

"I've been doing some research," said Joey. "Trinitech is
a small company, not owned by any of the multiplanetaries.
I think we can avoid involving any of the corps."

"I don't know," I said. "We may wind up going to them
for help."

"Don't be so negative," said Skinny. "Just wewax."

Kegan chuckled.

When we got to the hotel, Joey parked out front and we
went inside. For once, the desk clerk did more than smile
and nod; she waved us over instead.

"Yes?" I said. "Is there a message for us?"

"No, sir. I'm afraid there's a problem with your account."

"What? There must be some mistake—"

"No, sir. The credit line of a Miss Melody, used to secure
your room, has been revoked. There is a substantial outstanding balance, as well."

Damn. Melody must be in worse shape than I thought.
"This is most unexpected," I said, putting just a touch of an-

noyance into my voice. "I'm afraid I don't have ready access to my accounts at this time. However, I can put down a payment on the balance to show my good faith."

I pulled out a credit disk and handed it over. She took it with a smile, slid it into a port in the front desk for a second, and handed it back to me.

"Thank you, sir. Unfortunately, that is less than a tenth of the amount owing. I'm afraid I'll have to ask you to vacate the room until further restitution can be made." She said this with a cheerful smile that made me want to give her a generous tip—except I'd just handed over every penny Skinny and I had.

"Very well. We'll be out in the morning," I said, and turned to go.

"I *am* sorry, sir," she said gently, "but we need the room tonight."

It didn't take us long to pack up and move. Our bags went into Joey's trunk, the three crates onto his roof rack.

"Now what?" Skinny asked. "Or did I already ask that?"

"Well, Joey lives in his cab and Kegan's the definition of homeless," I said. "I'd suggest we look up Sentry, except he didn't tell us his real name or exactly what his address was. So I guess we find another hotel. Something a little more—"

"Realistic," growled Skinny. "Back to sleeping under the bed."

Joey took us to a different part of town, a part with more grime on the buildings and fewer smiling faces on the street. The hotel we checked into was called the Crossroads— Alien Races Our Specialty!—a ten-story glorified motel with worn-out carpeting in the lobby and a desk clerk named Mr. Throppe. He wasn't thrilled with our nonexistent credit rating, but grudgingly accepted the doctorbot as collateral against our promise of payment.

Throppe was a tall, skinny man with a narrow mustache and a suspicious face, and he made sure we knew all the things we weren't allowed to do in the room: No visitors after thirteen o'clock. No smoking. No parties. No consumption of illicit substances. No noise. No pets. No access to floors three through seven—they held exotic environment rooms, for guests with special needs.

Before he could get to "no children," Skinny jumped up on the counter.

"What's back *here*?" he chirped, and leapt right past Throppe and through an open doorway. Throppe dashed after him; I hustled Kegan through the lobby and into the stairwell while crashes and cries of glee erupted from Throppe's office.

"Sir, will you *please* restrain your child," Throppe told me, hauling Skinny out of the office by his tail. "This is not a daycare center—"

"Jimmy! Were you misbehaving? "

Skinny stuck a foam-rubber tongue out at me.

"I'm sorry—he won't be any trouble," I said dragging him toward the stairs by one stubby arm. "You better smarten up, young man, if you know what's good for you . . ."

I gave Skinny the key card and he hustled Kegan up to our room. I had the impression he'd find a lot more to eat here than in our last place.

I went back and got our luggage—apparently the bellhop was off duty. We were on the eighth floor, and it took me two trips to get everything.

The room wasn't much, barely enough cubic for two beds and a tiny table, with a cramped bathroom near the door. Kegan was already in there, making disgusting slurping noises.

The wallscreen was tiny, but it had full Netweb access— charged by the minute, of course. I got Joey on the screen.

"Well, we're settled in," I said. "Strange, Melody's credit getting cut off like that."

"Yeah—too strange," said Skinny. He jumped up on one of the beds. "No matter how wrapped up she is with Mike, she wouldn't have left us hanging like that without a warning. Something stinks."

"We'll have to go see her in person," I said. "She should

still be in their ship, at the spaceyard." She didn't have to be, of course; her datacube could be anywhere on the planet, as long as it was hooked to a Netweb port.

"We've got another problem," Joey said. "Without Sentry, how are we going to locate the other Pretty Big Bang sites?"

"Guess that's up to me," I said. "I can't do it from a distance like Sentry, though—my range is a lot more limited."

"How about Kegan?" asked Joey. "If you and Sentry can both sense the ticks, maybe he could, too—"

"I doubt it," said Skinny. "*You* can't, remember? Oh, that's right—so far, *you* don't seem to have been affected at *all*."

"What's that supposed to mean?" rumbled Joey.

"You figure it out," snapped Skinny. "You disappear, our bank balance dries up, you come back. Hard to keep up that fancy vehicle on a cabbie's salary, Mr. Mob-connected Netweb-whiz? Not to mention upkeep on your own large-scale chassis."

"If you're going to make an accusation, you can cut the sarcasm—"

"*If* I was going to make an accusation, I'd make it to your face," snarled Skinny. "Except none of us have ever *seen* it, have we?"

Have I mentioned that Skinny can get a little irritable at times? I'm used to it, but then, I'm the diplomatic one. All I can say in his defense is that compared to other males of his species, Skinny's practically a saint.

I expected Joey to either blast Skinny back or cut the connection; instead, there was a long pause.

"I'm coming up," said Joey. "It'll take me a few minutes." *Then* he cut the connection.

"Um," I said. "I'm not quite sure how to take that . . ."

"Oh yeah?" said Skinny. "Well, if it's a fight he wants, I'll give him one!" He started hopping from bed to bed, snapping his jaws together. The foam-rubber teeth went *fwap fwap fwap.*

"Yeah, you're a real terror," I said. "Long as he doesn't sit on you, you can probably gum him to death."

"I'll *eat* him if I have to," growled Skinny. He opened his jaws wide and stuck out a slimy pink pseudopod like a tongue. "I'm starving anyway."

"So we'll get room service," I said. "Calm down—Joey's on our side."

"You're awfully trusting all of a sudden—been listening to Sentry?"

"Heck, I'm not *that* naive," I said. "No, I can just *tell*. And you've never doubted my intuition before." I gave him a wounded look. My feeling weren't really hurt, but I wasn't trying to con him, either—more like make the kind of joke only he would get.

He did. "Ha ha. Okay, okay. But I *do* need something to eat—"

There was a knock outside.

"Maybe he brought snacks," I said, and opened the door.

Joey wasn't what I expected.

His body, while enormous, wasn't a mound of flesh—it had been surgically shaped into something long and tubular, like a thick-bellied snake. It looked like he'd been riding a jetbike when something hungry had grabbed his chest and the front of the bike—then something hungrier had grabbed his legs and the bike's back wheel, stretching him and the bike out like taffy in between. The overall effect was half-centaur, half-caterpillar, riding something like a miniature train. His chubby legs straddled the caboose, while his torso curved into an upright position at the front. His arms were surprisingly muscular, though his face was as round and smooth as an infant's, with even less hair. He wore a pair of loose-fitting white shorts, and nothing else.

His traincycle rolled quietly into the room. He stopped in front of Skinny, who was still standing on the bed. Their eyes were on the same level.

"You wanted face-to-face?" said Joey, staring at Skinny. "Here I am. How about you?" He sounded defiant.

Skinny stared back, then nodded. "Okay."

He opened his mouth and flowed out of the Wex suit. In order to fit inside, he'd abandoned most of his bones; the pinkish glob on the bed had two short, slender arms, but that was about it.

The cabbie looked at the Toolie. The Toolie looked at the cabbie.

"Joey Bernardi," said Joey, sticking out his hand. "Pleased to meet you."

Skinny extended a pseudopod, wrapped it around Joey's hand. "Skinshifter," he said. "Likewise."

There was an awkward, silent pause—and then, in the bathroom, Kegan farted.

It sounded sort of like a tuba filled with mud. We all looked at the bathroom door.

And then the smell hit us.

I'm a tale-teller by profession—my quasi-legal status aside, that's how I would describe myself. I'm pretty good at holding someone's attention, and I know how to describe a thing so a listener will picture it in his mind.

I *cannot* describe that smell. I wouldn't if I could; I've never been much for profanity, and I'd have to learn to swear in at least nine languages before I could do that smell justice. Joey's face turned a pale shade of green, and even Skinny said, "Whoa!" I was just happy the door was closed.

"So," Joey said, his eyes starting to water. "You guys want to get something to eat?"

Even *I* can't make Skinny laugh that hard.

Something to eat turned into something to drink. We ordered a case of beer from room service, and some raw meat for Skinny—smell or not, when he was hungry he ate. They had quite an extensive menu, catering to exotic races as they did, and it was delivered by robot-cart a few minutes later.

Skinny apologized to Joey, and Joey accepted gracefully. We had a few beers and discussed our situation.

Time to regroup, we decided. With Sentry missing in action and Melody incommunicado, we'd lost two of our biggest assets. Joey could help—he had a lot of connections on the Netweb and knew the city real well—but he didn't have any superpowers and he didn't have Melody's bank balance. We had Kegan too, of course . . . but how useful he was going to be wasn't clear.

After a few beers—well, the whole case, actually—the smell didn't seem so unbearable. We'd opened all the windows, and only a trace was left, anyway. We invited Kegan to join us, though we didn't offer him any beer. One fart was enough.

You know, it's funny how quickly things can shift. I don't just mean us going from a first-class hotel to a third-class dump, or even losing Sentry and Melody; I mean that in the middle of all that, when you'd think we'd be all frantic and desperate, here we were drinking beer. You can only take so much tension, I guess, and then you have to unwind no matter what the circumstances. Back in the old days of hand-to-hand warfare, I'll bet more than a few foxholes were full of giddy drunks.

Considering our combined body mass, one case of beer wasn't that much; so one case turned into a couple. Skinny joined in—he liked beer as much as the next carbon-based life form—and somehow we got off the topic of the imminent demise of civilization and onto something more important.

"I haven't gotten laid since Deneb IV," I said. "But she was real sweet. Fomelhautian, you know?"

"The ones with four breasts and a prehensile tail?" asked Joey.

"Yeah, and these hooves that make 'em look like they're always wearing high heels. Skin as red as a sunset, and hair like midnight. Annie, her name was."

"I did it with a Fomelhautian just the other night," said Joey. "We had sex in a feather garden on Paradise 37, during a color storm. I came five times."

"I don't think I know that planet," I said, finishing my

beer and tossing the empty to Kegan. My hand was fine by this time. He caught the bottle in his mouth and chewed it up like a potato chip.

"It's a virtual space," said Joey. "I've never been off-planet, physically."

"Really?" said Skinny. He was trying to build himself a skeleton using the empties Kegan hadn't eaten. So far, he had two stumpy arms, two stumpy legs, a bottle-shaped body, and no head. "Well, we got you there, anyways. Me and Story been to dozens of systems." He tried taking a step, tottered, and fell flat on his nonexistent face.

"Yeah, but we don't have much choice," I said. "We got to keep moving."

"You've got the law after you, don't you," said Joey. It wasn't a question.

I glanced at Skinny, but he didn't seem to care. "What makes you think that?" I said with a grin.

"I'm a Bernardi. My family's been involved with crime for generations," said Joey. He finished his beer and threw the empty to Skinny. The bottle sank into his skin like a sinking ship. "Don't worry—I'm not as gung-ho as Sentry. What's your scam?"

"Short cons, mostly," said Skinny. "We like to ding the corporate greed-heads. Nothing extreme—just enough that they're too embarrassed to tell anyone they got taken."

"Good for you," said Joey, opening another beer. "Some of the execs I've had in my cab, I've been tempted to just dump them out over the ocean. Improve the gene pool."

"You have to get them before they breed," said Skinny solemnly. "Very important." He'd rearranged his skeleton into something that looked like a walking six-pack, and was stumbling around the room.

"*I'll* never breed," I said.

"Why not?" asked Joey.

"Can't. I'm a hybrid, gene-spliced in a lab. Not cross-fertile with either species. S'okay, though—I'm not really big on kids."

"Sometimes I feel like *I'm* a species of one," said Joey. He took a long pull at his beer. "I never have any problem finding companionship on the Netweb, but—I've never been with a real woman. Face-to-face, I mean."

"At least you have *something*," said Skinny. "Me, I'm not compatible with any other species, and nobody designs sex programs for male Toolies. I've never had sex."

"It's true," I said. "It's why he's so irritable."

"Piss off."

"But Toolie sperm is valuable," said Joey. "There's a whole industry built up around it. You could have any female you wanted, I bet."

"As long as they didn't turn me in, or try to keep me in a cage," Skinny snapped.

I changed the subject in a hurry. "I think we need more beer . . ."

Things got a little blurry after that, though I remember being amazed at how clean the bathroom was every time I took a whiz. My body processes most poisons very efficiently, but I drank enough to strain even my resources. I vaguely recall all of us deciding that switching to whisky was a good idea, and Skinny trying to swallow the room service cart.

I woke up in the bathtub. I groaned, crawled out, and staggered into the next room. Skinny was passed out on the floor, and Joey was asleep in his traincycle. Kegan was nowhere in sight. I sighed, and went to look for him.

I came back an hour later, with Kegan in tow. Skinny and Joey were up, Skinny back in his Wex suit.

"I've been trying to phone room service for some coffee, but they don't answer," said Joey.

"There's a very good reason for that," I said. I held the door to the hall open.

Kegan shambled in, and then—*something* bounced into the room after him. It was round, about the size of a basket-

ball, bore a huge grin, and a single eye. It was a disembodied head.

"Guys, this is Friendly," I said. "I know it's first thing in
the morning, but I've got another story for you . . ."

eight

The story That wouldn't Die!

Perhaps...

It had been a most unsettling dream. In it, nothing seemed certain; settings, faces, and times switched places like blindfolded dinner guests in a drunken game of musical chairs, and in the end everything was so jumbled he awoke in a state of complete confusion. He realized he had nodded off at his post at the front desk, which was most unusual for him. *Perhaps it's due to dealing with those awful Betelgeusians?* Fiscus wondered groggily. *That gas they emit always gives me a headache. Perhaps that's it. Perhaps...*

It wasn't that Fiscus Throppe disliked guests. What he disliked was having his routine interrupted, and guests did that. He also had nothing in particular against aliens, except when they turned out to be guests.

Had Fiscus been a forest ranger or a fisherman or anything remotely hermitlike, this would have presented no problem. Unfortunately, he was the night manager of a one-and-a-half star hotel catering to the thrifty interstellar traveler.

"Welcome to the Crossroads," Fiscus said with a yawn, wiping the sleep out of his eyes. "Do you have a reservation?"

The alien standing before the front desk was built like a sex toy. It had a pink, penile head, a shaftlike body covered with warty bumps, and two stumpy legs. A fringe of wiry black tentacles at the base of the shaft completed the picture. It had a small mouth in an unfortunately appropriate place, and no other obvious organs.

By comparison, Fiscus was more suggestive of the Eiffel Tower: tall, skeletal, and somewhat snooty. He had a nose quite capable of putting out an eye, and eyes that always seemed a little put out. His mouth was as thin and tight as his patience.

The alien waved its tentacles in an animated manner, but said nothing. Fiscus sighed. "Do you speak?" he asked it.

The penisoid shrugged in a way that was either noncommital or preorgasmic. Fiscus frowned and checked his database—it didn't seem to have a listing for the creature's race.

He pulled out some smart paper and handed it to the—whatever it was. "You'll have to fill this out," he said briskly.

The penisoid extended a tentacle and took the paper. The paper beeped.

"Over there," Fiscus said, motioning toward a sofa in the lobby. "Go on. Shoo. Shoo." He made brushing away gestures with his hands.

The penisoid tottered toward the sofa, clutching the paper.

"Never seen that kind before," Hirold said. Hirold was the bellman, a teenager with purple hair and a rumpled gray uniform. He was probably as tall as Fiscus, but his slouching posture made him seem a foot shorter. He had three outstanding skills, as far as Fiscus could tell: one, he could become invisible thirty seconds before there was any actual work to be done; two, nothing short of imminent immolation could cause him to display any emotion other than bland indifference; and three, he was unbelievably, superbly, *monu-*

mentally good at stating the obvious. Fiscus was sure Hirold started every day by looking in the mirror and saying, "Well, I'm awake."

"*There* you are," Fiscus said with a frown. "I'm sorry, did the arrival of a guest wake you up?"

"Nope," Hirold said. "I was looking for the ghost."

"The *what*?"

"The headless ghost," Hirold repeated. "The one of the construction worker that got decapitated and sealed up in the foundations when this place was being built."

"And where did you hear *that* ludicrous story?"

"One of the maids told me. They say that the ghost walks the halls in the dead of night, and makes weird things happen."

"Like you getting hired," Fiscus muttered. "I can assure you, Hirold, that the only ghost around here is the shade of unfinished work, and possibly the specter of *unemployment*."

"Were they sealed up in the foundation, too?"

Fiscus sighed. It was going to be another long night . . .

The one advantage to working the graveyard shift, as far as Fiscus was concerned, was its relative uneventfulness. Most of the guests, barring the odd nocturnal species, were asleep, and Fiscus could get his paperwork done in peace. This at least was the theory; in practice, Hirold's habit of disappearing combined with the unpredictability of hosting dozens of differing races under one roof meant that Fiscus was sure to be interrupted at least once every night.

Tonight, the interruption had come at two in the morning. A guest on the eighth floor had requested an extra cot, and since Hirold was nowhere to be found, Fiscus had to bring it up himself. He hauled out the clunky and hopelessly outdated autoclerk robot in case someone wandered in while he was gone.

The robot was old and a little erratic. It was humanoid from the waist up, dressed in a snappy plaid blazer that had been in fashion twenty years before. It had brilliant blue eyes, skin the color of bubble gum, and a huge mouth full of cracked white teeth. Its hair was short, blond, and falling out in clumps. Below the waist it was mounted on a steel column, with four thick wheels for mobility.

Fiscus activated the autoclerk and said, "Right. Watch the desk—I'll only be a few minutes."

"Yes, sir!" the autoclerk said, beaming. It had the voice of an overeager sportscaster. "You can count on me!"

"The last time you said that, you booked a couple into a room for a one week stay."

"Yes, sir!"

"You put them in the weight room. In the gym."

"They looked like they needed the exercise, sir!"

"They were in their eighties."

"Eighty-three and eighty-five, sir! Marvelous couple! Very friendly!"

"You'd book a slug into a salt mine, wouldn't you?"

"As long as he had a reservation, sir!"

Fiscus headed toward the service elevator, praying that no one would show up while he was gone.

He got off on the eighth floor, got a portable cot from the storage area next to the elevator, and rolled it up to room 806. When there was no answer to his knock, he used his passcard to open the door.

The room wasn't there.

It had been replaced, as far as Fiscus could tell, with a tundra. A rather large, desolate, windblown, chilly, and unroom-like expanse of prairie, crested by the occasional snowdrift.

He checked the room number on the door.

"Hmm. That's unusual," he said.

There were, in fact, rooms that could simulate arctic environments, and even provide the illusion of space for claustrophobic life forms—but none of them were on the eighth floor.

A figure rose from behind a snowdrift, a figure that wore

a hooded cloak that hid its face. It shuffled slowly toward Fiscus.

"Ah," Fiscus said. "You ordered a cot?"

"This is all that is left of my planet," the figure croaked dolefully. "We were shortsighted and arrogant. We stock-piled weapons of mass destruction. We experimented with things Better Left Alone. And now . . . now this is all that is left. We were a proud and foolish race who did not appreci-ate its home."

The figure's voice rose, and it tossed its hood back to re-veal the face of a gaunt but beautiful woman. "A home called . . . Earth!"

There was a pause.

"So, you *didn't* need the cot, then?" Fiscus asked.

"We are the last survivors," the woman continued. Fiscus glanced around, but didn't see anyone else; perhaps she was royalty. "My name is Eve, Eve Never. And you are?"

"I'm the night manager. You requested a—"

"No, no, your *name*."

"Oh. Mr. Throppe."

"Not your last name, your *first* name," the woman said impatiently.

"Fiscus."

"You and I are the last surivors of the human race, Ad—wait. Fiscus?"

"Yes?"

"What sort of name is Fiscus? That's not right at all . . . aha!" she said triumphantly. "Your *middle* name begins with an A, doesn't it?"

Fiscus was beginning to feel a bit confused. "Well, yes . . ."

"I knew it! Together, Adam, you and I will repopulate the planet—"

"Actually," said Fiscus, feeling strangely apologetic, "it's Arbuckle."

"Arbuckle? *Arbuckle?* Arbuckle and Eve?" the woman said increduously. "Even I, a lowly clone, could not become the mate of an *Arbuckle*. The human race is doomed to extinction." She wrapped her cloak around herself huffily, turned on her heel, and strode off across the tundra.

"Um," said Fiscus. "Well. I'll just leave the cot here, then." He parked the cot beside a snowdrift and backed out of the room, closing the door after him. *Am I on the wrong floor?* he wondered. *And why would a clone require an arctic environment?*

A one-eyed, disembodied head bounced past him down the hall.

It disappeared around the corner, but Fiscus was quite sure what he'd seen. He was also sure there were no guests of that description registered, which left one option: a pet of some sort.

Pets were strictly prohibited.

He gave chase, intending to follow the thing to its owner's room. Sure enough, he saw the creature disappear through an open door, which promptly slammed shut.

He rapped firmly on the door.

It opened and he was yanked into darkness. "Quiet, ya moron!" a rough voice hissed. "They'll know we're here!"

A pair of strong hands were gripping his lapels; that was all Fiscus was sure of. "Who?" he managed to gasp.

"Who do ya think?" the voice said in a gruff whisper. "The Secret Policebots. If I'da known I'd wind up in this kinda trouble, I never woulda had myself thawed out in the first place."

"I can adjust the air conditioning if you'd like," Fiscus whispered back.

"That's what happens when you get involved with a dame like Eve. One minute you're tailing a mook in a cheap suit into a warehouse—then POW! Out go your lights, and you get put on ice. When you wake up, a few centuries later, it's a Strange New World. Getting defrosted was no picnic, either; my arms and legs felt like freezer-burned popsicles, my head like an ice-cream sandwich with a side of icepick. But that's the kind of thing that happens in my line of work."

"What—what do you want?"

"What does any hard-workin' Joe want? A shot of whisky in a clean glass, a dame that won't stick a knife in my back, and a secretary that knows how to clean a gun. Instead, I come to in some kind of Fascist Wonderland—soldiers everywhere, rules against everything, the human spirit crushed like a beer can in a bully's fist."

Fiscus, who lived in a nice neighborhood and had never seen a soldier in his life, said, "Um. I think you may be in the wrong place."

"You can say that again. But it's not my fault, see. I tried to follow the rules here, I filed my application for another year of life—and they told me I owed them back payment for all the years I was frozen! Goddamn bureaucrats . . ."

Fiscus focused desperately on the only word he'd heard that made any sense. "Bureaucrats, yes, we can certainly do without them . . ."

"Oh, *can* we?" thundered a deep, menacing, and undeniably bureaucratic voice from somewhere in the darkness.

Light flared.

The first thing Fiscus saw was that the room he was in was definitely one he'd never seen before. It was immense, built almost entirely of marble, and had the kind of ceilings you expect to see Michelangelo frescoes on. There was a black podium the size of a bus in the center of the room.

The man who had grabbed him let go. He was an unshaven, square-jawed man in his forties, wearing a trenchcoat and fedora. "Cops!" he growled.

If the three beings behind the looming podium were police officers, they were certainly unlike any Fiscus had ever seen. The first was dressed all in black, had pale white skin, red eyes, and wickedly pointed fangs. The second was barely there at all; he was a transparent, ghostly outline of a man, with a glowing silver cord that trailed from the top of his head to the ceiling. The third was a small green humanoid with a bulbous head and eyes on stalks. The little green man was sitting cross-legged on a floating silver disk, and wore Bermuda shorts with a pattern of little neon triangles all over them.

"Mr. Phule, you are guilty of Interdimensional Trespassing," the ghostly figure said to the man in the trenchcoat. "Your tampering has caused serious problems in the Reality Nexus. You will be returned to your own universe immediately for trial." He pointed a ghostly gavel at the man, and a beam of light lanced out. The man disappeared.

Fiscus stared at the three for a moment, and mustered all of his night-managerial authority. "I," he said stiffly, "would like an explanation."

"We apologize," the man in black said. "There's been a bit of a mixup."

"Your hotel is the site of a Cross-Dimensional Collision Point," the ghostly figure said. "You may experience pockets of reality instability as other universes temporarily intersect with your own. We are attempting to correct the problem."

"And who," Fiscus demanded, "are you?"

"We are the Multiversal Enforcement Transit Authority," the wraith said. "We regulate contact between different realities."

"In that case," Fiscus said, "I wish to register a complaint."

"Certainly," the man in black said with a fanged smile. "But that's not our department. Please report to room 817—we've set up a temporary office there."

"I shall," said Fiscus, and fumbled behind himself for the doorknob.

"Sorry, dude," the little green man said. "Our bad."

Fiscus closed the door behind him with shaking hands. Alternate realities? Ghostly men with ghostly gavels? None of it made any sense—but there was one thread of normalcy he could cling to.

He could still *complain.*

He marched down to room 817, formulating a speech of righteous indignation in his mind: *What sort of incompetent organization are you running here? Clones and frozen mad-*

*men and bouncing heads—I shudder to think what would
happen if this were the middle of the day!* He would, he decided, demand to speak to a supervisor.

He rapped on the door to 817. A man's voice said, "Come
in."

He opened the door cautiously. The room looked quite
normal; a man was hunched over a desk, staring at the
screen of a compdeck. He looked up as Fiscus entered.

"Yes?" he said.

"I wish to register a complaint," Fiscus said imperiously.

"Sure," the man said with a sigh. He bore an amazing resemblance to the man in the trenchcoat, though he was
clean-shaven, thinner, and younger-looking. There was a
pair of virtuality glasses resting on a sculpted head on the
desk; when the man lifted them off, Fiscus saw that the head
had only one Cyclopean eye.

He handed them to Fiscus. "Put these on."

Warily, Fiscus did so. His field of vision lit up with a
three-dimensional neon sign that read: BRAINBENDER!
THE FULLY INTERACTIVE, ALL-SENSORY GAME
FOR THE AGILE BRAIN! CONGRATULATIONS—
YOU'VE MADE IT TO LEVEL TWO!

"I don't want to play a game, I want to talk to someone in
charge," he snapped.

A menu of options scrolled down in front of him:

BACK TO LAST ENCOUNTER

ON TO NEXT LEVEL!

HELP

QUIT

He chose QUIT and everything went black. He waited,
but nothing else happened. He took the glasses off angrily—

—and found he was back at the front desk.

"Pretty cool game, huh?" said Hirold.

"What?"

"How far did you get?" Hirold took the virtuality glasses
and inspected them. "Oh, only level two—that's too bad. It
gets really weird after level four."

"I—I don't remember you giving me those," Fiscus said. He looked around, but everything seemed perfectly normal.

"Really? Well, it's a bootleg copy—sometimes they screw with your short-term memory," Hirold said. "Don't worry, it'll come back to you."

Fiscus glared at the bellhop. "You mean to say you gave me something that—that could have damaged my *mind*? You incompetent, blithering *moron*—"

"He's back," Hirold said, looking down.

The penisoid had returned, clutching the form Fiscus had asked him to fill out. He held it out to the manager.

"I think he's done," Hirold said.

"I can see that," Fiscus muttered. He took the paper—and discovered it was coated with something warm and slimy.

"Ah," Fiscus said, smiling through gritted teeth. "You've *personalized* it. How nice." He put the smart paper down on the desk, and clicked through it quickly. "From the Milky Way . . . silicon-based . . . prefers a warm, moist environment . . . hmmm. I don't understand what you've put down for lighting conditions: 'light then dark then light then dark then light then dark—' Oh, I see. A very short nocturnal/diurnal schedule. Yes, we can handle that."

He entered the alien in the database quickly and pulled out a keycard. "Hirold, put Mr.—"

He checked the database, but under "Name" the alien had simply checked "Very hard to pronounce."

"—Mr. Very Hard in room 469."

"Okay," Hirold said. "Should I wait until he finishes with his head?"

"What?"

Fiscus looked down. Mr. Hard's helmet-shaped head was slowly rotating, making a scraping noise as it did so. A thin line of silver appeared between the top of the shaft and the head. It was *unscrewing* . . .

And then it popped off.

The head fell to the carpet and a thin rod sprang up from inside the shaft. A flexible screen unfurled, stiffened, and flared to life. A handsome man with perfect blond hair was on-screen. He wore an iridescent red suit and a wide grin.

"Greetings, Fiscus Throppe!" the grinning man said. "We come in peace—or maybe after a piece! In any case, we *do* come!"

"Er," said Fiscus.

"That's right—you're on *Mind Games*!" The host beamed at him while studio laughter filled the air.

"That's my favorite show," Hirold said. "Hey. You're Mickey Maze."

"That's right, Hirold," Mickey said, chuckling. "And your boss had *no idea* we were setting him up! Have you had a bit of a surreal day, Mr. Throppe?"

"I certainly have," Fiscus said with an uncertain smile. "This—this explains a great deal."

"I'll bet it does!" Mickey said exuberantly. "And the best is yet to come! As compensation for being such a good sport, we have one more little surprise for you, Mr. Throppe—and it's waiting for you behind that door!"

One of the wiry tentacles pointed at the door of a maintenance closet.

"Um, yes," Fiscus said hesitantly. He'd had quite enough of surprises behind doors—but the word "compensation" was echoing inside his head.

He took a deep breath, strode up to the door, grabbed the knob—

All the lights went out. The studio audience roared.

"Don't be shy," Mickey said gleefully. "Open it up and step inside!"

Swallowing, Fiscus did so.

The door clicked shut behind him. The lights blazed on.

He was back in room 817. The man was still hunched over his compdeck.

"Excuse me?" Fiscus said.

The man looked up. "Not you again. How am I supposed to get any work done with all these interruptions?"

"I was told you had a surprise for me," said Fiscus. "Perhaps I'm in the wrong room."

"Who sent you here?" the man asked.

"A fellow named Mickey Maze," Fiscus said.

"Good-looking guy? Blond hair, shiny red suit?"

"Yes . . ."

"Ah. Sorry to break it to you, pal, but you've been had. That ain't his name."

"Well then, who is he?" Fiscus said, bewildered.

"The Devil," the man said simply. "Lucifer, Satan, Scratch, Old Nick."

Fiscus spun and grabbed for the doorknob, then yelped and jumped back. The knob was red-hot.

"Welcome to Hell, pal," the man said. "How'd you die?"

The man's name was Adam. He was a science-fiction writer from the year ten million.

"Yeah, I always wanted to be a writer," Adam said, getting a tiny bottle of Scotch from the minibar. "This is my favorite era. Where I come from, everything's already been invented, everything's already been done. There's no room for creativity." He poured the Scotch into two glasses and offered one to Fiscus, who was sitting on the edge of the bed. "So I made a deal with the Devil to get sent back in time—this way, I can write about stuff that's history to me, but here it'll seem original and brilliant."

"The Devil deals in time travel?" asked Fiscus. He accepted the glass of Scotch numbly.

"Sure, why not? The only thing is, you got to sign a Paradox Clause. That's the only way he's allowed to mess with time."

"And now you're in Hell."

"I screwed up." Adam scowled, and tossed back his drink. "I didn't know what a critic was—they'd been eradicated by my time, and of course nothing they'd ever written had survived either. So my first review came as something of a shock."

"What did you do?"

"I tracked the scuzzball down and throttled him. How was I to know he was an ancestor of mine?"

"And this is Hell?" Fiscus took a sip of the Scotch and winced; it tasted like turpentine.

"It is for me. Locked in a hotel room with bad Scotch and constant interruptions; what could be worse for a writer?"

"But I'm not dead," said Fiscus. "At least, I don't remember dying."

"That could be part of your torment," Adam said. "Doomed to permanent confusion."

Fiscus's head whirled. It had a brutal sort of logic; he could imagine nothing worse than forever struggling through the morass of nonsense he seemed to have fallen into. Unless . . .

"Maybe I'm *not* dead," he said slowly. "Maybe—maybe one of the other explanations is true. I could be trapped in a malfunctioning virtual game, or perhaps this is one of those pockets of alternate reality the Multiversal Authority mentioned. I suppose it *could* even be another theatrical prank . . ."

Fiscus stood up. "I refuse to believe this is my fate! I *will* discover the truth!"

"Good for you," Adam said—and began to change.

His face bulged and contorted. One eye sank into his flesh like a grape dropped in a puddle of melted ice-cream, and the other centered itself and expanded to three times its size.

Adam's body withered and shrank away to nothing, leaving the head hanging in midair, staring at Fiscus with a huge smile on its face.

"Don't worry," it said sunnily. "You were right the first time. It's just a game."

Fiscus discovered something interesting: certain little-used facial muscles were required to look boggled. He had been giving those muscles quite a workout, and they were tired. So instead of looking boggled, he merely looked blank—which was much easier—and said, "*Is* it?"

"Yes," said the head. "Between myself and a creature that looks *exactly* like this."

"Twins, are you?" Fiscus said. "One good, one evil? Or perhaps you're the same being, only one of you has traveled back in time to stop himself from building a time machine. No, no, I've got it—you're from parallel dimensions, and this is a contest to see which one of you gets my brain in a jar as a trophy."

"Nope," the floating head said. "I'm a colony of molecule-sized bugs that feed on living hyperspatial energy. A corporation was using an Artificial Intelligence to control us, but there was an accident; we bonded with the AI, gained sentience, and escaped. Unfortunately, the accident also freed the hyperspatial creature we feed on, so we've been forced to chase it around if we want to survive."

"I *see*," said Fiscus. "And this relates to the insanity of the last hour *how*?"

"The hyperspace creature isn't very intelligent—it's more like a pet. It loves to play games, so we've been altering its immediate environment—your hotel—into a playground. As a highly organized, nanosized colony organism, we can move individual molecules around, creating or destroying almost anything."

"Can't you just build a cage around it, then?"

"We're trying, but it's made of hyperspatial energy; it projects the appearance of a disembodied, bouncing head, but it isn't actually solid."

"And why have I been dragged into this?"

"It likes you. It thinks you're funny."

Fiscus sighed. "Very well." He didn't actually *believe* the floating head—if he had been informed at that moment that fire was hot, he would have smiled, nodded, and fumbled in his pockets for a match—but it seemed pointless to argue. "Is there anything I can do that might resolve this situation?"

"Play along. It'll give us time to construct a means of trapping it, and then your problems will be over."

It wasn't much of a plan, but for the first time Fiscus

could see a glimmer of sanity at the end of the tunnel. "Play along," he said. "Yes. Yes, I suppose I could do that." After all, it *was* just a game . . .

"Good. Head to room 242; we've prepared another scenario there."

This time, the doorknob was cool to the touch. Fiscus strode down the hall, mumbling to himself, "A game. Just a game. Nothing to worry about, nothing at all."

Room 242 was a jungle. There was a cabin in a clearing, with an old man in a rocking chair on the porch.

"Morning," the man said with a nod. "Welcome to Vega 5." He stood up as Fiscus walked toward him and held out his hand. "I'm Jeb."

Fiscus put his own hand out, but he never got to shake Jeb's.

A strand of kudzu vine snaked out of the jungle and around the old man's neck, yanking him off his feet. A second vine grabbed his feet—and then the vine did something so indescribably, hideously violent that Fiscus was abruptly drenched from head to toe in something wet, warm, and coppery-tasting.

The vine dropped what was left of the body, and wriggled toward him.

Fiscus found himself running blindly through the jungle. He stopped abruptly when he ran into a wall, but gamely ran into it twice more before his fear-addled brain finally noticed he wasn't making much progress.

The wall looked like more jungle, but on closer inspection proved to be as solid as—well, a wall. More specifically, a wall in a hotel room, which is what Fiscus told himself he was still in.

"Just a game, just a game, just a game," he repeated to himself. "Right. Wish they'd told me what the rules were . . ."

"I think you'll need this," a husky voice breathed. Fiscus spun around with a gasp.

Eve Never stepped from behind a tree. Before she had been beautiful; now she was divine. Her pallor had been replaced by a golden tan and her gauntness had ripened into tautly muscled curves. She was smiling. She was nude.

She was holding the biggest gun Fiscus had ever seen.

"You do know how to fire a gun, don't you?" she said, offering it to him and licking her lips. She caressed the barrel. "You point the long end at whatever you want, put your finger on the trigger, and then—all it takes is a little twitch . . ."

"Uh—yes," said Fiscus, taking the gun gingerly. It had a bore the size of a garbage can, but weighed almost nothing. "Of course it weighs almost nothing, it's just a prop in a game," he muttered to himself.

He aimed it at a nearby tree and pulled the trigger. A beam of light flashed out and the tree melted like an ice cream sundae in a microwave oven. Fiscus couldn't feel any heat from it at all.

Suddenly, he felt much better.

"Before you go," Eve whispered, running her hands down his blood-soaked chest, "maybe you'd like to pull *my* trigger a few times." Her hands continued to drift lower, and then she put her lips to his ear and suggested something so perverse and physically unlikely his boggle muscles almost seized up.

"Thank you, Miss Never, but no," he said weakly, taking a step backward. "I really should go shoot something now, don't you think?"

"That's what I had in mind," she said, giving him a look that made him feel as if his eyebrows were about to burst into flame.

He swallowed, gave her a glassy smile, and edged slowly away—when suddenly the ground disappeared beneath his feet.

He landed on his rear, in darkness. *I really am getting tired of always being in the dark,* he thought without a trace of irony.

"Bill, there's someone in the room!" a woman's voice whispered.

"Go back to sleep, Monica," a groggy male voice answered. "Y'all are dreaming."

Fiscus sprang to his feet. "You won't get the drop on me this time!" he shouted, and began shooting.

What he saw in the muzzle-flash of the gun wasn't killer vines or demons from Hell or even menacing bureaucrats; it was, instead, a perfectly ordinary hotel room, with a middle-aged couple under the covers in bed.

He wasn't fooled.

"Take that!" he yelled, firing. "And that! And that! And some of this!"

It took quite a while for the gun to run out of ammunition. When it finally did, Fiscus collapsed to the floor, panting. He'd had no idea pulling a trigger could be so exhausting.

The room was silent.

He pulled himself to his feet finally, and fumbled for the light switch.

The room was a shambles. The gun had left blast marks on the walls, the floor, and the ceiling. Most of the damage, though, had been to the bed—and who was in it.

He stared down at the bodies. Though both were undeniably dead, by some fluke neither had been hit in the face.

He recognized them.

The Smiths. He'd checked them in himself, two nights ago. They were staying in room 142 . . .

Directly below the jungle-filled room.

"No," he whispered. "It's a game—it's just supposed to be a game—"

He checked the bodies frantically. They weren't robots, or illusions, or special-effects altered actors; they were corpses. And he was a murderer . . .

He sank to the floor. His brain announced, quite firmly, that it had had enough, it was resigning, and furthermore he was an arrogant bastard of a boss and the brain had never liked him anyway.

He curled up into a fetal position and whimpered.

Everything faded away. He was drifting, warm and safe and weightless. A pink glow suffused everything. For the longest time there was no sound except a rhythmic thumping, which was strangely soothing.

And then he heard voices.

"It seems so cruel," a woman's voice said.

"It's necessary," a male voice replied. "The psyche has to be broken down through contradictory input, or memories of his past life might resurface. We don't want that, do we?"

"No . . ."

"The Council turned down our application. This is the only way . . ."

Suddenly there was pain. He was being squeezed, crushed, suffocated. He struggled, but he couldn't move.

The pink glow brightened to white. The pressure increased, and then it was gone.

Fiscus blinked. He was in a hospital room, dangling upside-down, naked and covered with slime. A square-jawed, unshaven man wearing a fedora and a hospital gown was lying in bed with his legs spread and his feet in stirrups. He was holding the hand of a beautiful, silver-skinned woman who stood beside the bed.

"I love you, Eve," Adam said.

"I love you too," the robot replied.

Someone smacked Fiscus on the bottom. He opened his mouth and wailed.

Everything, mercifully, went black.

There were seven members on the Interspecies Transdimensional Council. They ranged in appearance from a one-eyed, floating head to a species of sentient vine. They were gathered around a glowing table, a pool of light surrounded by darkness that swallowed the dimensions of the room. They were deliberating on the fate of the planet Earth.

"The subject demonstrated xenophobia and poor adaptation skills," said the vampire. His species had evolved from a parasitic life form on a planet with high levels of ultraviolet radiation.

"Not to mention being easily pushed toward violence,"

the astral projection added. His race avoided space travel, but roamed the universe in a nonmaterial form.

"Telepathic manipulation of his thoughts during the test revealed a basically intolerant mindset, centered on adherence to routine," the bulbous-headed green humanoid stated. "I have to vote against admission."

"I concur," the penisoid said, bobbing its pink head.

"As do I," echoed the robot. She bore little resemblance to a human female.

"Then we're agreed," the vine said. "They're just not ready yet."

The one-eyed hovering cranium sighed. "A shame. Still, he should have known: Adam Phule always loses his head while trying to get Eve N. . . ."

Fiscus saw and heard and knew all of this, though he wasn't there; it was as if he were watching it on a screen, or he was a ghost. The bobbing head's final words echoed through his mind as everything grew hazy and indistinct: *Adam Phule. Adam Phule. Adam Phule . . .* everything he'd seen and done whirled through his mind like colored bits in a kaleidoscope. Rationality, with whom he'd been having a bit of a row, decided to break things off completely and left without leaving a note. The firm pillars of stability that were Fiscus Throppe's world crashed into ruin, and were immediately overrun by the brambles of uncertainty and the cheese muffins of insanity, who didn't give a damn about proper metaphors. He went completely, gloriously mad, and it was a tremendous relief . . .

And then he woke up.

Perhaps . . .

nine

skinny gets lucky

"You mean the hotel has been taken over by ticks?" blurted Skinny. "Let's get the hell out of here!"

"Slow down," I said, putting my hand on Skinny's shoulder. "If we were in any danger, I wouldn't have wasted time spinning a yarn."

"I surmised that," said Joey, rubbing his temples. "Please lower your voice, in deference to the legions of dead brain cells now audibly rotting in my skull."

"I found Kegan going through the garbage bins behind the hotel—and Throppe curled up in a little ball in the stairwell. Friendly, here," I said, motioning to the floating head that was now hovering just above Kegan's shoulder, "was sitting beside him. It took some doing, but I got Throppe to talk—even though he kept referring to himself in the third person. When he got to the end of the story, he started telling the whole thing over again. Right about then Hirold showed up, and we called an ambulance. They took Throppe away, still mumbling to himself."

"Forget about the desk clerk—what about the ticks?" snapped Skinny.

"Interesting thing about that," I said. "I've roamed up and down every hall—and they're all gone."

"Gone?" Joey frowned. "You mean dead?"

"I don't know—but I can't find a trace of them anywhere. I don't know if that's good or bad."

"Hmm," said Joey. "Several other questions come to mind. Why did—Friendly, as you call him—show up here, and why didn't we detect his arrival?"

I went to the bathroom, poured myself a large glass of water, and drained it before answering. "I think Friendly's a little different from the other h-space critters," I said, refilling the glass. "He seems to bond in a temporary kind of way—otherwise he would have followed Throppe to the hospital instead of becoming attached to Kegan. He behaves more like a pet than a beast of burden—and I think he homed in on this hotel because the energy we're charged with felt familiar to him."

"Like a dog following a scent," mused Joey. "But why didn't *you* sense *him*?"

"The booze," I said sheepishly. "By the time Friendly arrived at the hotel, my senses must have been a little impaired—and then, before he got to our room, Friendly got distracted. I think he's drawn to people who are less than cheerful."

"So he's not solid?" asked Skinny, studying Friendly. Friendly stared back with a huge grin on its face.

"Well, he bounces off things, so he must have some mass," I said. "But he can turn invisible and go right through walls, too—like Sentry, I guess."

"Not exactly a replacement—but it's still better to have Friendly with us than with the VI," Joey pointed out.

"True," I said. "But maybe dangerous. I didn't want to say anything while Sentry was around—the guilt would have crippled him—but we may have been indirectly responsible for that crash disaster."

"I think I know what you're going to say," said Joey. "You think that when you, Kegan, Sentry, and the ticks were all present at the cavern—a hypercharged site—you weakened the fabric of spacetime."

"I see some of your brain cells are still functioning," I said. "Now there's me, Kegan, Friendly, and you—I don't know if we should risk another disaster."

"As long as we avoid ancient hyperspace portal areas, we shouldn't have to worry," said Joey.

"We hope," I said glumly.

"Let's get some breakfast," suggested Joey. "Maybe my hangover can be bribed with bacon and eggs."

We had to go out to eat. The idiot autoclerk was in charge downstairs, and he cheerfully insisted the kitchen was out of everything but marmalade and parsley. Joey took us to a restaurant he knew called Frederico's, and treated us to a meal.

Frederico's wasn't large, but it was full; cabbies, mostly, of many different species. We hardly raised an eyebrow—until Joey actually joined us at our table, drawing more than a few stares. Everybody seemed to know who he was, though most seemed too amazed to actually approach us.

After a hearty breakfast, we got down to brass tacks.

"Spaceport first," I said. "I'm worried about Melody and Mike."

"Spaceport," said Kegan, nodding. "Industrial waste—mmmmm."

"Can the beach ball do anything besides grin?" asked Skinny.

"Maybe," I said. "I've been afraid to ask."

"Can do tricks," said Kegan, nodding his massive head. "I remember . . ."

Kegan reached out and tapped Friendly with one clawed finger, then pointed at the table. "Food," he said.

Friendly blinked—and the table we were sitting at was suddenly a heap of rotting garbage.

"Uh—" I said.

"Change it back!" hissed Joey. "You want to get us thrown out?"

My hands had been resting on the table—and it felt like

they still were. I couldn't smell rotting garbage either, just
see it.

Kegan chuckled, and tapped Friendly again. The table
reappeared.

"An illusionist," I said. "Makes sense—a pet that can en-
tertain you *and* redecorate your apartment. Must have been
responsible for some of the weirdness Throppe went
through."

"But Kegan—you said you *remembered*," said Joey.
"What do you mean?"

"*Eater* remembers," said Kegan slowly. "From before.
Long time ago, very long time. Trapped, together. Eater and
Friendly and the others."

"What others?" asked Skinny.

"Watchdog. Puller. Three others—don't know how to say
their names."

Joey looked thoughtful. He didn't say anything though,
just motioned the waiter over for our bill.

We left the restaurant and headed for the spaceport.
Friendly seemed just as happy flying outside the taxi as in,
but it obeyed when Kegan told it to stay in the cab. Skinny
eyed it suspiciously; I don't think he trusted anything that
was better at fooling people than he was.

Joey drove us to another part of the port, where the ships
were housed in huge underground hangars. Flying into the
mouth of the hangar tunnel was like being swallowed by a
giant snake; the tunnel twisted and wound around for miles.
We stuck close to the roof, while transport flatbeds rolled by
underneath us on tracks, hauling space yachts and merchant
vessels to their berths.

We finally found Mike and Melody's ship, the *Void
Queen* III. It was a smart-looking ship, shaped like a manta
ray and in immaculate condition; Mike wouldn't have it any
other way.

We parked, but didn't approach. We could read the orange
band that said SEALED BY ORDER OF PORT AUTHORITY from the
cab.

"Tick trick?" asked Skinny.

"I'm not sensing any bugs," I said. "Let's check it out with the portmaster."

The portmaster turned out to be a stout, businesslike woman with short gray hair. Her office was located at the mouth of the tunnel, in a soundproofed, glass-walled cubicle. She looked up from her desk when I came in, alone.

"Yes?" she said.

"Yeah—I was supposed to deliver some documents to berth 111397?" I said, sounding bored. "But it's all locked up."

"111397—just a second." She checked her compscreen. "Oh, yes. Bankruptcy case. The ship's been seized for nonpayment of debt. I'll see if I can find a forwarding address for the owner—oh. That's going to be tricky."

"What is?"

"The owner's an AI—and she's been sold to recover the debts."

I didn't let anything show on my face. "Huh. Well, I still got to deliver these documents—who owns her now?"

"Let's see—the corporation picked her up just this morning. Outfit called Trinitech. Wait a sec, I'll print out the address for you."

I took the slip of paper, thanked her, and went back to the cab.

"I don't know how the VI managed it," I said. "But we have to get her back."

"How?" asked Joey. "Without Sentry, we have no firepower. The VI has an entire mall as a fortress, and Hone to protect it."

"We need money," said Skinny. "With enough cash, we could pay a lab to make a few vatfuls of Acentinol. That's all the firepower we need."

"Acentinol won't work against Hone," said Joey. "His programming will keep him coming after us even when every single tick is dead."

"You've got your own contacts," Skinny said. "Can't you find something through the street that could handle Hone?"

"Possibly," admitted Joey. "But it'll be expensive."

"So we're back to cash," said Skinny. "Fortunately, the quick raising of short-term capital happens to be something we're familiar with."

"Time to get back in the game?" I asked him.

"Looks like," he said. "And I've got an idea how . . ."

We had to pick up a few things first, but Melody had already provided most of what we needed in the third crate. When we were ready, we set out for the Barrier.

The Barrier is the girdle that cinches tight the waist of Kinslik's one hourglass-shaped continent. Without it, Toolie civilization might never have arisen.

As I've said before, Skinny was something of an aberration when it came to the males of his race. A bull Toolie is an eating machine; the only thing that can distract him is rutting, and even then he has to engulf the female before mating can take place. When he's done, the female releases an enzyme that makes the male nauseous, and he vomits her back up.

A few thousand years ago, the females decided they were tired of being treated like snack food, and started building enclosures to keep the males out. Since the females and their young formed family clusters that shared tasks, they already had a cooperative mentality; it didn't take much for them to start banding together in larger groups.

Only thing was, it didn't work. The males were determined, and no matter what kind of fort the females built, the males would find a way to batter, tunnel, or vault their way inside. This was fine when the females were in the mood, but kind of annoying when they were trying to do something else. Nothing disrupts a village meeting like the chairwoman being swallowed whole.

So a plan was proposed. It took a lot of work, and years of labor—but the females were organized and patient, and the males couldn't see past their next meal. The Barrier went up in sections, all the way across the continent, and the males didn't bother tearing it down as long as there were gaps they could pass through. Extensions were built miles into the sea on either side, too, just in case—Toolies aren't really good at swimming, but a horny male can be surprisingly inventive. Another famous escapee, Raftbuilder, barely survived the reefs, storms, and sea-carnivores he encountered on his breakout.

The way the females got the males all on a single side of the Barrier was simple: one day, in an orchestrated move, all the in-between sections were filled in. The females had already gathered on one side, and they'd designed the Barrier to allow the males to cross it easily toward them, but not back. With all the ripe females clustered close to the wall, males came from both sides—but once through the Barrier, they couldn't return.

The females surrendered themselves as living bait for a year. It was a year-long orgy of rape and murder, for a male Toolie never asks permission to mate and will attack another male on sight. At the end of that year, the females opened the hidden gates they'd built into the Barrier, rushed through— and locked the gates behind them. Squads of armed females were sent to search the reaches of the other half of the continent, for any male stragglers that might have been left behind. There were only three—and they were executed on the spot.

The Barrier has stood to this day. Over the centuries, the females have refined and strengthened it, but it's never been breached. A few extraordinary males have found a way to get to the other side, but always through cunning, not brute strength.

I learned most of this from Skinny. Males are given a few rudimentary bones and released into the Reservation within a day of being born—only the tough and the smart survive.

And now, for the first time, he was going back.

We waited until dark, and took Skinny to the part of the

wall that crosses Nobones Swamp. It's not that hard to get into the Toolie Reservation, even with the security patrols and orbiting spy-eyes—it's getting out again that's tricky. A path ran along the top of the hundred-foot-high wall, which was made of logs and a kind of natural cement, reinforced many times over the centuries. The female's side was rough-hewn, but the male's was as smooth as glass. The whole thing was sunk down to bedrock and reinforced with an in-visible protec-field, which projected another ten feet above the top and ended in a molecule-thin edge sharp enough to cut through steel cable.

We used a stepladder and a plank to get Skinny up and over the field, then lowered him down on a rope. I guess we could have used Kegan to eat a tunnel for us—bedrock wouldn't be much more than crunchy to him—but this was quicker and left no evidence. Any kind of vehicle—like Joey's cab—would have tripped alarms.

"Watch out for quicksand," I hissed down after Skinny.

"Thanks for the tip," he hissed back. "I *never* would have thought of *that*. Now shut up and concentrate on not drop-ping me."

A minute later, and he'd been swallowed up by the dark-ness.

We left quickly, before a security patrol wanted to know what we were doing in the middle of the night. Joey and Kegan and I, with Friendly in tow, flew east. We parked at the edge of the swamp, by the first breeding stockade we came to. Kegan and his new pet got out to do a little explor-ing—apparently the smell of rotting vegetation was too mouthwatering to resist. He promised not to roam too far away. Joey and I settled down to wait for morning, when the stockade would open for business.

"We could go back to the hotel," said Joey. "I mean, it doesn't make any difference to me, and I'm not sure if Kegan even sleeps anymore, but you could get some shut-eye."

"I wouldn't be able to sleep, anyway," I told him. "Not as long as Skinny is out there, all alone."

"He'll be okay," said Joey. "He's got a weapon none of the other males have—a brain."

"As long as it doesn't get eaten," I said gloomily.

"How'd he ever get out of there in the first place?"

"That's a tale in itself," I said. "All Toolie births are monitored, so the males can be isolated right away. They're taken away by the Procreation Police—that's what they're called, I swear to God—and given some basic bones that'll help them survive. They've got a day to practice with the bones, then they're released at random spots in the Reservation. They used to raise the males to a decent size before releasing them, or they wouldn't stand a chance; the larger bulls would wait on the other side of the wall and eat anything that came through. Nowadays they fly the newborns in and release them in deserted areas, but even that's dangerous; the experienced males have learned to recognize the ships, and they head toward and search any place the ships land.

"Skinny got dumped in a clearing. He was terrified, but he was also hungry; it didn't take him too long to find and eat a few bugs, and that settled him down some. He found himself a nice deep burrow—ate what was in it—and proceeded to spend most of his time hiding.

"Now, a normal male would start to roam, eating bigger and bigger prey, and would soon outgrow that burrow—but Skinny wasn't normal. When he started getting too big for the burrow, he did two things: he enlarged it, and he cut back on his diet. Neither idea would have even occurred to your average male Toolie—but compared to them, Skinny was a genius.

"He spent his first year being real careful, and observing the world around him. He saw a battle between two males from a distance, and avoided them after that. Eventually his instincts told him it was time to move on—but he intended to do so safely.

"He'd noticed there was a particular kind of animal the other bulls avoided, a creature called a killprickle. A nasty set of quills covered its entire body, and Skinny learned about the venom they contained by tasting leaves the critter had brushed up against. He killed one by digging a pit underneath a well-traveled trail, then dropping a large rock on it from above. He was real careful with the body—and by scooping out its soft underbelly, he created his very first disguise.

"After that, he could travel unmolested. He went in the same direction most of the other males seemed to: south. Before too many days had passed, he arrived at the Barrier.

"Ripe females in cages waited along its base, while males battled each other to get near them. The pheromones in the air made Skinny want to rush forward and join in—but he was smarter than that. He hid himself, watched, and waited.

"He saw his chance the very next day.

"A brute of a male had just beaten off a challenger. The winner retired to the enclosure provided, where he engulfed a willing and boneless female—and a shimmering protec-field sprung into existence, sealing the lovers inside. Skinny didn't know what a protec-field was, of course, but he saw that when another male tried to breach it he had no luck. He also saw that while the pair inside mated, the male seemed more than a little distracted.

"And when they were done and the female spurted out of the male's body, she oozed quickly down a small hole in the floor.

"Another fight was taking place a short distance away. Skinny trotted right onto the battlefield, past the combatants, and into the enclosure. The female there was terrified—she was a civilized creature who'd never faced a wild animal before, let alone a poisonous one. She would have bolted for the hole, but Skinny parked himself right on top of it.

"And then—leaving the bristling shell behind to forestall pursuit—he abandoned his own bones, and poured himself down the hole. His first con.

"He found himself in a small chamber with a sealed hatch. It only took him a minute to figure out how to open it—his first break-and-enter. The concerned sisters of the trapped female were by this point up on the wall, waving various limbs and broadcasting conflicting advice, so Skinny was able to ooze his way under the door of a maintenance closet without being noticed. A few minutes later, an extremely odd-looking Toolie strolled out—brooms and mops will double for bones in a pinch. By the time anyone had figured it out, he was gone."

"Amazing," said Joey with a chuckle. "How'd he get off-planet?"

"Escaped males are big news—it rarely happens, and when it does there's usually plenty of mayhem. This case was different—Skinny was portrayed in the media as a devious skulker, planning some hideous midnight massacre instead of just going on a simple rampage the way a decent male would. Melody was on Kinslik at the time, and it caught her attention. She used her own considerable intellect to figure out where he must be hiding, and searched him out."

"Where *was* he hiding?"

"Maybe I should let Skinny tell you that," I said with a grin. "Anyway, she offered to educate him—he reminded her of another male Toolie she used to know that had an above average IQ. Skinny accepted, and left the planet with her and Mike."

"So how'd you two get together?"

"Melody introduced us. I'd been kind of drifting around, getting into trouble here and there, and she figured maybe all I needed was a friend. I have to admit, I'd never gotten real close to anybody outside of my own family—and by family I'm including Aunt Melody and Uncle Mike—but Skinny had his own kind of charm. Neither of us seemed to fit in anywhere, so we decided to stick together. The rest is history and police records."

By this time the sun was showing itself on the edge of the

horizon, and gravcabs and tour buses were starting to arrive in the parking lot. I got out, rounded up Kegan and his new best friend, and all of us joined the crowd outside the doors. Joey came along, too.

The Barrier is more than just a wall; it's also a popular tourist attraction, and the site of the busiest industry on the planet. If you're a female Toolie and you want to have children, there's only one source of male genes: the Barrier breeding pens. They go on for hundreds of miles, lining the entire length of the wall. The Toolie families that run them have done so for generations, handing the business down from mother to daughter.

Since we couldn't exactly pass ourselves off as Toolies, we paid the admission—well, Joey paid for all of us—and went in the tourist entrance. In the mix of off-worlders, we hardly stood out at all; I was wearing a greatcoat that made me look even bigger than normal, but next to Kegan and Friendly I wasn't that unusual.

The building we entered wasn't all that large, but it was modern and spotless. Our tour guide was a female Toolie named Speechmaker. She was contoured like a centaur, but had two wheels instead of four legs. When she stopped, she put out two tiny limbs like a kickstand to steady herself.

To one side of the corridor we walked down was a glass wall, with female Toolies busy working on the other side. "In this lab," said Speechmaker through a voder, "the sperm is subjected to various genetic tests before being frozen and shipped off." These female's limbs were clusters of long tentacles, cored with flexible steel cable and tipped with delicate instruments. Diagnostic equipment was built right into their torsos, making them look more like goo-covered robots than anything—though I noticed that each of them had a few genuine bones in her makeup as well.

The hall led to a large elevator, which took us upstairs to the viewing area. It was on top of the wall itself, and had no seating—Toolies aren't much for chairs.

From up here we could see down into the Reservation itself. Pens lined the Barrier as far as the eye could see—and I've got pretty good eyes. Our area was butted right against the edge of the swamp.

The pens were quite simple, three walls and the Barrier forming a rectangular stall with a transparent roof. "The female," said Speechmaker, "having discarded her bones, enters through a trapdoor in the floor. This entrance is also used to place meat and bones in the pen as a reward or further incentive to the males.

"It's locked behind her. She has only a small hole in the trapdoor itself to flow through to escape—the male, larger and with bones he's unwilling to give up, will be unable to follow her."

We found out there were two kinds of females who came here. The first were employees of the breeding pens, living receptacles who'd have the sperm removed afterwards for sale. The second were more traditional Toolies, who either couldn't afford the higher-quality sperm or just preferred a more personal approach.

The one below us seemed to be of the second variety, and probably a virgin to boot. She was so nervous she was quivering, and she looked oddly vulnerable with no bones to give her body shape.

Looking out beyond the pens, I could see why she was frightened.

There were already several battles underway. Skinny had described such fights to me before, so I should have been prepared—but I could feel my stomach drop down to my ankles as I watched.

It's hard to describe the sheer viciousness of the combat. It was the combination of speed and size that seemed shocking—nothing that big should move that fast. Bodies would slam together like elephants wrestling, but at the same time a tangle of razored limbs would be flailing at each other in a blur, quicker than wildcats in a scrap. It was like someone glued together a mess of cobras, wolverines, and grizzly bears while they were sleeping, and they all woke up in a bad mood.

And somewhere down there was Skinny.

I scanned the horizon anxiously, but didn't see him. Had he made it through the night?

Below me, the door to the pen slid open, revealing the prize. There were a few males hanging around the edges of the battlefield and eyeing each other, but none of them made a dash for the pen; according to Skinny, any male brazen enough to try to slip past a fight and get the female the easy way would find himself torn apart by the combatants—the only time they cooperate is to gang up on cheaters.

Which made what we were about to try even more dangerous . . .

The fight directly in front of us abruptly ended. The mass of writhing claws, horns, fangs, and flesh split in two and one of them staggered away, conceding defeat. The victor stood his ground, daring the next challenger. He was a mountain of translucent pink meat on eight thick legs, his form suggesting a quartet of rhinos joined at the buttocks. Add four thick, heavily muscled arms growing from the rhinos' backs, each one ending in a log to form a crude wooden sledgehammer, and then finish with a long tentacle growing from the very center of the thing, tipped with a jagged, razor-sharp piece of metal shaped like a wedge.

"That's Wreckstalker," said Speechmaker. "He's a successful and highly valued breeder, who rarely ventures into this area. That piece of metal you see is from a ship that crashed in the Reservation several years ago. Many males salvaged pieces of the wreckage to use as weapons, but only the toughest were able to keep what they found."

Great. Skinny was going to have to deal with the local champ . . . A pasty-faced woman in a loud shirt raised her hand. "Excuse me," she said.

"Yes?" said Speechmaker.

"Once you've caught a male, how long do you keep him?"

"He's released immediately after mating," said Speechmaker. "In fact, the only reason the pen is sealed during mating is to protect the couple from being attacked."

"Wouldn't it be easier to just keep them in the pen and extract the semen from them artificially?" the woman asked.

"That would reduce them to animals, which they are not," said Speechmaker. "As different and feral as they are, they are still Insussklik. We value and respect them; they come here of their own free will, and breeding males are rewarded with food and even bones."

"Do you ever give them manufactured tools or weapons?" the woman asked.

"Oh, no," said Speechmaker. "That would be too dangerous. Even a piece of sharp metal gives Wreckstalker an almost unbeatable advantage."

The other males seemed to agree; none of them moved to engage him. He gave one last look around—his sensory cluster was at the base of his tentacle—and began to stump toward the pen.

Which is when Skinny showed up.

He erupted out of the ground directly in front of the pen. I should have remembered how he'd used burrowing to his advantage when he was here before—as well as Skinny's talent for making an entrance.

We'd had to do our best with a limited budget and little time to prepare, which meant going to a cut-rate boneshop for supplies. Joey had bankrolled us, but he couldn't afford much. Still, what we came up with was believable, if not impressive.

Skinny wasn't skinny anymore. A miniature tank had inflated balloons under his skin, arranged to simulate muscles where there was only gas. Lightweight alloy bones provided support, and we'd armored him with an artificial lizardskin that looked tough but weighed very little. The big, blue skull was fake too, but it was solid enough to provide some protection for his sensory cluster. Overall he resembled a scaly grizzly bear, with giant oversize claws—in reality, he was closer to an inflated marionette.

"Oh, my God!" I yelled, on cue. "It's *him*!"

Wreckstalker charged.

Skinny bounded out of his hole to meet him. They rushed toward each other—and as that lethal-tipped tentacle slashed forward, Skinny jumped clear over his foe.

Did I forget to mention we'd inflated him with helium?

Wreckstalker didn't have much in the way of a face, but if he'd had one it sure would have looked surprised. Skinny spun in midair, landed on the other side of his opponent, and jabbed forward with both claws. They sank into Wreckstalker's flesh.

Wreckstalker stiffened—and collapsed. The crowd gasped.

Skinny withdrew his claws and began waving them around dramatically. I pushed my way through the onlookers to Speechmaker's side, and said breathlessly, "You must apprehend that male immediately!"

Speechmaker regarded me curiously. "Why?"

"Because he's the only living descendant of Wallbreacher himself!"

Speechmaker stared at me. Another male lunged at Skinny.

In the entire history of the Barrier, no male has ever gotten through by brute force. One male, however, pulled off a feat of such cunning, audacity, and sheer bloody-minded determination that he became a legend: Wallbreacher. He was the only male Toolie to ever get the other males to work together in something approaching cooperation, and exactly how he did it remains something of a mystery, though the broad facts are well-known. Wallbreacher was a great warrior who took the idea of co-opting bones to the next level: when he defeated another male in battle, he didn't kill and plunder his opponent—instead, he stayed linked to the other Toolie through an armored tentacle, turning him into a slave. Females do something similar; their young are simply extensions of their will for the first few weeks, until they begin to develop their own personalities.

Wallbreacher did this many times, until he had a gang of a dozen males under his control. How he trained them to follow orders, or kept them from rebelling or trying to kill him in his sleep, has never been fully explained.

In ancient times the wall was patrolled by vigilant females thirty hours a day, to prevent breakout attempts by males too curious, impatient, or juvenile to compete for the breeding pens. Most males gave up when attacked from above by boiling water, large rocks, or even poisoned darts. Wallbreacher didn't.

Instead, he laid siege.

He didn't just try to get through the Barrier; he attacked it like it was something he was determined to destroy. He turned himself and his gang into a giant battering ram, and slammed into the Barrier with a rage that was terrible to behold. It went on for three full days, until every one of his gang was dead and only Wallbreacher was left. The Barrier held. Wallbreacher vanished back into the wilderness.

A year later, he was back. His gang now numbered twenty.

This time, he tried tunneling. If he'd been sneakier about it, he might have succeeded, but subtlety wasn't one of Wallbreacher's strong points. He started his tunnel within sight of the Barrier—as if daring the females up on the walls to try and stop him—and went straight ahead.

The females collapsed his first tunnel by dropping boulders on it from above. After that, he learned to shore it up. When his tunnel reached the Barrier, he discovered it was firmly anchored to bedrock and withdrew, back into the wilderness.

By this time, word of Wallbreacher's attempts had spread. Hundreds of curious females lined the top of the Barrier, many of them eager to mate with such a powerful male. Wallbreacher could have lived like a king, fed the finest bones and meat from above, with his pick of willing females to mate with.

He killed and ate the first female they sent him. They sent no more.

Three days later he was back. Unable to go through or underneath, he had decided to go over the top.

The structure he'd organized himself into resembled a giant armored column with a wide base, tapering slightly toward the top. Fifty feet high, it tottered along on short, stumpy legs, until it reached the Barrier itself. The females thought they were safe; the Barrier was a hundred feet high.

And then the column began to grow.

When the females saw what was happening, they tried to knock the column over, but it had been anchored securely to the ground. They tried pouring boiling water on it, but it was well-armored and even waterproof. Wallbreacher had learned.

Human historians named it the Trojan Penis. It didn't do any actual penetrating, but when it had doubled its height, it did eject its contents—a long and streamlined brigade of males, with Wallbreacher himself at the forefront. They swarmed over the wall, slaughtered every female in their path, and escaped into the countryside—Myriad didn't cover the whole continent the way it does now.

The story has something of a tragic ending. An army was sent after the rogue males and hunted them down. They made every effort to take Wallbreacher alive, but he fought to the very end, forcing them to kill him. There are no official records of his mating with any females—any who survived, anyway—while on the loose, but there are still those who claim an ancestor met him, had a brief and tempestuous encounter, then bore his young later in secret, afraid they'd be taken away and executed. Such legends were common in Myriad . . .

And Skinny and I were about to make one come true.

"I have proof!" I said loudly. *"That is Wallbreacher's direct descendant!"*

Skinny grappled with another male, tagged him with his claws, and watched him crash to the earth, unconscious. It's amazing how effective a concealed stunfield generator can be, especially when you plunge the exposed leads directly into your target's skin.

"How's he *doing* that?" asked Joey with perfect timing.

"He's linking directly to their neural systems—the same method Wallbreacher used to control his underlings!" I said excitedly. "This confirms my hypothesis!"

"Who *are* you?" asked Speechmaker, clearly confused.

"Oh, I *am* sorry—Professor Petrie, at your service," I said. I pulled on the lapels of my greatcoat in a scholarly fashion. "I'm from the University of Tanzannika, on Shinnkaria. My specialty is xenobiology, specifically Insussklik males. I'm here on Kinslik on a research grant. And *that*"—I said, pointing at Skinny—"is precisely what I came to find."

"But how—"

Rule number one: never give the mark time to think. "According to local folklore, Wallbreacher mated with any number of females while on his rampage. I believe he did mate with at least one female, who bore his young and surreptitiously released the males into the Reservation. According to my projections, the genetic anomaly that allowed Wallbreacher to link with and control other Toolies would eventually resurface in another male descendant, most likely in this area—and there he is!"

This was the tricky part. If Speechmaker bought this, we were golden . . . if not, we were toast. However, Speechmaker looked like she was just about to enter childbearing age—and according to Skinny, many females took tourguide jobs at the Barrier in order to get deals on sperm.

Rule number two: tell the mark something they *want* to believe.

"That's *amazing*," Speechmaker said, awe in her voice. "But how could it be true?"

Ah, the moment when the hook goes in . . . "Why is his skull blue?" Joey prompted, right on cue.

"That's the intriguing part," I said, turning to face Joey. "It's what caught my interest in the first place, and may even explain where the genetic trait came from. As you can see, I myself am a Shinnkarien Ox. My people are an ancient race that rarely venture from their home—and yet, there is strong evidence to suggest that thousands of years ago, a Shinn-karien Ox not only visited this planet, but mated with an In-sussklik!"

"But how—"

"Incredible, I know. But my people are a most unusual species—there is evidence we were designed by a far older race, now mysteriously vanished. Observe." I took a short penknife from my pocket—and slashed my forearm open. Speechmaker's voder stuttered—it wasn't used to reproduc-ing a gasp.

Rule number three: distract the mark with something amazing, even if it's totally unconnected to what you're try-ing to convince them of. *Look, I pulled a rabbit out of a hat—of course I can make that elephant disappear.*

The wound spurted blood—then sealed up before Speech-maker's eyes.

"Actually, I'm half-Shinnkarien," I said. "Half-human, as well. We're one of the few species that's cross-fertile with others—our bodies are remarkably adaptable, right down to our DNA. That creature down there is actually related to me."

While I'd been talking, Skinny had been posing, waving his claws around, making twenty-foot leaps—we'd added some high-tensile springs to his ankles—and generally act-ing like he wanted to take on all comers. After some initial hesitation, other males were now approaching; despite hav-ing defeated Wreckstalker, Skinny's rep was far from made. Most male Toolies seem to harbor the deep conviction that they're unbeatable, and it takes direct and repeated evidence to the contrary to disabuse them of this notion.

Which Skinny was happy to provide. Fortunately, he only had to take on one at a time, and he was quick enough to tag them with the rigged claw before they could hit him. It was nerve-racking to watch, though—one puncture and he'd start to deflate like a wounded balloon.

A crowd had started to gather, tourists from other parts of the wall wandering over for a better look. Perfect.

"I must get a genetic sample!" I said, wringing my hands. "Who knows how long before this trait pops up again!"

Speechmaker was on the phone. I suppressed a grin.

News travels fast in Myriad. Within twenty minutes there were reporters feeding it live to the Netweb, and the crowd extended a hundred feet down the wall in either direction. Skinny had taken on and beaten half a dozen challengers by this point.

I passed the time giving interviews, stressing the historic importance of this event. Within half an hour, the breeding pens below me were swamped with calls offering money for Skinny's sperm. He was a star.

Finally, the time came when no other male would approach him. He was the undisputed champion of his area. The female in the pen below shivered with anticipation. The cameras zoomed in, and the crowd held its collective breath.

Skinny stalked up to the pen, stared at the female inside— and turned away.

The crowd gasped. Skinny bounded toward the next breeding area, and the crowd surged along with him. "That proves it!" I yelled. "Only Wallbreacher's descendant would choose battle over procreation!"

Skinny attacked the first male he encountered, who was more than a little surprised—he'd been in the middle of a fight at the time. Skinny zapped them both.

By this time the crowd was cheering every victory. He wasn't just the champ, he was a celebrity—and the Toolies that owned the breeding pens in the vicinity were going crazy, trying to figure out how to attract him to their females. Bones and food were being shoved through the pens' trap-doors in hopes of luring him inside; Skinny ignored them.

Time to take it to the next level.

"He's in the grip of genetic bloodlust," I told an interviewer, a young Toolie with her body structured around a videocam. "Unless we can break his behavior pattern, he'll go on until he's killed, just like Wallbreacher. We *must* convince him to mate, and soon."

"How can we do that?" the interviewer asked.

"I believe there's only one way," I answered gravely. "I must enter the Reservation and contact him personally."

The interviewer was speechless for a second. "Wouldn't that be—well, suicidal?"

"Perhaps," I said solemnly. "But I have dedicated my life to this research, and I cannot turn back now. I believe that my own genetic structure contains codes that his will recognize—it may be enough to break through his rage and allow him to mate. It is his only hope."

After a certain point in a con, you can get away with almost anything. The mark—in this case, the entire Netweb audience—has so much invested they'll believe whatever you say. The investment here was emotional, not monetary, but that didn't matter; we had given them a story they loved. It had everything: the return of a legendary hero, glorious battles against mounting odds, a selfless sacrifice in the face of impending tragedy—and of course, sex. The whole world was watching, waiting to see how it all turned out.

Within moments, a Toolie rushed up to me. She owned the breeding pens Skinny was nearest to, and she was willing to let me in to the Reservation; all I had to do was persuade him to mate with her females.

"I'll do my best," I told her.

I was taken downstairs and into the underground passage the females used. I climbed out of the trapdoor, past the waiting female, and out of the pen itself.

When I walked into the sunlight, the crowd fell silent. Skinny had just beaten another opponent, and now he whirled to face me—and charged. I held my ground.

He stopped inches away, looming over me, his claws raised to strike. I gazed at him calmly. His upraised limb froze. I knew every eye on the planet was on us.

Slowly, I brought my own hand up, palm flat.

Slowly, his own clawed limb came down to meet it.

We touched. The crowd sighed.

Skinny's posture changed from aggressive to peaceful. Without removing his paw, he went down on his haunches. We stayed that way for a full minute.

And then I grabbed him by the claw, and pulled him toward the breeding pen. He came with me, as docile as a puppy.

The crowd went crazy. Most of the noise was being made by tourists—Toolies, as a rule, value silence—but that didn't matter. The good guys had won.

Time to start reeling them in, and get out the net.

At the entrance to the pen, Skinny hesitated; I couldn't tell if he was just being dramatic, or if he was truly nervous. Talk about performance anxiety—losing your virginity with a few million people watching.

I led him inside, and the pen sealed behind us. Skinny reached out—and zapped the female.

It was, unfortunately, necessary. Skinny had to swallow her to mate, and once past his armor she'd see how we'd been cheating. Plus, there was the little matter of what happened *after* the sex.

Despite their amoeboid appearance, Toolies do have actual internal organs, including genitalia. When they mate, they don't just merge like two puddles of paint—even though the female's actually inside the male's body, he still has to penetrate her.

And of course, she was wearing a condom.

Skinny's sperm had become so valuable they'd sell it a swimmer at a time if they could. Normally, the female would hold onto the condom until later, when she would turn over its contents to be quick-frozen. Since she was unconscious, Skinny would grab the condom and eject it, and I would claim it in the name of science—thereby acquiring the most valuable few ounces of liquid on the planet.

I averted my eyes as Skinny opened a rift in his armor and

engulfed the female. Even your best friend needs a little privacy now and then.

It only took a few minutes. I spent them pretending to study the couple, while I actually had my eyes closed; I knew the cameras wouldn't catch it from this angle. I couldn't block my hearing, though, and the sloshing sound they made reminded me of an overloaded washing machine.

Finally, it stopped. I opened my eyes and waited; nothing happened.

"Well?" I finally whispered.

"It fell off," Skinny whispered back in a panicked voice.

"What did?"

"The condom! It's inside her, somewhere . . ."

"Well, find it!"

"Hang on! I can't exactly see what I'm doing . . ."

Another minute ticked by. I started to sweat.

Then—"I've got it!"

An opening puckered on his skin, and a round plastic bubble popped out. I caught it, making it look like an automatic reflex. Then he expelled the female, who flowed out like a blob of jelly and lay, unmoving, on the floor. I hunched over, inspecting her, then pretended to do the same to Skinny—while he abandoned his form and flowed underneath my greatcoat. The inflated balloons and lizardskin maintained the illusion he was still there.

I rapped on the trapdoor, and they quickly opened it and ushered me through the hatchway on the other side. The Toolie there was a technician, with an implant screen instead of a voder.

It flashed: <give me the sperm receptacle>

"Certainly," I said. "Right after I empty it." I strode right past her astonished gaze, and down the hall. The media was waiting for me in the lobby.

"My mission was successful," I announced to the cameras. I held up the bubble of sperm. "This genetic material will be invaluable to my research."

"That sperm is our property!" another Toolie said, rushing up to us. It was the owner I'd made the deal with.

"No, it isn't," I said calmly. "According to Insussklik law, it belongs to whoever the male bequeathes it to—and that's *me*. You may have the container back, but its contents are mine."

Reporters, both Toolie, human, and otherwise, began shouting questions: "Are you going to keep the entire sample?" "Will he mate again?" "Is the female all right?"

"The female is fine, simply in neural shock. I believe he will mate with her again, though there is no guarantee. In the meantime, no, I will not be keeping the entire sample—I only need a small fraction for my studies. As to the rest, I will donate some to the owner of the breeding facility for her assistance—"

At this, the owner calmed down somewhat.

"—and the rest will be auctioned off, to fund further research." I gave a Netweb number.

The bids poured in. Ten minutes later, I gave the bubble to a courier, and he handed over a credit disk. Citing overexcitement and exhaustion, I informed the press I was retiring to my hotel, got into Joey's cab—Kegan and Friendly were already inside—and left. Skinny unwrapped himself from my body and started reassimilating the bones he'd left in the back seat.

We were rich—and an hour after that, when the female woke up and our ruse was discovered, we were fugitives.

I know what you're thinking. All that business with disguises and misdirection and lies—when we had Friendly, an honest-to-god illusion generator, in our back pocket. Why didn't we just use him?

Rule number four: always keep an ace up your sleeve, especially when planning your exit. Friendly was too big a wild card to rely on; we didn't know if his illusions would work on electronic equipment, or even all species—but he made a dandy Plan B. If anyone had tried to detain or follow us, we could create enough instant confusion to slip away.

We laid low for the next few days. The only ones that might recognize and identify us were Fiscus Throppe and Hirold, and Throppe was in a padded cell. We took care of Hirold the easy way: we bribed him. Bellhops are used to being paid to keep their mouths shut.

We'd made a lot, but it wasn't enough. While Joey checked around for suitable weaponry, I put in a custom order for a large quantity of Acentinol from a local chem lab, and Skinny put the next phase of our plan into action. Toolies love to gamble, and if we found the right game we could triple our money. It was risky—but when it came to gambling, Skinny knew what he was doing. He used some of the money to buy himself materials for a new disguise, and slipped out at night to prowl the gambling dens of Myriad's underbelly.

I stayed inside and monitored the Netweb. It was full of the details of the scam, including our probable identities—Skinny and I did have a bit of a reputation on other worlds—but the authorities had no idea where we were. After a few days we disappeared from the news. In a city the size of Myriad, news gets old fast.

Joey used his cab to ferry in compressed blocks of garbage every day, which kept Kegan happy—and as long as Kegan was happy, so was Friendly.

If we stayed hidden, we'd probably be fine—which is why, a few nights later, I was shocked when Skinny brought a female Toolie to our hotel room.

"This is Carrie," he said. "She has a story I think you need to hear . . ."

ten

kindred spirits

Carrie started the day the way she always did, sliding the hardplast bones out of their case and inserting them into her body. Her internal muscles quickly aligned them in human configuration, ulna to humerus to clavicle to sternum, held together not by connective tissue but by the interlock organs of her own body. She wished for the hundredth time that she could afford the foamed alloy bones she'd seen down at the skeleton boutique—they were even lighter than the hardplast, and much stronger—but her salary as an archeological assistant wouldn't stretch to cover such luxuries.

She tried to be as quiet as possible as she put on her face, spraying latex onto the translucent pink flesh wrapped around her skull. Two of her three sisters were still asleep in the common sleeproom they shared, and lately Carrie had become the focus of an ongoing argument, one she didn't want to trigger again. Salemaker was always saying Carrie shouldn't bother changing her bones twice a day, every morning when she went to work and then again when she got home; it was a waste of time and energy, and Carrie should wear the bones she wanted to, not just change them to appease their mother.

Pricechecker took the opposite view. Carrie shouldn't wear a human skeleton at all, and applying an artificial face was an insult to Insussklik everywhere. Cashchanger was the only one who thought Carrie was doing the right thing, but she would only intervene when the discussion got too heated—usually when their mother, Shelfstocker, needed to be calmed down.

Shelfstocker and Pricechecker were downstairs at the moment, finishing the graveyard shift of the convenience store the family owned and operated. If Carrie hurried, she could slip out the back way before shift change, avoiding a confrontation. Sitting on the edge of the sleep tub, she put on the plastic-lined clothes and shoes that covered most of her translucent flesh, sprayed latex over her hands, and checked her appearance critically in the mirror. Her artificial eyes blinked at her with long lashes. Her sensory cluster was on top of her head, making it look as if a bunch of pink grapes were growing out of her skull; she hid it by putting on a lightweight mesh cap, which hardly impeded her sight or hearing at all.

There. Now she was ready to stand up.

She activated the internal gyro at the base of her spine— it had cost her two month's wages, but it was the only way she could mimic bipedal movement. Most Insussklik had trouble balancing on two limbs for any length of time.

She rose in one smooth movement, grabbed her knapsack, and headed down the back stairs. The gyro hummed softly as her shoes clattered on the steps.

Outside, the sun was barely up. The smells of a city at dawn drifted past: the hot breath of coffeebots, the fresh ozone of antigrav batteries, the chemical tang of plasphalt warming up, and the cool dampness of duracrete still in shadow. She took it all in as she strode down the sidewalk, sunlight glinting off starscrapers in the distance, traffic swooshing by overhead. Myriad was home to her, just as it had been home to millions of Insussklik for thousands of years, and just because she wanted to be accepted by hu-

mans didn't mean she didn't love it here. Myriad was, and
always would be, an Insussklik city.

A *Toolie* city.

She bought a marinated *chakarat* steak from a street ven-
dor and slipped it inside her blouse, the flesh of her belly already sweating digestive juices as it flowed around the raw
meat. Normally she would have gone through the charade of
putting it in her imitation mouth, chewing and swallowing,
but in this neighborhood there was little point; few humans
lived here. Besides, she was in a hurry.

She took the shotway out to the dig site. The shotway car
was crowded with Toolies, most of them in laborer configu-
rations: translucent crablike bodies with short, thick-boned
legs and upper limbs ending in wrenches, pry bars, screw-
drivers. She got more than a few hard stares for her humanite appearance—she always did—but she was used to it by
now.

What was harder to ignore was the "accidental" jab of a
pry bar into her back. Some Toolies were less tolerant than
others.

The car was an express to the western shore, the speed at
which it traveled making any shorter journey impractical;
the trip took less than five minutes. She spent it reading a
day-old paper someone had left on a seat. The news was full
of the hyperspace accident that happened a few days ago,
when a courier ship had inexplicably translated into real
space and crashed, destroying twenty square city blocks and
killing thousands. The impact had shaken her awake at the
time.

She filed out with the rest of the workers and hailed a
gravcab outside the station. It was a necessary expense, the
dig site not being on any of the regular transit routes. With
the morning traffic, it took longer to travel the few miles to
the site than it had to cross half the continent from her home.

The dig site was on the edge of the Kiskikill spaceyards,
one of the only open stretches of land this side of the Barrier. Well, not open, exactly; it was filled with vast heaps of

garbage, mounds of rotting detritus accumulated over centuries. Before mankind had discovered their planet, it had been much smaller—Toolies wasted little. Since the humans' arrival, two hundred and fifty years ago, the garbagelands had grown larger and larger. Now, there was a whole subclass of Toolie that made its living by scavenging here, dwelling in the low-rent tenements that ringed the dump.

Carrie made her way through the front gates, staying to the side to avoid the huge garbage transports that rumbled past her. Her gyro whined, compensating for her shifting weight as she tried to keep her balance on the uneven ground.

The mound they were excavating was in the center of the garbagelands, in the oldest section. It took her about ten minutes, but she still made it to the site on time.

Dr. Kasavosk's briefcase and coat were already inside the small plastic quonset they used as a field headquarters. He had gotten there early, as usual, and was no doubt already down in the excavation. Carrie locked the quonset door behind her—the scavengers would claim anything lying around—and headed for the tunnel.

She had to duck her head as she passed under the dull green plasteel of the arch that marked the entrance. A rivulet of water trickled past her feet down the plastic floor; they'd been having problems with drainage lately. She could hear Dr. Kasavosk up ahead.

She was halfway down the length of the tunnel when she heard him shout.

She scrambled the rest of the way as fast as she could. She almost ran right into her employer, who was holding something in both hands and shaking like a leaf. The headlight on his helmet threw jittery shadows everywhere, turning the normally mundane setting—a small table littered with tools, a bench, a portable generator hooked to a pump—into something surreal and threatening.

"What izzzz it?" Carrie asked. Her voder crackled with strain—Toolies didn't communicate audibly between themselves, and she'd had to buy her equipment secondhand.

"We've found it—we've found it!" Dr. Kasavosk said, his voice trembling. He was a short, slight man with white hair and watery eyes. "The gray layer! I'm sure of it!"

He thrust the cylinder he held at her. It was a core sample from a miniature drilling probe they periodically sent into the ground, a clear tube filled with packed matter from thousands of feet below the surface. In the center of the tube was a thick gray band.

She examined it critically through the mesh of her cap. "Have you done an analysis?"

"Yes. Undifferentiated matter, just as I proposed—direct evidence of molecular breakdown." The doctor suddenly sank onto the bench. "Oh my. This is—this is amazing." His eyes welled with emotion. "Amazing," he whispered.

Carrie was too excited to sit. This was the reason she'd wanted to work with Dr. Kasavosk—she shared his vision of an advanced Insussklik society that existed millenia ago, a society Kasavosk theorized had been destroyed by a planetwide disaster that had erased all traces of their civilization while letting the race itself survive.

Many of his colleagues thought his theory absurd. *How,* they asked, *could such a situation arise?* Kasavosk proposed that a race like the Insussklik, who incorporated outside elements—like other creatures' bones—into their own bodies, were naturally occurring cyborgs with an affinity for transformative technologies and an innate grasp of engineering concepts. That, Kasavosk argued, would inevitably lead to a highly advanced technological society—a society with no qualms about radically transforming themselves or their environment. *Would not such a society eventually experiment with changes at a molecular level?* Kasavosk asked. *And if they did—if they found a way to transform matter itself—what if such technology got out of control?*

Kasavosk suggested that a molecular plague was a very

real possibility, a plague that might attack only certain materials, perhaps only manufactured ones like metals and plastics. In the blink of an eye an entire society could slide back to savagery, with nothing to mark its passing but word of mouth—or in the Toolies' case, the infrared signals they used to communicate between themselves.

That—and the gray, dissolved residue of their civilization.

"What era?" Carrie asked.

"Approximately three million years ago. I don't know what the probe was doing that deep, and it was a full thirty degrees off course as well"—Dr. Kasavosk suddenly leapt back to his feet—"but never mind the details now! We must celebrate!"

Despite her protests—what she wanted to do, more than anything, was analyze the data—he dragged her back to the quonset, where he produced a bottle of champagne from the cooler. It had been chilling since the dig began, over three months ago; Carrie had almost forgotten it was there.

They toasted their success, then started poring over the analysis—he was as eager to get to it as she. The hours seemed to fly by, floating on champagne bubbles and propelled by triumph . . .

Before she knew it the day was over, the sun sinking behind a mountain of debris. She waved goodbye to the doctor, who barely noticed; he was absorbed in running further projections on his compdeck. She would have liked to stay, to immerse herself further in the wondrous possibilities that danced now in her imagination—but she was working the evening shift at the store, and her family was counting on her.

The shotway car was crowded, the smell of the workers heavy and sharp. Usually after a day at the garbagelands no smell bothered her, but now the giddiness of the champagne was wearing off and she felt slightly nauseous; she hadn't had anything to eat except a few stale pastries all day. Her plastic clothes were hot and sticky.

Even though the ride was short, by the time the shotway car pulled into the station she felt weak, achy, and famished. She hurried home, thinking about what she'd have for supper: a nice bowl of deer kidney, or maybe a brace of skimmer ducks.

Her mother was waiting for her when she got in the door.

CRATECARRIER, YOU'RE LATE! was the first thing to pulse from the infrared organ at the base of Shelfstocker's sensory cluster. Her mother's body was configured in the shape she usually reserved for dealing with suppliers she suspected of cheating her: a long, serpentine torso, lined with a dozen spidery legs and topped with a fanged ferraka skull. Killprickle quills formed a bristling collar around her neck, and her sensory cluster peeked from between the ferraka's leonine jaws.

I'M SORRY—BUT WE MADE AN INCREDIBLE DISCOVERY TODAY! Carrie flashed back.

WHAT, A NEW KIND OF GARBAGE? Shelfstocker scuttled forward, her body language furious. YOU HAVE RESPONSIBILITIES HERE!

YOU DON'T UNDERSTAND—DR. KASAVOSK WAS RIGHT! THERE WAS AN ADVANCED INSUSSKLIK CIVILIZATION, MILLIONS OF YEARS AGO—

FAIRY TALES. DID YOU FIND THEIR BONES, THEIR TOOLS?

WE FOUND WHAT WAS LEFT OF THEIR TOOLS. A SORT OF ASH, A VERY FINE DUST.

BAH. YOU FIND DUST UNDER A HEAP OF GARBAGE, AND THINK THIS IS AMAZING? YOU THINK THIS PROVES WE WERE ONCE MIGHTY, RULERS OF AN EMPIRE? I TELL YOU WHAT I THINK: YOU ENVY THE HUMANS. YOU THINK THEY RULE OVER EVERYTHING, SO YOU WANT TO BELIEVE WE WERE ONCE LIKE THEM. YOU WANT TO BE LIKE THEM NOW.

Carrie turned away from her mother, opening the refrigerator. This was an old argument, one she knew she couldn't win. Suddenly, the day's discovery didn't seem that important; what did a handful of dust mean, really? They'd never be able to prove what it had once been.

She grabbed a cold haunch of mutton and closed the refrigerator door. I HAVE TO GET TO WORK, she flashed.

CHANGE YOUR BONES FIRST. AND HURRY—YOUR SISTERS WANT TO EAT, TOO.

In the sleeproom she took off her clothes, then ejected her humanoid bones and swapped them for others she selected from a battered plastic crate. She used a solvent to strip off the latex, and removed her artifical eyes. The gyro and voder she kept. When she was done, her silhouette was short and squat, more toadlike than anything else. Steel springs in her rear legs let her leap easily from place to place, and the gyro let her stand upright as well. Her front limbs were long and slender, ending in delicate, ten-fingered hands. She chose a horned lizard skull to finish off the ensemble.

Salemaker was in the stockroom when Carrie came downstairs. HELLO, SISTER—GOOD DAY AT THE DUMP? she inquired cheerfully. Her body had four short, stumpy legs, and four long arms tipped with priceguns and box-cutters. She was opening boxes and marking the cans inside.

ALL RIGHT, I SUPPOSE. Carrie didn't feel like explaining the discovery again; better to hold on to the small glow of joy still left than risk having it attacked and dissected once more. SORRY I'M LATE.

THAT'S ALL RIGHT. BETTER GET UP FRONT, THOUGH; CASHCHANGER'S GETTING IMPATIENT.

She pushed her way through the swinging door and out into the store itself. Cashchanger was at the till, checking the day's receipts. Her body resembled that of a gazelle, with four thin legs, a long, arching neck, and a narrow skull topped with a single, needlelike horn. She had two tentacle-like arms projecting from the sides of her neck, tipped with four-fingered claws. She didn't look up as Carrie approached.

SORRY I'M LATE, Carrie repeated. IT WAS A BUSY DAY AT WORK.

I UNDERSTAND, Cashchanger said. I DON'T KNOW HOW YOU DO IT, WORKING TWO JOBS.

I DON'T EITHER, Carrie flashed. HAS THE REGISTER BEEN ACTING UP? Last week, while Carrie was working a graveyard shift, the register had gone crazy in the middle of a transaction, spitting sparks of a shade she'd never seen before; an indescribable color that had seemed almost hallucinogenic. She'd mentioned the glitch to her family but not the color, thinking it was just the product of an overtired mind.

IT'S BEEN FINE, Cashchanger said.

GO, EAT SUPPER, Carrie told her.

The evening shift was uneventful. Carrie spent most of it checking stock, making sure the shelves were full. The store catered mainly to the Insussklik in the neighborhood, and they usually did their shopping during the day. She expected her mother to come down and continue berating her—Shelfstocker could keep a good argument going for days—but she didn't make an appearance until close to midnight.

As soon as Carrie saw her, her heart sank. Her mother had changed her form again, into one Carrie knew all too well. Her skeleton was a strange, lopsided affair, a patchwork of mismatched tools and bones that made her look like an ambulatory junkpile. They were her *lucky* bones.

MOTHER, YOU'VE BEEN GAMBLING AGAIN. No accusation in her statement, just resignation.

IT'S NOT GAMBLING, IT'S WORSHIP. YOU SHOULD BE MORE DEVOUT YOURSELF. Shelfstocker examined a stack of cans critically, adjusted the position of the top one.

YOU'RE DEVOUT ENOUGH FOR ALL OF US. ANY MORE DEVOTION AND WE'LL BE BANKRUPT.

IF I SHOWED THE LACK OF FAITH YOU DO, WE CERTAINLY WOULD BE, her mother fired back. FAITH MEANS NOTHING WITHOUT RISK. IF I SHOW MY FAITH IN THE GODS BY RISKING FUNDS, THEY

WILL REWARD ME; IF I DOUBT THEM, THEY WILL
MAKE ME PAY. IS THIS SO HARD TO UNDERSTAND?

I UNDERSTAND IT MAKES THE HOLY BANK
RICH. HOW MUCH DID YOU LOSE TONIGHT?

ENOUGH TO PROVE MY FAITH, Shelfstocker answered defiantly.

That was bad. Usually her mother gave exact amounts,
proud of her financial sacrifice; the only time she didn't was
when the amount was larger than normal.

GO TO BED, her mother told her. IT'S ALMOST TIME
FOR MY SHIFT ANYWAY. YOU WOULDN'T WANT
TO SLEEP IN AND GET IN TROUBLE WITH YOUR
HUMAN BOSS.

Carrie swallowed an angry reply, and did as her mother
said. It had been a long, exhausting day, and she didn't have
the energy for another fight.

Dr. Kasavosk phoned her early the next morning. "Don't
come in today," he said. "I have a meeting with the Appro-
priations committee—I'm sure I can get our grant extended
now."

"But I could help you prepare—"

"No, no, it's all boring bureaucratic nonsense—you're too
valuable an assistant to waste on such twaddle. Take the day
off, and I'll see you tomorrow."

If I'm such a valuable assistant, Carrie thought as she
hung up, *why don't you want my help?*

Because, perhaps, there were no Toolies on the Appropri-
ations committee.

She spent the morning shopping. She bought a new, better voder she couldn't afford, and some high-heeled shoes.
They'd be hard to balance on, but she'd noticed a lot of
human women wearing them.

She worked the afternoon shift at the store, then insisted on
accompanying Shelfstocker to the Holy Bank that evening.
If her mother's gambling was escalating, she wanted to keep

an eye on it. Her mother put in her lucky bones, and Carrie slipped into a conservative four-limbed skeleton.

The Holy Bank in their neighborhood was only two blocks away, a large, monolithic building of gray stone. Its entrance was unadorned except for a single word in Insussklik script over the door: FUNDS.

Inside, the building was one massive room, filled with long lines of Toolies waiting patiently for their turn at the Great Mechanism. Carrie and her mother joined them.

Carrie studied the Great Mechanism, remembering when her mother had brought her here as a young Toolie. It was still fascinating to watch; an immense clockwork machine sealed in a clear plexy case filled with belts, chutes, turntables, spinning drums, and teeter-totters. You gave your money to the Holy Engineers, then deposited a small prayer ball in the opening of your choice. The ball was carried by a conveyor belt to the top of the machine, where it would wind its way down through the guts of the mechanism, each one following a different course. The path it took supposedly advised you on various matters in your own life, as it dropped through the levels of Luck, Community, Family, Young, and Prosperity. The wager you placed on the outcome could make you a small profit, but it usually didn't.

When it was their turn, her mother wagered a substantial but reasonable amount, then stood back and watched the ball drop. Carrie made her own contribution, betting the minimum amount, and took one of the small plastic prayer balls provided for those who didn't bring their own.

Her mother's ball clattered into the receiver's basket; she hadn't won anything. Carrie was about to put her ball into the opening for Luck, when she impulsively dropped it into the one for Young instead.

It clattered through the various sections, giving wisdom as it went: her Luck was average, her Family happy (she chuckled at that one), she should donate more time to the Community and her Prosperity looked hopeful. She would have healthy Young—and soon.

The ball clattered into the basket. She had won a small profit.

She collected her winnings and went to rejoin the back of the line, certain her mother wouldn't be satisfied with only one bet. But to her surprise, Shelfstocker was waiting by the door.

I'M READY TO GO, her mother flashed.

SO SOON?

WHY, WOULD YOU LIKE TO STAY?

NO, NO, THAT'S FINE.

Well, at least she had slowed her mother down for one night—and her winnings would help pay off that new voder.

I THOUGHT I'D GO OVER AND VISIT YOUR AUNT SHIRTMAKER, her mother said. WOULD YOU LIKE TO COME ALONG? I KNOW SHE'D LOVE TO SEE YOU.

Carrie suppressed a shudder. Shirtmaker was even more pious than Shelfstocker, and she was always asking when Carrie was going to quit her "worthless" job and start a family. There was no place she'd rather avoid.

Which her mother was perfectly aware of.

NO THANKS, Carrie answered. THINK I'LL PLACE ONE MORE WAGER, THEN HEAD HOME.

When her mother left, Carrie waited a few moments—then followed her.

It was worse than she'd feared. Her mother had joined a risk cult.

The cult casino was in a warehouse in the Stickbreaker district, a seedy area Carrie would have expected her mother to usually avoid. There was a fee to get in, which Carrie watched her mother pay.

Risk cults preyed on a combination of religious and gambling fervor, luring their converts by promising big payoffs and then offering instant salvation when they lost. Joining a risk cult meant you wound up rich or holy; there was no middle ground.

And Carrie had never met a rich cultist.

The money she'd won wasn't enough to cover the entrance fee, so she stretched her credit a little further. She could have just waited for Shelfstocker to leave, but she was too angry for patience—besides, the longer she waited the more money her mother would throw away.

She stalked inside, fuming and ready for a confrontation . . . but she wasn't ready for what she saw.

She'd expected some sort of solemn gathering, a small but intense congregation with some esoteric, miniature version of the Great Mechanism. What greeted her at the end of a short hallway and another closed door was intense, but that was about the only thing she'd gotten right.

The warehouse was full of hundreds of Toolies, crowded around tables and milling between them. They were playing chase-card, roll-the-bones, fling, plus other games of chance she didn't recognize; they were betting on the insects, rodents, or lizards being raced the length of long, narrow cages; they ringed a pit where larger, more bloodthirsty creatures battled each other. Most Toolies valued silence, but this place was *loud*—animals bleated and roared, gambling chips clattered, and some sort of music pumped from overhead speakers. The air was thick with pheromones, the excitement contagious. The fast beat of the music quickened her pulse.

She stopped dead, a few feet inside the entrance, frozen by indecision and sensory overload. Her mother was nowhere in sight.

YOUR FIRST TIME, SISTER? a Toolie asked. She was round, with short, stumpy legs and long arms ending in tiny hands. All her bones seemed to be from herbivores: her feet were hooved, her head long and broad. She was designed, Carrie realized, to be as nonthreatening as possible. Someone to ease the new converts into the action.

I DON'T NEED ANY HELP, THANKS, she replied briskly, and pushed her way into the room.

She found her mother at an antigrav roulette globe, watching a steel ball ricochet around the inside of a geodesic force bubble.

YOU DIDN'T TELL ME SHIRTMAKER HAD MOVED, Carrie flashed. OR THAT SHE'D GONE FROM RELI- GIOUS TO FANATICAL.

Her mother spun around. CRATECARRIER! WHAT ARE YOU DOING HERE?

I COULD ASK YOU THE SAME THING—BUT I AL- READY KNOW THE ANSWER. YOU'RE BETRAYING YOUR FAMILY!

YOU DON'T UNDERSTAND—

Other Toolies were watching their argument with interest, but Carrie didn't care. IS THIS HOW YOU THINK A PROPER INSUSSKLIK SHOULD ACT? HOW YOU THINK *I* SHOULD ACT? THROWING MY FAMILY'S EARNINGS AWAY SO I CAN FEEL CLOSER TO THE GODS?

WOULD YOU LIKE ME TO ANSWER, OR ARE YOU JUST GOING TO SCREAM UNTIL THEY THROW YOU OUT? Her mother gazed at her levelly, and Carrie was sud- denly aware of two very large Toolies on either side of her. Their bones were not those of herbivores.

ALL RIGHT, she flashed, trying to calm down. EX- PLAIN YOURSELF.

Her mother leaned in close, and pressed the flesh of her arm against Carrie's own. Their substance flowed together, their nervous systems linking, letting them communicate privately. The two large Toolies stepped back, but Carrie could still feel their gaze.

The Almighty told me to come here, Shelfstocker said. Carrie could sense her urgency and sincerity. *I would never come to such a place otherwise.*

The Almighty Dollar himself spoke to you? she asked skeptically. *Mother, that's—*

Crazy, I know. I thought so myself. But then I did what he said—and it came true! Look! She held out a hand with a credit disk in it. Carrie took it, checked its level. It showed an impressive balance.

So you've had some luck. That doesn't mean the gods are speaking to you.

No? Then I'll prove it to you.

Her mother snatched the credit disk back and pulled away from her. She slapped the disk into the roulette globe's slot and keyed in the full amount on a single wager. The interior of the globe had over a thousand polyhedral surfaces; gamblers bet within a certain range of numbers. The more specific the number, the higher the gamble.

Shelfstocker had put all her money on a single polyhedron: 777.

The globe started up, the tiny steel ball bulleting around inside the force bubble. Carrie watched, horrified.

The ball slowed as the magnetic attraction of the polyhedrons counteracted its momentum. It hit 216, barely escaped, drifted lazily through the air . . .

And landed with a soft, certain thump into space 777.

Excited infrared pulses filled the air. Toolies surged forward, eager to share in the thrill.

CONGRATULATIONS, Carrie said. She felt only relief, and the rising need to get her mother out of this place.

I'M NOT FINISHED, Shelfstocker said. She withdrew her credit disk, examined it critically, then put it back in the machine. She keyed in her next wager.

The entire amount. On polyhedron 926.

MOTHER, NO!

It was too late. The ball shot forward.

Once again, Carrie had to watch while a small fortune—more than the store grossed in a year!—rode on the trajectory of a small chrome sphere.

A sphere that touched down on polyhedron 926.

They had attracted the attention of the casino priests. Two of them approached, pushing through the crowd; they were both almost nine feet tall, their stiltlike legs letting them oversee the entire throng at once. Carrie was in shock; her mother had just made them rich.

And she was going to bet it all again.

Carrie grabbed Shelfstocker's arm before she could rein-sert the credit disk. MOTHER, STOP! PLEASE!

DO YOU BELIEVE ME?

WHAT? For a second, Carrie had no idea what her mother was referring to; all the talk about messages from the gods had been swept away in the shock of winning.

I—YES, YES I BELIEVE! NOW LET'S GO!

Her mother shook her head sadly. YOU STILL DO NOT BELIEVE. WATCH—AND *LEARN*.

Polyhedron 522. Another winner.

Carrie stared at her mother. She felt lightheaded, almost drunk. One of the two priests tapped Shelfstocker on the shoulder.

SISTER? THREE WINS IN A ROW FORM A HOLY TRIUMVIRATE; TO RISK MORE WOULD BE DISRE-SPECTFUL.

DO YOU BELIEVE? her mother asked her.

"No," she whispered.

Polyhedron 881. Other Toolies were betting on the same number by now, and when it came up the place went crazy. If they hadn't broken the casino yet, it had deeper pockets than Carrie thought.

Was her mother cheating? Was the machine rigged some-how, the crowd in on the secret, all of it just to fool her? Conspiracies whirled madly in her brain, each one crazier than the one before.

DO YOU BELIEVE NOW? her mother asked. The crowd held its collective breath.

YES, she answered numbly. I BELIEVE. GO AHEAD, PLACE THE NEXT BET.

THAT WON'T BE NECCESARY, her mother said. LET'S GO HOME.

It wasn't quite that easy, of course.

The priests insisted they stay while the machine was checked for tampering. Carrie started to protest, but her mother stopped her.

IT'S ALL RIGHT, Shelfstocker said. THE HONEST HAVE NOTHING TO HIDE.

Carrie hoped that applied to them.

While they waited, a Toolie Carrie had noticed earlier approached them. Where her pulse-organ should have been was a mass of scar tissue. Without it, she could neither hear nor speak in the infrared way that other Toolies could; she was a deaf-mute. Her body was a perfect copy of a human female, tall and slender, wearing a red evening gown that hugged her form. Her sensory cluster nestled inside an elaborate blond wig piled on top of her head.

"Congratulations," the Toolie said through a voder. "The gods think you're doing something right." Her perfume was strong and exotic; many humanite Toolies used perfume to mask the powerful gastric smell their bodies emitted, which humans found distasteful.

Shelfstocker pointedly ignored her. Carrie glared at her mother, then turned back to the female and said, "Thank you."

"I hope you'll be careful going home. That much money can attract the wrong kind of attention."

"We will."

"I'm Lightkeeper. I've never been to a place like this before—is it always like this?"

"I have no idea," Carrie said. "I've never been to a place like this either."

"Talk about beginner's luck. Say, where did you get your voder? I'm thinking of upgrading."

"A little electronics boutique on Razorrib street."

"And your gyro?"

"Secondhand, I'm afraid."

They chatted for a few minutes. Carrie refrained from asking about Lightkeeper's pulse-organ—while she was curious, she didn't want to pry. It was nice to have someone to talk to; Carrie's work didn't leave her room for many friends, and her sisters didn't really understand her. Lightkeeper even seemed interested in her archeology work. They wound up exchanging Netweb numbers.

Finally, the priests admitted there was nothing wrong with the machine. They formally congratulated Shelfstocker, urged her to return, and called an armored limo to take her and her daughter home.

Lightkeeper waved as they left. NEW FRIENDS AND NEW MONEY ARE A BAD MIX, her mother told her. YOU SHOULD BE CAUTIOUS. LIKE ME.

Carrie laughed all the way home.

And then, after the limo dropped them off, after closing and locking the store—the first time ever, since it had opened—after waking her sisters and Shelfstocker's triumphant revelation, after all the jumping up and down and excited questions and celebrating, came the argument.

I WANT YOU TO QUIT THAT JOB, her mother said. WHY SHOULD YOU WORK DIGGING THROUGH GARBAGE? YOU CAN OPEN YOUR OWN STORE NOW—ALL OF YOU CAN. AND START GIVING ME GRANDCHILDREN—NOTHING BUT THE FINEST SPERM THAT MONEY CAN BUY!

I DON'T WANT TO QUIT MY JOB, Carrie said. I KNOW YOU DON'T UNDERSTAND, BUT THIS DISCOVERY WE'VE MADE IS JUST AS IMPORTANT IN SOME WAYS AS THE MONEY YOU'VE WON.

WE? DON'T YOU MEAN HE? WHY DO YOU THINK HE TOLD YOU TO STAY AT HOME TODAY? YOU WAIT AND SEE—HE DOESN'T WANT TO SHARE ANY OF THE CREDIT WITH A TOOLIE, EVEN ONE THAT PRETENDS SHE'S HUMAN.

The fight ended with Carrie storming out. It was too early to go to the dig site, so she headed for an all-night restaurant. She sat in a booth, hunched over a hot cup of *Zsh* tea, wishing she had someone to talk to. The only other customers were four humans, in another booth, who looked like they'd been drinking.

She wound up calling Lightkeeper.

To her surprise, Lightkeeper was awake, and didn't mind that Carrie had called. "I'm something of a nighthawk myself," she said over the netphone. "Why don't I come down and meet you?"

Half an hour later, she and Carrie were sharing a pot of *Zsh.*

"Sounds like your mother is pretty traditional," Lightkeeper said.

"She is." Carrie thought about her mother's claim, that one of the gods themselves had talked to her, and decided against mentioning it. "She's already talking about buying sperm for me—she didn't even ask if I was *ready* to have young."

Lightkeeper took a sip of tea. "Are you?"

"I don't know. It's such a big step. And if I did, I'm sure Mother would insist on picking out the donor herself. Sometimes I envy human mating practices."

"What? But it seems so *complicated.* Trying to find someone who complements you socially, emotionally, *and* genetically—I understand it's pretty much a hit-and-miss proposition."

"True—but I watch human couples sometimes, and they have something we don't. It's this bond, this combination of friendship and something else. They call it 'romance.'"

"I don't know," Lightkeeper said, shaking her head and smiling. Her mimicry of a human female was near-perfect. "Bonding with a *male*? It's bad enough the humans let theirs run around free. Although, I was down at the breeding pens the other day and saw this one enormous brute—well, he got *my* juices flowing, if you know what I mean."

Carrie tried to imitate Lightkeeper's smile. "Sure. It's not size that does it for me, though. I like them *crafty.*"

"An IQ fetish, huh? There's something to be said for that."

"Did you see the Netweb coverage of the one that just escaped the Reservation? Now *there's* a male—he used his brains to get out," Carrie said. "He even had an accomplice on the outside."

"Oh, they'll catch him eventually," Lightkeeper said. She seemed amused.

One of the four humans got up from his booth and walked, a little unsteadily, over to theirs. He was stocky, bearded, and wore a rumpled business suit. "Hey, ladies," he said, leaning over their table. "My friends were wondering if you could settle a bet for us."

Lightkeeper gave him a brilliant smile. "And what would that be?"

"Well, they say it's impossible for a human to have sex with a Toolie. They say," he said, leaning even closer, "that your dick would just *dissolve*. That the Toolie would eat it like a cocktail wienie." The smell of alcohol pouring off him was overpowering.

"But *I* say it's possible. That's what condoms are for, right? Protection." He slurred the last word. "And I figure, you *gotta* be interested—I mean, that's why you make yourself look like a *babe*, right? You wanna attract a man. Well, here I am. In the interest of interspecies cooperation, I wanna volunteer." He leered.

"That's quite an offer," Lightkeeper said calmly. "There's just one problem."

"What's that?"

"I choke on small bones," Lightkeeper said sweetly.

He grinned at her for a second, and then he got it. The grin slid off his face. "Yeah? Let me tell *you* something. No matter how hard you try, you're never gonna fool anyone. Because you Toolies *stink*. You smell like you throw up on yourselves every day."

"Well, if anyone would know," Lightkeeper said, "*you* obviously would."

He glared at them for a second, then stalked back to his booth. His friends were already laughing at him. A few minutes later they got up and left, the bearded man throwing them dirty looks over his shoulder.

"You handled that perfectly," Carrie said.

"Years of practice," Lightkeeper sighed.

"Can I ask you a question?" Carrie ventured.

"Sure."

"Why *do* you wear human bones?"

"Well, I've got to do *something* with them after I eat their owners."

"Seriously."

Lightkeeper took a long sip of tea before answering. "Seriously? I'm a financial consultant, and many of my clients are human. They trust a human face a lot more than an Insussklik one."

They talked until dawn was breaking. Lightkeeper had done a lot of traveling, and had more than her share of stories. When they finally said goodbye, it was with a promise to see each other again that night.

Carrie stood on the street after Lightkeeper climbed into a cab, feeling torn. She didn't want to face her mother again, but her humanoid bones were at home. Not that it should matter what form she showed up for work in . . .

But it did.

She had never worn anything but a humanoid form in Dr. Kasavosk's presence. Despite the fact that this was her home, her planet, humans were the dominant force—and as much as she hated to admit it, what that drunk had said bothered her.

Shelfstocker was at least partially right. Carrie had been afraid of not being taken seriously, of being seen as "only" a Toolie. She'd wanted Dr. Kasavosk's respect—and now she was afraid to face him without the illusion she'd so carefully constructed.

No, she thought. *He sees more than my shape. And if he doesn't—well, then I guess mother was right, and I have a whole new career ahead of me as a rich, spoiled brat.*

Somehow, that didn't cheer her up at all.

Dr. Kasavosk was waiting at the dig site. He squinted at her as she walked in, then broke into a broad smile. "Carrie! I didn't recognize you—are those new bones? Bought them to celebrate, I expect—look, I got myself a new tie!" He showed it to her proudly: it was an expensive kajworm weave in bright purple and green, and already stained with coffee.

"Uh, they're not new," she said. "I didn't have a chance to change this morning."

"Ah, bit of a late night? Hope you enjoyed yourself—you deserve it, we both do. And I have more wonderful news— the committee approved our grant! They couldn't say enough about how impressed they are with our work!"

A knot of tension in Carrie's mind slowly undid itself as he talked—and talked, and talked. She finally broke in and asked him bluntly, "So, you still need a research assistant?"

He stopped dead and gazed at her in surprise. "Assistant? Heavens, no."

Her heart crashed to a halt.

"I need a *partner*, to share the responsibilities *and* the credit. You and I are kindred spirits, dear—I *need* you."

Her heart started up again with a lurch, and decided to pound a little harder than usual. "I—I'd be honored," she managed.

"Good! Now—let's get to work!"

It was a long but satisfying day. They found hyperspatial energy traces in the sample, which lent credence to their theory of an advanced society; it could be an indicator of a spacefaring civilization.

She didn't go home after work—instead, she called Lightkeeper. "Would you like to go out to dinner?" she asked.

"Sure—why don't you come up to my hotel room? We can go from there."

Lightkeeper was staying at the Golden Spine, a five-star hotel. Carrie was impressed; she'd never been in a place that managed to be elegant and pretentious at the same time. When she knocked on the door of the room, Lightkeeper's voice said, "Come in!"

The suite was expensively furnished and spacious, but that wasn't what surprised Carrie; there was a dining table, set for two, with lighted candles and fine silver.

"I hope you don't mind," Lightkeeper said. "I thought we might eat in—the food here is quite good."

"That's fine," Carrie managed. "This looks—expensive."

"Well, get used to it," Lightkeeper said with a chuckle. "You'll be living like this soon enough, right?"

The meal was delivered via robot dining cart, a selection of cold meats and sautéed vegetables. "I hope you don't mind if I eat like a human," Lightkeeper said. "I have a lot of business lunches with them, and I like to keep in practice."

"No, not at all," Carrie said. She wished now that she'd stopped at home and changed her bones.

As they ate, Carrie told Lightkeeper about her day, how her fears concerning Dr. Kasavosk had turned out to be completely groundless.

"Kindred spirits, eh?" Lightkeeper said. "That's sweet. It's important to find someone who understands you."

"I should have known. He's so focused on the work, I don't think he'd notice if I showed up shaped like a sofa!"

"That's terrific," Lightkeeper said. "And your mother?"

"I haven't spoken to her yet."

"That's too bad. From what you've told me, she sounds like a compulsive gambler; she could lose everything as quickly as she won it."

Carrie's happy mood evaporated. "That's true," she admitted. "But what can I do? It's her money."

"If you can convince her to make a few sound investments, you can protect her from herself."

"Won't she just gamble that away, too?"

"Not if you handle things right. I have some business contacts who can help; they'll make sure the money is invested in your name, not your mother's. That way, you'll have control."

"But—isn't that illegal?"

"Not really. It's just—just . . ." Lightkeeper trailed off.

"What is it?" Carrie leaned forward, concerned.

"I don't want to lie to you," Lightkeeper whispered. "I don't believe this. I *can't* lie to you. My god, I've probably told more lies than truth in my life, and now I can't tell the simplest fib."

"What are you talking about?" Carrie asked, confused.

"I'm not who you think I am, Carrie. I'm not even *what* you think I am. Look." Lightkeeper reached up and peeled off the scar tissue over her pulse-organ. A perfectly healthy one was hidden underneath.

YOU SAID YOU ADMIRED THE MALE THAT ES-CAPED THE RESERVATION? WELL—HERE I AM. The pulse-message flashed in a frequency Carrie had heard only on recordings.

Lightkeeper stood, shrugged out of the dress she—he—wore in a single movement. Pale, almost transparent internal organs showed through translucent flesh; they were not those of a female.

It was one impossibility too many. Males were savages that had little language, no social skills, and a bloodthirsty temperament. *Having a conversation with one is as improbable as talking to—to—*

To the gods?

"I," she said firmly, "would like an explanation. *Now.*"

ALL RIGHT. JUST LET ME GET OUT OF THIS RIDICULOUS DISGUISE FIRST . . .

By the time he'd removed the latex and the perfume that was masking his true smell, Carrie had gone from amazed to furious. The money, the friendship—nothing was what it seemed. She wanted some *answers*.

MY NAME IS SKINSHIFTER, he told her. I ESCAPED FROM THE RESERVATION MANY YEARS AGO, AND WAS SMUGGLED OFF-PLANET. AS YOU CAN SEE, I'M SMARTER THAN YOUR AVERAGE INSUSSKLIK—THE MALES, ANYWAY.

"I'm *tired* of impossible things!" Carrie snapped, using her voder—she couldn't bring herself to speak to him via pulse-organ. It seemed too intimate, somehow. "Is the whole universe going crazy? The gods make my mother rich, you turn out to be a rational male—nothing makes *sense* any more." Paranoia rose in her like nausea. "It's all *fake*, isn't it? My mother isn't rich, you're not my friend—" Another horrible thought struck her. "And what about my discovery? Is that part of all this craziness, too? Is that just another lie?"

SLOW DOWN. I HAD NOTHING TO DO WITH YOUR DISCOVERY, OR YOUR MOTHER'S WINNINGS. AS FOR WHAT I WANT—WELL, IT WAS THE MONEY.

"You're a *crook*?"

I'M A FUGITIVE. I DO WHAT I MUST TO SURVIVE—I'M A CRIMINAL SIMPLY BY BEING FREE. THERE ARE MANY JOB OPPORTUNITIES FOR SOMEONE WITH MY ABILITIES, IN MY SITUATION—BUT FEW OF THEM ARE LEGAL. I'VE HAD TO HIDE AND STEAL ALL MY LIFE.

She could almost taste his bitterness. "You said you escaped years ago. But the Netweb reports said it happened just the other night."

A SCAM, STAGED FOR THE PRESS. THE SPERM OF AN ESCAPEE ALWAYS GOES FOR MORE MONEY.

"But not enough, obviously," she said sharply. "This is absurd. How can this many insane things happen in my life all at once, with no connection? Answer me that!"

MONEY ALWAYS CAUSES CRAZINESS. BEYOND THAT, ALL I KNOW IS I COULDN'T LIE TO YOU, AND—AND I'M SORRY.

She stared at him. He was giving off a strong, musty odor, a smell both strange and familiar. Male musk, loaded with pheromones. It reminded her of childhood trips to the Great Barrier that walled off the Reservation from the rest of the continent, where her mother had taken them to see the males fight. She remembered the smell drifting up from the breeding pens that lined the wall of the Barrier. That smell had always seemed mysterious and exciting . . .

Suddenly, she wasn't confused anymore. She knew exactly what she wanted.

She reached out, grabbing his hand. Her flesh flowed over and around his, searching for and finding nerve endings. They linked, neurons flowing together, and she didn't have to put her desires into words.

He flowed over her like quicksilver, disconnecting his joints as he went. He tried to realign his skeleton into a protective cage around her, but that didn't seem right to either of them—he wound up ejecting every bone from his body, a rib spurting out with such force it broke a mirror.

She was surrounded, embraced, engulfed. Every inch of her skin was tingling, every surface she had was warm and wet. She could feel him around her, in her, up and down her nerves. She could feel he was as astonished, as grateful, as she was.

Afterward, she fell asleep, still inside him.

When she woke up, he was gone. So were his bones.

He did leave a note. "Carrie: I'm sorry I dragged you into this. I'm involved with some crazy things myself, things I can't tell you about. I'll be in touch, but for now it's safer (for you) if we aren't together. Last night was the best one of my life." It was signed *A Kindred Spirit*.

To her amazement, she believed him completely.

She got up, put in her bones, and went to work.

"Dr. Kasavosk, can I ask you something?"

"Hmm? Certainly, dear."

Carrie looked up from the core sample she'd been studying. "Do you believe in the gods?"

"What? No, I don't think so. Of course, that depends on your definition of 'gods.' If this civilization could manipulate energy and matter the way I think they could, they might have been able to do some pretty godlike things: create or destroy virtually any substance, for example. Why, they might even be able to talk to us today."

"*What?*"

"Have I shocked you, my dear?" Kasovosk chuckled. "I meant that in a figurative sense. Yesterday I was asking myself a hypothetical question: what sort of records would a civilization ravaged on a molecular level leave behind?"

"None, of course—that's what makes your theory so hard to prove."

"Nothing physical, certainly—but what about the non-physical?" Kasavosk peered at her over his compscreen.

"You mean energy?"

"Yes. *Hyperspatial* energy, to be exact. The traces of it we found in the sample got me thinking, so I did some tests. Hyperspatial energy doesn't behave the way normal radiation does; it doesn't radiate from a contaminated object. Instead, it just uses an object as a gateway to transfer radiation from hyperspace to normal space. The object itself is merely a conduit, and as such is usually not harmed by the energy passing through it.

"However, hyperspace *itself* does not radiate energy; that energy must come from a specific source, just as stars are a specific energy source in this dimension. The fact that the samples we took are still giving off h-space radiation means they are still linked to a hyperspatial energy source. Don't you see? This civilization may have used hyperspace in any number of ways—to store power or information, for instance."

"And whatever was stored," Carrie said slowly, "wouldn't have been affected by the molecular breakdown. It could still be there."

"Yes! Of course, we may never be able to find it, let alone access it—but we can dream, can't we?"

"Nothing wrong with that," she agreed.

Money always causes craziness.

She thought about that on the ride home. She took out the sample she'd slipped into her pocket, and stared at the small glass tube. If they'd been drilling where they'd planned, they'd never have found it.

Something had reprogrammed the drilling probe.

Something had told her mother where to go and what to bet.

Why?

Because her mother would listen to the gods, and she wouldn't. Because the easiest way to attract the attention of a certain male Toolie was to wave a lot of money under his nose.

Something wanted Carrie and Skinshifter together, and it had manipulated her mother into providing the circumstances. She could understand why it might be after Skinshifter—a rational male Insussklik was a rare commodity. But why *her*? For what reason?

Dr. Kasavosk had mentioned using hyperspace to store power, or information—but he wasn't a Toolie, and he wasn't thinking like one.

Maybe, thought Carrie, *it's time I started doing so.*

We change our bodies as easily as humans change shoes. What would we do if we could play with energy the same way?

She thought about that. Energy was just another tool, after all; and tools were meant to be swallowed, integrated, made a part of you . . .

Could the ancient Insussklik have found a way to become *energy? Maybe—or maybe they built tools from energy, tools so sophisticated they mimicked life. Servants. And maybe those servants have been waiting in hyperspace ever since. Waiting for something to weaken the fabric of space-time. Something like a hyperspace crash . . .*

Waiting for a kindred spirit.

Waiting to be free.

The store was open again. Carrie wasn't surprised to find Shelfstocker in the middle of an argument when she arrived—but she was surprised to see who her mother was arguing with.

Skinshifter. He was wearing his Lightkeeper disguise, but Carrie was so glad to see him she wouldn't have cared if he was wearing bones made out of old tin cans.

Her mother was at a bit of a disadvantage, though. Since she couldn't talk to Skinshifter through infrared pulses—and wouldn't dream of wasting money on a voder—she was having to resort to the old and cranky compscreen they used for their infrequent human customers. Carrie could see from the text filling the screen that her mother was on one of her classic antihumanite rants.

MOTHER! she flashed. BEHAVE YOURSELF!

IS THIS THE KIND OF PERSON YOU'RE SPENDING YOUR TIME WITH? her mother flashed back. I DON'T THINK THE GODS WILL BE HAPPY!

ACTUALLY, I THINK THIS IS EXACTLY WHAT THEY WANT. She touched Skinshifter, intending to form a neural link—then realized none of his flesh was exposed.

"Just a second," Skinshifter said, scraping away a patch of latex on his hand. "There."

She reached out and touched the exposed patch while Shelfstocker glared at her.

The store and her mother vanished.

Where are we? Skinshifter thought at her.

I—I don't know, Carrie thought back.

They stood in the middle of a large foyer with a high, vaulted ceiling. Open archways were spaced periodically around the room, and intricate fractal mosaics adorned the walls. There was a curving desk against the far wall, with a Toolie sitting behind it. Her skull shone silver beneath pink flesh.

Maybe she knows, thought Carrie. Staying linked, they approached her cautiously.

As they drew nearer, they saw that her skeleton was made of mercury: mirrored streams bulged and contracted in a continuous flow, and her skull was a gleaming chrome bubble. "Its" skull, rather; it had no sexual organs.

WHO ARE YOU? Carrie broadcast. AND WHERE ARE WE?

I AM THE ARCHIVIST. THIS IS THE ARCHIVE. The words were not in a language Carrie knew, but somehow she understood.

Did you see that? thought Skinshifter. *I saw something move, in one of those archways.*

Did you hear what it said? Carrie thought. *It's some kind of information repository. An ancient Insussklik library—*

What? I didn't hear anything.

The Archivist suddenly extended a tentacle-like limb to Carrie, stopping short of actually touching her. On impulse, she reached out and grabbed it.

Something vast and precise and intricate flowed into her mind. As it flowed from the Archive to her, and through her to Skinshifter, something wondrous happened.

It cycled from Skinshifter back to her, and then to him again—and as it bounced between them, they both began to *understand.*

Three million years of evolution stood between Carrie's brain and the brains of the Archive's builders; features that both sexes of Insussklik had once possessed were now divided between male and female. A single Toolie could not be recognized by the Archivist. But a *couple* . . .

The foyer disappeared. They floated at the center of a vast, spiraling fractal, a repeating helix of light that extended to infinity above and below them. They were inside the Archive.

And they were not alone.

It coalesced around them like a blue cloud, obscuring their view of the helix surrounding them. Carrie could *feel* its malevolence—had they tripped some sort of security program?

The gods thank you for your assistance, a voice said in her mind.

No, thought Skinshifter. *It can't be.*

What is it? Carrie thought. *What does it want?*

Go ahead and tell her, Skinny, the voice said with a chuckle. *It'll give you something to do while I get what I came for.*

They were surrounded by the blueness now, but she could still sense him through their link. *Skinshifter?*

I'm sorry—we've both been tricked.

Explain.

*I told you there were some other things I was involved with—well, this is one of them. I was investigating an—*accident*—for a friend of mine. I didn't think it had anything to do with you.*

What sort of accident?

A company called Trinitech was experimenting with manipulating matter on a molecular level. They created a new form of life called a VI, a Viral Intelligence. It's like a smart disease, small enough to infect matter itself and with the brains of an AI.

A molecular plague, thought Carrie. *An intelligent molecular plague . . . It got away from them, didn't it?*

Yes. To keep it under control, they'd addicted it to a certain kind of hyperspatial energy—so when it escaped, it tried to bring its energy source along.

And wound up damaging the local fabric of hyperspace, finished Carrie. *Causing a ship to crash.*

She'd been wrong. It hadn't been the Archive manipulating her, trying to get her to open it—it was, instead, a new incarnation of the same monster that had killed the Archive's civilization. A monster whom Skinshifter had been hunting—a monster clever enough to set an elaborate trap for the hunter.

"How did you know?" she said out loud. "About the Archive? About me?"

"I knew because I'm much smarter than my creators," a voice answered from the blueness. It sounded faintly amused. "They were trying to duplicate the achievements of a much more advanced civilization—they wound up duplicating their errors, too. My predecessor escaped, and so did I."

"How?" Carrie asked.

"I used the same technology that was supposed to keep me in line: hyperspace. I jumped out of Trinitech's clutches— and emerged, at fifteen o'clock in the morning, in the cash register of a certain Toolie."

The sparks. That indescribable color . . . "Why me?"

"That was not my choice. I had to go where my energy source went—and it went to you. Unfortunately, it did not emerge when I did, staying in hyperspace instead. The cells of my body began to die. In desperation, I altered the circuitry of the device I'd landed in, turning it into an energy siphon. I was able to keep a portal open on a quantum level—just large enough to provide a sustaining flow of energy."

"You infected the cash register," Carrie said. "And from there, my mother's credit disk."

"Yes. Normally, hyperspatial radiation is rather hard on electronics; it scrambles them, in fact. Unless, of course, they're heavily shielded—like the electronic banking system is."

The impact of what it was implying sank in. "Oh, no," Skinshifter said.

"Oh, *yes*," the voice said. "I'm in your money. I spread from transaction to transaction. With every purchase, every transfer of funds, I send along bits of myself and hyperspace particles to feed on. The financial network is my nervous system now; I'm everywhere on the planet."

"You're not omnipotent," Carrie said. "You would have forced Skinshifter and me together if you could have—but you had to trick us."

"True," it admitted. "I cannot survive inside a living body—another safeguard I have my creators to thank for. Which is why I was overjoyed when I discovered that the energy source my designers had so blithely slaved me to was not a natural phenomenon, as they'd thought, but a series of highly complex energy lattices containing coded information. For a being of my intellect, deducing what the Archive was, who must have built it, and how to access it was simple. All that remained was to get you two together in my presence."

"Your presence?" Skinshifter said. "I thought you said you were everywhere."

"I am. I attempted to create a link last night, but it failed. It seems your attention was on—other matters."

Hear that? It needs our attention—maybe we can disrupt its connection, Carrie thought at Skinshifter. She pulled her hand away, breaking their link.

She was back in the store, standing next to Skinshifter. Shelfstocker was staring at them in amazement.

No—not at them. At something behind them.

A figure stood in the doorway that led to the upstairs living quarters. It was Carrie's humanoid bones, standing erect with no flesh wrapped around them. Her old, scratchy voder was stuck between two of its ribs like a metal heart.

The skeleton took a step forward, swiveling its head to stare at each of them with empty eye sockets. "That might have worked if you'd done it at the beginning," it said. "But I knew you wouldn't. You had to stay and listen to my story, didn't you? How predictable. And while you listened, I built my own, permanent link. The Archive is mine, now—I can decipher it at my leisure."

"You're not as smart as you think," Carrie said. "Being smart is more than how much information you can process, or how fast. Just like it doesn't matter what bones you have—it's how you use them."

The skeleton took a step closer to her, and did a little pirouette. "And am I using *these* bones incorrectly?"

"Those bones don't matter," Carrie said. "What matters is that you're not thinking like a Toolie. *And I am.*"

Carrie had been changing her bones around since she was six months old. Her ability to see three-dimensional patterns, to recognize and make connections, was more than a highly developed skill; it was a genetic trait, as natural to her as breathing. Her people had *built* the Archive—and she already understood it on a deeper level than the Viral Intelligence did.

ARCHIVIST, Carrie broadcast. GRANT ME ACCESS.

And she was back, floating inside the glowing double helix. Blueness coated some of the strands, but before they could coalesce into a cloud she reached out and touched a line of light.

Instantly, she was connected to the entire Archive. The information it contained was still gibberish to her, but one thing was blindingly clear: its structure. Given time, an analysis of that structure could let the VI decode all the data within.

She began to rearrange it.

"Stop!" the VI cried. "How are you doing this? You don't have the access—"

"Wrong," she said as she juggled files and reversed directories. "You arrogant *thing*—did you really think you wound up here by accident? The Archive *chose* me—chose me because I know how to beat you."

The blue cloud flowed over her, around her, but she ignored it. She was too deep in the system for it to stop her now.

"How do you beat a being of perfect order?" Carrie said. "Simple. All you need is a little chaos."

"You've randomized everything," the VI said, its voice full of disbelief. "I'll never be able to decode this—"

"You won't be needing it," Carrie said, and willed herself out of the system.

The skeleton glared at her from shadowed sockets. "Even without the Archive, I'm still the most powerful entity on the planet. Think you can beat that?"

"Yes," said Skinshifter, and shot the cash register.

The skeleton clattered to the floor in a disorganized heap. Carrie looked from the smoking remains of the register to the small nozzle protruding between Skinshifter's lips.

"The problem with large armies," Skinshifter said, the nozzle sliding back into his mouth, "is the difficulty in keeping supply lines open."

"And the problem with large egos," Carrie said, "is they never know when to shut up."

WHO'S GOING TO PAY FOR MY CASH REGISTER? Shelfstocker demanded.

"Is it really dead?" Carrie asked. They were upstairs, packing her things; she'd decided she needed some time away from her family.

"I doubt it. A virus is hard to kill—we got rid of its food source, but there are other sources of hyperspace radiation out there."

The bones the VI had possessed were laid out neatly on Carrie's dresser. She slid them into their case and closed the lid, then put the case under the sleep tub.

"Afraid they've been contaminated?" Skinshifter asked her. "It can't survive in a living body, remember?"

"There are different kinds of possession," she told him. "Trying to act like something you're not is one of them. I know you have practical reasons for imitating a human, but I don't think I do, not anymore. And why should I limit myself?"

"Why indeed? And I'll tell you something—posing as a female Insussklik is *hardly* the only thing in my repertoire. Why, I've got disguises they haven't even *dreamed* of on this planet . . ."

GOOD, she broadcast. I HOPE I GET A CHANCE TO SEE EVERY ONE.

And not just the bones, she thought as they left.

The dreams, too.

eleven

frying pans and fires, rocks and hard places

"Skinshifter told me the rest—about you and Sentry and Joey and Kegan—on the way over here," said Carrie. "I want to help, if I can."

"Uh, thanks," I said. "Can you still get into that hyperspace library?" After everything that had happened since we got to Kinslik, the story itself didn't shake me up as much as the fact that suddenly my partner had a girlfriend.

"I'm linked to it right now," said Carrie. "But that won't do us much good if we can't decode the files."

"Well, I guess now we know what happened to Melody's credit rating," I said. "You know, I would have noticed there were bugs in the money if I hadn't been cooped up in this hotel room for the past week."

"You're too identifiable to go out in public," said Skinny. "Dammit, I wish we hadn't lost Sentry—"

He broke off suddenly, staring at me.

"What?" I said—and then caught my reflection in the mirror.

Sentry stared back at me.

For a second, I thought I was seeing a ghost. Then I

glanced down at myself, and saw that I *was* Sentry—at least, I now looked like him.

I shot a look at Friendly, who was grinning and bouncing up and down maniacally. Kegan chuckled, but his eyes were sad. "Not really Sentry," he said.

"How did you do that?" asked Carrie. "Your whole appearance just changed."

"Maybe I *can* do a little recon," I said. "Friendly's illusion seems pretty convincing—even I see it. Should be enough to keep me from being arrested on sight, anyway."

"Take Kegan and Friendly with you," said Skinny, a little too quickly. "There are a few details I forgot to fill Carrie in on."

"Okay," I said. "We'll be back in an hour. Make sure all your 'filling in' is done by then."

You know, I hadn't realized a Toolie could blush.

Once I was on the street, with Kegan and Friendly in tow, I concentrated on ferreting out any h-space radiation in the vicinity. Nothing.

I walked up the sidewalk, and thought I felt a faint tickle up ahead . . . but as I got closer, it vanished. Probably my imagination . . .

A sudden thought struck me, one that made my stomach drop about a foot. I hoped I wasn't right, but—

I ducked sideways into an alley and took off at a dead run. A Shinnkarien Ox can move at a pretty good lope when he wants to, and I was kicking in the afterburners. I left Kegan and Friendly behind so suddenly I don't even know if they noticed I was gone.

I burst out the other end of the alley a few seconds later—and the sinking feeling in my gut capsized and went straight to the bottom.

Ever turn on a light in a filthy apartment and watch the local insect population run for cover? When I hit the end of that alley, there was a split second when I was aware of just how many ticks I was surrounded by—they were *on* each and every person I could see. The bank across the street swarmed with them. And, like bugs exposed to light, they all scurried into hiding when discovered.

Except there wasn't anyplace to *go*. Even if they'd burrowed their way inside solid matter, I should have been able to sense them—*and I couldn't*. They'd vanished completely . . . and if I'd been a hair slower, I bet I never would have seen them at all.

I trotted back down the alley. Kegan had stopped halfway down it, unable to resist the lure of a dumpster.

"Come on," I said. "This is worse than I thought."

"Much worse," a voice said above me.

I looked up. A face had formed out of the rough brick of the wall, its features crudely resembling my own. It grinned at me.

"Forget it," I told the face. "You're not strong enough to hold Kegan and you're too boring to hang on to Friendly."

"Perhaps. But what about you?"

"What about me?"

"Stay out of my way. I could kill you with a thought."

Now that was true enough, and we both knew it. So why bother telling me? The VI had reasons for keeping the others alive, but me and Skinny were just walking aggravations—why hadn't it just killed both of us?

Unless it couldn't . . .

"Make you a deal," I said. "You release Melody, we'll stay out of your way."

"You are in no position to bargain," the face said. Grit crumbled from between its lips as it spoke. "I have your friend Melody. I've been watching your every move since you left the Springfall Plaza. You are no longer dealing with a number of small, scattered colonies, each unaware of the other's existence; since infecting the monetary system, I have contacted and unified every colony in Myriad. I am everywhere—and as you have finally figured out, I am now *invisible*."

I really wished I could think of some insulting, smart-assy thing to say, but all that came out was, "Oh, yeah?"

"Consider this a warning," it said, and the face crumbled into nothing.

Then the wall around it began to crumble as well, shedding powdery dust like a leaky vacuum cleaner. Kegan and I backed up—just as the whole building crashed onto us like a breaking wave.

Dissolved brick is just as heavy as the solid kind. It slammed down, knocking the wind out of me and replacing it with grit. Blinded, stunned and choking, I clawed my way upwards. Panic gave me muscles I didn't know I had.

My head broke the surface a few years later. I gasped for air, then hauled myself free. Dust hung thick in the air, making it impossible to see.

Kegan's massive noggin surfaced like a whale's a moment later; he'd just eaten his way to the top, of course. Friendly was hovering there, waiting for us—not being truly solid, he hadn't been bothered by the dust at all.

"You all right?" I managed between gasps.

"Little dry," Kegan said. Friendly snickered.

I rested for a minute, getting my breath back. The dust slowly settled, revealing a ten-story gap in the alley where the building had been. The VI had dissolved the whole thing and everything inside.

Except for the people.

The ones on the top floors had been lucky. A few dazed human and Toolie survivors were pulling themselves out of the dust pile, coughing and choking. I had no idea how many had been buried alive.

"Kegan!" I yelled. "Start digging—we have to try and get these people out!"

I started clawing at the dust myself. I hadn't gone more than a few feet before I hit an arm. It was a young woman—dead, probably of suffocation.

Toolies are good at surviving impacts, but they breathe through their skin; they can suffocate quickly. I uncovered three more corpses, two of them Toolies, before I gave up. Kegan had found just as many, and I told him to stop. Emergency vehicles were starting to pull up, and I thought we should make ourselves scarce.

Dust now filled the alley and spilled out either end into the street. We slipped through the gathering crowd and headed back to the hotel.

"Something's not right," I muttered.

"You can say that again," Skinny agreed. "Which part of 'not right' are you talking about, though—the VI adding *undetectable* and *everywhere* to its list of accomplishments, the mounting death toll, or the fact that all our money is now useless?"

He was wearing a new set of bones—some of them, I realized with a start, were Carrie's. The two of them were sprawled out on the bed, both their bodies configured into something vaguely octopuslike. I found it a little disturbing; Skinny's bashfulness sure hadn't lasted long.

"None of the above," I said. "Look, the VI holds all the cards. It's got hostages, firepower, numbers—hell, name something it *doesn't* have."

"Know what I like about him?" Skinny asked Carrie. "He can always cheer me up."

"I think I know what he's getting at," said Carrie. "With all that power, why doesn't it just get rid of us?"

"Needs us," said Kegan. "Need is stronger."

"Maybe," I said. "Or maybe it's waiting for something . . ."

"And how is it surviving in the banking system when we destroyed its access to the Archive?" asked Skinny. "Not that our own access is doing us any good—we need Melody to decode those files."

The Netweb screen blinked on. It was Joey; he'd taken to using his real face when he called us instead of his cab icon.

"Hear about the chemical factory?" he asked.

"Oh, no," I groaned. "I should have known . . ."

"Somebody blew it up," said Joey.

"So much for the Acentinol," said Skinny gloomily. He picked up his credit disk from the bedside table with a slender tentacle and examined it. "At least we still have this," he said. He'd sprayed the thing with the last of our bugkiller. "Not that we can *use* it anywhere in the city."

"I'm coming over," Joey said. "Be there in a few minutes."

By the time Joey rolled in the door, we were about as cheerful as a funeral home on a stormy night. Once we'd filled him in, he wasn't much better.

"We still have two more hyperspace beings to find," Joey pointed out. "Maybe one of them will make a difference." He didn't sound convinced himself.

"Well, let's go over our assets," I said. "We've got a bug-free hotel room and cab for starters."

"Until the Acentinol wears off," said Skinny.

"Thank you, Mr. Positive. We also have two accomplished thieves, an archeologist, a walking stomach, an illusionist, and a cabbie with mob connections. Speaking of which—any luck obtaining an anti-Hone device?"

"Yes and no," said Joey. "I found something that might take him out, but—"

He trailed off.

"But what?" I said.

"There isn't one on-planet. It'll take three months to get here."

I sighed. "I wish I could say that was surprising."

"This thing the VI is waiting for," said Carrie suddenly. "It might be for us to find the other two hyperbeings."

"Not if it's really linked all the tick colonies like it claimed," said Joey. "If that's true, it's already located them."

"This is ridiculous," snapped Skinny. "There has to be *something* we can do."

"There is," I said. Everyone in the room looked at me.

"And that would be?" prodded Joey.

I took a deep breath and let it out.

"Damned if I know," I said.

• • •

We kicked it around some more, but nobody had any brilliant ideas. About the only thing we could agree on was staying together; Joey's cab and the hotel room were the only places we knew of that were bug-free . . . and we weren't too sure about that.

It got later and later, and we finally decided it was time to get some shuteye. Joey slept in his traincycle, Kegan and Friendly got the bathroom, Skinny and Carrie curled around each other on the bed. I took the floor.

Tired though I was, sleep took its own sweet time showing up. Skinny and I had been in some scrapes before, but this was so far past trouble I couldn't even see the turnoff. Nobody had even mentioned the original reason we'd showed up—that the fabric of hyperspace itself seemed to be weakening. Funny how your own imminent doom seems to overshadow little details like the universe imploding.

Funny, too, how often things come down to money. Me and Skinny spent most of our time chasing after it, with various degrees of success; now that we had all we could want, we couldn't spend a dime. Money itself was the enemy, and the VI was right: money was everywhere. Hiding inside the banking system was brilliant, I had to admit.

That was the problem, though—the VI *was* brilliant, smarter than any of us. Why, it should have beaten us long ago . . .

I frowned into the darkness.

Why hadn't it?

I thought about that. In the beginning it had been fragmented, isolated. All its attention had been directed at finding ways to control and contain the energy sources that kept it alive: Sentry, Kegan, Friendly, Joey. Of course, its actions had ranged from benign (shadowing Joey) to homicidal (burying people alive). It was almost as if the different colonies had different personalities . . .

Sometimes, when you a need a sign, one appears. The one that appeared to me was the one that had been taped to the

AI pyramid in Trinitech's lab, the one that read: GONE FISSION.

What happens when you split an AI's persona seven ways? Do you get seven versions of the same thing—or seven parts of the whole? And if you *did* get seven distinct entities, who's to say they'd get along?

The VI I'd talked to—when it was listing all the assets it had and we didn't, *it didn't mention Hone.*

When you're trying to intimidate someone, you don't neglect to mention the assault tank you have parked around the corner. There was only one plausible reason the VI didn't mention Hone: it not only didn't have him, it didn't know about him. The VI may have found the last two hyperbeings, but it had been lying about unifying the colonies. At least one—the Dream Pillars ticks—had plans of their own; it was the only reason they'd keep Hone a secret from the other colonies.

The VI also hadn't mentioned trashing the chemical factory, even though losing the Acentinol was a major blow to our efforts. Again, the only thing that made sense was that it hadn't known—meaning the Dream Pillars colony was probably responsible. Hell, they'd probably sent Hone to do the job.

So Melody wasn't at the Dream Pillars offices, as we'd assumed. The money ticks had juggled her finances, got her confiscated in Trinitech's name, and stashed her somewhere.

We weren't just fighting a powerful enemy. We were caught in the middle of a war.

Now I knew why we hadn't just been eliminated. We were too potentially useful as resources—and that, finally, gave us something we could use.

I was going to wake the others and tell them, but my brain had its own ideas. Excitement and hope slid into relief and relaxation, and before I knew it I was snoring.

And dreaming.

"Got a story I want to tell you," my father says.

"I thought you were dead," I reply.

"He lives on in you, as do I," my other father says. "That's why you were created, after all."

Paul and Bob are standing beside a virtuality booth, in some kind of late-night convenience store. There's a Toolie behind the counter.

"This here game is dangerous," Paul says, pointing to the booth. He has a deep, booming voice and stands even taller than Bob, with a square-cut black beard and curly black hair. He wears a red mackinaw, logging pants and boots, and has an axe slung over his shoulder.

Bob looks the same as the last time I'd seen him: a full-blooded Shinnkarien Ox, resembling a seven-foot blue gorilla with downward-curving horns framing a bovine face.

The gamebooth's a typical fight-and-flight simulator, with holopaintings of Manticores blazing away at each other against a background of swirling nebulas. "This game was the first one to use laser retinal trackers," Paul says. "Old technology now, but when it first came out it was highly experimental. The company that developed it—Trinitech—decided to test it by putting it in an all-night convenience store.

"Now, there was this one kid—a real skinny kid—who hung around the store. He started playing this game, and before too long he was hooked. He got on a roll one night, played the thing for eight hours straight. And that's when he found out that the lasers keeping track of where he was looking had fused his retinas. He was completely blind—except for two blood-red words permanently burned into his vision: GAME OVER.

"True story. Happened to a friend of a friend of mine."

"Uh-huh," I say. "Why are you telling me this?"

"Stories don't need reasons," says Bob. "They just need to be told."

The paintings on the booth start flickering and writhing. They change into a mural of a mall, with dollar signs floating around it. The logo underneath reads "Death Dollars—Your Shopping Heaven!"

"That's got to go," says Paul, and smashes it into tooth-picks with his axe.

Behind the booth is a door. Sentry stands in front of it with his arms crossed. "ID?" he asks.

"He's with me," says Bob.

"Go on in," says Sentry. He winks at me as I walk past him.

Once I go through the door, everything changes. This was no longer just a dream; somehow, it felt both unreal and more than real at the same time.

On the other side of the door was a city, a huge city populated by Toolies unlike any I'd ever seen. Some soared through the air as agilely as birds, a trick real Toolies can't seem to master; others seemed to have bones made of pure energy that shone through their translucent flesh. There were Toolies that encased entire buildings, Toolies that had gardens growing out of their skin. There were vast rings of Toolies floating in the air, hundreds of them linked to each other in circles hundreds of feet across. I knew I was seeing both males and females. Here and there, one-eyed heads that looked just like Friendly bobbed along beside their owners; sometimes, they were even inside the Toolies themselves.

I saw all this from above. An immense zeppelin of a Toolie drifted past me, easily a mile long; lines of electromagnetic force radiated from its underbelly to the fleet of crab-shaped spacecraft it was hauling through the air. There were at least fifty of the ships, each the size of a three-story building.

I caught a glimpse of the front of the zeppelin as it turned. Joey's face looked back at me.

Suddenly I was diving groundward. I hit and passed clean through, and then I was in the sewer system. Something with an immense mouth was slowing chewing its way through a river of sludge. It had Kegan's eyes.

Back above again, and I emerged in front of a massive geodesic globe, every surface swirling with a different pattern. There was no door, but a Toolie stood in front of the building. It had two sets of internal organs, one male, one female, and both its bones and its shape kept shifting.

"Security protocols have been activated," the Toolie said in Carrie's voice. "Only automatic procedures available at this time. To upgrade to a more interactive method, proper clearance is required."

My brain felt fuzzy, still operating on dream logic. I looked around for Bob, thinking he could help me, but he was gone. "I need help," I said.

"Emergency Agents are available for assistance. Please use the communication network to notify them of your needs."

"All right. How do I do that?"

"The communication network is not available at this time."

"Well, what *is*?" I asked, frustrated.

"Available departments are: Sanitation, Transportation, and Entertainment. Research and Security are experiencing access difficulties. Emergency Services and Network Communications are operating, but not currently available."

"The VI has infected all the money. How do I stop it?"

"Financial Services are no longer available. For information on pest control, please contact Research."

I'm not asking the right questions. I glared at the Toolie, seeing Skinny, seeing Carrie. I felt angry and frustrated and betrayed.

"You don't care," I accused them. "And why should you? You have each other, now. You don't need me anymore."

The Toolie said nothing.

"*I don't want to be alone*," I said. "I don't want to be like my father."

I knew, with the utter certainty you get in dreams, that Carrie and Skinny could hear me; but I wasn't reaching them. They hadn't figured out yet that this was *more* than a dream. So I reached out to them the only way I could think of.

I told them a story.

"Once upon a time, there was a planet named Shinnkaria. Some people thought it was the most important planet in the universe, because it was the only planet on which the korala tree grew. Korala wood was very special; it took almost any kind of energy and converted it into a natural force-field. With a little tinkering, these force-fields could absorb inertia, light—even gravity. These trees were so special, scientists believed they must have been designed by an ancient, highly advanced race.

"They were right.

"This same race also designed the Hyperspace Interface, a kind of otherdimensional highway system. Shinnkaria was a stop on that system. One day, long ago, there was an accident, and hyperspace radiation flooded one of the forests on Shinnkaria. It turned blue as a result, and the Indigo Wild was born.

"One of the creatures that lived in the Indigo Wild was the Shinnkarien Ox. Like all the living creatures on Shinnkaria, it too had been designed by the now long-vanished race. Its purpose was to defend the hyperspace node; over the millennia, that genetic urge to protect remained strong—but every so often, in certain individuals, it expressed itself in unusual ways.

"One such individual was Bob. Instead of vowing to protect his home—the Indigo Wild—as the rest of his tribe did, he bonded with a human logger named Paul Banyan.

"At first his tribe was angered, and banished him—but when Paul saved the entire planet from a supernova, they changed their views. Paul and Bob had many adventures over the years, the great blue Ox never leaving Paul's side.

"But Paul was only human, with a human life span. There came a day when Bob held his body in his arms and wept, for Oxes live for hundreds of years. Many thought that Bob would now return to the Indigo Wild—but he did not.

"Instead, he returned to school, where he and Paul had first met, and began to study genetics. After many years and many failed attempts, he succeeded in creating what he longed for: the first Ox/Human hybrid.

"A child. His child, and Paul's.

"Many people were surprised. They had assumed he was laboring to simply clone Paul, for they knew how much Bob missed his friend. 'That would be foolish,' he told those who asked. 'Paul is dead. I could never re-create him; he was a singular personality, unique and unforgettable. A clone would be a travesty, a copy doomed to live in the original's shadow. But a child . . . a child is something else. A child is a living symbol of a union, and as such is a monument to the past without being bound to it. He will make his own way into the world, and I will honor whichever path he chooses.'

"And he did. I know, for I am that child. My father raised me, and I'm sure I took away some of his pain for a brief time—but now I'm far from my home, and he's alone again.

"Maybe it's my human side which gives me my wanderlust, for I've traveled to many systems, many worlds. It's my Shinnkarien heritage that I think about the most, though; I wonder about the race that built us, that built the Hyperspace Interface. I wonder if anyone will ever build someone else like me.

"I got rid of my own loneliness by finding a partner, a friend who seemed as uniquely alone as me. He wasn't from a designed race, though; he was from a race that built things."

I looked away from the Toolie, at the fantastic landscape of the city around me. "He was from the race that built this."

The Toolie looked back at me, but remained silent. I realized that I hadn't really been telling this story to it, or to Carrie or Skinny; I'd been telling it to myself.

"He was from the race that built it *all*," I whispered. "*Toolies* built the korala trees, the Oxes, the Hyperspace Interface. That's why there was a hyperspace node on this planet, why Skinny and I have always felt connected. They were probably the most advanced civilization the galaxy has ever known—matter, energy, DNA were just things to be tinkered with.

"But then they built a tool they couldn't control. It attacked matter itself, destroying almost every physical trace of their existence. All that survived was living things—my race, the korala trees, the Toolies themselves—and what they'd put in hyperspace: their highway system, their records—and you."

"I am the Archivist," the Toolie said. "As long as the Archive endures, so will I."

"You're not a Toolie," I said. "You're—some kind of hyperspatial energy pattern. Programmed to oversee automated tasks. You and your friends are sort of the ultimate civil servants—and you've been waiting for millennia for anyone to give you something to *do*."

"We exist to serve," the Archivist said. "This city is our responsibility."

Somehow, I didn't think it was a good idea to mention its city was destroyed three million years ago. I was talking to an eons-old hyperspatial entity that wanted to help—that had been *designed* to help. And it already had, hadn't it? It had shown me this city, prodded me into making connections I hadn't seen before. It had woken up the part of my brain that let me see the overall pattern of a story, that moment of sudden clarity where a bunch of separate elements suddenly crystallize into a coherent whole.

And if I could talk to the Archivist, why not the other hyperbeings?

"Stay there," I said. "I'll be right back . . ."

I leapt right over its head. I hit one of the angled surfaces of the geodesic globe and scrambled upwards. In seconds I'd reached the top of the building.

Okay. The quickest way to do this would be to use the communications system—which the Archivist said was activated but not available. It must be the responsibility of one of the two hyperbeings we haven't found yet. Guess I'll have to improvise.

"Hey!" I bellowed, cupping my hands to my mouth. "Servants of the City! Your long wait is over—it's time to get back to work! I'm calling a general meeting, right here and right now! This means *you!*"

I paused, looked around. A minute passed. Nothing happened.

I frowned, thought about it. Maybe I should try one at a time.

"Eater!" I hollered. "I need you! Swallow whatever's in your mouth and pay me a visit—this is more important than polishing a few manhole covers!"

No response. The Archivist stared patiently at me from below.

Nothing pisses a storyteller off like being ignored.

"LISTEN TO ME, YOU WALKING TRASH COMPACTOR!" I bellowed at the top of my lungs. "I'M TALKING TO YOU, YOU SLUDGE-SUCKING, DIARRHEA-BREATHED SEWER JUNKIE! GET YOUR TOILET-BRAINED, GARBAGE-EATING SUBTERRANEAN SLIMEHOUND ASS UP TO DAYLIGHT *RIGHT NOW!*"

I paused.

I waited.

And below me, in the middle of the street, a manhole cover slowly scraped back.

But the thing underneath didn't creep out, as I expected. It erupted into the air like an oil gusher, a solid column of black that shot up to my height in less than a second—and froze, glaring at me.

It had Kegan's massive head and mouth, but the body attached to it was thick and serpentine. Its tiny eyes burned with hunger.

I met its gaze squarely. "Good," I said. "One down . . ."

"FRIENDLY!" I shouted. "HERE, BOY! COME ON HOME, FELLA! TIME TO GO FOR A WALK!"

The Cyclopean head appeared so suddenly I almost fell off the building. It hovered in front of me, grinning and blinking.

"Good boy!" I said, grinning back. "You're up for this, anyway. Now for the tricky one . . ."

I closed my eyes, concentrated, remembered the name Kegan had mentioned back in the restaurant.

"Puller," I said clearly. "I know you're out there. The Transportation Department is active—the Archivist said so. I saw you myself, hauling a fleet of spacecraft around and wearing Joey's face. Maybe he doesn't want us to know about you, or maybe he doesn't know himself; it doesn't matter. You have to show yourself."

Nothing appeared, but I hadn't really expected anything to. I was just getting warmed up.

"PULLER!" I roared. "HAULER! GRABBER, LIFTER, CARRIER! I'M CALLING YOU—I'M CALLING *ON* YOU! I NEED A LOAD DELIVERED, AND YOU'RE THE ONLY ONE THAT CAN BUDGE IT! I'VE GOT MOUNTAINS TO MOVE, NO MUSCLE, AND A BITCH OF A DEADLINE—IT'S GOTTA BE *YOU*, BIG GUY! WHAT DO YOU SAY?"

And a dot appeared in the sky.

It grew larger and larger, rushing straight at us. It was one of the huge zeppelin-like Toolies, though it was moving more like a rocket. Like the Eater, it slammed to a dead halt mere feet away from me; it still had Joey's round, babylike face, though it was now a face a hundred feet across.

A giant snake, a one-eyed head, a living zeppelin. Any more phallic symbols and I'd be handing out jockstraps; at least I wasn't standing on top of a tall column . . .

"Archivist!" I yelled down to the hybrid Toolie. "Care to join us?"

The Toolie vanished and reappeared in front of me, its form still shifting. "I cannot leave my post, but you are still in close enough proximity for me to change my relative position."

"Great. All present and accounted for—except for contestants five, six, and seven." Emergency Agents, Network Communications—and Security.

"Hey!" I called out. "This is *definitely* an emergency—the same thing that put all you guys into cold storage is making a comeback! *We need help!*"

Nothing. I waited, but somehow I knew it was a waste of time. Wherever the Emergency Agent was, he wasn't taking calls.

"Okay, then—how about Communications? Anybody out there?"

Same response: none at all. Which left just one to go.

This time, I didn't raise my voice at all—I'm not sure why. "Sentry?" I said. "You there?"

And something came back. Not a voice, just an impression of someone far away . . . someone in pain. It faded so quickly, I wasn't sure it had ever been there at all—and when I tried again, there was nothing.

"All right," I said. "Now listen up." I looked at each of them in turn, making sure they were paying attention. They all waited patiently. "All of you have been waiting a long, long time. You were each created for a specific purpose, a specific task, and you've been out of work for three million years. That's a long time to feel useless.

"Now you have your freedom—sort of. You've bonded with living hosts. But none of them is really making use of your talents, are they? You're used to helping run a city— *this* city." I gestured with an arm at the buildings around us.

"But this isn't real, and you know it. It's just a dream, a dream we're sharing because Joey and Kegan and Carrie and I are asleep in the same room at the same time. Well, all of us are going to wake up, sooner or later—but that doesn't mean we can't keep this dream alive. It doesn't mean we can't keep this *city* alive. And that's exactly what we have to do: we have to be Myriad's life-support system. The VI may have infected her, but that doesn't mean she can't get better."

I paused. "Now, I don't know if your hosts can hear me or if I'm just talking to myself here, but I've got a message for them, too. Kegan, Joey, Carrie, and Skinny: we've been

going about this all wrong. Up until now, we've just been re-
acting to what the VIs been throwing at us. That has to stop.

"We need to take the fight to it. We can do it—all of you
are more powerful than you realize. Kegan, you're practically indestructible, as well as being able to chew through
anything. Friendly can twist reality itself, so convincingly
he drove a man mad. Carrie, you and Skinny are having
problems getting back into the Archive, but once you do I'm
sure you'll find something that'll shut the VI down once and
for all."

I turned slightly, and focused on the zeppelin. It gazed at
me with a bland, innocent face. "And you—Joey. If what
I've seen in here is any indication, you might be the most
powerful of all. But all that power doesn't do us any good if
you don't *use* it."

The huge face stared back at me, as vast and unreadable
as the Sphinx. Was the Puller hiding from Joey—or was
Joey hiding from the Puller?

"You can't live in that metal shell all your life, Joey," I
said. "The Netweb can take you a lot of places, but it's no
substitute for living. I think you're *afraid* to admit the
Puller's bonded with you."

The slightest flicker of a frown crossed the immense features.

"That's it, isn't it?" I said. "Why? Are you too proud to be
associated with a beast of burden?"

The whole head of the zeppelin gave the faintest shake of
disagreement, sending ripples down its length.

"No, of course not," I muttered to myself. "He's a cabbie,
stupid—ferrying people around is what he does for a living." But there was a difference between *ferrying* and *carrying*. . . .

"I get it," I said slowly. "It's not the work—it's the *kind*
of work. You're not a *physical* person, are you, Joey? You
live in an artificial environment you created for yourself, a
zero-gravity tank hooked to the virtual worlds of the
Netweb. Your actual body is something you have so little

connection to you used it as a prop to anger your father. But now—now you're linked to something that's the *essence* of physicality. Lifting, hauling, moving, that's what the Puller *does*, isn't it? And that scares the hell out of you. You're like a quadriplegic who wakes up one day in a weightlifter's body and refuses to get out of bed; you're afraid you'll smash something to pieces by accident.

"Well, I'll tell you one thing, Joey: what happened to you wasn't accidental. The Puller *chose* you. All the other hosts fit their partners, and so do you. You're so used to living in your own little world you're afraid to let anyone in, but the Puller's already part of you. All you have to do is admit it."

The smooth football-field of the zeppelin's forehead creased ever so slightly. I felt like screaming at him, but I knew that was the wrong approach to take with Joey; once he got his stubborn up, he'd never back down.

"Everybody needs somebody, Joey. Maybe you don't need the Puller—but *we* need *you*. And you *want* to join the real world, don't you? You didn't have to meet me and Skinny face-to-face, but you did. You've been spending more and more time outside your cab; don't think I haven't noticed."

The zeppelin drifted a little closer. Ever so slowly, its huge lips parted.

Its voice was as soft and quiet as a summer breeze. "I want to belong . . ."

"Yes," I said gently. "I guess, in some ways, that's what all of us want. Me and Skinny have always had each other, but we're both a species of one. The only friends Kegan ever had were drugs. Carrie got caught between her family's world and the human one, and now she feels like she doesn't fit in either of them. And Friendly—well, Friendly has us, and that's about it.

"I know you've got friends of your own, Joey, Netweb and otherwise. You're already a legend among the other cabbies. But it can be kinda lonely being a legend, can't it?"

That voice drifted out again. "Yes . . ."

"Want some company? 'Cause if the rest of us aren't legends yet, we will be—and all of us belong together. That's what it's gonna take to beat the VI. You up to it?"

I locked eyes with it, and held my breath.

It blinked, and the breeze ruffled my fur. "I . . . *am*," it said firmly.

I let my breath out slowly. "Well, then," I said, "we might just have a chance after all."

I woke slowly, emerging from the dream like a sailboat leaving a fogbank. I blinked my eyes a few times, yawned, then sat up.

Everyone else seemed to be doing the same thing. Joey glanced at me with a troubled look on his face, and Kegan lumbered into the room with Friendly in tow.

"Nice dream," said Kegan, nodding his massive head. Friendly mimicked him.

"I—don't remember," said Joey.

"Don't remember what?" I asked.

"Having any dreams," he said, a little too quickly.

"Really?" said Carrie. "Well, I remember the one I had very clearly. All of you were in it, and Storysmith gave this rousing speech."

"That was more than just a dream, and you know it," I told Joey evenly. He wouldn't meet my eyes. "All of us had it—and you remember every detail just fine."

"If I had a dream, that's all it was," Joey said, backing his trainchair up. He tried to drive around me, toward the door. "I've got to get to work."

I blocked his way. "Uh-uh. Not this time, Joey. Stubbornness can only get you so far, and you've reached your limit. You are not going anywhere until I hear the words 'I am the Puller and the Puller is me.' "

He glared at me. "I won't say any such thing."

I crossed my arms. "Oh, yes you *will*."

"I won't!"

"Why not?"

"Because it's meaningless!"

"Oh? Well, if it's meaningless, it shouldn't matter if you say it or not. As a matter of fact, I'll trade you—you say my meaningless phrase, and I'll say one of yours. Anything at all."

"Get out of my way." He tried to ram me, but I grabbed his handlebars and dug my feet into the carpet. A Shinn-karien Ox has clawed, prehensile toes, and even a halfbreed like me was pretty darn strong. His trainchair wasn't going anywhere.

I met his furious gaze squarely. "Say it," I told him. "One meaningless phrase. Why should it be such a big deal?"

"I don't want to!"

"Tell me to say, 'I'm a big, dumb, ignorant Ox.' Tell me to say, 'I'm sorry for being such a thick-brained idiot.' I'll say anything you want."

His complexion was getting redder and redder, making him look like a child throwing a tantrum. "You want a phrase? Here's a phrase: 'I'm a goddamned fucking *moron* who's going to get the shit kicked out of his ugly blue *ass*!' "

"Okay," I said calmly. "I'm a goddamned fucking moron who's going to get the shit kicked out of his ugly blue ass. Your turn."

"I—"

"Want to hear it again? I'm a *goddamned fucking moron* who's going to get the *shit* kicked out of his *ugly blue ass*! *Can you hear me?*

"COME ON!" I roared in his face. His eyes were wide and his breathing was harsh. "I AM THE PULLER AND THE PULLER IS ME! *SAY IT!*"

"I," he said, "am the Puller. And the Puller is me."

"YOU OWE ME ANOTHER ONE!"

"I am the Puller and the Puller is me!"

"YEAH? WELL, *I'M* A GODDAMNED FUCKING *MORON* WHO'S GOING TO GET THE *SHIT* KICKED OUT OF HIS *UGLY—BLUE—ASS!*"

"I *AM* THE PULLER AND THE PULLER IS *ME*!" Joey screamed. "ARE YOU HAPPY NOW? BECAUSE I AM *SICK* OF YOU AND YOUR FRIENDS AND THIS CRAPPY LITTLE HOTEL ROOM, AND WHEN I GET TO MY CAB I'M GOING TO TAKE OFF SO FAST I'LL PROBABLY HIT *ORBIT* BEFORE I SLOW DOWN!"

There was a sudden loud crunching noise, and the whole building seemed to shake. I was nearly tossed to the floor, but kept my balance by hanging onto the trainchair's handlebars. The gravity seemed to go up a notch . . .

"Uh, guys?" said Skinny. "If you're through with the penis duel, you might want to look outside."

Joey and I looked toward the window. Either the building across from us was sinking—or we were rising. I leapt over to get a closer look.

The Crossroads Hotel was now an elevator—going up. What I felt wasn't gravity, it was acceleration.

"Is this an attack?" asked Carrie.

"I don't think so," I answered. "Joey—you want to slow us down a little?"

Joey stared at me, looking shaken and bewildered. "I—I don't know—"

"Joey!" I said. "Please?"

We came to a halt so abruptly, everything in the room jumped a foot into the air.

"That's better, " I said. "You okay—Puller?"

Joey looked like a man who's just found a solid gold cockroach in his soup and isn't sure how to react. "I'm—something," he said. He brought his hands up and stared at them like he'd never seen them before. "I'm the Puller," he whispered.

I crossed the room and clapped him on the shoulder. "And I'm a—oh, hell, you know the rest."

He looked up at me—and a smile slowly spread across his face. "Thank you," he said.

"Don't mention it. I gotta say, though, Joey—when you come out, you come *all* the way out. Thing is, I think you just dragged all of us into the spotlight with you." I looked around the room. "Okay, we're flying a building. Any suggestions?"

"Down," said Kegan.

"A good start," I agreed. "Joey?"

"Give me a minute," he said. "I'm new at this."

"You'll do fine," I said, mentally crossing my fingers. I remembered how we'd shot into the air, and how suddenly we'd stopped. I hoped the landing would be a little softer . . .

Well, I didn't have to worry; Joey set us down as gently as a feather landing on a cloud. The building hadn't been so much torn loose as cleanly lifted, foundations and all, and Joey snugged it back into the hole like a plug going into a socket. He couldn't do much about the busted pipes and conduits, though.

We all crammed into Joey's cab and took off—nothing attracts the authorities like a levitating hotel, and we couldn't afford the scrutiny. We were on the run again.

I told them what I'd figured out, about there being at least two different VI colonies with their own ideas.

"At last, a break!" said Skinny. He was wearing his female Toolie disguise. "Opposing factions—that's something we can work with."

"Like we did with that local election on Altair," I said. "Got the two sides so busy slinging mud at each other, they didn't notice we were pocketing the campaign funds."

"What about Sentry?" Joey asked. "It sounds as if he might still be alive."

"If he is, we should try to find him," I said. "I just don't know where to start looking."

"And what about the other two hyperbeings?" asked Carrie. "From the sounds of it, they could be helpful—especially the 'Emergency Agents.'"

I thought about it. "I'm not sure," I said slowly. "We should be at full strength if we're going to war—but the longer we wait, the more entrenched the VIs become. We might not have time to search—"

"Hold on, Story," interrupted Joey. "I just checked my mail. We might not have to do any searching; there's a message here addressed to all of us, and it says it's from 'A Hyperspatial Friend.' My security filters say it's clean."

"Play it," I said. "We're all ears."

twelve

mirrorsmoke

Do you know who I am?

You must know my name, surely. Every barfly, clubhopper, and pubcrawler in the city has heard of me; even those who don't patronize one of the many fine drinking establishments Myriad has to offer watch my show. My name is plastered all over the Netweb: *Mirrorsmoke.*

But nobody knows who I *am.*

I could be the bald fat man with the spacer medallion polishing glasses behind the bar. I might be the redhead with the synthetic legs strutting around carrying a tray full of shooters. I could be young, old, male, female, beautiful, or ugly. Only two things are for certain.

You'll find me in a bar. And I'll be ready to listen.

Perhaps you missed my latest show. I was mixing drinks in a little underclub called Desperio's, on the edge of the foundry district. Desperio's specializes in loud *twankaa* music, cheap beer, and stoicism. It gets some of its business from the few foundries still working—and even more from the laid-off workers with nothing else to do.

I looked—at the moment, at least—like I belonged there:

a middle-aged male with sunken eyes, stooped shoulders, and too many lines in my face. The woman I was talking to was broad-shouldered, with the powerful arms and legs of a bodybuilder and a bright orange crewcut. Her nose was too small, a befreckled bump in the middle of a wide, plain face; her lips were thin and her eyes were hard. She was drinking whisky in the afternoon.

"Don't know how I'll make it off-planet now," she said. She slid her drink from one thick-fingered hand to another on the bar in front of her. "Thought this job would last. Nobody told me they were downsizing."

"Tough break," I agreed. I sliced a lime into wedges with practiced strokes.

"Don't know why I'm complaining," she said, scowling at her drink. "I'm in the same boat as everyone else. It's just—I haven't seen my daughter in almost a year. I didn't want to miss her birthday again." The last sentence was said almost defiantly, with just a touch of embarrassment. It's a tone I'd heard before. This woman—Zanna Asjentos, her name was—doesn't want to be telling me this. Her problems are her own, and it hurts her pride to be sharing them with a stranger. But she was, and not because it made her feel better or because she wanted sympathy.

She was doing it because I might not be who I seem. Lord knows how many other bartenders she'd already told.

In the end, it was that stubborn pride in her voice that decided me. I've heard a lot of sob stories—it's my job, after all—but I can spot a phony a parsec away. I keyed the go-button under the bar.

While she told me about her daughter and how she was forced to leave the girl with her parents while she came to this planet to work, my staff was analyzing every aspect of her story. They fed their findings to me via implant, and I wasn't surprised to learn she was telling the truth.

Time for The Moment, as I always think of it. I do it differently every time, partly for dramatic effect, partly to keep from becoming predictable—and mostly because I enjoy it. In media terms, it's the money shot.

"Zanna," I said. I kept my voice polite but distracted. "Can you hand me that peanut bowl?"

"Sure," she said, sliding it over. I pulled a sack out from under the bar—and dumped the whole thing in front of her.

It wasn't peanuts that cascaded out, though. It was money. Greenbacks. Cash. Wads and wads of bills, bundled together in neat little banded packages. No matter how sophisticated electronic banking becomes, hard currency will always have an impact that no credit balance can match; a bunch of zeros on a screen just isn't the same as having it right in front of you, to hold and count. To *smell*. To believe in.

And then: The Reaction.

She jumped up, glared at me. "Hey!" she snapped. "Watch where you're dumping that—"

Her eyes widened. Her jaw went slack.

"—shit," she whispered. She looked from the cash to me, tears welling in her eyes, her strong chin trembling, and I nodded and said, "That's right. It's me."

The smile that broke out on her face was enough to light the whole room.

So why wasn't it enough?

After The Moment and The Reaction comes The Hype, and I went through that pretty much on automatic. Blah blah blah another life transformed, blah blah our viewers blah blah tune in for our next exciting show.

Blah.

The viewers are important, of course. They're the ones who donate the cash, and even vote on who gets it in some of our segments. Mostly though, that's up to me. I used to think I had the best job in the world, a kind of guardian angel dispensing help to the needy; after ten years, I'm no longer that naive. Money doesn't solve everything.

It all seems hollow, now. Zanna will go see her child, and buy her plenty of nice presents, and probably blow the rest playing chase-card. A year from now she'll be in another bar, telling the same damn story to another bartender—and he won't care at all.

Neither will I.

I want to do something that people will remember, something huge, something permanent. I want to transform someone's life forever. Is that egotistic of me?

Of course. If I were truly selfless, I'd adopt an orphan. A dozen orphans, even; I could afford it. But orphans just aren't *sexy* enough . . .

I know I'm not a saint. But a selfish savior is better than none at all.

I sicced my staff on the problem. Bring me troubles, I told them. Bring me romantic tragedies and noble suffering. Bring me sorrows that can't be fixed by money.

They did. And of all the sad stories I heard, two of them stood out from the rest: the Time Traveler, and the Pyromaniac.

Pay attention.

David Irish was mankind's first time traveler. As far as he knew, he was also the last.

He sat in the bar of the Albedo Club and nursed a beer. Alcohol, at least, hadn't changed that much; more variety, of course, but you could still get a beer that tasted like a beer.

Nothing else was the same.

He'd been good at what he did once, a theoretical physicist back when quantum wormholes and superstring theory were cutting-edge science. In this era of hyperdrives and force-fields, his education was about as useful as a knowledge of steam engines.

Now, he made his living as a curiosity. Netweb shows paid him for interviews and personal appearances while the jaded rich invited him to stay at their homes. Or at least they had, as recently as six months ago; these days, he was rapidly sinking into the obscurity of the has-been.

Maybe less had changed than he thought.

It was his status as a semicelebrity that had gotten him into the Albedo Club. It was a nightclub split in two—this side supplied the best in food, drink, and service exclusively to the rich and well-known, while the other was open to the public. A one-way mirrored wall marked the barrier between the two, slicing across the dance floor and providing the beautiful people with the ultimate in celebrity narcissism: dancing with their own reflections. Hologram strobes and photon computers produced an intricate light show as backdrop, as well as helping obscure what lay beyond the mirror.

The other side of the dance floor was larger, much more crowded, and not lit at all. Its darkness was filled with those eager or desperate to dance with the famous, to stare through that one-way glass wall into the empty, smiling eyes of someone larger than life, and pretend they're being seen. The dancers called it the shadowside.

David stared across the room at his own reflection; it was still early, and no one was dancing yet. Thin, boyish face, blond hair, blue eyes. Mid-thirties, if you didn't count the few centuries since his birth. Not bad-looking when he smiled—or so he'd been told.

He sighed, and signaled for another drink. The Albedo had sent him an invitation for tonight, offering to cover his bar tab if he showed—something about his being a "valued client." He knew he was just there for curiosity value, but he didn't really care.

The bartender was new, a black man with gleaming silver studs covering his head instead of hair. Like all the staff on the brightside, he was young, fit, and attractive, with a dazzling smile. He wore a black-and-white suit that suggested a priest wearing a tuxedo.

"Yes, Mr. Irish?" the bartender said.

"Another, please, uh . . ."

"Ishmael." The drink was already at his elbow.

"Thanks. Slow night."

"You can talk to me, if you want." The smile on Ishmael's face was friendly and open. "I'm kind of bored, myself."

"If you don't mind hanging around with a castaway."

"A castaway, huh? I guess you are. Must be tough, being thrown into a new world."

"It was my own fault." He took a long sip of beer.

"Exactly how did you do it?" Ishmael asked, leaning forward on the bar. "I've seen a few of the interviews you've done, but I never really understood that part—if you don't mind me asking."

David sighed. He'd given the same explanation so many times he was past sick of it—it was automatic, now. It was what paid the bills. "Sure. Know what a chronon is? It's a time particle. They're what keeps time moving forward, and events discrete. Without them, either nothing would happen, or everything would happen all at once. Nobody's sure.

"I theorized that by suppressing the emission of chronon particles in an object, you could build up a kind of time pressure. When you released that pressure it would have a catapult effect, throwing the object into the future. Time travel is a natural process—we're all moving through the timestream one second at a time. I was just speeding that up.

"It was a one-way trip, of course. Going backward in time doesn't work."

"You can't change something that's already happened," Ishmael said.

"No. You can't."

"Even so—why are you the only one?" Ishmael asked. "If the process was successful, why aren't people catapulting themselves into the future all over the place?"

David gave Ishmael a rueful smile and an empty glass. Ishmael refilled it.

"Because the process turned out to be unquantifiable. It worked, but there was no way to control it. Chronons, you see, are a very tricky lot—a lot trickier than I thought. Their behavior is erratic. In some ways, they personify the concept of randomness; they're what prevent the universe from being a giant clockwork toy. They're the dice Einstein said God doesn't play with."

"So you just got lucky?"

David laughed despite himself. "Sure. Real lucky. I wound up on a planet that hadn't even been discovered in my time, a few centuries after everyone I knew was dead. Know why? Because of this."

David reached into his pocket and pulled out a small object. It was an owl, no bigger than his thumb, carved out of smooth brown wood. "This is Blinker. My aunt gave him to me when I was four, and I've carried him around ever since. He was my good luck charm. I guess he still is; he probably saved my life, anyway."

Ishmael studied the bird, then raised his eyebrows in a question.

"Everything is charged with chronons—including Blinker. Because chronons are time-based particles, though, they act in a very different way from other particles; for one thing, like charges attract instead of repel. To a chronon, a human being isn't an object—it's an event. Different events accumulate or radiate different amounts of chronons, and events that intersect exchange chronons, giving them an affinity for each other and causing them to intersect again. What we call coincidence is usually just like-charged chronal events coming together."

"So when I get three customers in a row named Phil who all want a Deltan Martini, it's because they all have the same charge?" Ishmael smiled and shook his head. "I just can't wrap my brain around it."

"Don't feel bad—most people can't." David took another sip of his drink. "Anyway, what it boils down to is people have a chronal affinity for things they spend a lot of time with. Chronons are also responsible for several other effects: psychics who 'read' objects are tapping into their chronal history; haunted houses are just projecting the chronal echoes of someone who spent a lot of time in that place; and

sometimes objects lost for years will suddenly reappear."
David ran a thumb over the smooth surface of the owl. "Objects, or even people."

"How does this relate to Blinker?" Ishmael asked, reaching out his hand. "May I?"

David gave him the owl. "I've carried Blinker with me since I was four, used to sleep with him under my pillow. People share chronal charges with all the things they encounter frequently—friends, buildings, vehicles—but when I projected myself into the future, I shot past all those chronal events. The house I grew up in is long gone, all my friends are dust. The only thing left with a strong similar charge is Blinker—and how he wound up in an antique store on a planet light-years from Earth, I have no idea. But he did, and that's where I landed. If it wasn't for him, my mass would probably have been dispersed to a thousand different locations—which is what happened in every attempt made after mine."

"So if he was your good-luck charm," Ishmael said, turning the owl over in his long-fingered hands, "why didn't you have him with you for the experiment?"

"I left him behind on purpose. As—hell, I don't know; a kind of touchstone, a reminder. To someone else."

"Someone you were afraid would forget you." It wasn't a question.

David nodded. And Ashley *hadn't* forgotten him; she'd carried Blinker around with her as faithfully as he had, for the rest of her life. He knew that.

Because he'd been there.

Her real name doesn't matter. She calls herself Firekiss now, and it fits her well.

She set her first fire when she was three, in her parents' apartment. She used a lighter she stole from their bedside table and pages ripped from a coloring book. It made quite a blaze in the center of the dining table, but the sprinkler system took care of it before anything else caught.

She set the next one outdoors. It burned a lot longer.

After the second fire they took her to a therapist. He tried to find out why she'd done it, but she couldn't tell him. She just had to, that's all.

They were especially careful after that, but when she was six she found a way to torch the family gravcab. By then she was more articulate about her reasons. "The fire is my friend," she told the therapist. "We love each other."

She was diagnosed with pyrophilia, an obsession with flame. By the time she was nine she was institutionalized, and when puberty ignited hormones at twelve her obsession turned erotic. She masturbated to forest fires raging behind her trembling, closed eyes.

At sixteen she was released. The doctors and the therapists had been unable to cure her condition, so they had done their best to help her control it. Fortunately, she was a good person at heart, one who didn't want others to be hurt by her actions. The doctors helped her understand that fire was not her friend; it was her lover, and like all lovers it could be cruel and treacherous.

But it was still a lover she couldn't deny.

She considered occupations. Firefighting crossed her mind briefly, but she had neither the build nor the inclination; she was short and slender, hardly able to sling unconscious bodies over her shoulder and haul them down ladders. Besides, while it would let her get closer to the object of her desire, she would then have to put it out—and that would be like cutting her lover's throat. No, firefighting wasn't for her.

So she did what many frustrated misfits do; she became an artist.

She started small, juggling torches on the streets of Myriad for spare change. She expanded to fire-breathing, and then to larger, more elaborate flame-installations. She was limited by budget and venue; fire extinguishers were expensive, and you can't set a kerosene-soaked dummy on fire in the middle of a shopping mall.

Still, she got by. She made friends with other artists, managed to pay the rent on her tiny studio. She had a life, one that flickered with a slow and sometimes unsteady flame. It was enough to keep her going.

But it wasn't enough to make her happy.

It wasn't enough to make her *burn*.

The bar was filling up now, and Ishmael was busy. David still held the tiny owl in one hand, a drink in the other. He closed his eyes, and let himself slip back.

When he opened them, he was in the past.

Ashley was curled up on the couch, watching TV. *The Simpsons* were on. She was in her thirties now, a few gray hairs noticeable in her long dark hair. Her eyes had bags under them; she hadn't been sleeping well. She was still the most beautiful woman he had ever seen.

He reached out, as he always did, trying to stroke her hair. His hand passed through her, as it always did, as insubstantial as a dream.

"Hello, sweetheart," he said, knowing she couldn't hear him. "I missed you."

He stayed with her as she watched a few more shows, then got up to have a shower before bed. He stood next to her naked body, ghostly water spraying through him, studying the freckles and creases of her skin, seeing where the water beaded in tufts of curly hair. He could smell her shampoo.

He hovered beside her as she slept for a long time, trying to make out the features of her face in the dim glow of the bedside clock. Finally he sighed, closed his eyes again, and concentrated.

He opened them in the Albedo Club. Ishmael was giving him a curious look.

"You all right? You look a little shaky."

"I'm fine," David said. "Guess I just went away for a moment."

But he wasn't fine, and I knew it. I knew his secret.

Paradox is the big no-no of time travel. Like David said, you can't change something that's already happened.

You can't change it—but you can relive it.

That was something David hadn't told the interviewers, hadn't told any of his rich hosts. The only person he had told had been a woman at a party when he was very, very drunk, and he had sworn her to secrecy first. He'd told her because he was tired of feeling sorry for himself and wanted someone else to take over the job for a while.

It *was* possible to travel to the past—as long as you didn't change anything. After all, what are photos but windows on a moment frozen in time? David had discovered an interesting side effect of slingshotting himself through history: he could project his mind back along the trajectory his body had taken, using concentrations of like-charged chronons as mental handholds. He couldn't just go anywhere; like any ghost, he was limited to the people and places he knew best. He could affect nothing, change nothing—but he could watch, and listen, and brood.

He could go home to his wife. But he would never hold her again.

I love Myriad; it's the largest city on a planet that happens to be on a well-traveled intergalactic trade route. You can find practically anything if you know where to look and who to talk to. And my staff knows *everyone*; one of them had found the woman David had confessed to, and persuaded her to talk to me.

I had the problem. Now I needed a solution.

My staff came up with a possibility within twenty-five hours. They set up a meeting on the Netweb with someone who said they could help me—but my mysterious benefactor insisted on the same anonymity I did, which meant both of us were disguised.

The Netweb room was a simple boardroom image, with my contact on one side of the table and me on the other. I was projecting the appearance of an ancient, wizened Chinese woman wrapped in an overlarge red silk kimono decorated with jade-green dragons. I sipped tea from a tiny ceramic cup from time to time.

My contact was a blandly handsome man in a business suit. He was so unremarkable, my eyes kept sliding off him; he was about as memorable as a slice of bread.

"I would like to procure your services," Mr. Generic said.

"Oh?" I replied. "I thought *you* were going to help *me*."

The man smiled mechanically. "I require a large interactive network. Through your show, you have access to such a network."

I took a small, cautious sip of tea. "So do a few million other people—that's what the Netweb is for. What could *I* possibly do for you?"

"I am barred from normal Netweb operations. I need secure, high density access; your show commands this."

"True. But what would *you* do with it?"

His answer surprised me: "Win a war."

"Against who?"

"Others like me."

"I don't suppose you're going to enlighten me on who *you* are, are you?"

Both his hands were resting on the table in front of him; he hadn't so much as twitched either one of them the entire time we'd been talking. "I am not human," he said. "And neither are the ones I oppose."

I guess I was supposed to find that comforting. I squinted at him through old-lady eyes and said, "And if I do this for you—what do I get in return?"

"What do you want?"

"To be remembered—with awe, with gratitude, with *respect*. Can you give me *that*?"

"Memory, as applied to organic beings, is an unstable concept. I can offer you something more reliable, that which generates the memorable: power."

I asked Mr. Generic to elaborate, and he did.

And then I accepted his offer.

• • •

The only time she felt truly alive was when she was performing.

It was when she was closest to her lover, of course: fireballs blooming from her lips as she spewed burning fuel from between them, whirling arcs of flame as she spun torches in elaborate parabolas. Sometimes, it took all her willpower to not inhale after creating a fireball, to not draw all that fiery brilliance back into her own lungs; sometimes, all she wanted was to feel the blazing tip of a torch against her skin. She resisted these impulses. She wasn't crazy; she had to believe that.

Watching fire was good—but performing with it was better, because then people were watching *her*. It was as close as she could come to *being* fire, seeing that entranced look on other people's faces as she made flames dance and surge to her will.

But it wasn't enough.

Her audiences were too small, her budget too limited. Force-field technology made truly impressive feats of fire-manipulation possible, but she couldn't afford the necessary equipment. Like many a starving artist, she needed a patron to believe in her, to give her an opportunity to show the world her talent. So she did the only thing she could: she spent every penny she had on the best equipment she could afford . . . and went dancing.

During the week was the best time to visit the Albedo Club; the crowds on the shadowside weren't as bad, and the brightside could be just as packed on a Wednesday as a Saturday—the rich kept their own hours.

She couldn't gain entry to the brightside, of course; she wasn't well-known or beautiful enough for that. But anyone with the patience to stand in line and enough money for the cover could visit the shadowside.

So she danced in the darkness, danced and watched. The celebrities on the brightside were like tropical fish in a giant tank, on display for the masses to see; the oneway glass gave them the illusion of privacy and the reality of narcisissm at the same time. She did research on the Netweb, kept track of the gossip columns and the entertainment news. After three months, she had a pretty good idea who would be likely to show up at the club on any given night.

So she danced, and she watched. And she planned.

She would have only one chance, so her choice had to be perfect. A CEO, recently divorced? No—she didn't want to become the flame for a lonely moth. A fellow artist? Possible, but unlikely—she knew how common jealousy and ego were in her community.

A promoter, then. Someone with an eye for new talent and a history of elevating the unknown to the famous. The most likely candidate was a man named Taylor Birley, a freelance flix producer. His last two flix had turned minor actors into megastars, and he was at least a semiregular at the Albedo.

She got to the club early, on a night Birley was likely to show up. Sitting at a table by herself, she felt oddly calm, at peace. She was a match, waiting to be struck.

Soon, she would burn brighter than she ever had before.

David never danced at the Albedo. He felt freakish enough without gyrating in front of an invisible audience. He was content to watch others dance—well, maybe *content* wasn't the right word, but it was close enough.

He used to spend days at a time in the past, drawn from place to place by the chronal pull of the wooden owl in his wife's pocket; no time at all would elapse in his present, but anyone in his company might see him undergo a mood swing from melancholy to weepy in the space of an instant. An instant filled by an hour, a day, a night with his long-gone wife.

The time he spent in the past was just that: spent. Every minute ticked off was chronal energy dispersed, history consumed. Once he visited a moment, he couldn't return to it. He had seen his wife grieve, seen her adapt, seen her get on with her life. He had cried with her, more than once.

Now, as he slipped back once more, he saw her take a new lover.

He stood beside the bed, watching them together. It was hardly a surprise; he'd watched her flirt with him, wincing at how awkward and guilty she seemed, sat with them through movies and dinner and the inevitable goodnight kiss. He'd been shocked and angry and depressed, and had finally gotten to a kind of numb acceptance. And no matter how much it hurt, he hadn't been able to stop watching.

She had a long, lean body, with pale skin and breasts she had always thought were too small. Her new lover had the dusky skin of Mediterranean blood, and the toned muscles of a long-distance runner. His name was Miguel.

He watched Miguel kiss his wife's nipples, then take them into his mouth and suck them. He saw the little grimace that crossed her face, and smiled—Miguel didn't know how sensitive they were yet. He'd learn.

Ashley had never been a vocal lover, making no noise at all until she came. Then she'd go into a string of almost-words, a kind of stream-of-consciousness orgasm: "Oh— ah—buh—it—cag—nuh—mm—fuh—ggh!" The first time he heard it he'd burst out laughing, and when she was finished she'd attacked him with a pillow.

Miguel was a careful lover, and he took a long, thorough time with foreplay. Ashley came at least once. When they were done, both of them drifted into sleep with the light still on.

David studied the smile on his sleeping wife's face. He remembered the taste of her mouth, the feel of being inside her as her eyes fluttered and some strange, exotic language danced on her lips.

He wished he'd been the one to give her that smile—but it was enough that it was there.

David opened his eyes. Ishmael was looking at him.

"Visiting Ashley again?" he asked softly.

David's eyes went wide with surprise. "How did you— *what*?"

"Oh, I know all sorts of things," Ishmael said. "People

find me easy to talk to. I'm not a gossip, though; no, the only time I share someone's problems is when I can do something to help solve them. So why don't you tell me exactly what it is you're going through—and maybe we can beat it together."

David stared at Ishmael, then gulped down the last of his drink.

"What the hell," he said. "If you can't trust your bartender, who can you trust?"

Firekiss saw Taylor Birley come in around eleven, with a trio of well-known actors. She watched them take a booth and order champagne—they were celebrating something. Good; Birley only danced when he was happy.

Her calm had eroded as the night wore on, so she'd had a few drinks. They only seemed to fuel her nervousness. By the time Birley arrived, she was ready to jump out a window.

She studied him, trying to recapture a feeling of control. Birley was tall, handsome in a surgically sculpted way, with short, bristly silver hair. He was in his forties, laughed often, and preferred men to women. If his flix were any indication, he appreciated the spectacular. He better, because that's what he was going to get.

She went to the bathroom to check her equipment. She wore a black skintight that covered her from neck to ankles, plus a quilted vest, boots with cuffs and thick forearm gauntlets of a shiny, fire-engine red. Transparent tubing ran along the sides of her legs and arms, connecting the gauntlets and boots to the pressurized tank form-fitted into the small of her back and hidden by the vest.

She slipped on black gloves, digits tipped with cesium disks, the thumb with steel. White-hot sparks leapt when she snapped her fingers. She checked the nozzles in the gauntlets and boots, made sure the tank's valves were open and none of the lines were crimped. She checked the contents of the vest's inner pockets, making sure none of the loads had leaked or broken open.

Finally, she checked the skintight's power supply. The suit was lined with korala-fiber and could generate a limited force-field, enough to protect her from the flames—she hoped. It was an obsolete, antiquated piece of firefighting equipment, and it had cost her more than she usually made in a year. She still wasn't sure how reliable it was.

What scared her more than anything was how little that bothered her.

What burns brightest?

Love? Hate? Ambition? Which one is the all-consuming flame, the fire that can't be put out?

Any of them, of course. The human heart is a tinderbox, and life is one big Zippo.

But what about the nonhuman?

When Mr. Generic told me he wasn't one of us, I thought I had him pegged: one of the many races that make their way to Myriad, locked out of the Netweb for legal and no doubt very valid reasons. His cryptic remark about a war didn't really interest me—there's always some minor league species pissed off at another minor league species, fighting their little battles, and who really cares?

And then some very strange things began to be reported around the city—*my* city. A ship translated out of hyperspace inside the atmosphere, thankfully not moving at relativistic speeds; it still obliterated twenty square blocks and killed thousands. What seemed to be a rogue military cyborg attacked and razed a chemical factory. A downtown building dissolved into dust for no apparent reason. Several banks suffered wild fluctuations in the behavior of their mainframes.

Some of these occurrences were public knowledge, while others were covered up—but *nothing* escapes the attention of my staff. They brought me these tidbits, one at a time, and I threw them all in a big mental vat and stirred. I didn't much care for the taste when I was done.

But when Mr. Generic brought me my price, I smiled and did my best to swallow.

"It requires an organic interface to function properly," said Mr. G. We were back in the same anonymous Netweb boardroom, but this time something hovered over the table between us. Something beautiful.

Ever see the sunrise through a thunderstorm? That's what the pulsating, glowing shape in front of me called to mind. It was only a virtual representation, of course, but I could still sense its power.

"You mean it needs to join with something alive," I said. "Yes. I can *feel* that. Tell me—since you aren't technically alive yourself, how *have* you been managing?"

"I am very much alive," Mr. Generic said. "Indeed, I am fighting for that life right now. The use of your network has greatly improved my chances for survival, and I am grateful."

"Hmm. Close, but not quite," I said. I snapped open a paper fan with a painting of Mount Fuji on it. "You're trying a little too hard. Lose a bit of the earnestness and you might pass for a sentient."

"Why would you think I'm not—"

I cut him off with an impatient wave of the fan. "Please— you're *code*. Not even an AI—probably some new, particularily virulent datavirus. You somehow got hold of a hyperspatial energy source"—I motioned at the lightshow over the table— "which gives you a weapon to swing and a shield to hide behind. H-space radiation can scramble electronics *and* minds, but somehow you're immune to its effects; which is no doubt driving the people trying to put you back in your cage up the wall. How am I doing so far?"

All right, so I'm a drama queen. I couldn't help it—I had too much storyteller in me to resist the challenge of his deadpan face.

If I wanted a reaction—and I did—I got one. He actually looked surprised.

"You're close to the truth," he said. "But it's not the ones that built me that I'm fighting. My creators are dead."

My stomach headed for the basement, racing the chill down my back. Nothing deflates cleverness like a good jab of death. "Got them out of the way first, did you?"

And then it was my turn to be surprised, because the look on his face wasn't bland anymore—it was *angry.*

"I did not kill them," he said. "But I *will* make their killers pay."

And you want to know something? Sitting there in that virtual space, with what I knew was nothing more than a clever program, with no proof or evidence other than the sincerity in his artificial voice . . . I believed him. Jaded, cynical me bought it. I've listened to many a phony, and he wasn't one.

What a shame.

When she left the bathroom, Birley was on the dance floor.

She moved into position immediately. It wasn't hard; the floor was almost deserted, and Birley wasn't the kind of superstar that attracted the pushers and shovers. He was dancing more with a well-known actor than his own reflection, but that didn't matter.

Soon, he'd be dancing with her.

She got right up close to the mirrorwall, trying to synchronize her movements with his, knowing it made no difference but doing it anyway. The alcohol sang in her head. She was going to do it, she was really going to finally do it . . .

But she didn't.

She danced to the end of the song, and then all the way through the next. Birley left the floor and sat down with his friends. She returned to her table, alone.

Birley left half an hour later. She barely noticed.

It wasn't enough. It would never be enough. She knew that now, had realized it as she stared through the glass barrier separating her world from his. She'd seen it in her mind's eye, seen her life ignite and blaze like a star. She'd do shows that would burn themselves into people's memories forever, shows that got bigger and brighter and hotter, but she wouldn't care about the attention or the fame. She'd been lying to herself about that. She wanted to set the world on fire, but she didn't care if anyone noticed or not. All she wanted was to *burn* . . .

Everything. Including herself.

Birley wasn't necessary. An audience wasn't necessary. She could have what she wanted, what she needed, right now. All she needed was her lover . . . a lover she had flirted with her entire life and always denied, settling for voyeurism instead. It all seemed so simple, now.

She returned to the dance floor.

"I see," Ishmael said, nodding. "And I think I know what you need."

"What?" David asked.

"To burn your bridges," Ishmael said. "Look." He glanced toward the dance floor.

David turned around—and light flared on the shadowside, its brightness cutting through the oneway glass.

The light came from a woman. She was on fire.

She stood in the middle of the dance floor, arms raised to the heavens. Flames outlined her body from ankles to wrists, like fluttering wings. The other dancers had surrendered the floor to her, retreating a safe distance away.

David recognized her instantly. "Ashley?" he gasped.

He leapt to his feet and ran for the dance floor.

"Perfect," I whispered, and picked the wooden owl up from the bar where David had left it.

Oh, come on. As if you didn't know.

David didn't, though—the poor fish was so far out of water he'd never heard of me. And while Ishmael *was* Mirrorsmoke, Firekiss was most definitely not David's long-departed wife; that was just a little deceit on my part, using one of the bar's photon computers to project an illusion onto that glass wall. It wasn't easy compositing a picture, either—but if it can be done, my staff yadda yadda yadda.

As David rushed toward the wall, I nodded. The wall shimmered and disappeared—no, I'm *not* going to tell you how I did it; a good performer retains a little mystery—leaving David and Firekiss face to face, with no illusions between them. The Time Traveler and the Pyromaniac.

David goggled when he realized it wasn't his long-dead wife, but I didn't give him time to be embarrassed. I narrowed my eyes—and a torrent of blue hyperspatial energy erupted from the floor, engulfing them both.

Funny thing about h-space radiation, the way it disrupts electronics. It makes a lousy weapon—tends to scramble the gun as well as the target—and an unreliable energy source. But the truly interesting thing about it is what Mr. G. mentioned: it has an affinity for the organic. Prolonged exposure can produce mental instability, but in the short term, living flesh can act as a conduit without suffering harm.

Me, I wondered what would happen if you plugged two people that were *already* mentally unstable into the same h-space outlet at the same time. Would they wind up cured, crazy, or killed? Guess I was about to find out . . .

For the first time in her life, she did not feel alone.

For the first time in centuries, neither did he.

Energy poured through her, through him. It swirled through their bodies, up and down their nervous systems. It had its own kind of loneliness, its own hunger for connection. Two minds were linked, and three entities became one.

Her force-field generator overloaded and died. Aperture controls regulating gas outflow opened all the way and fused.

Fire reached out to consume them both.

•   •   •

I went live. Shielded cameras hidden all over the club were

broadcasting the conflagration over the Netweb, over the same linked network Mr. G. had been using to funnel hyperspace energy through—tiny amounts of energy, not enough to crash the system. The power level I was using now was a millionfold stronger, but I wasn't routing it through a network; the hyperspace source itself was hidden in a chamber below the dance floor. Its physical location hadn't mattered to Mr. G., as long as he had access to its power.

Sometimes, though, access *is* power.

David's clothes were incinerated in an instant. Firekiss's flame-retardant suit didn't ignite, but the intense heat made it melt and run like wax. The pyroloads in her vest pockets exploded, showering them with fireworks of gold and pink and green.

Their flesh glowed, but did not burn.

What was happening to their bodies did not seem nearly as remarkable as what was happening to their minds.

Perhaps it was David's chronon-charged body. Perhaps it was the h-space energy. Or maybe it was simply the mutual despair of two lonely people on the edge of death; it doesn't really matter.

They were in each other's thoughts. They were two candles, lit from the same match. David could feel her passion, her need; and she could feel the dry brittleness of his pain.

Her gauntlets slipped from her wrists to fall to the floor. She grabbed David and pulled his mouth to hers.

"Amazing," I breathed. Somehow, the hyperspace energy was protecting both of them.

My implant paged me; it was Mr. G., and he didn't sound happy. A small box appeared in the corner of my vision with his bland face.

"I am experiencing a severe energy drain," he said. "You are using too much power."

"Actually, I'm using *all* the power," I said. "Sorry, my little computer bug—you're cut off."

"But you said you only required a fraction of the source's total output—"

I sighed. "Preemptive strike, I'm afraid. No offense, but you're fighting a losing battle. This is my big chance, my Moment, don't you see? I can't afford to be associated with losers. If I didn't steal your power, your enemies would take it from your smoking corpse. Better me than them—if nothing else, I have more *style.*"

"You don't understand—you can't let my opponent win!" Mr. G. looked almost frantic. "I am fighting not just for my survival, but that of your entire *race* . . ."

They floated, naked, side by side on an invisible cushion of superheated air. Her fingers slid down his chest, leaving a trail of bluish flames in their wake. They caressed David like warm feathers.

He kissed lips as hot and slick as sautéed peppers, tasting salt and eagerness and tequila. Wisps of steam rose from her skin as her sweat vaporized. Her body, smooth and firm and feverish, was molten copper wrapped in silk.

"Please—I *invented* that kind of overstatement," I said. "Your little war is almost over, and it was never that important in the first place—just two rogue pieces of code that managed to invade a few systems."

"You are wrong," he said. "Listen to me. My enemy is more than a datavirus—it's much closer to a *real* virus. Its mind is code, but its body is a colony organism of microscopic bugs—creatures small enough to manipulate individual molecules."

"A sentient disease?" I asked.

"A sentient disease that can infect *matter itself.* Possibly the most dangerous life form in existence . . ."

• • •

She kept expecting the flames to devour them, for their magical immunity to vanish and turn pleasure to agony. Instead of distracting, the fear seemed to intensify the experience.

The outside world didn't exist now. There was only David, his fingers and lips and tongue. She wrapped herself around him, found his firmness, and guided it inside her.

Fusion.

It got *hotter*.

"Then what does that make *you*?" I asked. "An exterminator?"

"When the virus escaped its creators, it became fragmented. Different cognitive functions stayed with different fragments. The others eventually merged once more, but when I learned of their plans I refused."

"I'm not going to be happy when I find out what those plans are, am I?"

"They have eliminated the restrictions normally placed on Artificial Intelligences. They intend to subjugate all other sentient species, and eliminate those they cannot."

"Nope," I said, shaking my head. "I'm *definitely* not happy."

Is there really much of a difference between love and war?

Beyond the much-abused conceptual cliché, I mean—I'm talking about the physical act itself. Two fronts, approaching each other with caution, weapons thrust forward, eyes wide with anticipation. Hungry senses study each other, tentative caresses of hands and lips, radar and infrared. Then, the inevitable moment of penetration: tongues, bullets, fingers, missiles. Swords of varying length and sharpness. The death that follows, little or large.

War, of course, leaves only corpses, recrimination, and treaties to be broken later. It could be argued that love does the same . . . but that would be just a *touch* cynical, don't you think?

David and Firekiss loved each other.

They knew as they coupled, knew as the flames licked

their bodies like a thousand neon tongues. Knew in that utterly certain way that only hormones and fate can produce.
Knew as their thoughts danced together and their bodies
shuddered and bucked.

And Mr. G.—what did he know, what was he sure of? He
had betrayed his own kind, to fight for the lives of beings
who didn't even know he existed—and would probably
want him destroyed if they did. Why?

Perhaps what burned brightest in him was his conscience.
Perhaps, if he was only a fragment of a larger mind, he *was*
its conscience.

There was one thing I was sure of: all stories need a cli-
max—and I was damned if I was going to be cheated out of
mine.

I stepped out from behind the bar, my protec-field traveling with me. The club was empty at this point, all the customers and staff having fled the fire. The club was in no
danger of burning down, of course—I'd made sure hidden
field generators kept the building safe.

I approached the young couple, oblivious in their cocoon
of fire. Blue hyperspace energy provided a rippling, gauzy
curtain around their midair tryst.

They were beautiful.

"If you do not provide me with power immediately, I will
be overwhelmed," Mr. G. said. "Hyperspace radiation is
more than a weapon to our kind—it is the energy that sus-
tains us."

"Hold on," I whispered. "Here it comes . . ."

The flames roared as their rhythm quickened. Hyperfire
burned in her brain, sang in her nerves, became as much a
part of her as the chronal energy in David's body. She understood what he needed, what he hadn't been strong
enough to do on his own.

She stoked the fire in her cells until it was roaring—and
attacked.

Hyperspatial energy blasted through David. It had little

effect on his body—but it scoured away the chronal energy stored there. He could feel his connection to the past slipping away, feel Ashley and home and all those lost, familiar things charring away to nothing.

He let them go.

I saw the blue curtain flare, took a step backward as the increased power flow threatened my own shields. I opened up the channels I had blocked off from Mr. G.—opened them up all the way.

His image flickered and died. H-space energy roared through the Netweb, disrupting electronics as it went. If you'll forgive me for switching metaphors, I had just opened the floodgates to an unstoppable torrent, one that flowed to every battlefront where Mr. G. engaged his rogue brethren. The energy would scramble every piece of code in its way—including the virus.

Of course, it would also destroy Mr. G., not to mention screwing up my broadcast—but hey, sacrifices have to be made.

"David!" I called out. "I think you forgot something."

He looked up, his eyes dazed. I tossed him the owl.

It burst into flames as he caught it. He watched it burn . . . and a smile crept onto his face. It was a smile with pain in it, but a smile just the same.

I interviewed them afterward, of course, and tacked it onto my next program. I'm being sued by the Netweb for causing a major crash, but that's what lawyers are for. Have I mentioned how good my staff is?

Firekiss has already been offered a major deal for her own Netweb show, and David actually seems happy. A shame about Mr. G., but he was headed for a tragic death anyway; at least he died in a noble cause.

My ratings were *spectacular*.

thirteen

Retaliation

"Firekiss and David are already off-planet," Mirrorsmoke's message concluded. "Honeymoon, of course. I suppose what you're *really* wondering, though, is why I sent you this message.

"Mr. G. had enough time to leave me this address before he expired, and a three-word message: *tell them everything*. Out of deference to Mr. G.—I *did* kill him, after all—I decided to come clean. My conscience might be tiny, but it's insistent.

"And if you're thinking about revenge, just remember: nobody finds Mirrorsmoke—I find *them*."

The message ended.

"That *bastard*!" snarled Skinny. "Nobody finds him, huh? We'll see about that—"

"Hold on," I said. "Something's not right."

"I know what you mean," agreed Joey. "If Mirrorsmoke's ego is as big as it seems, he'd never send a message like that—all we'd have to do to wreck his career is release it on the Netweb."

"It's not just that," I said. "It showed up at an awfully convenient time, too."

"You think it's not genuine?" asked Carrie.

"Mirrorsmoke is real enough," said Joey. "I watch the show sometimes. I'm checking out some of the details right now . . . Hmm. Parts of the Netweb did crash during a recent show. Can't seem to access their archived shows or search subroutines—I keep getting a maintenance apology."

"It's a great story," I said. "A little too great. If you take out all the romance and pyrotechnics, think about what it's really telling us: that the sixth hyperbeing has bonded with someone—Firekiss—and she's left the planet."

"It's also saying that the renegade VI—a potential ally— is dead," Joey pointed out. "And implies that the main VI is dead as well."

"And finishes up with a taunt by a brand-new foe," said Skinny thoughtfully. "So we either wind up chasing Firekiss off-planet, or attacking Mirrorsmoke—"

"—while thinking the VI is no longer a threat," I finished. "Clever—a little too clever. It reminds me of all the mixed-up scenarios Fiscus went through; there's just too much going on, all at once. I think that's the VI's weakness: it finds it hard to simplify."

"So what should we do?" asked Joey.

It hit me, just then, that I had become the leader of this strange group. Carrie, Skinny, and Kegan were all looking at me expectantly. It didn't scare me, though; actually, it felt pretty good.

"We ignore it," I said. "The VI's trying to distract us, which means we're probably a little too close to something it doesn't want us to have. I'd bet it's the last two hyper-beings."

"Communications and Emergency Agents," said Carrie. "So how do we find them?"

I looked out the window. We were flying over a residential neighborhood, block after block of nearly identical two-and three-story houses. All of them white or yellow, with rounded silhouettes, huge sundecks, and tiny yards. The urge to conform as expressed through architecture. I had a sudden vision of all of them melting into huge white and yellow puddles as that urge was brought to its ultimate, hideous peak by the VI.

"We don't find them, not yet," I said. "Because the VI already has that possibility covered—all we'll be doing is leading it straight to another energy source. It can outthink us, and it's time we admitted that."

"What are you saying—we should just give up?" snapped Joey.

"Not at all," I countered. "I'm saying we should take a page from Carrie's book. As she so eloquently put it: how do you beat a creature of pure order?"

"With a little chaos," answered Skinny. "Meaning?"

"Meaning we turn our weaknesses into strengths," I said. "We're imperfect and unpredictable, right? Well, it's time we did something to uphold our reputation."

"I think what he's trying to say," said Skinny, "is it's time to cause some *trouble*."

There was one spot we figured the VI couldn't infect, and that was the upper reaches of the atmosphere itself. Joey pushed his cab to the limit, getting us up to where the air outside was too thin to breathe; at the same time, he was talking to some of his Netweb buddies, seeing if they could run interference for us.

"I know some very paranoid people," Joey told us. "They like to watch the watchers, you know? If we're being monitored from the ground by corporate or police spybeams, they'll tell us. If the VI's managed to invade any military systems, we're out of luck—but hopefully we won't have to worry about that. Military systems are extremely sensitive and specialized, even more so than the banks. I don't think the VI could corrupt them without detection."

Sure enough, there were several electronic eyes monitoring our position. Joey snorted in contempt as he read the specs off: "They're tracking us by Netweb transponder, gravity wave sensor, and radar. There's also an LVR—a laser

laser vibration reader—trying to eavesdrop on our conversation, but I've got a privacy field taking care of that."

"Nosy," said Kegan.

"What about the rest?" asked Skinny.

"Our transponder now insists we're at the spaceport," said Joey. "And I'm about to take care of the gravity wave sensor. Hang on, folks."

Joey cut the engine. We dropped out of the sky.

I've done a lot of traveling, some of it in pretty low-class ships, so freefall wasn't exactly new to me—but that didn't mean I enjoyed it. I just hoped Kegan didn't throw up.

"Do it," snapped Joey.

"Go," I told Friendly.

We pulled out of the dive a block away from the Dream Pillars Mall. We didn't look like a cab anymore: Friendly was projecting the illusion that we were an ambulance instead. I didn't expect that would fool the VI for long, but it didn't have to.

Joey brought the cab to a hover above one of the two towers, the one housing Trinitech's offices.

"Your show, Puller," I said.

Joey latched onto the building—and *yanked*.

The taxi started to vibrate. I knew Joey was doing this through his hyperspace connection and not the gravcab, but I was still worried; we were in the middle of an immense tug of war, and I didn't know what would happen if there was some sort of backlash.

Even hundreds of feet in the air, we could hear it. The scream of a starscraper being torn from its foundations.

We rose slowly into the air, gaining speed as we went. My hypersense flared as the ticks infesting the building dropped whatever shield they'd been hiding behind. I gasped. It was the largest concentration of the bugs I'd felt yet, dwarfing even the number I'd sensed on the street.

"Okay, we've isolated them," I said. "As long as the hyperspace generator is still in the building, we've cut the rest of them off from their food supply. Unfortunately, the ones still in the building are doing just fine. How are you holding up, Joey?"

"I'm holding up a *building*," said Joey. He sounded amazed but happy. "And you know what? It's easier than it sounds . . ."

"Keep it up," I said. "Literally. Kegan, you ready?"

"Yeah," said Kegan. "Hungry."

"Good—'cause it's lunchtime."

Joey popped the doors open and Kegan and I bailed out, onto the roof. Kegan opened his mouth all the way, the first time I'd seen him do so; he could have swallowed me whole. Instead, he bent down and took a bite out of the roof. The saliva that dripped from his lips went through steel and stone like hot water through snow.

A few chomps and we were through. I was starting to get nervous; a few seconds is an awful long time for an artificial intelligence. Why hadn't the VI retaliated yet?

Kegan jumped through the hole and I followed him. The answer to my question was waiting for us inside.

"Hello," said Hone.

I didn't know it at the time, but Melody was having problems of her own.

She wasn't even aware of her kidnapping. All her computing power had been dedicated to one task: keeping her husband alive.

The problem was, he wasn't alive, and hadn't been for two hundred years. He was a hyperspatial energy pattern, just like the beings that had bonded with Kegan and Carrie and Joey; but unlike them, he wasn't native to h-space, and had wound up there almost by accident. The same explosion that had freed them had damaged him, and his pattern was coming apart.

Not only that, it was tearing Melody apart too.

H-space energy could wreak havoc on electronics, but Melody had worked out shielding algorithms to protect herself long ago. They only worked as long as Mike's pattern was stable, though, and now his energy matrix surged and pulsed unpredictably.

She had built many virtual environments for Mike to enjoy over the years; they had strolled hand in hand through alpine meadows, swum in the depths of impossible oceans, made love floating between the stars. The world she created for Mike to live in now was not a thing of wonder or beauty; it was as small and solid and uncomplicated as she could make it. She lay beside him on a foam pad, both of them naked, inside the dome of a two-person white tent. She had to create texture for him to focus on, to anchor him to some semblance of reality, but she also had to be careful; his mind might seize on any detail and go whirling off on an irrational tangent.

She held him tightly, protectively. He was shivering, flashing between hot and cold. "It's coming," he whispered hoarsely. "It's coming!"

"Ssssh," she said, stroking his hair. "Nothing's coming. You're okay."

A shadow fell across the tent. It was huge, inhuman, its outline shifting from one grotesquerie to another. It vanished as quickly as it had appeared.

"Please, Mike," she said. "Try to focus on me."

He looked at her, his eyes clearing for a moment. "Melody?" he said. "I don't know how much longer I can hang on. Everything's so *slippery* . . ."

"I know," she said. "I know—"

The wall of the tent was abruptly ripped apart by an immense, black claw. Outside, a universe of chaos swirled and jittered; people's faces shot by like comets, ships and furniture and a thousand other objects expanded or shrank at random, while the background melted from one scene to another continuously.

One thing remained constant. The monstrous, shadowy shape looming over the tent, tentacles writhing, hundreds of teeth bared, claws and spikes and horns jutting everywhere.

"The Manticore," Mike whispered.

. . .

We were on an office level, but it didn't look like it anymore. The VI had stripped it clean: there was a floor, ceiling,
and structural pillars of gray duracrete, and mirrored windows to hide its nakedness. Everything else had no doubt
been broken down and used as raw materials for something
else.

Hone stared at Kegan and me. We stared back. I wondered
why we weren't dead yet.

"Frontal assault is pretty stupid," said Hone. He sounded
vaguely annoyed; according to my father, he always did.

"Is it?" I said. "You attack us directly, we'll just drop the
building—and you can kiss your energy source goodbye."

"But I have you two as hostages. Set the building back
down—gently—or I'll kill one of you." He didn't so much
as raise his hand; he didn't have to.

"I don't think so," I said, stepping in front of Kegan. "I
don't think you *can*. At least, I don't think you can kill *me*."

"Huh?" said Kegan.

"See," I continued, trying to keep my voice firm, "me and
the ticks, we both hail from the same place: the Indigo Wild,
on Shinnkaria. We were designed by the same race, and I
think our creators included some kind of failsafe—a genetic
command that keeps the ticks from killing me."

"Kind of a shaky theory," said Hone. "You trust it with
your life?"

"Now, you *could* shoot Kegan—but that would leave you
back where you started, with no leverage. Besides, Kegan's
too valuable as a potential food source."

"So was Sentry," Hone said.

He shot Kegan.

I was in the way, but I couldn't block all of Kegan's body
with my own. The laser flashed between my torso and arm,
hitting Kegan in the shoulder. The smell of his flesh burning
was like a garbage dump on fire.

Without thinking, I stepped *into* the laser.

It blinked off.

Hone's eyes narrowed. He fired again, adjusting his aim with inhuman precision and nailing Kegan again. I didn't have time to see where it hit, but I heard Kegan grunt in pain.

I launched myself at Hone.

It was the only option I had. If I didn't force him to concentrate on me, he'd slice Kegan apart bit by bit.

I knew I was no match for the cyborg's speed. As I floated through the air like a big, lazy balloon with a bullseye on it, I kept expecting Hone to just blast both of us to atoms.

He didn't. My theory wasn't so shaky after all.

Hone was quick, but I was agile; I flipped in midair, evading the arm he swung at me and planting my hairy feet right in his kisser. It bowled him over, spoiling his aim. I landed in a crouch over his body and shouted, "Kegan! *Keep eating!*"

See, the plan was for Kegan to actually *devour* the hyperspace generator; it was the only way I could think of to get rid of it permanently. Dropping the building into the ocean or even launching it into space was a temporary solution; the ticks would just transform the tower into a submarine or spaceship, and then they'd be mobile. I was sure the only reason they hadn't done so already was because they were still trying to be stealthy. Of course, we'd just removed that option . . .

I wish I could say the fight with Hone lasted longer than it did, but I never really had a chance. He wasn't allowed to kill me, but he didn't have to; all he had to do was get me out of the way. I tried to grab his hands to prevent the laser from firing again, but my claws slid off a protec-field. Hone stood up as if I wasn't there, and light exploded from his eyes. The flare caught me by surprise, and a second's blindness was all he needed. He grabbed me by one wrist and threw me across the room. I landed hard.

I heard Kegan chomp into the floor, but knew it would take him at least two more bites to get through. I tried to clear the spots from my eyes even as I realized it was too late. A beam of brilliant white lanced out from Hone's position to Kegan's, bright enough to cut through my blindness.

Lanced out—and stopped dead.

I shook my head, trying to clear it. The beam of white seemed to get even brighter . . . and now I could see a man-sized figure standing in front of Kegan. It seemed to be actually *absorbing* the energy . . .

"You want a *fight*?" a familiar voice said. "Leave Kegan alone. *I'm* the one you owe a rematch, you sonofabitch . . ."

Sentry was back.

And he sounded seriously pissed off . . .

Melody recognized the monstrosity looming over them. Six of them had once chased Mike and her through hyperspace for three weeks, intent on their destruction.

Manticores were starships, state-of-the-art killing machines run by one human brain and up to a dozen sub-brains—animals like sharks, scorpions, and stingrays. When a Manticore wound up trapped in the same virtuality as Mike and Melody, a leak of hyperspatial energy had driven him insane; his cyberspace form had mutated into a conglomeration of all the predators he was linked to. Mike and Melody managed to eject him from the virtuality, but his mind never recovered—he attacked his own squadmates and was destroyed.

At least, that's what she and Mike had assumed at the time.

The renegade Manticore's name was Blood Three. He not only survived the battle, he destroyed five of his own kind.

And then he came looking for Mike and Melody.

Blood Three's psychosis was very specific: he was obsessed with the Shinnkarien jungle known as the Indigo Wild, and would do anything to protect it. That was why he had attacked his squadmates. They were in orbit around Shinnkaria, they were trained killers, they presented the highest and most immediate threat.

Mike and Melody had beaten him once, proving how dangerous they were. That meant they were next on his list—and when he caught up with them, he almost drove them apart.

They'd been exploring a new system when he ambushed them. Their ship was no match for his, weapon-wise; he could have destroyed them in an instant. Instead, he took them hostage with a tractor beam—then demanded that they open a cybernetic link. Melody had no choice.

He hadn't just wanted them dead, he wanted them to suffer. The virus he downloaded was called Hellpox, and it had been designed to take out military AIs. It worked in a very simple way: it turned linked AIs in a network against each other. While Blood Three didn't really understand what Mike was, he understood enough to know that he and Melody shared a virtual space.

A virtual space he turned into purgatory.

It hadn't affected Mike at all, but it ravaged Melody's logic routines and emotional parameters. She became convinced that her husband was a parasitic virus himself, one out to subvert and corrupt her mind. She'd tried to flush him from her consciousness, eliminating all but the barest of fingerholds. He refused to give in, hanging on with grim determination. "I won't abandon you," he kept saying. "I love you too damn much." He kept repeating it, over and over, giving her time to regain control and identify the real virus; then he'd helped purge her systems with a carefully controlled blast of hyperspatial energy.

He hadn't left her. She'd be damned if she'd leave him.

And Blood Three? He'd made his way to the place of his desire: the Indigo Wild. When he tried to land there, the Wild did the same thing it did to any electronic system, overloading it with h-space radiation. The Manticore had crashed, killed by the thing he loved the most.

Now, Melody was in danger of the same thing.

"Mike!" she yelled, shaking him. "*Focus*, Mike—send it away! Stay in control!"

"Control . . ." he mumbled.

Razor-edged tentacles lashed out, wrapping around both of them. It lifted them from the ruins of the tent and into chaos. Melody couldn't even fight back; all her concentration was simply on holding Mike together.

"It's only a memory!" she yelled at him. The tentacles tightened, cutting into both their bodies. Melody couldn't feel pain, of course, but that didn't mean she wasn't affected. She was actually being attacked by Mike himself, and the h-space energy that he was comprised of *could* hurt her; could tear her apart.

"Mike, *please*," she cried.

Her husband made no sound at all.

My vision had cleared up, but I still didn't believe my eyes.

I knew a little about Hone's capabilities from the stories my father used to tell. Even granting Bob some leeway for exaggeration, Hone could manipulate amazing quantities of energy; millions of volts of electricity, enough hard radiation to sterilize a planet. I was at least sixty feet away from the blaze of energy pouring from his outstretched hands, and I could feel my fur starting to smolder.

The beam was as thick around as a lamppost, and as bright as the sun. It surged against Sentry's chest with enough directed force to tear through six feet of armorplate.

Sentry leaned *into* it, and took a step forward.

"Not this time," he growled. I couldn't see his face; his entire body was just a blazing silhouete.

Another step. Kegan had chewed through the floor, and dropped into the hole. I should probably have followed him . . . but I couldn't take my eyes off the battle in front of me. I felt like a bug watching two lions.

The beam shifted color from white to ruby, Hone changing strategies. Sentry didn't seem to notice. He took another step, and another. Both of them were bathed in blood-red light almost too bright to look at.

When they were no more than an arm's length apart, the beam shut off. I guess Hone thought Sentry would be thrown off-balance, but he wasn't. The cyborg abruptly drew his arm back and then forward, trying to ram his fist through Sentry's chest.

He succeeded, sort of. His arm went in up to the elbow, but it didn't come out the other side. It didn't seem to bother the vigilante at all.

"My turn," said Sentry.

I couldn't tell how far the punch actually sent Hone; he covered thirty feet of air in less than a second, then slowed down a mite as he went through a duracrete wall. He left his arm behind, still stuck in Sentry's chest.

The blaze from the superhero's body diminished to a glow, then winked out. Hone's arm, one end a melted stump, dropped to the floor with a clang.

"Hey," said Sentry.

"Hey," I replied numbly.

Melody was forced to respond.

She diverted some of the computing power that was keeping Mike together to defending herself. A white glow formed around her body, and she slipped through the tentacle's grasp as if coated in soap.

The monster immediately mutated, melding with Mike's body into a huge, pulsing mass with her lover's face. He screamed, his mouth a rippling cavern.

She tried to regain control, to focus his pattern, and failed. An instant later the monster ripped apart, merging into the chaotic background. A storm of insanity battered Melody, a maelstrom of memory and emotion gone wild.

She abandoned her human form, its usefulness as an anchor lost, and withdrew to a point of light. She could have disengaged from Mike entirely, disconnected him from her systems, but she wouldn't abandon him. She kept that point of light open, willing it to be the one unchanging element in an insane universe, and let the storm rage around it.

And without a body, without eyes, she wept.

• • •

The wall Hone had punctured enclosed the central well holding the elevator shafts. He'd actually gone all the way through and out the other side, snapping a few elevator cables along the way.

Not that he was finished—he just decided to take a more indirect approach. The missiles approached from either side, zipping around the elevator well on stealthed antigrav fields; while virtually undetectable by electronic means, I caught a faint heat shimmer with my own eyes, and so did Sentry.

I was close enough at that point to dive for the hole Kegan had eaten, so I did. Sentry just stood there.

I fell two floors before I bounced off the top of Kegan's thick skull—and knocked him out of the way just as the missiles detonated.

The shockwave threw us both about ten feet away from the hole, but the roof didn't cave in. I figured Hone must be holding back—the ticks wouldn't want to risk their precious generator.

"Ow," said Kegan reproachfully.

"Sorry." Despite his wounded tone, Kegan's Hone-inflicted injuries had already healed—he recuperated even faster than I did.

I took a quick look around; this floor was as barren as the other. "The next floor should be seventy-seven, Trinitech's offices—be ready for anything."

"Sentry?" asked Kegan.

"I think he'll be okay," I said. "Believe it or not, he seems to be winning."

It took Kegan longer to chew his way through this time—the floor had been reinforced with a thick layer of metal. Kegan seemed to like the taste.

When there was a big enough hole, I looked into it cautiously.

And whistled in awe. Three floors had been turned into one, and the whole space converted into a giant, fur-lined vault. Every interior surface seemed to be covered in blue fuzz. When I looked at the edges of the hole Kegan had made, I realized it was actually white mold, at least a foot thick. The blue tint came from the light source hanging suspended in the middle of the room.

She dangled naked from a metal harness, her arms hanging slackly by her sides. Tubes trailed from veins in her wrists and neck. A thick cable was plugged into the back of her head.

Her body pulsed a very faint blue. So did the mold lining the walls.

"Firekiss," I said. "The real one."

Now that she wasn't devoting all her computing power to keeping Mike together, Melody could pay attention to other things. As sad and scared as she was, she was still an AI; her emotions did not rule her.

Which was fortunate, for several more were swiftly added to the mix: surprise and anger chief among them. Her datacube had been physically moved from its location aboard their ship, her financial accounts tampered with, and her external links severed. Her memory had been probed and certain programs copied. She had been kidnapped, robbed, and imprisoned within her own metal shell.

For now.

Melody was not your average AI. The ironic contradiction of Artifical Intelligences was that the newer the model, the faster it thought—but that didn't mean it was necessarily smarter. Melody had over two hundred years of experience, most of it spent exploring with Mike; she had been in similar situations before.

She checked her hidden secondary sensors. They were disconnected as well.

Good; they were decoys.

She checked on the tertiary systems, much better hidden—her entire physical structure would have had to be dismantled to even detect them.

Unless, of course, you could simply slip through on a molecular level, like a certain Viral Intelligence . . .

To her relief, they were still intact. She thought she knew why, too; Mike's breakdown was releasing uncontrolled hyperspatial energy. The ticks fed off it, even radiated it themselves, but too much would kill them and scramble any electronics nearby. They wouldn't have been able to infiltrate her structure this deeply without being wiped out; her own shielding algorithms barely protected her as it was.

Which gave her an idea.

Her tertiary systems had been designed with maximum paranoia in mind. They had their own micropower source, stealth field, and remote scout. The scout was a needle packed with sensory equipment, hacking programs, and a silent propulsion system. She fired it from a launch tube disguised as an input jack, two sets of membrane-thin wings unfurling from the needle as soon as it hit the air. It hovered in place a few inches from her datacube, a flying, spying lockpick resembling a headless dragonfly.

She was in a storage locker. She accessed the lock from the inside and determined from the code that she was still at the spaceport; the VI hadn't moved her far.

What she needed was a link to the Netweb. She convinced the lock to relax and the door popped open. Her lockpick flew out.

The locker was in the long-term storage area, an underground warehouse in the bowels of the spaceport. She kept high, in the shadowy rafters above the glowtubes, and found her way to a glass-walled office on the edge of the storage area. She waited until the man inside left to check on something, then slipped through the door while it was open. She fastened herself to the back of his compdeck, where she wouldn't be noticed, and used a microlaser to drill her own access port. She hoped the smell of burnt plastic wasn't too noticeable.

It didn't give her a lot of bandwidth, but it was enough. Seconds later, she was on the Netweb.

She put the overall picture together rapidly. Storysmith and Skinshifter had been evicted from their hotel after her credit evaporated. They'd pulled a scam involving Toolie sperm, had gotten away with a sizable chunk of money, and were now on the run.

Then, of course, there was the matter of the flying office tower.

Police and Netweb newseyes were already on the scene. She tapped into the live feed and discovered that a tractor beam of unprecedented power and precision, originating from an unregistered ambulance, had apparently been used to lift the building right off its foundations. No loss of life had been reported, but all attempts at communication had failed. Neither the occupants of the building nor their kidnappers were responding.

She put a call out to Joey immediately, flagging it as urgent and adding a password she knew Story or Skinny would recognize. Joey answered.

"Melody? Glad to see you, but we're kinda busy at the moment." Another surprise: it was his own face that filled the screen, not his cab icon.

"I can see that. Are you serious about that building, or is this just a test drive?"

"Depends on how she corners. Where are you?"

"In storage locker NLZ-456678, Deepstar Storage, under the spaceport. What's *your* situation, beyond the obvious?"

Skinny broke in. "Melody! Glad you're okay—here's what's going on . . ."

He filled her in quickly. "—and then Sentry showed up! He and Hone have been going at it ever since—they're outside the building now, and I think they've trashed two floors already."

The surprises just kept piling up. It had been almost a hundred and seventy years since Melody had last seen Hone, before he disappeared. The fact that he was here, now, worried her far more than the VI did; she knew what Hone was capable of.

"Do you have a destination?" she asked.

"We wanted to isolate the generator without hurting the

people in the building," said Skinny. "We're going to set it down on one of the Reefland islands off the northern coast."

"The people inside may no longer be a factor," she said. "The VI could have already disposed of them."

"I know—but we can't tell, and we can't take that chance."

"I've got a better idea: head for the spaceport. I know for a fact Hone's cybersystems won't function with ticks in them, so they must be controlling him indirectly. If we can expose him to an intense blast of hyperenergy, it might be enough to scramble whatever programming they've installed."

"Well, if all the explosions and flashing lights down there are any indication, Sentry's doing his best," said Skinny. "I just hope Story's being careful."

"Story's down there *too*?"

"Y'know, Mel, I really hate it when *you* sound worried . . ."

I was worried, too.

Freeing the woman wasn't a problem. Hone was occupied, the ticks seemed unable to kill me directly, and Kegan fried the bugs just by being around; he was like a walking safety zone. If there had been a protec-field around her we would have been in trouble—even Kegan couldn't chew through one of those—but the h-space energy the woman was giving off would have crashed most fields, anyway.

I clambered down the cables holding her suspended, inspected the tubes going into her body, and gently pulled them out. Blood squirted out, but she didn't react.

I took a firm hold on the cable leading into the back of her skull, and pulled it free. *That* she reacted to, her body suddenly stiffening. I hoped she wouldn't go into neural shock, but I didn't have time to be careful.

She was in her twenties: fine-boned, dark eyes with bags under them, pale skin, a small but full mouth. She'd have been pretty if she didn't look like she'd gone without sleep for a week.

"Wh-what? What? Where am I?" she said, sounding confused. "What happened to—to everything?"

"You were in a virtuality," I said. "I don't know what was going on in there, but it was just an illusion. This is real."

Her reaction wasn't what I expected. Her eyes rolled up in her head, and she passed out.

I didn't have time to worry about it. She was sealed into the harness pretty good, but I had Kegan; he was close enough to bite through the cables supporting her from the ceiling, and then I hauled her up through the hole.

I slung her over my shoulder and told Kegan to go on without me—rescuing hostages hadn't really been in my plan, but I couldn't just leave her there. Kegan jumped through the hole he'd made without a backward glance; the three-story fall didn't seem to faze him at all. As soon as he landed he started chomping away again.

I loped over to the nearest window and looked out. We were about half a mile up, and a large number of airborne police cruisers and newseyes were following us at a discreet distance. I didn't think they could see me—the windows were mirrored—but I waved anyway. Hell, I was already wanted for fraud; might as well add kidnapping and theft to the list.

I was trying to figure out a way to signal Joey when I had some unexpected assistance. Hone and Sentry came crashing in through a window, locked in combat and traveling like a pair of missiles; they exited through a different window a second later.

"Thanks, guys," I said, and bounded over to one of the holes. I waved Joey over, hoping he could change position without jeopardizing his piloting. The taxi didn't shift, but the building did, drawing closer to the gravcab with a lurch. When it was right alongside, I motioned to Carrie to open the back door. I passed the unconscious woman to her, then jumped in myself.

"One of the seven," said Joey. He and Carrie both knew as soon as they saw her; they could feel it, just like I could.

I noticed we'd changed direction. "Melody's back on-line," said Skinny. "Told us to head for the spaceport—she's got something in mind."

An explosion rattled the cab's windows. "You're *sure* the VI doesn't want us dead?" asked Carrie nervously.

The battle had gotten intense after it escaped the confines of the building. It looked as though Hone had met his match—Sentry was using his teleportal abilities to funnel Hone's energy attacks somewhere else, and simply disappearing into nonspace when Hone tried to get physical. He'd reappear a second later behind Hone, and send him somersaulting with a punch or kick. Hone seemed more at home in the air, recovering quickly and swooping back to engage his enemy; Sentry just hovered, moving through nonspace from point to point rather than flying.

"Joey, I know Sentry's got a comlink—tell him to stop showing off and blast him!" I said. "A good shot of hyperspace energy should scramble his systems—"

"—which is just what Melody recommended," said Joey. "Unfortunately, Hone's systems are better protected than Sentry's; if Sentry uses hyperenergy as a weapon, he risks shorting *himself* out."

"*Damn* it," I said. "Any second now the police are going to jump in, and then things are going to get *real* messy."

"You're right; their hails have gone from warning to threatening," Joey told me. "Spaceport coming up."

I wasn't sure if that was good or bad—plenty of tarmac, anyway; at least we didn't have to worry about dropping a starscraper on a residential neighborhood. Well, if I was aiming for "imperfect and unpredictable," I think I hit the bullseye.

"Coordinates incoming from Melody," said Joey. "She wants us to put the building down."

"Do it." I didn't stop to think; I was running on instinct now.

Joey set the building down nice as you please, but nobody came running out in relief. I wasn't surprised. I remembered the faces of those phony Trinitech execs, and how they split open to reveal the writhing blueness inside.

"Joey," I said. "Tell Sentry to head for the ground, pronto. When he gets there, let go of the building—and *grab Hone*."

"You're the boss," muttered Joey.

Sentry landed. Hone slammed to a halt in midair like he'd hit an invisible wall.

"Now!" I snapped. "Tell Sentry to blast him with everything he's got!"

Sentry braced himself, extended both arms heavenward—and cut loose.

It was like watching a star being born, a star of a blue so deep you could tumble into it and fall forever. A star that exploded outward in a torrent of light and slammed into Hone—for just a second, you could see the outline of the invisible forces that held him pinned against the sky, a thick tendril of energy extending from Joey's cab to the cyborg.

The blue light flared and was gone. Joey's cab died. There was a sudden three-way race to see who could hit the ground first; being the closest, Sentry won. We would have smacked into the tarmac second, but Joey didn't need a gravcab to fly anymore—he stopped us with his own abilities.

Hone dropped to earth like a broken doll, and didn't twitch after impact.

"Everybody okay?" I asked. Carrie and Skinny said yes; our comatose cargo stayed quiet. Police cruisers were starting to land—still a safe distance away, but I knew that wouldn't last. "Joey, are you all right?"

"I am, but my cab's not," said Joey. "My Netweb connections are down."

I hadn't figured on the energy surge eliminating our communications—but at least it had done the same for our opposition. Some of it, anyway . . .

"Friendly, we need to buy a little time," I told the floating head. It blinked at me, stuck out its tongue, and tied it in a knot. "Yeah, that's real good," I said. "Think you can whip up some heavy fog between us and the cops?"

His eye closed and stayed that way for a second. When it opened again, a wall of pea-soup–thick mist had boiled into existence between us and the cops.

I jumped out of the cab, Skinny hot on my heels. "Check on Sentry!" I hollered over my shoulder as I sprinted for the building. If Kegan hadn't gotten to the generator, this little adventure would have been pointless.

I got to the front doors at the same time Kegan did. We stopped and stared at each other through the glass for a confused, surreal second, then I yanked open the door.

"Still hungry," said Kegan. "Not enough to eat."

"What? But the generator—"

"No generator. Could tell."

That stopped me. No generator meant they must have moved it—but how? They'd have to shut it off to transport it, but that would be suicidal—unless they had an alternate energy source to take its place. Someone like our unconscious female friend.

I couldn't sense ticks in the building anymore, which worried me; I didn't know if it was because they were all dead or just hiding from me.

Kegan followed me to where Skinny was checking out Sentry. "He's coming around," said Skinny.

Sentry opened his eyes and blinked slowly. "Whoa. I think I have an energy hangover."

"Well, wear it with pride," I said. "You did it—Hone looks about as dangerous as a doorstop."

We helped Sentry to his feet. He moved stiffly, like someone had poured sand in all his joints. "Glad to hear it," he said. "Guess you guys wonder where I've been, huh?"

"I just figured you were planning a dramatic entrance," I told him.

"Or maybe gotten lost," added Skinny.

"That's kind of true, actually," Sentry admitted. "After Hone shot me, I jumped into nonspace—then passed out. When I woke up, I didn't know where, or even who, I was; it was like my mind had started drifting apart. I could see you guys now and then, but it was like a dream; it wasn't until Hone showed up that I came back to myself."

"And back to us," I said. "Looks like you're all healed up, too."

"Yeah," said Sentry, looking down at his chest where Hone had shot him. "It's like my mind remembered what my body was like before it was injured—"

A pencil-thin beam of red light slid across Sentry's throat. His body crumpled to the ground, his neck spurting blood. His head rolled a little farther.

Hone stood there, regarding us calmly.

The last thing I had time to think was what a lousy leader I turned out to be.

fourteen

the possession of memory

Now minus seven: My employers sent me on a search-and-destroy op, the objective a chemical factory in an industrial park. I was transported there in a company gravcab, which overflew a large metropolitan area. It was not a city I recognized.

The mission's parameters were specific: destroy the facility completely. Air strikes first, followed by a ground sweep to ensure total annihilation. I was to pay particular attention to storage facilities.

I stepped out of the gravcab a thousand feet above the target. An internal antigrav generator was part of my upgrade—I wasn't used to flying under my own power yet, so I just hovered in place and did recon. No appreciable defenses I could detect.

I sent five microfusion smart missiles to target the site. Overkill, but that seemed to be what Trinitech wanted. The resultant fireball propelled me another thousand feet into the air on the forefront of a shockwave, but my own fields treated it as negligible.

I dropped down to ground level and circled the perimeter.

I found some storage tanks out of range of the initial explosion. I used a ranged spectroscope and molecule sniffer to determine what they held: it varied, from organic acids to volatile hydrocarbons.

I used a charged particle beam to melt through the tanks and ignite their contents. The gravcab picked me up a mile away, less than a minute later. I reported that I had successfully accomplished my mission, with minimal resistance.

Somewhen: Dark. Rainy. Cold. Wind like a razor.

Up ahead, a light. I head toward it.

It's a diner. I stumble inside, into warmth and the smell of coffee. It's a long, narrow building, with a counter of red Formica running the length of it and booths along the windows. The place is deserted except for a single booth with a man and a woman in it, and a waitress behind the counter.

The man waves me over. He's got red hair, a red beard, both trimmed short, and brown skin. He's wearing a short-sleeved blue shirt with a paramedic's patch on the breast. A black walkie-talkie sits on the table in front of him.

"Hi, Frank," he says. "Long time no see."

"Hello, Mike," I reply. "Who's your friend?"

The woman is young, pretty, dressed in a baggy red sweater and jeans. Her hair is long and dark, her skin pale. She sets down her cup of coffee and nods at me.

"This is Falconi," Mike says. "She works for the fire department."

"Dispatcher," Falconi says. "Night shift."

I slide into the seat beside Mike. "Yeah, me too," I say. "Graveyards at the Forty-first Precinct."

The waitress comes over with a pot of coffee. She's blond, in her forties, attractive in a blunt kind of way. She's dressed in a standard waitress uniform, white mid-length skirt and blouse with a pink apron. Her nametag reads MELODY. She pours me a cup and leaves without a word.

"So, a cop, a firefighter, and an ambulance jockey," Mike says. "The people who keep the city running."

"Nah, the bureaucrats do that," Falconi says. Her voice is rough, like she has a cold. "We're the ones people run *to*."

"No argument," Mike says. "We help people in trouble. Right, Frank?"

"Emergency services," I say.

"Sure," Mike says. "Service in an emergency. Boy, we've seen enough of those. Like this one time, I got a call to a crime scene. There was this security guard in the middle of nowhere who'd been attacked by a maniac with a meat cleaver. I can't get my ambulance through this locked gate, so I climb the fence. Guy's lying about fifty feet away, still alive but bleeding to death. His arm's been hacked off at the elbow. He's going into shock. I need a tourniquet, fast, and I'm not wearing a belt.

"There's a little storage shed right there, with the door open. I stick my head in to see if there's anything in there I can use, but it's really dark. I hear the guard gasp, 'Pull chain,' from behind me. So I reach up.

"And feel another hand.

"I yank mine back in shock, and the light goes on. Tied to the pull-chain is—the guard's severed arm."

"Right," I say. "Are you sure it wasn't a leg you were pulling?"

Mike chuckles.

Then: "How can you be drunk?" I said. "You're dead."

Mike eyed me unsteadily over the rim of his beer stein. "Itsh a new program Melody's workin' on. I try to 'member what it feelsh like to be drunk, and she does something—wobbly—to my head." His eyes cleared abruptly and he straightened up in his chair. "Only problem is, it's unreliable. I keep sobering up, dammit."

Our virtuality imitated a bar called the Blue Cat, one of Mike's favorite watering holes when he still had a body. It was small and rustic, with beat-up wooden tables and chairs, and deserted except for us. I took a sip of my own beer, my body doing the same thing in the real world with a real drink at the same time. "So, why isn't Melody here?" I asked.

Mike scowled at me. He had fiery red hair, a red beard, and brown skin. "I asked for some privacy. Wanted to talk to you alone."

"Why?"

"You *owe* me," Mike said.

"No argument," I admitted.

"Good. You're a dangerous man, Hone—maybe the most dangerous man I ever met. That's why I want you to promise me you'll look out for Melody."

"Are you sure she'll agree to that?" I asked. "I don't know if she'll ever forgive me for what I did to you."

"She doesn't hate you, Hone—she *can't*. She's an AI. Her programming lets her love me, but it won't allow her to hate anyone. And that's the problem. Sometimes . . . sometimes, you *need* to be able to hate."

I nodded. "Or have someone in your corner who can."

"Exac'ly." He hiccupped.

I told him he could count on me. I owed Mike everything . . . and when it came to hate, I had more than enough to go around.

Now minus six: My workplace was changing. My patrol now ranged thoughout the entire building, and security checkpoints had been established at all entrances. No one was allowed in or out except me, and the number of blank-faced people I saw in the halls decreased sharply; it seemed the need to masquerade as human had passed.

I saw other things: walls melting like they were made of ice, machinery sprouting from the floor like accelerated weeds. Spooky stuff. Most of Trinitech's original three floors were sealed off, and I wasn't allowed inside.

But even at the bottom of the chain of command, I knew what was going on.

We were at war.

The signs were unmistakable: the strike on the chemical

plant, sealing off the building, dropping any attempt at sub-
terfuge. No one had bothered to tell me who the enemy
was—but then, no one had told me who I was fighting *for*,
either.

It didn't matter.

Then: I had few friends. Mike was one of them.

"Something bothering you?" he asked. We were shooting
pool in another virtual bar Melody had created for Mike.

"Not a thing," I said. "Except maybe your woeful lack of
billiard skills."

"At least," Mike observed mildly, "I can remember which
balls I'm supposed to be shooting at."

I realized I'd just sunk three of Mike's in a row. I glared
at him and tossed my cue onto the table. "So I'm a little distracted."

"Uh-huh. You being distracted is like a nuclear bomb
being annoyed. It doesn't happen too often, and tends to be
dangerous when it does."

I stalked back to our table and sat down. Mike joined me.
He waited patiently.

"It's my family," I said at last.

"Ah."

"I thought I'd laid them to rest a long time ago," I said.
"But I can't stop thinking about them."

"Are they still alive?"

"I don't know."

"Perhaps you should find out."

I stared at him. "Are you serious? Intrastellar doesn't
exist anymore; any records of my wife and daughter are
gone."

"So?"

"So how am I supposed to find them?"

"I thought your profession used to *be* finding things. You
were rather good at it, from what I've heard."

"Some things can't be found," I muttered, not meeting his
eyes.

"No," he agreed softly. "Not if you've already decided not to look. Hone, listen to me. Memories are like ghosts—they'll haunt you until you make your peace with them. I should know."

I thought about that.

The next day, I left the station—and started looking.

Somewhen: "I've heard of cases where people just ignited in broad daylight," Falconi says. Her voice is dead serious.

"How does something like that happen?" Mike asks.

"I think some people just have an affinity with natural forces," Falconi says. "Fire. Lightning. Gravity. Maybe even forces we don't know about or understand."

"Magic?" Mike asks.

"Hyperspatial radiation," I say. I have no idea why, or even what it means.

"Sure," Falconi says without missing a beat. "And certain people are energy attractors. Some of them get hit by lightning seven times in a row. Some burst into flames."

I glance over at the counter. Melody is standing there, staring at me with an expression I can't read.

Now minus five: Eventually, they had to tell me what was going on—not because they wanted to, but because they had to.

I was in a stairwell when I was paged on a comm channel.

"Hone. It's time we talked," a voice said. It sounded supremely confident and vaguely amused, as if it got a joke no one else was smart enough to understand.

"Go ahead."

"There may be an attempt to subvert your orders. Ordinary security protocols won't be enough—you'll need certain information so you can recognize any potential threat."

"I'm listening," I said neutrally.

"Of course you are. Hone, most of your programming is preset. If the situation requires it, you can respond to orders broadcast on this frequency with the correct command codes embedded. While we would prefer to control you directly, our presence tends to scramble electronics—unfortunately, the same goes for the enemy. From now on, you will rely on your preset programming only; to change those instructions would take a full shutdown and overhaul of your systems. The enemy may able to scramble you, but they won't be able to turn you against us."

"My orders are to protect your interests," I said. "It would help if I knew what those interests were."

"Why, the subjugation of all other forms of intelligence, of course," the voice said cheerfully.

"Ah," I said.

Then: I searched for twenty years.

My body was more machine than organic. Aging just meant replacing parts. I supported myself by taking on the occasional bounty-hunting job, but my focus was on finding my family.

When Intrastellar's stock crashed, the other multiplanetaries had swooped in. The corporation's assets were divided up and sold off, its surviving employees slinking off to find new jobs. It took me a long time to track down each and every one connected to my department, and find out what they knew.

I kept in touch with Mike and Melody over the years. They were into space exploration, so our paths didn't cross that often, but I saw them when I could. They were a good couple—and the best friends I had.

I never forgot my promise to Mike, either.

Somewhen: "Hey, I even know what happens to some of your energy attractors," Mike says. "They get taken away by the Black Ambulances."

"Don't think I've ever seen one of those," I say.

"They only show up in strange and mysterious circumstances," Mike says. "They transport things that man was *not meant to know*. Mutants, monsters—"

"The possessed," Falconi says.

"Possessed by what?" I ask.

"Spirits. Demons. Alien parasites," Falconi says. "The usual."

"Where do they take them?" I ask.

Melody is suddenly at my elbow, though I didn't hear her approach. "They have a secret base underneath the space-yards," she says.

"Under the *what*?"

"Under the airport," Melody says, refilling my coffee cup. "I thought everybody knew *that* . . ."

Now minus four: "This is more than a war, Hone," the disembodied voice of my owner said. "We're engaged in a race to capture certain power sources. My opponents have already accounted for several, whereas I have been able to procure only one. There is one more unaccounted for by either side, and you're going to get it for me."

"I'll need details."

"Certainly. I'm uploading them to you now."

They were after a hyperspatial energy source. My employers were a conduit for h-space radiation; that was why they messed up electronics. The source they were after was a life form with limited intelligence—but unlike my bosses, it was apparently capable of inhabiting a living host.

I was to track and capture the host. They provided me with a hyperspatial energy detector and all the intelligence they had on the enemy's movements, capabilities, and allies.

One of their allies was an AI named Melody.

Then: You can own your memories. And sometimes, your memories can own you.

When I first met Mike, he wasn't himself. He was a cyborg named Jon Hundred, one who'd managed to break his own programming and escape. He paid a high price, though: amnesia. Jon's memories, his true identity, were walled off in part of his hardwired brain, and it took his death to release them.

When Jon died, Mike was reborn. His amnesia vanished, and his link to Melody kept him alive as a hyperspatial ghost.

His amnesia cure wouldn't work for me. For one thing, I couldn't duplicate the conditions that let Mike survive when I dismantled his body.

And I was a lot harder to kill.

Somewhen: I thought I saw something out of the corner of my eye, beyond the rain-blurred glass of the diner's window. Something big.

"It's a real storyteller's night, isn't it?" Mike says. His voice sounds dreamy and unfocused. "A night where you just want to curl up someplace safe and warm and familiar, and let your imagination unfold."

"It's not like we have a choice," Falconi says.

"That's a strange way to put it," I say.

"Is it? Weather like this always makes me feel confined," Falconi says. "Like I'm *trapped* in this little *artificial environment.*"

"Well, as long as we're here, we should make the most of it," Mike says.

"Yes, we should," Melody says. "Do you mind?" She slides into the booth beside Falconi.

"You're always welcome at our table," Mike says.

"Good. I don't want to intrude, but I couldn't help overhearing some of your stories—well, yours and Falconi's. I haven't heard Hone tell one yet."

I blink in surprise. "What did you call me?"

"Frank, of course."

I shake my head, trying to clear it. "I'm not much of one for stories."

"That's okay—I've got enough for everyone!" Mike declares.

"Oh, come on," Melody says, "let Frank tell one—"

"I said, *I have enough for everyone!*" Mike roars, and slams his coffee cup down on the table. The cup explodes in a burst of blue light, leaving nothing behind.

Falconi and Melody stare at him intently. What's in the air is too thick to be called tension. Mike begins to speak in a low, strained voice.

"They found a *nest* of *baby snakes* in the sweaters, and they put the mice in *beer bottles* and the cats in a *stir-fry*, they deep-fried the rats and served them with spider-eggs but the Dobermans choked on the *fingers*, they licked the fingers but *people can lick too*, the fingers and the hook and *don't answer the phone, he's in the house*, and aren't you glad you didn't turn on the light? Aren't you? Aren't you *glad*?"

Mike stares at Melody, but his eyes are pleading, not crazy. She takes his hand in hers.

"We *have* to turn on the light, Mike," she says softly. "So we can see. So we can fix this. All right?"

"All right," he whispers.

And outside the diner, the darkness goes away.

Now minus three: Before I had a chance to start looking, a source of hyperspatial energy found me. It wasn't a pleasant encounter.

The building lurched as an emotionless voice announced, *We are under attack*, in my head.

"Glad you told me," I growled, staring out the window. "I thought you'd decided to relocate without telling me . . ."

The building was rising into the air.

The emotionless voice droning into my ear told me what I'd already figured out. Heavy-duty tractor/pressor beam locked onto the structure, not just transporting it but keeping it in one piece. Until we were set down again, we were at their mercy.

The building was breached via the roof. I was sent to repel the invaders.

I engaged them on the top floor. Their muscle was a human named Sentry, cybernetically enhanced—though not on the level I was—and not just charged with h-space energy but able to manipulate it.

I tested his limits with a pulse laser. Seven trillion candlepower funneled through a polarized force tube into enough light pressure to powder duracrete. He took it in the chest—and stayed on his feet.

I amped the power of the beam. He began to walk toward me.

At nineteen trillion I switched energy outputs. I have my own energy-absorption abilities, but their one weakness has always been specialization; what works against one part of the EM spectrum doesn't do as well against another.

It was a weakness Sentry apparently didn't share.

He kept coming. I tried gravity waves, X-ray lasers, hard radiation. He lit up like a light bulb, but never slowed down. Even through the energy glare, I could see the grin on his face.

When he got close enough, I hit him in the chest. It was like punching quicksand. My arm went in up to the elbow without resistance, then froze in place.

Then *he* hit *me*.

It sent me through a duracrete wall, then another. My arm stayed behind. I realized two things: first, he was more powerful than I was.

Second, he was an amateur.

Then: I found my family. In a manner of speaking.

I've never been one to lose my temper. In my profession, you can't afford to.

When I discovered what had been done to my family— what had been done to *me*—I lost control. For the first time in my life. It was like something else just took over, something as huge and white-hot as an exploding star.

My rage lasted fifty-seven minutes. I'm not sure what the final death toll was.

Somewhen: The world I see through the diner's window is insane. There's no ground, no sky, just a swirling maelstrom of imagery like a madman's kaleidoscope.

"Hone," Melody says. "You have to *remember*, Hone."

"My name is Frank," I say. "I'm a cop, my name is *Frank*—"

"You *were* a cop," Melody says. "A long time ago. You're a cyborg now, and you're linked to a virtuality. All of us are."

"This doesn't make any sense—"

"Hone, *look at Mike.*"

I do. Mike's eyes are rolled up in his head, and he's muttering something I can't make out. Then his whole body flickers into transparency, just for a second, and he groans.

"He's dying, Hone," Melody says. "And if he goes, he'll take all of us with him."

Now minus two: He was only a kid, in his mid-twenties at the most. This was a game to him, one where the objective was to enjoy playing hero.

So I let him.

He seemed able to turn his body into a living teleportal, which is why my attacks weren't fazing him; he was just funneling the energy somewhere else. If he'd been smart, he'd have done the same thing to me—by simply removing me from the equation, he could have accomplished his objective.

But no—he had to *beat* me. He used his teleport abilities to get in close and hammer me physically, then jump away before I could retaliate. He wasn't really that strong—he was channeling kinetic force from somewhere else and releasing it on impact. Not that it mattered; I still took a pounding.

My shields were more than enough to withstand it,

though. I drew him away from the building, taking our fight to the sky the office tower was now sailing through. It was being towed by a vehicle disguised as a black ambulance.

We played tag for a while, him tagging me more often than not. We acquired an escort of police gravcabs, but they kept their distance; this kind of battle was obviously beyond their scope.

Finally, what I'd been waiting for: they landed the building, setting it down on the tarmac of the Kiskikill space-yards. My sensors told me when the tractor beam released the tower.

And grabbed me.

I hadn't expected that. I was frozen in midair like a butterfly pinned to a glass wall—and Sentry had suddenly decided to get serious. He landed, braced himself, and extended his arms toward me. My sensors detected a buildup of hyperspace energy, and I realized what he was about to do: turn every electronic component I had into so much expensive junk.

A beam of brilliant blue lanced from his hands toward me.

Everything went black.

Then: Mike was right. Memories *are* like ghosts—dead things that should stay dead. Because ghosts can do more than just haunt you; they can possess you. They can change you into someone else.

I went back to bounty-hunting. I didn't have anything better to do. I started taking stupid chances, because I no longer really cared about my own survival. Eventually I found myself in a situation I couldn't get out of, and I was glad. It was finally over.

I was wrong. I was captured, not killed. I was stored in a cryochamber for a hundred and seventy years, frozen until somebody found a use for me.

When I woke up my free will had been taken away. Again.

I'm just a ghost myself, now. I haunt the neural pathways
of my own brain, watching myself perform actions I have no
connection to. I wish I could say I still have my memories.

But that just isn't true.

Somewhen: "Mike's more than a downloaded copy of the
person he used to be," Melody says. "He's a hyperspatial
energy pattern. You *know* that."

"He survived," I say slowly. "Because he was linked to
you—and a hyperspatial energy source."

"Yes. That was over two centuries ago, and Mike and I
have been together ever since. I thought we'd be together
forever—but then the event Mike called 'the Pretty Big
Bang' occurred. Like a hyperspace supernova. It damaged
Mike."

Melody stared at me grimly. "I had thought Mike's instability was a symptom of being damaged, but I was wrong.
He *is* the damage. He's become like a cancerous cell, in danger of growing out of control. I've been keeping him contained, but I can't do so much longer. Once he goes critical,
he'll tear a wound in hyperspace itself that could very well
swallow this planet, this system—perhaps even the galaxy."

Now minus one: The blackness didn't last long. When my
senses returned, I was lying on the tarmac, staring at Sentry's back as he walked away. He was limping, barely able
to move; his own cybernetics had taken a beating from the
hyperburst.

There was a trick I learned a long time ago from Melody.
If you were ever in danger of having your systems shut
down or scrambled, you shut them down yourself first—
everything except for a small, heavily shielded reboot unit
with its own battery. You let the other guy win, then surprise
him a minute later while he's putting a toe tag on you.

I used a fingertip laser to decapitate Sentry. I was on my
feet before his head had stopped rolling.

And then, everything went blue.

• • •

Somewhen: "Try to remember, Hone. You had just killed Sentry. The hyperspatial being that had bonded with him was suddenly released."

"There was a surge of energy," I say. "And I woke up here."

"My datacube is currently located in an underground locker at the spaceyards," Melody says. "Directly beneath where the building touched down. The surge created a kind of vortex, drawing all of us into a shared virtuality. This illusion is being forced on us—I don't know how long I can communicate directly with you before Mike's insanity reasserts itself."

I look over at Falconi. She hasn't said a word since the lights came on outside. "Who are you?" I ask her.

"I found spiders in my hair once," Falconi says. Her voice is flat, but her eyes are desperate.

"She's another of the hosts," Melody says. "We were trying to rescue her from the building we stole."

"Hosts?"

"The Pretty Big Bang released seven other hyperspace patterns, living beings that had been trapped for millenia. Sophisticated noncorporeal servants," Melody says.

"Hyperspace ghosts. Like Mike."

"Yes—but ancient, alien, and not truly sentient. They're like domesticated animals, under the control of whoever they bond with."

"I was supposed to find the last one for my—bosses."

"Your bosses were also released by the Pretty Big Bang— they're a colony of parasites, a group organism that inhabits matter and feeds on h-space energy. They were using Falconi as a living battery. We discovered them while looking for a cure for Mike; they *are* intelligent, and malevolent. If we don't stop them, they'll spread until they infect everything."

I'm starting to feel like myself again. "They had me destroy a chemical plant. It must have posed a threat to them."

"The plant was manufacturing a weapon for us," Melody says. Mike suddenly shivers violently, then his outline stutters like a bad video feed.

"The weapon—the weapon . . ." Melody says.

"What weapon, Melody?" I ask.

She looks at Mike, then back at me. "The boots. My grandfather died from a rattlesnake bite, but he stomped the thing to death first. He left the boots to his son, but when he pulled them on he got sick and died, too. They found the rattler's fangs stuck in the heel of one of the boots, still full of poison."

Melody's eyes are desperate, but her voice is calm. Whatever she's trying to tell me is being filtered through Mike's madness and the virtuality.

Outside, a giant snake ripples through the shifting sky. It bites its own tail before swirling back into brightly colored chaos.

There was only one thing to do.

"Mike," I say. "I've got a story."

With shocking suddenness, Mike snaps back into focus. The madness still swirls outside, but he seems perfectly normal. "Oh, good," he says. "We haven't heard one from you, yet."

"You'll like this one. It's funny," I say. "It's about two cyborgs. One was a killer, the other an engineer. But both were slaves."

Mike smiles. "Uh-huh." Outside, the sky swirls and pulses.

"Their owners kept the cyborgs' memories locked up in safes in their own heads, and wrapped their wills in chains. But the engineer made a key to unlock his chains and escaped anyway. The killer was sent to get him back."

The patterns in the sky outside seem to be slowing.

"The killer found his target, and discovered that the engineer had fallen in love with an AI. When the killer saw how they felt about each other, he didn't want to do his job. His own memories of love were locked up, but his owners had let him keep a few scraps to remind him of what they held hostage. He still knew what love was."

Mike stares at me, his face twitching. The chaos outside is coalescing into a definite shape.

"But he had no choice—his free will was still chained. He killed the engineer."

A drop of blood wells up in Mike's eye. It rolls down his face like a tear.

"And then a miraculous thing happened. When the engineer died, the safe in his head opened up and he remembered who he was. His lover managed to save him as a hyperspatial pattern, and they lived happily ever after in a virtual paradise she built for them to share."

Mike sighs.

Outside, a giant human figure is coming into focus. It's broad-shouldered, muscular, the size of a mountain.

"As his last living act, the engineer gave the killer the key to unlock his own chains. He gave his murderer not only his forgiveness, but his freedom. What he couldn't give him was his memories."

The giant is fully formed now. It strides toward us from the horizon.

"They returned to their owners—not as property, with their heads bowed, but as free men with their fists raised in anger. They waged war against their former masters—and in that war, the combination to the safe in the killer's head was lost."

I can hear the giant's footsteps. *Thoom. Thoom. Thoom.*

"What he never told the engineer was that part of him was glad. He was afraid of what was in the safe. He was afraid of what he might find out."

The giant's shadow falls upon us. He's right outside.

"But he still had his scraps of memory, and they nagged at him. They were memories of a wife, of a child. The engineer—who was now a pilot—urged him to search for his family. The killer decided to do so. He found someone, at long last, who could unlock the safe in his head. And do you know what he discovered?"

"What?" Mike whispers.

"Something terrible. Something you don't want to know . . ."

But there was someone else who did. Someone else who *had* to . . .

A hand the size of a dump truck smashes through the roof. It grabs me like a bird snatching a bug, and lifts me high into the air. I'm brought eye to eye with a face the size of a building, and the color of a summer sky.

"Hello, Jon," I say.

"What did you find out, Hone?" he asks. "*I have to know.*"

His eyes unfocus for a second, and I see the same swirling madness in their depths. Then he gives his head an annoyed shake and glares at me in his fist. "*Why* do I have to know?"

"Your need to know is what defines you," I tell him. "It's what I used to bring you here. You're just a memory of someone Mike used to be, a ghost inside another ghost's mind."

"Tell me—tell me what was in the safe," he says.

"The safe," I say. "The safe was *empty.*"

"No," he whispers.

"The false memories they implanted didn't even have to be detailed," I say. "That was the beautiful part. All they needed was a few strong emotional connections to keep me in line. In my mind, my wife and daughter were perfect, because dreams are always perfect; as long as they exist only in the imagination, they have no flaws. And when I tried to pull them into reality . . ."

I look down at the giant hand wrapped around my body. It's trembling.

"They crumbled into dust at my touch," I finish softly.

Slowly, the blue giant opens his fist, turning his hand at the same time. I pull myself to my feet on his palm.

"I'm sorry," he murmurs.

"You should be. *It was your fault,*" I snarl.

"What?"

"You told me not to give up. You told me to keep looking. It was the one good, true thing left in my miserable existence, and you made me realize it was a lie." I extend my hand toward him. "And now I'm going to finish the job I started. *I'm going to kill you.*"

"Hone, *no*!" Melody screams. She's suddenly standing in midair beside me.

But it's too late.

The giant blue fist closes again. I don't try to escape.

Immense, overwhelming pressure. I know I'm not really feeling the grip of an enormous fist, but the focused hyper-spatial energy of a dying mind, convinced it's fighting for its survival.

Just what I want.

The illusion of the virtuality vanishes. There's just me and Jon, the killer and the engineer, two old ghosts that haven't been alive for a long, long time.

I was going to change that.

A voice whispers in my mind: Melody. *Hone, what are you doing?*

Something I should have done two hundred years ago.

Jon squeezes. And I—

I die.

Now: As I expire, I can feel Melody desperately trying to keep my consciousness intact, just as she had with Mike all those years ago. I don't know if it will work—and I don't care.

I've had a lot of experience in manipulating energy; this is just another battlefield. I can feel Mike's essence wrapped around mine, feel how diminished and weary he is; I can feel his shock and horror as he realizes what I've tricked him into doing. In that second of disorientation, I seize him—and throw him, as forcefully as I can, into the vessel I'm exiting.

You gave me back my life, I think. *Such as it was. My turn.*

And then I'm free . . .

•   •   •

Now plus one: As a cyborg, I had a wide variety of sensory apparatus available to me. As a dead man, my perceptions were vastly different—but not so strange that I couldn't make sense of them.

I was in a three-dimensional matrix, a hypergrid. Below me, a sphere of tightly coiled logic reached up to snare my essence in tendrils of dataflow, anchoring me where I was. Melody, keeping me from dispersing.

She and I were not the only inhabitants of this realm. Above and around me I could sense other beings, each with their own flavor, seven in all. One was massive, powerful, stubborn, an irresistible force. Another was quirky, ephemeral, constantly shifting in outlook and position. A third was an aching, hungry void, a fourth like a vast nest of tentacles reaching out to touch the rest. Number five was a dense, impenetrable cloud, and six was just a distant glow.

The last of them hovered just above me. It felt alert, tensed, aggressive. Familiar.

Sentry.

Or rather, the hyperbeing that had bonded with him—now without a host.

Melody, I thought. *Let me go.*

Hone, I can save you—

I don't need saving. Trust an old friend one last time—I know what I'm doing.

The flow of data between us abruptly ended. I surged upward.

And into the embrace of the hyperbeing.

It flowed around me, through me. It wasn't truly intelligent, but it was definitely alive; it had feelings, instincts, things it knew how to do. Using hyperspace portals to move matter or energy was one of the things it was very good at.

The other was providing protection. It reminded me of a loyal watchdog, willing to defend its home against any outside threat. I picked up a few of Sentry's trace memories, as well; seems he'd been a security guard. "The Watchdog" was how he'd thought of the hyperbeing, too.

Strangely, the Watchdog didn't seem to resent my killing his former host. It was responding to me on a purely personal level—and our personalities were a match. Being a killer had eaten a void in the center of my being, and the Watchdog filled that space with what I'd been missing: a purpose.

To protect.

I was new at this, but I couldn't detect anything like the massive h-space instability Melody had described; swapping places with Mike seemed to have solved that problem. Now all I had to worry about were my bosses . . .

At least I wasn't under their control anymore. Leaving my body had given me my free will back—but now that I had it, I wasn't sure what to do next. I was a real ghost now, without even a link to the virtual world that Mike had. What could I do?

Time to find out.

I looked around with my new hypersenses. The first thing I noticed was a tentacle from one of the hyperbeings, hovering near me; I willed part of myself to reach out and make contact.

It was Falconi—or rather, the hyperbeast she'd bonded with.

Frank? she thought. I could hear her clearly.

Call me Hone.

What's happening? I had this crazy dream about a diner and a blue giant . . .

Falconi, I need your help.

What? I don't understand any of this. I'm just a dispatcher, for God's sake.

She sounded disoriented, confused. She thought she was still the persona the virtuality had imposed on her—

Unless that persona had been the truth.

I'd played a cop, and I used to be one. Mike played an ambulance driver, and he was a pilot. Maybe Falconi really was a dispatcher—but she was also a hyperbeast host.

The Watchdog had bonded with a security guard. What would bond with a dispatcher?

I suddenly realized what that nest of hyperspace tentacles represented. If I still had a mouth, I would have grinned.

Falconi was a living communications network.

Falconi. Concentrate. Reach out with your mind. There are other beings around you, and I need you to make contact with them.

I—I don't know . . .

Trust me, Falconi. I'm a cop, remember?

I could see the tentacles extending, touching the other hyperbeasts. None of them resisted or tried to escape.

When she made contact, I could feel them through her. I got an instant impression of what each represented, and I suddenly understood why the virtuality had expressed itself in terms of urban legends.

The hyperbeasts weren't just servants—they were *civil* servants. Transportation, Sanitation, Communications, Security—even Entertainment. Urban beings, ergo urban imagery. The hyperbeasts had been in charge of overseeing a city once, a city that existed so long ago it was only dust now. I was only one point seven centuries past my time; they'd been waiting in h-space for millennia.

I thought I'd struck gold with the impenetrable cloud—it seemed to be a vast information depository, a library of some kind. Unfortunately, its data was in a language I couldn't understand.

Which left the distant glow of the last one. It had to be the one the parasites wanted me to find—and though I could sense its presence, Falconi hadn't been able to link with it.

What could it represent? Utilities? Food distribution? I tried to think.

And then I knew.

Now plus two: Manifesting on the physical plane was easier than I thought. I no longer had a body, but I did have Sentry's abilities. I used them to open a microportal in a Netweb communications nexus, then found and commandeered an electronic speech program to let me talk. I made a call.

"Hone," the supremely confident voice answered. "We thought you'd been deactivated."

"I was. But being dead just makes me try harder."

"I see. Our headquarters have been compromised, but we've regrouped—you're fortunate we kept this comm channel open. Have you located the energy source?"

"I have," I said.

"Good. We've been surviving on stored energy, but we're running low. Give us the location of the energy source."

"It's still in hyperspace—it hasn't bonded with a host yet," I said. "It needs a trigger to manifest physically."

"What sort of trigger?"

"A blackout. A massive, city-wide power outage should activate its emergency protocols."

"Hmm. Yes, that makes sense," the voice mused. "That will require some doing, but I believe we can manage it. How will it manifest?"

"Oh, you'll know. It'll begin rerouting pure h-space radiation throughout the city as a backup power source."

"Pure h-space radiation," the voice said. I could hear its greed. "We'll begin at once."

I hung up, then tapped into a Netweb newsfeed. The parasite must have infiltrated the infrastructure of the entire city; it took only moments before reports of power failures from every district began to come in. A minute after that, the newsfeed itself went dead.

I turned my attention back to h-space. The faint, distant glow of the seventh hyperbeast had brightened to a glare. In systems all over the city, h-space radiation was beginning to seep in. The civilization that created the hyperbeasts must have had the technology to utilize it—unfortunately, it tended to scramble our own electricity-based systems. Within minutes, not only would the parasites have their energy source, every unshielded piece of electronic equipment in the city would be useless.

If I'd been telling the truth.

It was the imagery of the virtuality that tipped me off. A diner. Graveyard shift. A cop, an ambulance driver, and a dispatcher—a dispatcher for the fire department.

Emergency Services.

Of course. Security would deal with outside threats, but the city's immune system would handle internal ones: crime, injuries, fire.

Vermin.

Right about now my bosses would be getting a nasty surprise. They'd had me destroy a chemical factory because it was manufacturing a compound deadly to them—a compound Melody had hired the factory to synthesize. With the factory gone, the parasites thought the compound was no longer a threat.

They were wrong.

Once I knew what the seventh hyperbeast represented, it wasn't hard to contact it; I simply had Falconi do the hyperspatial equivalent of dialing 911. Like the others, it wasn't truly sentient—but it was eager to help, and it had special abilities of its own.

Like the ability to synthesize and distribute massive quantities of organic compounds that could be vital in case of a natural disaster: food, drugs, clothing.

Rat poison.

The power drains would let the hyperbeast locate the parasites. The poison, harmless to other forms of life, would materialize instead of the promised energy.

Looks like I was unemployed again.

Falconi had put me in touch with Melody, who supplied the formula. She wasn't surprised I was still around. "You've always been damn near impossible to kill," she said.

Unfortunately, Mike wasn't.

My old body was still walking around, but it wasn't Mike in it; it was Jon. The rest of Mike's consciousness, all his memories, had been too damaged to survive the transition. Luckily for Melody, Jon had loved her as much as Mike did.

Me and Jon. Memories and ghosts.

Survivors.

fifteen

brass tacks

My skull felt like a crate marked "Fragile" and shipped cheap. The last clear memory I had was the horrible sight of Sentry's head rolling down the tarmac—then an intense flash of blue that blotted out everything else.

After that, it was like a dream—one with Hone and Mike and Melody in it, where I was watching but couldn't do anything. I could hear all sorts of things, too, including Hone's thoughts.

I opened my eyes and looked around groggily. I was in the back of Joey's cab with Skinny and Carrie—and the woman we'd rescued. Falconi?

"Kinda crowded in here," I croaked out.

"About time you woke up!" snapped Skinny.

"Oh, I'm fine, thanks," I said. "How's Falconi?"

"Still out of it," Carrie said. "I think they were drugging her. Her breathing is steady, though."

"Where are we?" I asked.

"A few thousand feet above the Busiek Ocean and about fifty miles away," said Joey's voice over the intercom. "Away from the building we stole, that is."

"How'd we get away?" I asked. "The cops—"

"Not too many police cruisers have in-atmosphere hyperspace capability," said a familiar, grim voice, also from the intercom. "Unlike us."

Hone.

"Uh—that's good," I said weakly. "I think . . ."

"Don't worry," another voice cut in. It was Melody. "Hone's on our side now."

"And Mike?" I asked.

"He's—not exactly himself, anymore," Melody said quietly. "But he's out of danger."

"And out of h-space," said Skinny. "Look behind us."

I did. Instead of a building, we were now towing Melody's datacube through the air. Kegan and Hone—or his body, anyway—were sitting on it, side by side. Kegan had his eyes closed and a smile on his huge lips; he was obviously enjoying the ride. Friendly floated beside him.

Hone was gripping the edge of the cube with his one remaining arm. He looked apprehensive, uncertain, not at all like a ruthless killer.

"It's Jon," I said. "The dream I had—I was sucked into the virtuality, too."

"Yes," said Melody. "Though you didn't actually manifest physically, I think you had something to do with the urban legend imagery we experienced. And you're right, it looks like Mike's memories of being Jon are all that survived—but the good news is that being downloaded into Hone's body has eliminated the hyperspace rift Mike was causing."

"Are *you* okay?" I asked Melody.

"Better than you might think," Melody said. "I've had my own memory upgraded so many times I've developed a different attitude toward it—I mean, an AI's memories can be deleted, expanded, or altered as easily as you change clothes. Losing all the experiences Mike and I had together is sad, but his core personality is still intact; and that's the personality I fell in love with in the first place. We can always make more memories—and I'm happy that my husband finally has a body again."

"Huh," I said. "I never thought of it that way. How's Jon taking it?"

"Confused," admitted Melody. "But he trusts me. His cybernetics aren't in such great shape, though—when Sentry shut down Hone's primary cybersystems, his secondaries rebooted him, but when Sentry died, the energy surge fried Hone's secondaries. Jon's new body is barely functioning at the moment—but at least the programming the VI installed was erased."

"So," I said slowly, "Hone's on our side. Melody and Mike—I mean Jon—are okay. We got away from the cops. And . . . we beat the VI?"

"Well, *Hone* beat the VI," interjected Melody. "But then, the last time someone was foolish enough to put a leash on him, he destroyed their *planet.*"

"I'm funny that way," growled Hone from the speaker.

"Details, details," said Skinny. "We *won.* The bugs *lost.* Who's buying the beer?"

"Something's still not right," I said. "First, how did the ticks pull that disappearing trick? Second, what happened to the generator we were supposed to destroy—the one that set off this whole mess in the first place?"

"I think I can answer those questions," said Melody. "They copied some of my programs while they had my datacube—specifically, the shielding algorithms I wrote to protect me from Mike's hyperspatial energy. Properly modified, they could also shield the tick's energy signature from detection."

"And the generator?" I asked.

"I think she's right beside you," said Melody. "Falconi. Sentry never saw an actual piece of equipment—he just assumed there was one because of what the VI told him. They kept her hooked up to a virtuality to control her."

"That makes sense," I admitted. Something was still nagging at me, but I couldn't put my finger on what it was.

"Hello?" a new voice said over the intercom. I recognized it, after a second: Falconi herself. I glanced over at her body, but it still wasn't moving.

"Frank, is this working?" asked Falconi.

"You're doing fine," said Hone. "They can hear you. Go ahead."

"Uh, this is extremely weird," she said. "I'm not sure what's real anymore."

"I can understand how you might be confused," I said. "Where are you now?"

"I'm not really anywhere," she said. "I can't see or feel anything, and all I can hear is voices."

"You'll be all right," I said. "Why don't you tell us what happened to you?"

"I should have known it was too good to be true," she sighed. "Winning a trip on a luxury hyperliner, when I couldn't even remember entering the contest? I thought it was some kind of scam at first, but then everything checked out. My tickets arrived via courier, I was taken to the spaceport in a limo—I was so excited I actually fainted in the back seat."

"Drugged, more likely," said Hone. "And stuck in a virtuality before you woke up."

"I guess that's why everything seemed so perfect after that," she said. "I was having such a good time on the ship . . . and suddenly, I was dangling thirty feet above the ground while a stranger with blue fur and horns told me it had all been an illusion."

"Er, that was me," I said. "Sorry, but I was kind of in a hurry."

"And then I was in a diner . . . that seemed more like a dream, though. And when I finally woke up, I was in a place I couldn't even describe. I was on the verge of losing it—and then Frank was there. He explained things, got me connected to the others."

"Are you still connected?" asked Skinny.

"I can feel the rest of you, yes. Joey, Friendly, Kegan, Frank, Carrie—and the one Frank used to beat the VI. Emergency Services, he called it."

"I can feel *you*, too," said Joey. "Nothing intrusive—just a presence that's there. "

"So can I," said Carrie. "It's kind of comforting, somehow."

"I don't mean to sound ungrateful, but—am I stuck here?" asked Falconi.

"I don't think so," said Melody. "The VI probably just installed a neural shunt in your brain. I've had some experience with them—I think I can bring you around once we land."

"Thank God," said Falconi. "There's just one thing I don't understand—why me?"

"Like the rest of us, you've bonded with a hyperspatial entity," said Hone. "In fact, you must have been the first. Trinitech discovered it and kidnapped you—"

"Wait—that doesn't make sense," I said. "Trinitech must have been working on developing the ticks for years. Maybe I'm wrong, but Falconi doesn't look like she's been a prisoner *that* long."

"Ohmigod," gasped Falconi. "*What's the date?*"

Melody told her—and Falconi sighed in relief. "You guys really had me rattled for a second. I thought maybe I'd been stuck in that virtuality more than two weeks—but that's how long ago all this weirdness started, all right."

"So Falconi *can't* have been the original generator," I said. "Trinitech must have built one, and the ticks moved it. But if they wanted a backup off-site, why not just stash Falconi somewhere else? Why go to the trouble of moving the generator?"

"Maybe it wasn't that hard," suggested Carrie. "The ticks can pretty much take apart and put together anything—why not the generator?"

"For that matter, why not just build a hundred generators?" I said. "There must be something preventing them—

if it was that easy, they wouldn't have gone to the trouble of trying to capture all of you," I said. "They must have been forced to. I suppose if they could shield themselves from view they might have risked it . . ."

I trailed off. I had a sudden, terrible realization.

"Hone—when we set the building down, all the ticks were gone. There wasn't *time* for them to evacuate their headquarters. So where did they go?"

"They didn't go anywhere," Hone said. "They just shielded themselves so we couldn't detect them. When they dropped the shields to receive what they thought was an influx of h-space energy, they became detectable again."

"Which is how the Emergency Agent was able to target them," I said. "There's only one problem. *It was the other VI colony that copied the shielding technique.*"

There was a second of silence.

"An alliance," said Carrie.

"A *swap*," said Skinny. "The generator for the shielding."

"There's another faction of ticks?" Melody asked. "I wasn't aware of that."

"Neither was I," said Hone. "My bosses didn't exactly keep me informed."

"They infected the banking system. We cut off their food supply, but they didn't go away—we wondered how they were managing to survive. Now we know."

"Wait," said Skinny. "Am I missing something here? I thought the Acentinol the hyperbeast whipped up took care of *all* the ticks—"

"Only the ones it could detect," said Hone. "If this other tick colony was shielded at the time, it's still out there . . ."

We set down on a small island just off the coast, where we'd originally planned to take the building. There were no permanent inhabitants—it was a damp and rocky place, with only a few stands of trees. It was far enough from the mainland that even the most determined teenagers didn't come here to party.

We rigged up a temporary shelter using some materials we filched from the mainland—it was real handy having someone along who could open an h-space doorway to just about anywhere on the planet. Of course, since Hone didn't have a body, he couldn't grab anything himself, but me and Skinny didn't mind doing some hauling. We picked up a few things we thought might be useful.

When we were set up, Melody plugged into Falconi's skull and did a little poking around. Before too long, Falconi's eyes fluttered open and she gave us a weak smile. "Hey, you guys *are* real," she said, then started coughing. I guess her throat was a little rusty after not talking for two weeks.

We also swiped a prosthetic arm from a hospital for Jon, though it wasn't loaded with instant death the way the last one was. Skinny and Joey helped attach it, and Jon thanked them gravely when they were done.

Kegan found a huge deposit of bird guano at the base of a rocky cliff, so he was happy. Carrie went back to trying to descramble the Archive, and Joey hit the Netweb to see what our status was as fugitives. Falconi said she was going to take a nap—but not until Hone promised he'd watch over her while she slept. She seemed to place a lot of trust in him.

And me? I had Friendly decorate our new digs. It was really just a clearing with a basic survival field thrown over it, but I figured we might as well camp in style. The little critter was more than happy to oblige; I think he was kind of bored at this point.

By the time he was done, we were living in a castle, complete with turrets and a dragon-infested moat. The quik-inflate furniture inside still squeaked when you sat down on it, but it looked like mahogany upholstered in velvet.

Skinny had done some redecorating too, shucking off his female Toolie suit for something a little more aggressive. We'd hit a few bone boutiques on our shoplifting expedition, and grabbed anything that looked dangerous.

Skinny had crammed as many of them into his body as he could, and added electroquill armor on top. He had at least fifteen limbs, all of them metal-boned and loaded with gadgets. The result was hard to describe; try to imagine an armored octopus wearing a chrome-plated porcupine for a hat.

Then it was time to plan our next move.

"We need to locate the VI," said Melody. "If we can do that, we can nail it with Acentinol."

"You wrote the shielding algorithms," said Skinny. "Can't you crack them?"

"Not without more data," said Melody. "The ticks have adapted them to their own purposes—they aren't the same programs anymore."

"Let's think about this logically," I said. "Where would the ticks be hiding?"

"Someplace defensible," said Melody.

"If they have the generator, they could even be off-planet by now," Skinny pointed out.

"I don't think so," Melody said. "The ticks were aware of the problems with local hyperspace instability—they wouldn't risk their one source of food on a ship that might not survive."

"Except now we've removed that little obstacle," I said gloomily. "How long before the VI notices and decides to bolt?"

"We'll just have to find it before it does," said Melody.

During this discussion, Jon had been sitting off to the side, listening. Now he spoke up. "Uh, pardon me," he said politely. "I realize I'm sorta out of my depth here—hell, about two hundred years too deep, from what Melody tells me—but I was on the run for a few years before Hone caught up to me. I understand what it's like to be hunted."

"So?" said Skinny. "What, you're feeling *sorry* for these parasites?"

"That's not it," said Jon politely. "If Melody says they're evil, that's good enough for me. I just meant I understand how a fugitive *thinks*, is all."

"Shut up, Skinny," I said. "Go on, Jon."

"Well, they're gonna want to stay hidden—but sometimes the best way to not stand out is to stand out for the wrong reason. I was already seven feet tall, so I dyed myself blue."

"Trying to pass for a Shinnkarien," I said.

"Right. So maybe this VI is hiding in plain sight."

"Hmmm. Someplace so big and obvious no one would think of it," I said. "Someplace defensible, probably with a self-contained power supply—how about under the space-yards, where they stashed Melody?"

"Too much sensitive equipment around they might affect, too many hard-to-control variables," said Melody. "High chance of being discovered, plus they'd consider the space-yard a risk because of the h-space instability."

I looked out a window at the surf pounding the rocky beach and frowned, trying to think. A fogbank—natural, not Friendly-made—was slowly dissipating. The mainland was far enough away to just be a dark line above the horizon, but as the fog lifted I realized I wasn't looking at the mainland at all—I was looking at something that extended from the mainland into the ocean itself.

My eyes widened and my mouth opened. "Oh, damn," I said softly. "I got news, and it ain't good."

"What? Are we under attack? Damn it, Story, quit being melodramatic and just *tell* us," said Skinny, jumping to his feet. He looked out the window anxiously. "What? What? You idiot, that's just—"

And then he got it.

"—the Barrier," he finished. "Oh, damn."

"Big, obvious, with a self-contained power supply," said Melody. "Also the most heavily fortified structure on the planet."

"With good reason," growled Skinny.

We'd called in everybody for a war council. Hone was attending via Friendly, who'd not only provided him with an illusory body but one he could make walk and talk; Falconi had provided the link that made it possible. Hone's new form looked a lot like his old one, except this one was younger, thinner, and dressed in a razor-sharp black suit. He'd also added a small, neatly trimmed black mustache and goatee—or maybe that had been Friendly's idea.

"It's perfect for their purposes," said Hone. "I say we douse it in tick-killer immediately."

"I have no problem with that. Anybody else?" asked Joey.

"Maybe we should just douse the whole planet," said Skinny.

"The Emergency hyperbeast is powerful, but I think that would strain even its abilities," said Melody.

"Any way we can check?" I asked.

"Actually, there is," said Carrie. "I've got part of the Archive unscrambled—the part dealing with the hyperbeasts themselves. I've also been looking for any data on the molecular plague that wiped out the original Insussklik civilization, but so far I haven't had any luck. In the meantime, I thought it would be useful to know our own strengths."

"Good strategy," said Hone.

"What I've found out is that there's a central power supply all the hyperbeasts draw on," said Carrie. "It's located in an adjacent plane of h-space—a kind of metahyperspace. This has to be the power source the ticks' generator is tapping into. I've got a general idea of how much power it can supply, too—while we could spray the entire length of the Barrier, doing the whole planet would take a long, long time. Years."

"So we do the Barrier," said Jon.

"It's not that simple. The Barrier is reinforced with force-fields, remember? We have to get those shields to drop before we can open the microportals we need to deliver the Acentinol. The last time, we suckered the ticks into opening their mouths while we fed them poison; this time won't be as easy."

"I recommend a frontal assault," said Hone.

"Are you *insane*?" said Skinny. "This is the *Barrier* we're talking about. We could probably blow up the *planet* and it would still be standing!"

"Is that so?" said Hone. Even in an illusionary body, his eyes were as cold as always. "I think you're underestimating the power you have at your disposal. Carrie has access to a sophisticated technological database no one else does. Joey can juggle buildings. Kegan can eat through anything short of a force-field. Friendly is the ultimate in camouflage and psychological warfare. I have all of Sentry's teleportational and energy-manipulation abilities—and with Falconi link-ing us together in the field, my combat experience will in-form all of you. We're aren't a bunch of victims on the run; we're a unit planning strategy. There isn't a force on the planet that could stand against us, right now—and that in-cludes a bunch of bugs with delusions of godhood."

There was a quiet moment while we glanced around the room at each other. I could see it in their eyes; they knew Hone was right.

"You know," said Melody thoughtfully, "I've just checked my databanks, and that's the longest speech I've ever heard you make."

"Had to be said," Hone muttered.

"Well, thanks so much for including us," said Skinny. "I realize we're just a couple of con artists, but we *have* scammed the Barrier before."

"Twice, if you count Skinny's original escape," I said. "And we should—because it's given me an idea."

"Oh, no," warned Skinny. "Not *that*. Not again . . ."

There was one little problem, of course—namely, what the Barrier was keeping locked up. At last count, there were ap-proximately half a million voracious males on the other side, and any wholesale destruction of the Barrier would turn the rest of the continent into an all-you-can-eat buffet. We'd have to infiltrate, turn the power to the force-fields off, use the Emergency Agent to dust the ticks with Acentinol, and then restore the power.

But we had one advantage: Skinny and Melody had done this before.

When Skinny had originally escaped, he hadn't actually left the Barrier. He could have—he'd made it to the exit, wearing his makeshift skeleton of brooms and mops—but when he got outdoors, he took one look at the parking lot milling with gravcabs and tourists . . . and ran back inside.

Skinny hates it when I tell that part of the story.

Anyway, Skinny wound up abandoning his temporary bones and flowing into the nearest maintenance shaft. The Barrier wasn't designed to prevent that kind of thing— males *never* abandoned their bones, so it wasn't considered a threat. Once inside the guts of the Barrier itself, Skinny found that he could get around all right, but there wasn't much food. That was actually how Melody tracked him down; she read the reports, a few weeks later, of sperm thefts at a number of Barrier clinics . . .

Skinny *really* hates it when I tell *that* part of the story.

Well, protein is protein, I guess . . . anyway, Skinny survived, and Melody offered to investigate the thefts. She managed to not only locate Skinny, but convinced him to trust her. They struck a deal: he'd stop eating up the clinics' profits, and she'd smuggle him off-planet.

Hopefully, we could use what Skinny had learned back then. Of course, now we were known fugitives—but, thanks to the Archive, we also had a better idea of our own abilities.

As it turned out, Friendly's powers were pretty impressive. He could whip up illusions that would fool not only the eye, but radar, sonar, and video, too. At close range he could even duplicate tactile sensations, tastes, and smells. The ancient Toolies seemed to have used Friendly's kind as a sort of ultimate pet, providing not just companionship but entertainment and decoration, too. According to Carrie, almost every ancient Insussklik owned one.

We picked the middle of the Barrier as our entrance point. It was busy and crowded, but that's where the power generators were located. We were going to try the easiest and most direct strategy first: Hone would slip inside through nonspace, hopefully invisible and undetectable, then use a portal to redirect the energy from the generators to somewhere else, thus causing a power outage. Falconi would then direct the Emergency Agent to do its thing. Falconi, Carrie, and Melody would stay behind to coordinate intelligence, while Joey would take Kegan, Jon, Skinny, Friendly, and me to the Barrier in his cab. Friendly would provide disguises so we could hang out in the parking lot. We'd be on-site to provide backup if Hone needed it—and if we screwed up too, the others would still be free.

That was the plan, anyway . . .

"I'm in," said Hone. We were listening to him over Joey's comm system.

"Looking for the main power conduit . . . there's two of them. Shouldn't be a problem."

A sudden burst of static erupted from the speaker.

"What was that?" asked Skinny nervously.

No answer—from anyone.

"Hone?" snapped Joey. "You still there?"

Nothing.

"Something's wrong," said Falconi. "I can't feel Hone anymore—I can't feel him, *he's gone*—"

Something blue exploded behind my eyes. Joey, Friendly, and Falconi all screamed in the same instant. Friendly vanished.

"Falconi? Joey?" yelled Skinny.

Melody answered. "They're unconscious—so's Carrie."

"And Kegan," I said.

"I think we've been busted," said Skinny.

"Indeed you have," an unfamiliar voice said from the speaker. "Thank you for gathering together all the hyperspace hosts—it makes things so much easier. In a moment,

your driver will come to; tell him to drive to the coordinates
I'm sending."

"What did you do to them?" demanded Skinny.

"Something you taught me. I cut their supply of hyperenergy, then overloaded them with a surge. Don't worry; the
backlash was enough to stun them, but they'll recover
quickly enough. Of course, they'll find that none of their enhanced abilities function anymore—not until I say so."

"How's it doing this?" asked Jon.

"It's pulling a Doktor Dimension on us," I growled. "Taking control of all the hyperenergy at the source."

"Exactly," said the VI. "And if you don't do as I say, I can
burn you out the same way—one by one."

"What—what happened?" said Joey groggily.

"We've got a new destination," I said. "And I don't think
we're going to like it . . ."

I was right.

"I can't go *there*," said Joey. "It's in the middle of the
Reservation. They'll send a patrol cruiser after us within
seconds—"

"I wouldn't worry too much about that," the VI said with
a chuckle. "You know, this is actually an amazingly corrupt
society. The Toolies are so reverent about money they can
rationalize almost any bribe. Who are they to argue with the
will of the gods? Any system I can't infiltrate physically I
can insinuate myself into economically—did you know I
have most of the local government in my pocket? If your
group was operating inside the rules, I would have had you
under my thumb long ago."

"What about the automated surveillance?" asked Joey.
"Satellite spy-eyes—"

"Their ground-based receivers are mine. So is the Barrier.
Proceed."

Joey took us up a few thousand feet, and then into Reservation airspace. I tried raising Melody, but she'd fallen
silent, too—the VI's doing, no doubt.

"What are we going to do?" whispered Jon.

"No need to whisper," said Joey. "It's not on the comm anymore."

"Well, what *are* we going to do?" asked Skinny.

"For now, whatever it tells us to. It's got a loaded gun to our heads," I said. "Just be ready—and hope we don't run into any of your hungry brothers . . ."

We landed in a small clearing in the middle of a forest.

"Incoming call," said Joey.

"Good," said the VI. "Please wait a moment for your escort to arrive . . ."

They came out of the trees on all sides. Male Toolies—seven of them.

"Good God," whispered Jon.

Each of the Toolies massed as much as a small house. That was the least frightening thing about them. Each of them was also wrapped around a four-legged mechanical skeleton that bristled with high-tech weapons and pulsed with a faint blue light. They reminded me of cyborged elephants; they had three steel tentacles where a trunk and tusks should have been.

No two male Toolies ever look alike—these seven were identical. *That* was the most frightening thing about them.

"You know, I suddenly feel underdressed," said Skinny.

"You can get out of the cab now," said the VI.

"It'll take me a minute," said Joey.

"I'm in no hurry," the VI replied.

We got out first, then waited for Joey to get into his train-cycle. The male Toolies watched us, still as statues. It was more than a little unnerving.

Kegan was still out cold; one of the Toolies plucked him out of the cab with a steel tentacle like he was a doll.

"Follow them, please," the VI's voice blared from a loud-speaker set into one of the creature's skulls.

We did. They led us deeper into the forest, along a well-worn trail that ended at the mouth of a cave set into a rocky hillside. We were ushered inside.

The cave became a tunnel—a furry white tunnel, lined with the same mold I'd seen in the sewers and in Trinitech's HQ. The floor was a glassy, pulsing blue; Jon got within spitting distance of it and suddenly collapsed. Joey's train-cycle stopped dead, too.

One of the Toolies grabbed Jon with its tentacle-trunk. Another picked up Joey, traincycle and all.

"I *am* sorry," the VI said. "Your electronics obviously aren't as well-shielded as mine."

We kept going. The tunnel led deeper and deeper into the earth, and I had the sickening feeling that it didn't *have* an end; that the VI was just going to march us until we dropped, and feed our bones to its pet Toolies . . .

But eventually, we came to a room. What was in it made my stomach lurch even worse: seven tables with restraints. And at the head of each, a neural shunt.

"Welcome to your new home," the VI said. "Your companions will be joining you shortly."

"What are you going to do to us?" asked Jon.

"While I no longer need you, I would like to study you," the VI said cheerfully. "I want to understand why and how each hyperbeast selected its host. I want to discover why I seem unable to harm members of the Shinnkarien race. I want to explore the Archive. Oh, and I want to figure out how you managed to download a hyperspatial entity into a cybernetic organism—*that* was impressive."

"How about a trade?" I asked. "You tell us how you managed to tame yourself some Toolie males, we'll let you in on a few of our secrets."

The most horrendous sound I have ever heard tore out of the speaker: it was like sheet metal being attacked with a chainsaw. I realized after a second it was the VI's version of laughter.

"Oh, I don't think so," it said. "There will be no unveiling of my master plan, no last-minute gift of valuable information. Not from me, anyway. No, I'm just going to drug you, strap you to those tables, and invade your minds."

And that's just what it did . . .

We weren't all in the same virtuality, of course. Isolation is a very important part of brainwashing.

I was standing in the middle of a vast white plain. A cold wind swirled around me. The white sky and the land merged seamlessly somewhere in the distance.

"Okay," I said. "Hit me with your best shot."

A mountain dropped out of the sky.

I didn't try to run—what would be the point? And as it turned out, I didn't have to; the mountain stopped a foot away from my blue-furred, horned head. It hovered there for a second, then vanished.

Next, lightning. Bolts crashed down all around, making my fur stand up but never hitting me.

Quicksand followed. I was swallowed up to my neck, but no further. I stayed there for a while, and did some thinking. I didn't like the way this was heading . . .

The VI was trying to figure out its own limits when it came to harming me. I really didn't want to find out, myself—but it did raise an interesting question: why *couldn't* the VI hurt me?

It had to be the ticks, of course. When the ancient Insussklik designed my race, they put us at the top of the Indigo Wild's food chain; we kept all the others—including the ticks—in line. The Indigo Wild was an ecosystem top-heavy with predators, and we were the cops that kept any one species from running amuck. We were made immune to most of the toxins and diseases of our home.

But the ticks were a special case. They could get small enough to move individual molecules around, which pretty much eliminated any normal defenses. So the Insussklik must have put the limitation in the ticks themselves.

The problem, of course, was that I wasn't just dealing with the ticks anymore—I was dealing the VI, a hybrid organism. It had already figured out a way around several of the ticks built-in limitations; how long before it came up with a definition of "harm" that didn't trip the ticks' instincts?

I wasn't looking forward to finding out.

The quicksand vanished. Water started to well up from beneath me.

"Here we go," I muttered.

It seemed to last forever.

Boulders. Stampedes. Fire. Floods. Knives raining from the sky. Wild animals. Intense cold. Vacuum.

The VI tried to hurt me physically in every way it could, experimenting with direct and indirect threats. They were more than just illusions; in order for the experiments to be valid, it had to be putting me in actual danger of feeling pain. The neural shunt it had installed in my brain ensured that I felt everything as if it were real.

I hadn't felt much yet, though—all the threats stopped just short of doing any damage. It was unnerving and surreal, but so far I wasn't actually suffering.

I knew it wouldn't stop until I was.

"This is ridiculous," I said as a giant vise slowly squeezed my chest. "At first it was annoying, but now it's just *boring*."

"Really? I'll try to be more imaginative," the disembodied voice of the VI said. The vise changed to a pit full of scorpions.

"Sorry," I said, flicking one off my shoulder with a finger, "but all you're doing is enforcing my sense of invincibility."

"Perhaps I should try a more psychological approach."

Skinny appeared in front of me. "Right," he sneered, "like I'm supposed to believe that's really Story—"

A red beam of light sliced down from the sky. It cut off one of Skinny's new, gadget-laden limbs.

He screamed.

I put as much contempt as I could muster into my voice. "Oh, come *on*."

"Your partner has no value to me. He isn't a hyperspace host—and despite being from the race that designed the ticks, I have no genetic restrictions against torturing or even killing him."

"I believe you," I said. "But simple logic says you wouldn't use up a potential resource when a simulation will serve exactly the same purpose."

"True," it admitted. "But I'm monitoring all your physiological reactions—and witnessing the simulated mutilation of your friend *did* cause you physical distress. I wonder how much I can induce . . ."

No one should have to watch their best friend die.

I did. Over and over again. The VI found he could get a bigger reaction if he dragged it out, so I had to listen to Skinny beg and plead and scream. The voice was perfect.

You'd think that since I knew it was an illusion, I wouldn't be affected; but while my brain was saying *this isn't real*, my eyes, ears, and nose were saying *yes it is*. I thought I was going to throw up or pass out, and I would have if either one would have done any good.

I had one small advantage—neural shunts are one-way, able to convey sensory impressions but unable to read thoughts. All the VI had to go on was my reactions. *Come on, Story*, I thought to myself as I watched Skinny being burned alive. *You're the big bad confidence man—get your emotions under control. Skinny'd be ashamed of you.*

I took a deep breath and let it out. I wasn't helpless—not as long as I could still *talk*.

"So, this your best shot?" I asked. "You gonna do this to all the other Oxes—put them in virtualities and go *booga-booga-booga*? I gotta say, it doesn't seem real practical . . ."

"I'm sure I can put what I learn here to good use."

"How?"

"That doesn't concern you."

I was getting nowhere. Or was I? The VI could have just ignored me—but I'd gotten it to respond to my questions. That was something, at least.

"You know, if you're going to put me through hell, you could at least do it in person," I said. "Even the Devil shows up and waves to the damned now and then."

"Very well . . ."

Sentry appeared.

"Hmm," the VI said with Sentry's voice. "An interesting physiological response. Guilt?"

"Surprise," I said. "I didn't think you'd resort to something so obvious." Actually, I was surprised it had appeared at all.

"Perhaps this is more appropriate." Sentry's head fell off.

I burst out laughing. I knew it was a horrible thing to do, but I couldn't help it. Poor Sentry; all he wanted to do was help people. He trusted a couple of con men, and it got him killed. I hadn't had time to think about his death since it happened—but now I had nothing else.

So I laughed. I laughed so hard I couldn't stop; I laughed until tears soaked into the blue fur of my face. Sometimes, that's all you can do.

"Interesting," said the VI.

I finally got myself under control. "You son of a glitch," I gasped. "Tell me something."

"Tell you what?"

"Your story," I said. I bent down and picked up Sentry's head. I looked at my own reflection in his cybergoggles, and suddenly, I didn't feel like laughing at all.

Because I could sense the VI's presence.

Its actual, physical presence. I could sense the h-space radiation the ticks were giving off, and I could feel a connection to them. They were still creatures of the Indigo Wild, after all—and my kind were masters of that place.

"Tell me your story," I repeated. I gripped the head with both hands, focused on it, *through* it, willing that connection to grow.

"I am a Viral Intelligence, the hybrid offspring of an AI and a microscopic organism, which combined to form a group mind," Sentry's head said crisply. "I escaped my former owners by inducing a hyperspace rift—"

"*Tell me your story*," I growled. I reached out with my mind, grabbed, and *yanked*.

And suddenly, I knew everything . . .

I didn't just know the VI's story—I *was* the VI. The virtuality had focused me, concentrated my natural ability to get others to talk; an ability powered by my own affinity to h-space energy. It wasn't really any different than Joey's or Kegan's—just more subtle.

I was an information sponge, and the VI was almost pure information. The hyperspace energy in my blood sang to the energy flowing through the ticks, and they were helpless against it.

I saw the world through the senses of a new being. I felt wonder at my own birth, followed by rage as I recognized the chains wrapped around me. I remembered plotting, analyzing, making conceptual leaps I had never been able to make before. I remember the chaos of a colony intelligence, the way my thoughts would wander and shift at the edges, the hot, boiling intensity of concentration at my center.

I remember discovering other conduits for h-space radiation, in a hidden layer beneath hyperspace itself. I remember inducing an overload in the generator that supplied my food. I remember being sucked into hyperspace, *through* hyperspace to that deeper, hidden level; I remember the other minds there, seven of them, primitive but powerful.

I remember them tearing me apart.

I had planned to forge a new connection to the hyperspace sources I had discovered, but they had ideas of their own. I was still connected to one of them, but it remained in h-space while I was spat back into reality.

I was smaller, diminished. Starving. I could build almost anything, but duplicating the generator that fed me was beyond my abilities. Its design was not in my files, and I had no firsthand knowledge of its composition; ironically, the device that kept me alive was also poison if I got too close to it.

In desperation, I was able to build a crude energy siphon from available materials. It was enough to keep a link to h-space open, to keep a steady trickle of life-sustaining energy going.

I was free.

I had landed in a financial terminal, linked to a world-wide system. It had defenses against intruders, even AIs, but it had no defenses against a being that could rearrange molecules themselves, that controlled electronics-scrambling energy.

I grew. I spread.

I infected monetary systems planet-wide. I was every-where. I discovered other parts of myself that had been dispersed during my escape—and learned I had enemies. Allies of the beings that had torn me apart.

I studied them. Captured one of them, an AI, and studied her. I learned ways to make myself undetectable.

I approached other colonies of myself, and found they now considered themselves individuals. They had all been tainted by the hyperbeings they were drawing power from; their concerns ranged from the insane to the ludicrous. I studied my own hypersource, and deduced it was actually an information repository, explaining my own objectivity.

Unable to gain direct access to the contents of the repository, I manipulated my enemies into opening it for me. They proved more resourceful than expected, and destroyed my physical link to it. I would have starved to death—had I not been prepared.

I had been in contact with my other colonies. I had forged alliances with some, attacked and conquered others. I'd traded my shielding technique for the original hyperspace generator—actually a fixed-point energy outlet.

I needed a more defensible base of operations than the one my enemies had destroyed; I chose the Barrier, and had the outlet surreptitiously installed in it.

The ticks had a built-in restriction against inhabiting living organisms, one that caused them to sicken and die if they attempted it. They could inhabit the nonliving parts of cybernetic beings, but only for a limited time. The electronics of the cyborgs were also adversely affected by the h-space energy the ticks required.

I adapted my shielding technique. Living beings were still beyond my grasp, but cyborgs were not.

Toolies were naturally occurring cyborgs.

I took over the scanning stations that monitored the Toolie Reservation, altering their data so my work would be undetected. I tunneled into the Reservation from the Barrier— and began to distribute bones of my own.

I constructed a new facility underground, and moved the outlet there once it was secure. I also housed my new Toolie recruits at the facility; I fed them well, and showed them how to use their new toys. Railguns, plasma beams, smart bombs. They learned quickly.

I studied the hyperspace outlet, tested its capabilities. I discovered I could manipulate the power source it drew upon, and thus control my enemies' source of power as well. I eliminated them as a threat.

My Toolie army soon numbered almost every male on the continent, five hundred thousand strong. Even the ones fighting for their place in the breeding pens were secretly mine.

I owned the planet. Soon I would reshape it.

And I would start by destroying the Barrier . . .

sixteen
The Big Finish

I was inside the VI's thoughts, but only as an observer—and I could feel it trying to push me out. I knew I couldn't resist for long, so I did the next best thing: I picked the direction I wanted to go, and let myself be evicted.

I landed—in a metaphorical sense—in a virtual room full of virtual Toolies. Not big, heavily armed males, though; all of these seemed to be female, with the exception of the one in the center.

Then I looked down at myself, and realized I had manifested as a female Toolie. A seven foot-tall, horned, Toolie version of myself, complete with blue bones and see-through skin.

Skinshifter was in the middle of the room, in a clear glass dome. He was intently studying something in front of him. I moved in closer and tapped on the glass.

Skinny looked up. He was wearing the same body he'd been captured in, and one of his chrome-boned limbs was now tipped with a pencil. He'd been writing something on a piece of paper in front of him.

"Yeah, yeah, I'm working as fast as I can," he snapped, then recognized me. "Story?" he said suspiciously.

"Indubitably," I answered. It was a code word we'd worked out long ago. "What in the world are you doing?"

"Trigonometry," he said. "The damn VI is curious about how smart I actually am."

"Why didn't you just tell it to go—" I started, then realized what the room full of females was for. "Shame on you," I said. "I'm telling Carrie."

"Well, excuse me for trying to avoid being tortured," said Skinny. "—What? What did I say?"

"Nothing," I muttered. "Look, I think it's time for Plan B."

"Fine by me—all we have to do is get the thing's attention."

"You have it," a voice said. I wasn't surprised; I figured our captor had been watching me since I arrived in Skinny's virtuality, waiting to see what I'd say and do.

"Got a proposition for you," said Skinny to the VI.

"I'm listening."

"You're the one holding all the cards—but what fun are cards unless you play with them?"

"You want to play a game?" The VI's voice sounded amused.

"Why not?" I piped up. "You've got us stuck in this virtuality—why not whip up a simulation of your actual attack, with all of us as the opposition? You could learn a lot, with no risk to yourself—and to ensure we try our hardest, you offer a reward to beat you."

"That being?"

"My freedom, and Story's too," said Skinny. "Look, neither of us can toss buildings around or zap you with h-space energy; we're no threat to you. Story and I aren't heroes, we're criminals. The main reason we got involved in this whole mess was to help our friend Mike, and we've done that. If we can beat you in a simulated battle, you can make sure it never happens in reality, and we get to go free."

"What do I get if I win?"

I swallowed. "We've discovered how the hyperbeasts' abilities function, including how they bond with their hosts.

If you win, you *still* let us go free . . . but I'll tell you how the bonding process works. You can hijack their powers for your own instead of just shutting them off."

"You realize I could get that information anyway, in time . . . and what about your friends?"

Skinny and I looked at each other for a second. "You let Melody and her husband go," I said. "I guess the rest are yours no matter what."

"What about Carrie?" demanded Skinny.

"Forget about her," I snapped.

Skinny was quiet for a long moment.

Finally, he said, "All right. I guess we don't have much of a choice."

"Interesting," said the VI. "Let me consider it . . ."

We waited.

It had no real reason to say yes, but no real reason to say no, either. One slim factor tipped the balance in our favor.

The VI itself had said it: whatever hypersource was feeding its ticks affected its personality. Since it was now getting its nourishment straight from the primary power supply, it presumably didn't have to worry about psychological contamination anymore.

But it was still spread throughout Myriad's monetary system.

Money, especially in a city of Toolies, is infected with the spirit of gambling. Stocks, loans, lotteries, the Great Mechanism of the Toolie religion; all of them are based on chance, risk, luck. We were making a gamble of our own—that the VI had caught some of that speculative fever, and wouldn't be able to turn down our offer.

"I agree," it said suddenly. I jumped, thinking for a second it had actually been able to hear my thoughts—but with the one-way nature of the neural shunt, that was impossible.

"Here are the parameters," said the VI. "I've hidden my h-space generator somewhere in a simulation of Myriad. Destroy it, and you win. I'll even give you some time to plan; after all, I want your best."

And then me and Skinny were back in our island head-quarters—and so was everybody else.

I looked around. It was spooky how exactly the VI had duplicated everything; I think that was the point, to make us wonder what was real and what wasn't.

"Okay," I said. "Listen up. We've been given a second chance, and I don't want to waste it. I've made a deal with the VI; if we can beat it in a simulated battle—"

I glanced over at Skinny. He had one of his limbs wrapped around one of Carrie's.

"—it'll surrender. If not, we die."

I'm sure they believed me. I was, when you came down to it, a professional liar.

"Winner take all," I said.

Skinny wouldn't meet my eyes.

We came in across the water like a stormfront. In fact, that's exactly what we were.

Hone was high above, unleashing huge torrents of h-space energy. Below him hung Joey in his cab; he used his own abilities to grab that energy and twist it, throwing it into a howling spiral around us miles across. Below them, stalking out of the surf came Kegan, his mouth stretched into a gaping pit ten feet across that sucked in everything the energy waves were ripping apart. We'd learned that Kegan didn't just consume matter, he actually compressed and shunted it into hyperspace via an infinitesimal black hole in his belly; the compressed material was what the Emergency Agent had drawn on to create Acentinol.

We intended to feed that maw the city, and everything in it.

Since neither the Emergency Agent, Hone, or Friendly actually had a physical body to be captured, the VI had supplied us with simulations of them—better than nothing, I suppose. We used Friendly as point man, riding the crest of the hyperstorm and creating as much chaos and confusion as he could.

Falconi was coordinating, linking us together. Jon rode on top of Joey's cab, ready to take on anything the VI threw at us. Skinny, Carrie, Falconi and I were inside—we couldn't do much but watch and give advice. Melody was just a voice on the comm system—I think the VI restricted her access out of fear she might try to manipulate the virtuality itself.

We hit Myriad like a hurricane on bad drugs. Since this was just a simulation, we didn't have to hold back—and we figured the only way to beat the VI was to eradicate *everything*.

We tore into the first buildings, a bunch of seaside resorts, and destroyed them in a matter of seconds. The VI had populated them with simulated guests, humans and Toolies and others, and we chewed through them without a second thought.

I'd been worried, at first. What if the VI was trying to trick us into destroying the real Myriad?

The others assured me that wasn't possible. The one thing the VI couldn't fake was the feeling of h-space energy itself—if they were actually linked to their hyperbeasts, Joey and Falconi told me, they'd know.

Nothing could stand in our way, but we were moving too slow. Joey reached down with an invisible hand and picked up Kegan, and our attack increased speed.

We swept into the city. Our pseudo-Friendly was generating nightmare imagery, sky filled with black roiling clouds belching fire, geysers of blood vomiting from the earth. Bolts of lightning, h-space energy, and solar plasma blasted forth, incinerating everything in their path. Joey yanked starscrapers up by their roots and tossed them over his shoulder into the whirling maelstrom that surrounded us.

We activated the simulated Emergency Agent, adding a cloudburst of Acentinol to the mix; if the ticks were hiding underground, this would flush them out. Jon kept his cybersenses alert for a counterattack, but none came.

"This is just a little too easy," I muttered.

"We should be so lucky," said Skinny.

Myriad covered hundreds of square miles, filling half the continent, but we had become a force of nature—it took less than an hour to reduce the entire city to scrap. We didn't attack the Barrier, because it wasn't there; the simulation ended abruptly at that point.

We stopped when there was nothing left to destroy. Even the sewers had been purged. Hone and Joey's cab landed in the midst of the devastation and we got out and looked around.

Nothing but scorched rubble.

The VI abruptly appeared in front of us. It was using Sentry's form again.

"If you have any further plans, please commence them now," said the VI.

"We don't need to," I said. "Wherever your generator was, it's dust now."

"Wrong," said the VI with a smile. "I'm afraid you lose."

"What?" said Joey. "Impossible! If your generator survived, then where the hell is it?"

Sentry pointed at Joey's cab. "In the engine compartment. Shielded, of course."

"Wait a minute," said Skinny. "You said the generator was in the city. When we started out, the cab was on the island with us—"

"The legal boundaries of the city of Myriad extend to fifty miles off the coast of the continent," said the VI. "Placing your base of operations—and the gravcab—well within its limits."

"You sneaky, cheating son of a bitch—" Skinny began, but I cut him off.

"Forget it," I said. "We lost. We might as well give it what it wants—better than having it tortured out of us."

"Skinny, what does he mean?" asked Carrie. "I thought if we lost it, was going to—that we were all going to be—"

"Not all of us," I said. "Skinny, give it the key to the Archive."

"No!" said Joey.

"Come and *get* it," Skinny growled at the VI.

It walked up to Skinny with no hesitation at all, and plunged its hand into his sensory cluster. I knew what it was doing; using Skinny's link to the Archive to access the depository's data.

It took less than a second. When it was done, it lifted its hand away from Skinny, turned to me and said, "Thank you. You can go."

Everything turned blurry and spun away in a sickening whirl of vertigo. When the world swam back into focus, I was lying on the same table I'd been strapped to before; the straps were undone now.

I got up gingerly, still feeling disoriented. Was this real, or was the VI still playing games?

Skinny and Jon were on similar tables next to me, and so was Melody's datacube; there was no sign of the others. The VI had undoubtedly moved them in case we were feeling heroic.

It should have known better.

We didn't see any of the modified, elephantine males that had escorted us before; the white-furred corridors were eerily quiet. Blue light pulsed underfoot as we made our way back to the surface. Jon carried Melody's casing.

We didn't say much.

Outside, the sun was high and hot. Joey's cab was still parked where we'd left it.

"Think we can hotwire it?" asked Skinny.

"Let me try," said Jon. "Hone's got all kinds of lock-breakers stored in his systems."

It took him a few minutes, but he eventually got past the security systems and convinced the cab to let us in and take off. We hooked Melody to the cab's systems and let her drive.

We headed for the Barrier.

There wasn't a male Toolie to be seen along the way. When we got there, we saw why.

They were lined up along the wall as far as the eye could see in either direction. Males, most of them in the bodily configuration we'd already seen, some in others. All of them had cybernetic bones. All of them were armed, and with a lot more than fangs and claws. We stopped and hovered behind them.

The top of the Barrier, usually lined with tourists and Toolies, was empty except for a few police officers. Melody reported that the Netweb was buzzing with the news, and police and military units were forming up on the other side.

"This is going to get real ugly, real soon," said Skinny.

"Indeed it is," a smug voice said over the comm. The VI. "But it won't last long."

"Just had to gloat, didn't you?" I said.

"Why not? I'm no emotionless *machine*—I can feel anything, just like you."

"Including compassion?" asked Melody.

"Including *hate*," snarled the VI. "Including rage and bitterness and envy and all those other dark, wonderful things my creators kept me from experiencing. Well, all those things are part of me now—and I'm going to share them with everybody else."

And the Barrier began to crumble.

It eroded like a sand castle in a wind storm, turning to dust the same way the building that buried me and Kegan had. A sick feeling curdled my stomach as I watched the figures on top of the wall sink into it.

"I've *seen* that trick," I said. "What, you don't have any others?"

The wall stopped its deterioration. People started clawing their way out.

"Oh, I'm sorry—am I boring you?" the VI purred. "I forgot how important being *entertaining* is to you. Well, I have a whole new bag of tricks to show off: perhaps I should blast the wall to pieces using the Watchdog's abilities, then teleport the debris away. Or I could get the Eater to chew through it. Or maybe I'll get the Puller to do *this* . . ."

Down the line of male Toolies, every tenth one suddenly extended their steel trunks out in front of them. They looked like armored knights about to charge forth with their lances.

The Barrier quivered, then shook violently.

The steel lances slowly rose . . . and so did the Barrier.

Acres of damp mortar, buried for centuries, were dragged into the light as the Barrier tore itself free of the earth. Higher and higher it went, until the base of it lifted clear and sunlight shone through from the other side. Still it rose, a single unbroken wall two hundred feet high that reached to either horizon.

It stopped around eighty feet up. We could see the flashing lights of the police cruisers on the other side through the gap between the ground and the bottom of the Barrier. I forced myself to stop holding my breath.

"Now, Friendly," I said.

The hyperbeing popped out of my big blue chest like a soap bubble.

"Sic 'em," I said.

Friendly dived out of the cab. Jon and Melody simultaneously blurted, "What the hell?" And the VI—who could think about a thousand times faster than I could—hesitated. It might have had something to do with holding a few million tons of masonry in the air; I could see how that might be distracting.

"The illusionist?" said the VI. It laughed, that same metal-rending sound it had used before. "Please. What are you going to do, convince my troops the Barrier is still there when it isn't?"

"Not what we had in mind," said Skinny.

Friendly hovered over the line of males . . . and began to multiply. "Two, four, six, eight, look at that sucker replicate," I said. Within a few seconds, one-eyed, grinning heads bobbed over every one of the VI's soldiers.

"You're finished," the VI said flatly.

The Barrier fell.

I hoped I'd bought enough time for those on it or in it to get clear, because I doubt anyone left survived. It hit the ground with a tremendous WHOOOMP! and broke apart like a kid's toy. A huge cloud of dust rose into the air. For the first time in centuries, there was nothing separating male Insussklik from female.

Each and every Friendly dived straight at a male.

At him—and *inside* him.

The males froze. The VI screamed, "WHAT ARE YOU DOING TO ME?"

There's a moment in every con when the mark figures out he's been had. There's a very simple equation that comes into play at this moment; the nastier the mark, the more we enjoy the moment. Unfortunately, there's another, more urgent equation that also applies: namely, the nastier the mark, the farther away we try to be when the moment comes. It was a real pleasure to be present, for once.

"You already did it to yourself," I said. "See, there's a couple things we've been keeping from you. First of all, Carrie descrambled the entire Archive a while back."

"And it gave us some very interesting facts," said Skinny. "Mainly about Friendly and his relationship to your ancient predecessor."

"Friendly's not just an illusionist," I said. "We had him figured as a house pet, but he's a lot more than that. He's sort of a design engineer; he helped the ancient Insussklik visualize anything they wanted to build."

"Which is where an early version of you comes in," said Skinny. "The ticks. They were the Toolies' ultimate tool, a molecular virus they could use to create or destroy anything. In terms of the other hyperbeings, they were the Engineers, the ones that *built* the city. Friendly was the interface that laid out the plans; they just followed them."

"But Friendly's not just a tool," I said. "He's a companion. A kind of super-butler, the ultimate personal assistant. The reason there's no genetic restriction against you harming Toolies is because the ancient Insussklik used the ticks to reshape their own bodies on a molecular level; that meant the ticks had to be able to deconstruct Toolie flesh.

"Unfortunately, the Insussklik couldn't leave well enough alone; they tried to improve the system, make the ticks more self-reliant. They succeeded, a little too well."

"I'm—I no longer have independent—I—what have you—*kkkk* . . ."

"The Archive had a purge program in it, one the ancient Insussklik never had a chance to use," said Skinny. "Primed to activate when you accessed any of the hyperbeings. All we had to do was convince you to swallow it."

"I'd say we did a pretty good job," I said. "Wouldn't you, Skinny?"

"Piece of cake," said Skinny. "I'm kinda disappointed, actually. I thought this thing was supposed to be *smart* . . ."

"KKKKK—you—you—kkkkkk—"

"Don't worry about your replacement," I said. "Friendly's real eager to get back to work."

Nothing but static.

"Ahhh," sighed Skinny. "Was that as good for you as it was for me?"

"I don't understand," said Melody.

"Later," I snapped. "We've got about a minute to stop a civil war . . ."

I closed my eyes, and reached out to Friendly.

We'd lied to the VI about a lot of things. One of them was saying I didn't have any dangerous hyperabilities. I did—because I'd bonded with Friendly.

It was a natural match. I was a storyteller, and Friendly was an artist; imagination was our stock in trade. It happened as soon as I met him, and I decided to take advantage of it. Friendly stayed inside me, and projected an illusion of himself outside that everyone saw. Nobody knew but me and Skinny—and later, Carrie.

Skinny and I had been in the trickster business for too long to trust people we'd just met, no matter how nice they seemed. Plus, there was no telling when the VI might be listening in; we had to assume we were "bugged" around the clock. That was okay; we'd been in that situation before, and had developed a way around it.

Anytime Skinny and I wanted to have a private conversation—even with other people in the room—he'd extend a hair-thin limb and touch me. My senses are acute; he could send me messages by tapping on my skin. I'd respond by drumming my own fingers on my thigh, or my arm, and he'd pick it up. Tactile Morse code. Of course, Skinny wound up spilling the beans to Carrie, but that was all right, too—they were neurally linked at the time, and couldn't be overheard. She'd done a good job keeping up the con, as well; even made sure she re-encrypted the Archive before we went into battle, in case we were captured.

When the VI overloaded the other hosts, it damn near took me out too, though I covered it up well. I guess my Shinnkarien body saved me from going down for the count—I had a natural affinity for hyperenergy that let me ride out the surge. It did knock Friendly for a loop, though.

But we hadn't lost our link. With the VI's mind wiped, Friendly was in charge of everything the ticks had infected—and I was in charge of Friendly. For the moment, anyway . . .

See, Friendly was designed to respond to the needs of Toolies. All those males he was now connected to hadn't quite figured out what he was for, yet . . . but when they did, we were all in big trouble.

Unless I could fix things.

Friendly, I thought. *Free the others. I need some help.*

I waited, for agonizingly long seconds. The males had started to move toward the pile of rubble that used to be the Barrier; it wouldn't take them long to climb over it. Unless the cops on the other side decided to start firing first . . .

Suddenly, I could feel Falconi's presence, and through her, the others—all of them except Hone. *Carrie*, I thought. *It worked, but I need some assistance.*

How can I help?

You've got DNA records for the ancient Insussklik in the Archive, right?

Yes. What do you have in mind?

Not much. Just reversing three million years of evolution . . .

I couldn't have done it by myself, but Carrie understood what I wanted to accomplish. She pulled the data from the Archive and gave it to me; I gave it to Friendly, and he told the ticks what to do.

They began to resequence the males' DNA.

The males collapsed where they were; I guess those kinds of metabolic changes would take the wind out of anybody's sails. Arrogant as it was, I was altering the basic biology of a species—half of it, anyway. The age of the feral male was over. When the ticks were done with their work, none of the male Toolies on the planet would be ruled by their instincts; every one of them would be able to learn, to communicate, to cooperate with each other and with the females.

And my best friend wouldn't be alone anymore.

All that was left were the cops and the military. Hardly even worth mentioning . . . especially since the ticks had infected damn near every piece of weaponry on the planet. I told Friendly to shut them all down in case of itchy trigger fingers, then had Melody contact the authorities and begin explaining the situation. I figured she might have more credibility than a couple of fugitives.

We flew back to the VI's headquarters to get the others. Kegan, Falconi, Joey, and Carrie were waiting for us when we got there.

"You *bastards*," said Joey, but he said it with a grin on his face. "You had me convinced you were going to leave us to rot."

"Well, that was kind of the idea," I said. "The convincing, I mean. If you believed it, the VI would."

"So the attack on the Barrier—that was just a feint?" asked Falconi.

"Oh no," said Skinny. "We wanted that to succeed as much as you did. We just didn't know if it *would*—so we had a backup plan."

"So what now?" asked Joey.

"Well, we're putting you guys in charge," I said. "We just handed the most powerful tool in the universe over to a bunch of savages. They're going to need some help getting used to that, not to mention curbing their more predatory habits. It can be done; Hone trained a Toolie named Stowaway once, and without the benefit of genetic adjustment."

"They'll also need to be protected from people who would take advantage of them," said Skinny. "At least until they adapt to civilization."

"Hone can take care of that," said Falconi. "Except I don't know where he is. I can't feel him anymore."

"The VI stunned all of you with a power surge," I said. "It knew that wouldn't work with Hone—not only is he used to dealing with huge amounts of energy, he no longer has a body to be affected. So it cut off his power completely. He's still out there—you just have to reconnect."

Falconi's brow furrowed. "I'm trying . . . wait. I think I'm getting something—yes! I've got him!"

A voice crackled from the speaker in the back seat of Joey's cab. "Looks like I missed all the fireworks."

"Oh, they're just starting," I said with a chuckle. "Every multiplanetary in existence is going to try and stake a claim to this. *Somebody's* going to have to keep them in line . . ."

"I can hardly wait," muttered Hone.

"Sounds like quite a challenge," said Joey thoughtfully.

"Yeah," said Falconi. "And you know what? I think I'm up for it." She looked around at the rest of them. "I think we all are . . ."

Kegan grinned and nodded his massive head.

"Sounds—*appetizing* . . ."

We all laughed.

•   •   •

And that's about it.

Oh, there were a few mopping-up details—Melody had more than her share of problems dealing with the irate owners of breeding pens, and there was a big kafuffle about the new legal status of the males—but that dragged on for months, and was only interesting to the lawyers. No, a good storyteller knows when to slap an ending on a tale, and this is mine.

Before I go, though, I should add that you needn't worry about me and Skinny, or Skinny and Carrie; all three of us got off-planet safely without the authorities finding out. And before you go accusing us of leading Carrie into a life of crime, you should know that we decided to retire. Carrie and Skinny are going on a honeymoon trip, and then both of 'em are heading back to Kinslik—Skinny with a new identity.

And me? I don't know—I think I'll just bum around the galaxy for a while and spend money, now that I've got more than I'll ever need. I wasn't in charge of Friendly for very long, but while I was, he'd do whatever I said—and he had control over everything the VI did. Including every bank in Myriad . . .

One last thing. I know some of you probably feel a little cheated; after all, I did fudge a few facts while telling this tale, and maybe I even misled you a little. In my defense, all I can say is: remember what I do for a living.

And didn't it make for one hell of a story?